# TRACES OF VIRTUE

## COVENTRY SAGA BOOK 4

### ROBIN PATCHEN

JDO PUBLISHING

*For Tricia.*
*Old friends are the very best kind.*

# CHAPTER ONE

Cᴀʀʟʏ Gᴀʀᴄɪᴀ's choices had dwindled to two—a lifetime of hell or an eternity there.

When she was a little girl, back when home meant the scent of tamales and the sound of lullabies sung in lilting Spanish, back when she was the only daughter of the most generous, most beautiful woman on the block, Carly had thought the world a magical place. She'd believed in laughter and beauty and angels. She'd believed in goodness. She'd believed in God.

She still believed in God. Everything else was gone.

She shoved the offensive plastic stick with its two blue lines back into the packaging, then wrapped the whole thing in toilet paper and shoved it deep in the trash can. Nobody would discover it there. It wasn't as if it would occur to her stepsisters to take out the trash. And her stepfather's contribution to the household included the paycheck that barely covered the bills—and little else. He was skilled at home improvement. At least he could do that— fix a running toilet, repair a gouged wall, paint. He'd even tried to teach her some of his skills, but she wasn't dumb enough to take those lessons. Whatever she learned to do would become her job, and the last thing she needed was to take on more responsibility around the house.

They might as well rename her Cinderella. Except there'd be no prince in her future. Not now.

She'd suspected the truth for more than a month. Today had been the first day she'd had the courage to confirm it.

A loud knock on the door was followed by Sophia's demanding voice. "What are you doing?" her stepsister asked. "I need to fix my makeup. Some of us have plans, you know."

"Just a sec." Carly checked her reflection in the mirror and saw her mother—dark brown hair, dark brown eyes. The biggest difference between them was the skin. Mama's had seemed perpetually tanned, but Carly's was lighter, closer to her pale father's—or so she assumed—than her Puerto Rican mother's.

*Oh, Mama. I'm sorry.*

Sophia banged on the door again. "Come. On. I need to get ready."

Carly opened the door and forced a smile for the oldest of her three stepsisters. At eighteen, Sophia was six years younger than Carly and thought she had life figured out. Unlike Carly, who'd lived long enough and been through enough to realize there was no figuring it out, only getting through it and surviving. "If you'd put on your makeup in the bedroom—"

"The light's better in here." Sophia pushed past Carly into the bathroom and yanked open the top drawer of the vanity. It fell off its runner, landing crooked in the opening, but Sophia made no effort to fix it, just snatched her makeup bag. "Hannah's gonna be here in ten minutes."

Carly leaned against the doorjamb and surveyed her sister's attire. Practically painted-on skinny jeans, a bright red top—long sleeved, low-cut, and cropped so the material ended about an inch higher than the jeans' waistline. Sophia had a lot of curves, and this outfit showed off every one. She'd added boots with two-inch heels to the ensemble. Now, she plastered on enough makeup to hide her pretty freckles and the little bit of teenage acne dotting her chin. She'd curled her long blond hair, which fell down her back in waves.

"Where you going looking like that?"

She shrugged. "Nowhere special."

Which meant she and her friends would be hanging out on the street, hoping to catch men's eyes. In that outfit, she had no doubt her sister would be successful. "Sweetie—"

"Don't start with me." Sophia glared at Carly's reflection in the mirror. "You wanna live like a nun, power to you. But I'm gonna have a little fun."

"What you're going to have will end up being anything but fun." Carly thought of the new life growing in her womb. She'd done everything in her power to prevent that. But she'd learned there were some things far outside her power.

That was the problem, wasn't it? She'd been given the task of taking care of herself and her family, and she couldn't do it. Though she tried and tried, all she did was fail over and over again. And now she'd be adding one more to be fed and cared for.

But when Carly's mother had lain on her death bed, Carly had promised. Mama would be so disappointed if she knew about the baby. The least Carly could do was keep her word.

"No man will ever value you if you don't value yourself." Carly had learned that the hard way.

"Oh, they value me all right." Sophia winked into the mirror, then resumed applying a second coat of mascara.

While Carly tried to think of something, anything, she could say to get through to Sophia, her stepsister stowed the makeup back in the drawer, shoved it closed—it ended up cockeyed in its space— and scooted out of the room.

"See ya!" she called over her shoulder.

"Be home in time for dinner."

Sophia didn't answer, just rushed down the stairs and out the door.

Carly didn't want to think about the trouble Sophia would get into that afternoon. It was a holiday, which was why everybody was home on a Monday morning in February. Everybody but Pete, who'd lumbered out the door for work that morning with hardly a *thanks for breakfast.* Two months before, when Carly had moved back in, her stepfather had acted as if he were doing her a huge favor. As if he could take care of the house and his daughters all by himself. What a joke. The man was barely more of a father than Carly's, and she wouldn't be able to pick hers out of a police lineup.

What kind of a father would Ian be?

The thought sent acid to her already-churning stomach. At least now she had a cause to blame for the sickness she'd felt off and on every day for a couple of weeks. She'd tried to chalk it up to nerves, stress, and fear. But it was morning sickness, though it wasn't kind enough to stick to mornings.

She needed to think.

She needed help.

She grabbed her backpack from the floor of the tiny room she shared with Sophia, threw on her sneakers, and headed down the stairs, careful not to trip on the books and bags and stack of toilet paper near the bottom. Once, she'd hidden a twenty-dollar bill beneath the stuff she set on the steps to be taken up, thinking to reward the sister who helped. After a week, she'd grabbed all the items herself and pocketed the twenty.

*Cinderelly, Cinderelly.*

The song from the movie played in the back of her mind, repeating the only two words she remembered. The cartoon version at least had animal friends to help her out.

Laurie and Danielle were seated on the couch, staring at one of their phones and giggling. YouTube, TikTok, Instagram... Who knew what had their attention?

"You girls finish your homework?"

Sixteen-year-old Laurie said, "Duh. On Saturday."

Danielle looked up and smiled. She was fourteen, but she hadn't developed any of the attitude that usually came with the early teen years. Thank heavens. Between Sophia and Laurie, Carly couldn't handle any more teenage nonsense. "I did mine after school Friday. You going somewhere?"

"I'll be gone a couple of hours. Can you two please clean up the kitchen?"

"Sure!" Danielle said.

Laurie didn't respond.

Danielle, for all her eagerness, was as flighty as a hummingbird. She'd forget, and Laurie wouldn't even try to remember. Carly had no doubt that, when she got home, she'd be washing all the dishes that'd piled up in the sink since the night before, her reward for not doing them right away.

This was what she'd signed up for when she'd moved back in. It was a small price to pay for the safety the home provided. Pete would never win father-of-the-year, but even Ian wouldn't mess with him.

After slipping on her jacket, she pushed out the back door into the dull February sunshine, climbed on her bicycle, and started out, thankful that last week's snow had melted. The cold air stung her cheeks, but with the energy she expended pedaling, she'd be warm soon enough. The streets were quieter than usual, thanks to the holiday, so she had little trouble dodging traffic and potholes. There were no bike lanes, and biking on the sidewalk was a no-no, so she kept to the right and hoped her bright red jacket would help drivers see her. She didn't own a car, and since she rarely left the South Boston neighborhood of Dorchester, she was able to get to most places by bike, except when there was snow on the ground—meaning most of the winter.

She'd hardly allowed herself to think about how her life would change if she were pregnant. Was it okay to continue riding her bicycle, or would a doctor tell her to stop?

She didn't drink alcohol, but coffee... She knew enough to know caffeine was bad for unborn babies.

If this had happened a year or two earlier, she'd have gone straight to an abortion clinic. She had plenty of friends who'd been there, who'd reported that it was easy. "No big deal," according to an older girl who'd lived next door. Their lives hadn't been forever altered by babies they couldn't care for. They'd suffered a day or two of discomfort and then gone on as if nothing had happened.

Except not all of them had. One of Carly's dearest friends had undergone an abortion when they were in high school, and she'd never been the same. She'd slipped into a depression that lasted for years. Everybody told her she'd made the right decision.

Carly could still hear Patricia's tear-filled lament. "I killed my baby. My own baby."

At the time, Carly had been one of the many encouraging Patricia to get over it. Move on.

Now, everything was different. Now, she not only believed in God, she'd accepted Him into her heart, just like her ex-boyfriend had wanted her to do years before. Braden had asked her, begged her, to consider becoming a Christian. At the time, she'd thought of herself as a good Catholic girl. She went to Mass every weekend. She lit candles and made her confessions. What else did Braden want from her?

She understood now that going to church didn't equal faith, that ticking Mass off her to-do list didn't a relationship with God make. When she'd gotten right with God, her life had changed dramatically. Suddenly, the liturgy meant something. It touched her, deep in her heart. The scripture the priest read whetted her appetite for more. She'd grown in faith, grown in knowledge.

And, thanks be to God, she'd finally had the courage to end the relationship with Ian, which had kept her practically imprisoned for nearly two years. She'd trusted God and followed Him to the best of her ability.

And look where she'd ended up.

CARLY BRAKED in front of the house.

*His* house.

Braden's parents had been at the hospital when Mom lost her battle with cancer. Braden had been off at college, though of course he came home to attend the funeral, but his parents had helped Carly through those first few torturous days. They'd organized meals. They'd held her hand and let her cry. They'd been her support.

Carly's stepdad hadn't been much help. Sure, Pete had tried to comfort his daughters, who'd lost a stepmom, but he'd been unsure how to help Carly. They'd never forged the bond her mother had hoped they would. Pete never seemed anything but uncomfortable around Carly, and the feeling was mutual.

If not for the Reillys, Carly wasn't sure she'd have survived.

And here she was again, needy and pathetic.

The yellow house glowed in the winter sunshine. The blue skies and white puffy clouds reflected off the second-story windows. How could Carly take her ugliness into such a beautiful place?

The storm door opened, and Mr. Reilly stepped onto the stoop. "You just going to stand there, or are you coming in?"

Despite everything, she smiled. "I'm caught now."

He looked like an older version of the man Carly had once thought she'd love for the rest of her life. Sean Reilly had dark brown hair, silvering at the temples, and light blue eyes. He wasn't as tall as Braden's six feet, but they shared the same easy manner. "Well, hurry up," he yelled, "before we let all the heat out."

Leaving her bike leaning against the porch rail, she climbed the steps and slipped inside. She hadn't seen the Reillys in a year or more, but nothing had changed. This house was more than a century old, just like the one her stepfather owned, but it was tidy and clean, and it had been updated this century. The walls were a pale sage color and contrasted beautifully with the gleaming hardwood and the white woodwork.

The living room looked just as it always had. Overstuffed sofas and throw pillows and cozy blankets, orderly but lived-in. The TV was on, a news conference. She recognized the man on the screen, a local politician named Richard Lynch. He was running for

Congress. The caption below him read, *Candidate defends his record.*

"The race is getting pretty heated." Carly rarely paid attention to politics, but Richard Lynch was local. Everyone she knew was pulling for him to win.

"The other guy's slinging dirt," Mr. Reilly said, "but so far Lynch hasn't gotten into the mud with him. Did you know him?"

"Nope, but I've heard of him, like everybody else."

"He was a friend of Shannon's, back in school." The older man watched the politician on the screen. "Imagine that, huh? A Dorchester boy running for Congress."

She grinned at the word *boy*. The guy had to be in his mid-thirties.

Mr. Reilly called up the stairs, "Anna Beth, guess who's here."

Mrs. Reilly hurried down from the second floor. "Oh, Carly! How wonderful to see you." She wrapped her in a hug, and Carly held on tight, maybe too long, reveling in her warmth and comfort.

It had been ages since anybody had hugged her. It had been ages since anybody had seemed genuinely happy to see her.

Mrs. Reilly leaned back, gripping Carly's shoulders. "Let me get a look at you." But when she did, the perpetual joy in her expression dimmed. "What is it?"

"What is what?" How did she do that? How did she *know*?

"That's all right, dear. I'm sure you'll tell me everything." To her husband, she said, "Don't let us stop you. And please turn off the TV."

Mr. Reilly chuckled as he grabbed the remote. "Looks like I've been invited to leave. You ladies enjoy." The front door closed just as Carly and Mrs. Reilly stepped into the kitchen. The space looked like it always had. Bright, shiny, clean. Happy.

"Sit, sit. What can I get you?"

Carly removed the backpack and settled in a wooden chair, the same one she'd chosen for all the years she and Braden were together. Braden had taught her algebra at that table. They'd laughed together. They'd eaten together. They probably would have done more kissing if Mrs. Reilly hadn't carefully planted herself in the next room. "I don't need anything."

A little *pfft* escaped Mrs. Reilly's lips. "Did you ride your bike? It's chilly out there. I can heat up some coffee. Or hot tea?"

Carly would love coffee. She'd been drinking it, as well as soda—and eating lunch meat—for two months. She was already a terrible mother.

Assuming she was keeping the baby.

But how could she?

Mrs. Reilly's eyebrows hiked, waiting.

"Just water."

Mrs. Reilly fixed two glasses along with two plates of coffee cake. The woman loved to bake. There was always some yummy confection on her counter, and the slight paunch in her belly only added to her charm. She sat beside Carly at the round table. "Tell me everything."

Carly wasn't quite ready for that yet. "How are you guys?"

"Fine, fine. Shannon and Mark just had their second." Mrs. Reilly pulled an iPhone from her sweatshirt pocket, tapped the screen, and turned it to face Carly. In the photo, the Reillys' oldest child, and only daughter, sat with her husband on a couch. Shannon was laughing, and Mark was watching his wife with a look of such affection that tears stung Carly's eyes. A toddler girl, maybe two years old, sat on her daddy's lap. Shannon held an infant.

The baby—another girl, based on the pink cap—had rosy cheeks and wide blue eyes.

"They're beautiful."

If Mrs. Reilly heard the hitch in Carly's voice, she didn't say anything about it. She held the phone to her chest. "My little darlings. I love being a mom, but being a grandma is the greatest joy of my life."

"They still live nearby?"

"Couple of blocks over." Mrs. Reilly filled Carly in on what all the kids were doing—all but Braden. Carly had heard he'd graduated and gotten a master's—some science or tech degree. He was successful, Carly had no doubt. Probably married, maybe with a kid on the way.

She didn't want to know.

Mrs. Reilly understood, had always understood, that mention of Braden only chipped away at Carly's broken heart.

"Now that we've gotten that out of the way," Mrs. Reilly said, "tell me what brings you here. And don't sugarcoat it. I can tell by the look in your eyes something's wrong."

"I'm sorry. I'm sure you have better things—"

"Enough of that. You know we love you like our own. What's going on?"

Like their own. Wouldn't that be something, to be loved, truly loved, by a family like this one? Carly didn't deserve such love. She didn't deserve these people. Braden probably thanked God every day that she'd rejected his proposal.

Dodged a bullet, he had.

How could she confess this to Mrs. Reilly? But she had to. She needed counsel, and she didn't trust anybody else to offer it.

"I was dating this guy for a while."

"Ian Murphy, right? I heard you two broke up."

Carly shouldn't have been surprised. News traveled faster than a February wind among the old neighborhood families. They were all connected somehow, a giant web that held too many of them captive. "About a year ago."

"That's good news. Very good news." The older woman's lips pinched.

"Do you know him?"

"I went to high school with his father. The man had a fierce temper. There were rumors about him for years, that he used to beat poor Marilyn. That he stepped out on her." She shrugged. "Maybe the rumors weren't true."

Carly knew Ian's father well enough not to doubt the gossip.

"Not that Ian's like his father," Mrs. Reilly added. "It's wrong of me to assume he is. It's just..." She shrugged but didn't finish her statement.

"He was very sweet, at first." Mrs. Reilly sat back and waited, so Carly continued. "But yeah, things got bad. Most of the time, he was kind to me. Generous and encouraging. But sometimes, he'd lose his temper." She let the memories of those days roll over her. He was fun and happy—until he wasn't. He'd never hit her, but he'd shoved her, had knocked her over a couple of times. He hadn't caused that much pain. He hadn't needed to. The threat of violence, the fear, had kept her in line. "Anyway, he wanted me to move in with him. Meanwhile, my roommate kept telling me about Jesus. I mean, I knew about Jesus. I went to Mass all my life. Went to confirmation. But for the first time, I started to understand what Braden"—her voice stumbled over his name like her bike on a pothole—"tried to tell me. I put my faith in Him."

"Oh, sweetheart." Mrs. Reilly gripped her forearm. "That's such good news."

Carly reveled in the woman's touch. Mama had been so affectionate, always stroking her hair, rubbing her back, hugging her hello and good-bye. Since her death, Carly'd had to choose between hardly being touched at all or allowing Ian's touch—sometimes tender, often not.

How pathetic she was.

"It wasn't easy, breaking up with Ian. I kept doing it, and he kept coming back, convincing me I needed him." She focused on her coffee cake, unwilling to meet Mrs. Reilly's eyes. "I guess I thought I did. Need him, I mean. In a lot of ways."

Mrs. Reilly squeezed Carly's arm. "I'm sure it felt like that, like you were all alone."

Carly forced down the sob rising in her throat. She had to get through this. She needed somebody to tell her what to do. And Mrs. Reilly was the only woman she trusted not to share her news with the neighborhood like a plate of cookies.

She just had to get it out there. Just say it. Aloud. Maybe, when she said it, it wouldn't feel so terrible.

"I'm pregnant."

Mrs. Reilly sat back. "Oh, dear."

Carly had been wrong. The words hadn't taken away any of her shock. It felt just as terrible, worse than before, thanks to the expression on Mrs. Reilly's face. Shock.

Disappointment.

No, she was imagining that, imagining what her own mother would look like.

This was a mistake. She stood. "I'm sorry. I shouldn't have—"

"Don't do that. Just"—she waved to the chair—"what happened? If you two broke up, unless... it is Ian's, right?"

Unfortunately, yes. Carly only nodded. The story was too ugly to tell. Too ugly to remember.

She didn't want to get into it with Braden's mother. The facts of the baby's conception wouldn't change anything now. She was carrying Ian's child. And she had to deal with it.

"You could give the child up for adoption," Mrs. Reilly suggested.

"He'll find out I'm pregnant, and he'll know it's his." Or maybe he'd think she'd been with another man, which would be worse. Either way... "If I give his kid up, he'll kill me." She'd meant the words as hyperbole, but as they escaped her mouth, she feared they might be true. Maybe, at first, he'd try to understand. But eventually he'd drink too much, and then he'd get angry. And then, who knew what he'd do?

But Mrs. Reilly didn't understand. "He'd be upset, but in time he'd move on. Maybe that would get it through his thick skull that you're not interested in taking him back."

If only Carly hadn't gotten involved with Ian from the start. If only she'd been stronger and wiser. If only she'd trusted her instincts instead of giving in to her need for love.

If only Braden hadn't left her.

If only Mama hadn't died.

The last few years had been nothing but one long series of if-onlys.

"If I tell him, maybe he'll step up." But what would that look like? Ian owned a successful business. He had money. He could provide for them. But would he accept that they were never getting back together? Would he treat their child with tenderness and respect?

Would he leave Carly alone? As the baby's presence in her body testified, that wasn't likely.

"Maybe he will," Mrs. Reilly said. "You have a choice. If you set boundaries and don't let him cross them, maybe he'll surprise you. As much as I'd like you to get away from that man, he is the baby's father. You just have to be strong."

Carly wasn't strong, though. She never had been. She'd always been a people-pleaser, a keep-the-peacer. How would she ever lay down boundaries and enforce them?

Ian would barrel over them, just like he'd always done.

"I don't have a choice." Carly's voice was high, small. "I have to get an abortion."

Mrs. Reilly leaned back as if pained by the suggestion. "That's not the answer."

"It's the only answer that doesn't result in me having to deal with Ian for the rest of my life."

But the thought of it, of killing her own child...

Carly'd done everything in her power to prevent a pregnancy. She'd been on the birth control pill for years. But after she'd broken it off with Ian for good, she'd gone off it, determined not to fall for another sweet-talking liar. She wanted to be pure, to be true to her God.

Stupid. She should have just kept taking the things.

"Is that why you came here," Mrs. Reilly asked, "to tell me you're going to get an abortion?"

The idea was so ludicrous that Carly almost laughed.

"No." The older woman's voice was filled with certainty. "You knew what I'd say. You came here to be talked out of it. You came here for a different solution."

"Do you have one?"

"In fact, I do. If you don't want to tell Ian—and I don't blame you for that—then you need to get out of town. Go somewhere and start over. Get a job, get an apartment, find a church, begin a new life. When the child is born, you can give him up for adoption. Or raise him in peace. Sean and I will do everything we can to help you."

Carly tried to force words past the tightness in her throat. That Mrs. Reilly would offer... so kind, exactly what Carly should have expected. "You're so generous to offer, but—"

"Why not?" Mrs. Reilly asked.

"Pete and the girls need me."

"They are *his* daughters, not yours." For the first time that day, Carly heard irritation in Mrs. Reilly's voice. "They are *not* your responsibility."

"Mama made me promise—"

"She shouldn't have. If she'd had any idea what that was going to look like, I'm sure she wouldn't have."

Mrs. Reilly must've heard how Pete neglected his girls and their home. How she'd heard, Carly didn't know, but she obviously knew more than Carly had shared.

Just as likely, Braden had told her why the two of them had broken up. It seemed Mrs. Reilly felt the same way Braden did on the matter.

But Carly's refusal to marry Braden hadn't just been about her stepsisters, about her promise to Mama. She'd still been mired in grief. Everything, everything had been tinted with it. Reds, yellows, blues and greens had all turned to gray. Her life had become colorless, joyless, loveless. Her future had felt hopeless. Braden's proposal, perhaps offered as a lifeline, had seemed ludicrous. She'd been too young, too scared, too sad.

And when Braden had become a Christian, he'd changed too much.

How could she have accepted his proposal?

And why, years later, did she still regret the decision she'd known was right?

Mrs. Reilly said, "Your mother never meant for you to put your life on hold for them."

Frustration and irritation rose in Carly's heart. "Mama loved them." Her mother had been an amazing woman, open and tender and generous. She didn't need defending. And yet Carly added, "She knew they'd need me."

"If she were here right now, what would she say?" Mrs. Reilly gentled her voice. "Would she tell you to abort her grandchild?"

"No. Never."

"What would she tell you to do?"

"I don't know." Carly pushed back and stood. She leaned against the kitchen counter, crossing her arms. "I have no idea what she'd say. She's not here, so she doesn't get to decide what I do."

"Your mother adored you."

Maybe. But she also adored Pete and Sophia and Laurie and Danielle. The day she'd married Pete, their family had changed forever. Carly didn't mind. She loved her stepsisters. But she'd been jealous of the attention her mother paid to them. She'd missed those years when it had been just the two of them.

Carly's tears spilled over. What started as a trickle ended with a sob. She dropped her face into her hands and wept. Mama wasn't there. Mama wasn't there, and Carly was alone, and there was nothing she could do. The thought of leaving the home Mama had created, of leaving the people Mama had loved so well... "They're the only family I have in the world."

Carly heard Mrs. Reilly's chair move, then felt the gentle pressure of a hand on her abdomen. "You have this family now. You have a child who needs you. Unlike Pete and your stepsisters, this child truly *is* your responsibility. You have to do what's best for him. Even without the baby, you have to take care of yourself. Baby or not, you're worth protecting."

# CHAPTER TWO

THis was a bad idea.

A terrible idea.

But if she was going to keep her child, she had no choice. And getting an abortion wasn't an option. It never really had been. The baby in her womb wasn't guilty, no matter what his father had done. Or maybe *her* father.

A child. A real child. She was slowly coming to terms with that.

This baby would not pay for Carly's mistakes.

She would tell Ian everything. She would set boundaries and do her very best to make sure Ian didn't cross them. If he did, if he ever hurt her, if he ever lost his temper around the baby...

Well, then she'd figure it out. She'd have to.

As she pedaled along the city streets, leaving the peaceful residential area for the business district, she prayed for help. For guidance. Only God could get her out of this mess.

Ian's machine repair shop was a few blocks from Upham's Corner in an old warehouse. The place didn't look like much, but Ian had a handful of employees, younger men Ian liked to claim as his protégés. He made a good living. She figured, with the other guys there, Ian would have to behave himself. Not that she was afraid of his reaction, not really. He'd probably be sweet and make lots of promises. But he could be volatile, so telling him about her pregnancy at his place of business would give him time to process the information, and it would offer her relative safety as he did so.

She rode her bike through the alley and to the back of the shop. Ian's car was there, a green '69 Chevy Camaro. His baby.

His *car* baby.

She settled her hand on her abdomen, not sure what to hope for. Did she want Ian to consider this child his, to provide for him or her, to be a real father? A very human, very lonely part of her longed for that. For her child to know a father's love like she never had.

But Ian couldn't offer her baby what he didn't have himself. And the man didn't understand love. He equated love with possession.

What was she doing? She should run from here, from him, from Dorchester. But she couldn't leave her sisters. Moving into an apartment had been bad enough, but she'd still been very much a part of their lives. She'd managed their groceries and kept their place clean. She'd tried to be a mother to them. If she left for good, what would happen to the girls? Pete wouldn't step up. He'd proved that over and over. They needed Carly.

She had to do this.

Though the classic car was shiny and clean, the area around it was littered with trash, broken-down machines she couldn't identify, and an overflowing dumpster. She leaned her bike against the brick wall. It would be safe there, and she wouldn't be long. She didn't bother with the chain.

The rear garage door was closed—unusual, even in the winter. The machines inside generated enough heat and noise that the men usually preferred the fresh air. She pushed open the back door and stepped inside, surprised by the silence. No banging of metal against metal. No whine of a grinder or hiss of a blowtorch. No voices. No music.

Had Ian closed the shop for the holiday? That wasn't like him.

What should she do? Get this over with now, or come back when the other guys were there?

Footsteps sounded, and Ian rounded the corner and stepped into the hallway at the opposite end. His brown hair was longer than usual and disheveled. He wore his normal jeans and a T-shirt tight enough to show off his muscles, but something was off.

His hazel eyes narrowed as he took her in. "What the...? What are you doing here?"

She'd expected a triumphant smile, considering how long he'd been trying to get her back, but he looked surprised and not at all happy to see her.

She should have left when she'd had the chance. "It's nothing. I'll come back."

He walked toward her and stopped at the door halfway down the corridor. "You're here now. Do you need something?" He flipped on the light in the office.

"Really, I don't—"

"Just get in here, Carly."

It was too late to retreat. She stepped past him into the small, dingy room. Like the rest of the shop, it carried the scents of motor oil and sweat.

He stayed near the door, his gaze flicking around the space as if searching for an enemy. So unlike the Ian she knew, all confidence and swagger.

To put distance between them, she walked to the other side of his desk.

He yanked open the bottom drawer of a file cabinet that was probably older than his classic car. He dug his hand deep inside and came out with a paper grocery sack that had been folded around its contents. He tossed the sack on the desk between them and faced her. He ran his hand over his hair, almost as if he were nervous. Also unlike him.

"I'm sorry... about what happened. It was"—he looked toward the ceiling, maybe searching for a word—"not okay."

*Not okay.* Was that what he called it?

"Is that why you came, for an apology?"

As if that would cover it. "What's wrong, Ian? Has something—?"

"I have to go away for a while. I promise, it'll never..." His words faded, and he looked up again. Then, he hopped onto the desk and reached toward the ceiling tiles. He started to move one, then glared down at her.

She was too close to him, but there was nowhere to go now. Wall behind her, desk—and Ian—in front of her. Fear pulsed in her veins. She couldn't do this.

She couldn't tell him.

His gaze flicked from her face downward. His eyebrows lowered, scrunched together.

She looked to see what'd caught his attention, realizing then that her hand was covering her abdomen. Something she'd never done. Some bizarre protective instinct. She dropped her hand, but it was too late.

He cursed, loudly. Then said it a few times more as if by repeating her Savior's name—in vain, as the commandment put it— He might come and help.

Something was wrong. Something was very wrong. Because Ian was a lot of things, but he wasn't... this. He wasn't afraid. He wasn't the kind of guy to be angry to learn he'd fathered a child. If anything, she'd expected him to be proud. She'd expected him to see this as an avenue to worm his way back into her life.

She had no idea why he was still standing on the desk. None of this made sense. "You're obviously busy. I wanted you to hear it from me. When you have time to talk about it..." Her words trailed as Ian popped up one of the ceiling tiles and reached through the hole.

A hiding place at work, to add to the ones he had at his apartment. She'd discovered one accidentally. The other, she'd once caught him digging into. All she'd spotted was a notebook. Not exactly the Crown Jewels.

When he'd seen her watching, he warned her to keep her mouth shut.

As if she would have told anybody her boyfriend was paranoid.

What secrets was he hiding?

His hand came out with another grocery sack. He tossed it on the desk, then returned the tile in the ceiling and hopped to the floor.

He lifted both bags as if weighing them, then tossed one to her. "Take it."

She caught it. It wasn't heavy. "What is it?"

"Just take it!" The words were practically shouted, not angry but desperate. "I'll try to get in touch. Don't tell anybody the kid's mine."

"What? Why—?"

"You gotta go. Don't come back. Stay away from here and my place. Far away."

Her heart pounded, and her hands shook, her body registering some fight-or-flight instinct. Flight. Definitely flight. She pulled off her backpack and shoved the paper bag inside, hoping it wasn't drugs. Hoping she wouldn't get caught with it and sent to prison.

No, Ian never used drugs. Liquor, plenty. But not drugs.

She slipped the backpack on. "Whatever's going on..." What did she want to say to him? Be careful? Take care of yourself?

She left the sentence unfinished and started around the desk, trying to keep space between herself and Ian.

A door slammed down the hall. Back or front? She couldn't tell.

Ian swore again. With wild, terrified eyes, he shoved her back, pushing on her shoulder until her legs crumpled. "Down," he whispered. "Stay down."

What was happening?

She crouched and crawled under the old metal desk. She barely fit, especially with the backpack taking up so much space, but she dared not move.

Ian hurried out of the room. She heard his footsteps on the concrete hallway. He was running. But more footsteps came. More than one person.

A man shouted, "It's over, Murphy."

"Look." Ian's voice came not far from where she hid. "We can work something out. I won't tell anybody anything."

More footsteps, the sound of a struggle, though it was over fast.

"What's this?" the stranger asked, his voice high, almost effeminate. "Figured you'd take the money and run?"

"I don't want any trouble." Ian's words were coming fast. "You guys just do what you gotta do. I'll stay out of the way."

"It's too late for that." The man seemed calm, a glaring contrast to Ian's obvious fear. "You had your chance to join us, and you refused."

"These are my people. I promised to protect—"

His words were cut off by a thud, and Ian grunted.

"Promised to protect them?" the high-voiced man said. "Is that what you call it when you extort money from your neighbors?"

"For..." Ian wheezed the word. Had they knocked the wind out of him? "Protection."

Protection? Carly had heard about someone running a protection scheme in town, extorting money from business owners on threat of violence.

Ian was behind that?

If so, were these people law enforcement? No, police would arrest him, not beat him.

"I understand why you did it," the other man said. "My guess is that this crappy little operation barely pays for itself."

Ian ground out, "My neighbors." He gasped. "Didn't want them to lose—"

The sound of a slap, and Ian quieted.

"Spare me your philanthropic BS. You were trying to protect your income."

Ian had no answer to that.

"Is there any more of this?" the man asked.

"In the bank. Invested." Ian's voice was returning. "This is all that hasn't been scrubbed. But I can get you whatever you want, however much."

"I don't need your money," the man said. "Though we'll take this for our troubles. Hey, get that tarp."

Carly heard the sound of plastic rustling, lots of footsteps. They seemed to be moving toward the shop.

Did she dare run? Could she escape without them seeing?

"Sorry it had to be like this," the man with the high-pitched voice said. "We could have used you on our side."

"Please don't." Ian's plea was like a physical blow. She didn't love him, could barely stand him, but he was her child's father.

A gunshot reverberated around the giant space. It seemed to rattle the metal desk, her bones, her veins.

*Oh God, oh God, oh God. Help me.*

She tried to make herself smaller. Tried to disappear. Her arms wrapped around her abdomen, protecting the child she'd considered aborting.

The men's voices sounded far away. The one in charge shouted orders.

"Grab that corner."

"Get his phone."

"Wrap him tight."

"Bring the bleach."

Others added remarks. There was movement. There were footsteps.

But Ian was silent. Ian was gone.

"Bet his car's in back," one of the men said. "We should put him in it."

The high-voiced man said, "Then we search the place."

They'd find her.

She had to escape. She had to run, now, before they discovered her. If they discovered her, they'd kill her for sure.

Everything in her wanted to stay hidden beneath Ian's desk, but if she did, she'd die.

She crept out of her hiding spot. Stood. Moved to the door. Peeked into the hallway.

Nobody was there. Nobody was looking.

She took a deep breath. Prayed for help.

And bolted. She reached the back door. Pushed it open. Stepped out, and—

"Hey! Stop!" The man's voice only propelled her forward.

She climbed on her bike and pedaled hard over the gravelly asphalt. She rode down the alley that ran behind Ian's building, racing for the street, away from the men.

Behind her, shouting, calls of *Get the truck!* and *Don't lose her!*

She didn't let up or slow down. Just pedaled, pedaled...

She glanced behind and glimpsed the front of a black SUV coming down an alley where it barely fit.

She turned down another alley, around another corner. Her tires slipped, and the bicycle went down, sending her tumbling on the asphalt. Her forearm hit the hard ground. Her opposite wrist flailed and smacked into the handlebars.

She scrambled up with the bike, ignoring the pain, and started off again.

She'd lost seconds, precious seconds. She turned back toward the machine shop. Trying to throw them off.

She needed people. She needed crowds.

She pedaled toward the shops at Upham's Corner. There were cars. Shoppers. Kids.

Witnesses.

She reached the area, kept pedaling, taking random turns, keeping to side streets, glancing behind her often. After a few minutes, there was no more sign of the SUV, but she didn't slow, though her lungs burned and her legs shook with exhaustion.

Finally, she hit a straightaway and pedaled as fast as she could, putting as much distance as she could between herself and the machine shop, the killers, and home.

~

She'd been pedaling for twenty minutes before it occurred to her to call the police. She found an alley on a quiet street, straddled her bike, and dialed 911.

"A man's been murdered." She blurted the words the moment the dispatcher answered. "Ian Murphy." She rattled off the name of his shop and the address. "I was hiding in his office, and I managed to get away." As the words came out, emotions bubbled up. Terror, grief, and a million other feelings she couldn't hold onto long enough to name. She pressed her hand against her abdomen and tried to keep it all from spilling over.

"Slow down, ma'am. What's your name?"

"Carly Garcia. I live in Dorchester. I was there visiting my friend, and he was murdered. They shot him." Hysteria bubbled over, raised the pitch of her voice. The dispatcher confirmed that she was safe—was she safe? He seemed convinced, or perhaps he didn't care that much. He asked her more questions, most of which she couldn't answer. He told her they'd be in touch.

Be in touch. As if she'd called to report a stray dog. Did they get calls claiming murder every day? The man's calm demeanor grated, his casual attitude infuriated.

Carly forced deep breaths. It was the dispatcher's job to be calm. He dealt with this kind of thing every day. He didn't know her enough to care about her.

Very few people did.

Carly stowed her phone back in her pocket and started pedaling again. She couldn't go home. She couldn't lead the killers to her sisters or Pete. She couldn't risk putting them in danger.

She could go straight to the police station. The new headquarters building was outside of Dorchester but not too far away. But would the killers assume that was her destination? Would they be watching for her?

By all reports, the police were overextended. Even if she made it there without being spotted, they'd take her statement and send her on her way. As soon as she stepped out of BPD headquarters, she'd be vulnerable, more so because she'd be at the most obvious location for the killers to find her.

No. She wouldn't go to the station. She'd called and made her report. That would have to be enough. After it got dark, she'd go home. Sneak in the back and try to figure out where to hole up until the killers were caught. Pete would help.

An hour passed, an hour of choosing random paths along busy streets and through parks, sometimes on bike trails, sometimes in traffic. When she felt she was far enough away, she allowed herself to slow down. An old green line train rumbled past, surprising her. The green line was nowhere near Dorchester. Good. The goal had been to get away, and she'd gotten as far as her bike could take her before her whole body wanted to collapse in exhaustion.

She dismounted and looked for a street sign. Huntington Ave. If she went left, she'd end up in Jamaica Plain, one of the many neighborhoods that made up the city of Boston, though much smaller than her own Dorchester. To her right... A giant structure loomed on the opposite side of the street. The Museum of Fine Art. She'd been there on a field trip in eighth grade. She remembered it as being soothing. Even fifty middle schoolers hadn't been able to detract from the peace.

Carly crossed the wide avenue and train tracks and rode her bike along the circle drive, already soothed by the pretty landscaping. She chained her bike to the rack. When she stepped inside the spacious marble lobby, it seemed as if she had left all her troubles on the street outside.

The tickets weren't cheap, but nobody would think to look for her there. Maybe she could find a bench and rest. Maybe she could crawl under one and sleep.

Probably not.

As she approached the ticket counter, she pulled her backpack around to the front and shoved her hand into the outside pocket for her wallet. If she were still a student, she'd get a discount, but she'd given up school when Mama died. She'd given up everything when Mama died.

She paid for the ticket with cash and turned toward the guard who was allowing people entrance.

She watched as the party ahead of her removed their bags and held them open. The guard poked through them, studying the contents before shuffling them along.

At the acid-drop feeling in her stomach, Carly froze.

The paper sack Ian had given her... What was in it? Maybe nothing important. But what if...?

What had the high-voiced man said? Something about Ian taking the money and running?

Maybe it was cash. Maybe it was *evidence*.

Of what, she had no idea.

Whatever it was, she didn't want to—couldn't if she *did* want to —explain it to the guard.

He waved her forward. "Open your bag for me."

Carly stood frozen, unsure what to do.

His lips pressed together. "Ma'am. There's a line."

She backed up, bumped into somebody.

"Pardon me," the woman said, irritated.

But Carly couldn't think what to say. She just turned and bolted for the door.

She reached the cold February air, hurried to her bicycle, and took off again.

A few minutes later, she locked her bike up outside one of the old white Northeastern buildings and followed the signs to the student center, where she found a deserted corner.

She pulled the paper bag from her backpack and peeked inside. Then, she stuck her hand in to ensure what she saw was real.

She closed the bag again and hid it at the bottom of her backpack.

Money. Though it was piled neatly, it wasn't like the bundles of cash they showed on TV, all crisp and tidy in machine-formed stacks. She'd seen hundreds, twenties, tens, held together by rubber bands. They were crumpled, well-used bills, money that had been used to purchase coffee and office supplies and lunch. If what the man had said at Ian's shop was true, then this money belonged to Dorchester business owners. It was money Ian had extorted.

Was his machine shop mostly a front? A place to... to launder it?

She wanted to hate him for that. For being a criminal. For stealing from their neighbors. For lying to her. But Ian was dead. He'd paid for his crimes and more. She didn't know who'd killed him or why. Maybe, when she went back over what she'd heard, she'd find some clue. But at that moment, she couldn't do anything but close her eyes. The murder, the exertion of her bike ride, the pregnancy... Her body had given more than she'd have expected, but it was done. She laid her bag on the cushioned bench seat beside her, dropped her head on top of it, and closed her eyes. Nobody would bother her there.

Nobody would care.

It was after dark when Carly rode back into Dorchester, shivering in the cold winter air, legs wobbly, arm and wrist achy from when she'd fallen. If she avoided main roads, surely the killers wouldn't see her. They'd only seen her from behind, anyway. If she cut her long hair, maybe dyed it blond, they wouldn't recognize her.

She'd get a new bike. This pink one Mama had given her was too conspicuous. Or maybe she'd give up riding until she had the baby, settle for taking buses and using her own two feet. Probably safer anyway.

She'd worry about all that later. Right now, she just had to get home. When she did, she'd tell Pete everything. They weren't close, but he cared for her, even if only because she was his late wife's daughter. He didn't have any idea how to raise children or run a home, but he knew people in town. If he didn't know what she should do, he'd contact someone who would help them figure it out. She could trust her stepfather with that. And she needed somebody else to take charge. Her exhausted, terrified, and pregnant brain couldn't manage.

She saw her house in the distance, and the stress of the ride melted away. Yes, she'd tell Pete everything, but not until she'd had a good night's sleep. She could barely push herself the last block.

She dismounted in front of the yard—smaller than her bedroom and less tidy—and caught movement in the picture window. Pete always closed the blinds the second the sun went down. Was he not home yet?

No. He was there. Sitting on the couch, facing outside. Sophia sat on one side of him, Laurie and Danielle on the other.

All four on the same sofa. That was weird. They never watched TV together as a family, and even if that was what they were doing, they wouldn't sit together, not with a loveseat and club chair in the room.

A tall, well-built man paced in front of the window, gaze on Carly's family.

Another man stood behind them in the dark space between the living room and the kitchen. She couldn't get a good look at his face, but he was shorter, thinner.

Sophia and Danielle's eyes never left the man in front of them. But Laurie looked toward the window, and her gaze snagged on Carly. Eyes wide, she shook her head slightly, then looked away.

A warning.

Somehow, the killers had tracked her down. They knew where she lived. How? *How!*

Had they seen her face? No. They couldn't have.

Did they know her history with Ian and guess that she was the woman who'd been there? Maybe, though she and Ian hadn't been together for a year.

Or was it the 911 call? Was it possible the killers knew somebody on the police force? Had somebody tipped them off?

However it had happened, the killers held her family captive. They were probably waiting for her. If she went inside, would they leave her family alone? Just take her?

No. She couldn't give herself up, not with a child inside her.

And the killers wouldn't let any of them live. How could they, if they killed Carly?

She mounted her bicycle and rode away. When she'd gone a few blocks, she shoved her Air Pods in and dialed 911.

"I need to report a home invasion." She rattled off her address. "The people in the house are the same ones who murdered Ian Murphy today."

She didn't know for sure, but it was a safe guess.

"Is this Carly Garcia?" the man asked. "We have a few questions for you about—"

"You need to get to my house. They're going to kill my family!"

"Ma'am, I've dispatched a patrol car already. Meanwhile, we need you to come in and file a report."

Come in. Come into the police station, where it was possible somebody was feeding the killers information. Maybe. She didn't know.

What she did know was that she needed to get out of town, fast. Before her loved ones got hurt.

Carly stopped in a driveway between two houses, keeping to the shadows cast by the streetlights. From there, she could watch and make sure her family stayed safe.

A few minutes later, a police cruiser parked at the curb in front of Carly's home. The cops knocked on the door. A minute, maybe two, passed before Pete answered and ushered them inside.

Carly waited for the intruders to be taken out in handcuffs. But it didn't happen.

Ten minutes later, the cops walked out, climbed into their cruiser, and drove away.

Either Carly had read the situation wrong—she didn't think so—or Pete had covered for the men.

And if that happened, that meant they'd threatened him.

Probably threatened the girls.

Carly could only guess what those men had said to Pete.

Whatever it was, it meant she couldn't go home. Not now. Not until Ian's killers were brought to justice.

# CHAPTER THREE

Carly put a couple of miles between herself and her home before calling the police again, telling them she believed her stepfather and stepsisters were in danger. The dispatcher listened politely, asked a few questions, and said someone would call her back.

"Just keep them safe." She'd tried to put force behind her words, but her voice cracked on the last one. She ended the call, prayed for Pete and the girls, and dialed again.

Mrs. Reilly answered right away. "Hello?"

"It's Carly. I need help." She peddled north as she related the story, ignoring Mrs. Reilly's gasps of shock as she did so.

When she was finished, Mrs. Reilly said, "You need to go to the police."

"They're not going to help me," Carly said. "They'll take my statement, but what else would they do? And anyway, what if they're the ones who tipped off the killers about who I am?"

That question was met with silence. After a moment, Mrs. Reilly sighed. "I see your point."

"I have to get out of town. I'm just not sure where to go. And…" Carly's eyes filled with tears, but she shook them off. Riding a bike at night wasn't exactly safe, and crying would only ramp up the degree of difficulty. She was so confused, so tired. "I don't know what to do. I'm headed to South Station. I thought a bus or a train. I just need advice."

"Forget that," Mrs. Reilly said. "Come here. We'll protect you."

"No!" Carly's bottom lip quivered. How lovely it would be to go back to their peaceful home. To step into Mrs. Reilly's comforting arms. "It's not safe. I won't put you or your family in danger. If anybody were to see me—"

"We can keep you hidden."

"I'm not coming to your house. Anywhere else. Just... New York? It's so expensive, though." She thought of the money in her backpack. That money wasn't hers. And how long would it last in a city like New York?

"Hold on, dear." Mrs. Reilly said something, but the words were muffled, and then Mr. Reilly came on the line. "We have an extra car. You can take it."

"I don't want—"

"You called us for help," he said. "Let us help. Tell us where you are, and we'll come to you."

She turned into a gas station parking lot and stopped, needing to rest. Needing to think. She inhaled the frigid night air, trying to ignore the sharp scent of gasoline. She had called them, and she did need help. For her child, she would take what they offered. "Okay. If you don't mind my borrowing your car."

"Of course we don't mind. It's nothing fancy, just that old Monte Carlo Braden used to drive."

She remembered it. He'd bought it for a couple of hundred dollars back in high school and then spent more time fixing it than driving it. "You don't think he'd mind?"

"It's mine now," Mr. Reilly said. "He got himself a fancy new truck and gave it to me. We use it for family emergencies, and I'd say this qualifies."

Family. If only she were part of their family.

She pulled in another deep breath, a plan forming in her mind. "Meet me at South Station." She pushed off and started pedaling north on Dorchester Avenue.

Fifteen minutes later, she chained her bike outside the bus station and went inside. Her nerves were shot, her senses registering danger everywhere. People sat on chairs and leaned against walls, many staring at a TV in the corner, but most focused on their phones. Buses idled outside, and the scent of exhaust permeated the space.

She got in line and stared at the bus schedule. The next bus was leaving for Albany in five minutes, at seven. She bought a ticket, smiling at the man behind the counter and making conversation. Hoping to be remembered, if anybody should come looking.

Ticket in hand, she went out the doors to where the buses waited, then walked between two and reached the street. She was tempted to take her bike, but if anybody came looking, its presence at the station would add to the story she was trying to tell—that she'd boarded a bus for New York. It killed her to leave it. That trusty bicycle had been with her since she was barely tall enough to ride, a gift from her mother on her twelfth birthday. It had been her freedom, her refuge after Mama's death. As of that day, it had saved her life.

The old gold Monte Carlo was idling at the curb. When Mr. Reilly saw her, he nodded forward and drove away.

She followed two blocks on foot, keeping her head down. Not that the people looking for her would have access to street cameras —were there street cams?—but it didn't hurt to be cautious. That was what Mr. Reilly was doing, trying not to get her caught on camera getting into his car. Smart.

He turned down a narrow side street and was climbing from the driver's seat just as Carly turned the corner. When she approached, he opened his arms, and she fell into them. He smelled like Old Spice and safety, and it was all she could do to hold it together and not crumble into a bawling mess.

Another car turned onto the street, and Carly backed away, realizing she'd been holding on too long.

Mrs. Reilly got out and ran to her, pulling her into another hug.

Carly needed to get on the road, but she didn't want to leave these two kind people.

While she reveled in the woman's embrace, Mr. Reilly spoke over them. "Father, we commit Carly and her precious babe into Your arms. Protect her and bring to justice those who are pursuing her. We trust You with this."

The simple prayer washed over her like a warm breeze, and her tears bubbled up and spilled over.

"It's okay, sweetheart," Mrs. Reilly whispered. "You're going to be all right. You're safe now."

Carly pulled herself together and stepped away. "I don't know where I'll go, but—"

"We do." The older woman pressed a slip of paper into Carly's hands, along with a wad of cash. "It's not much, but it'll help."

"I can't take this." She tried to give the money back, but Mrs. Reilly wasn't taking it.

"Go to Braden," the older woman said.

"What? No, I—"

"I wrote his address down. He's in New Hampshire, far from here. He can keep you safe."

"I can't..." What was she saying? How could Carly go to Braden?

Mrs. Reilly took Carly's shoulders and met her eyes. "Braden can protect you. He has a house big enough for you. He can help you."

"He won't want me—"

"You need time to regroup." She squeezed Carly's shoulders. "From there, you can figure out what to do next, but you need somebody to take care of you."

She didn't, did she? She was the one who took care of everybody else. And the thought of seeing Braden, of telling him everything. It scared her. She couldn't do it.

But part of her wanted to, more than anything.

"That's the deal." Mr. Reilly stood beside his wife, expression kind but firm. "You take our car, you go to Braden."

"Oh."

Mrs. Reilly was quick to add, "Because we want you to be safe, and you'll be safe with him."

A police car's siren blared from the main street beside them, and Carly jumped. "I have to go."

"We're serious," Mr. Reilly said.

"I'll warn him you're on the way," his wife added.

"Go." He held open the door. "Hurry, before someone sees us."

Carly tossed her backpack across to the passenger seat, hugged them both, and climbed in. With shaking fingers, she plugged Braden's address into her phone and drove away, watching the kindest people she'd ever known fade in the rearview mirror.

She was relieved to be getting out of town, terrified and excited, all at the same time.

She was going to see Braden.

# CHAPTER FOUR

Braden Reilly poured more tortilla chips into the bowl, trying not to think about the events of the day.

"Mind if I grab another soda?" Reid asked, stepping into the kitchen from the living room.

"Help yourself."

From the other room, James called, "I'll take a Dr Pepper."

"Since when am I your errand boy?" Reid yelled back, but he snatched two cans from the fridge.

"What kind of shot was that?" Thomas's voice carried through the doorway.

He and Garrett talked strategy as if their decisions might affect the final score of the basketball game.

Sodas in hand, Reid leaned against Braden's counter. "Figured you might invite Andrew tonight." The new guy, the guy Jacqui had hired without consulting Braden. The guy she'd been so excited to tell him about.

Braden thought he'd done a good job stepping into the management vacuum Jacqui's partner had left. When Jacqui'd mentioned a month before that she was creating a business manager/researcher position at BNB, Braden had assumed she was creating the position for him, considering he'd been doing the job for months. But it seemed that, despite all Braden had done on the business end of things, Jacqui didn't trust his judgment or didn't think he'd been doing a good job—or both. Not that she'd come right out and announced that Andrew Middleton would be given the job Braden craved, but it was clear in the way her eyes had sparkled when she'd mentioned Andrew's MBA that she would ultimately offer it to him.

Usually, it wasn't awkward that Braden's best friend in Coventry was also his boss's fiancé, but it felt that way tonight as Reid studied him.

"I didn't think of it," Braden said.

"Okay." The way Reid drew out the two syllables, studying Braden all the while, told him his friend wasn't as clueless as Jacqui about Braden's ambitions.

Braden did his best to sound lighthearted. "I'll invite him next week."

Reid headed back to the living room.

Braden followed with the chips and a fresh bowl of salsa. He hadn't watched a lot of sports in recent years, too busy in college and grad school and working, but now that he was living in Coventry, he had more time on his hands. And he had friends, actual friends, to come over and watch with him. It had started in the fall with Monday Night Football. When the season ended, the guys kept coming. They watched whatever game was on, basketball or hockey in the winter. They'd add baseball come spring.

Thomas and Garrett were on the couch, eyes fixed on the screen. Braden had met them at church, single guys who were, like him, new to Coventry.

James sat on a kitchen chair he'd dragged to the side of the sofa, unwilling to snuggle up beside the guys. He snatched a handful of chips as Braden walked by.

Reid reclined in the love seat as if he owned the place. The guy didn't get out alone much, what with a little girl to take care of, but Jacqui urged him to watch the games with them on Mondays while she and Ella had a girls' night.

Braden slid the chips and salsa onto the coffee table beside the plate of cold cuts James had brought from his restaurant. "Anybody need anything else?"

After grabbing a couple more sodas, he settled back into his chair and focused on the screen. He wasn't a huge fan of watching sports for no good reason, and he couldn't have cared less who won this matchup. Mondays were about the camaraderie. It'd been years since he'd been able to nurture friendships. Without a girlfriend or a wife, living so far from his family, he needed people.

Until today, he'd loved everything about his new life. The house he'd been able to buy—something he could never have afforded back in Boston. His new church. His new job. Now, though, thoughts of that job soured his stomach.

But the new guy hadn't been given the title of manager yet. At this point, Andrew was just another researcher, like Braden. Braden would have to demonstrate to Jacqui that he could handle the management position before she offered it to Andrew. His plan to seamlessly step into the role obviously wasn't going to work. He'd need to come up with something unique, something to prove his value.

As the thought came to mind, so did an idea. The biggest obstacle BNB had faced since they'd moved from Boston to Plymouth, New Hampshire, was the lack of a suitable employee pool. They needed more researchers, but most candidates weren't eager to move to central New Hampshire. They didn't understand what a great place it was to live, to own property, and to raise a family. Tonight, Braden would put together a comprehensive plan to educate potential employees about the benefits of central New Hampshire—the lower-priced real estate, the excellent schools, the many places to enjoy the outdoors all year round, and the quick access to the interstate. And that was just off the top of his head. Braden had been leery of making the move, but now that he was here, he had zero desire to move back to Boston. He felt confident other researchers would feel the same way if they gave it a chance.

While his friends watched the game, Braden tapped on his

laptop, recording his ideas and coming up with new ones. If Jacqui accepted this proposal, he'd be one step closer to becoming BNB's permanent manager and securing his place with the company.

As far as Braden was concerned, the only minutes worth watching in basketball games were the last four. This game was down to one. The Celtics were losing by three and had the ball.

Someone banged on the door. Who in the world could that be? Everybody he cared to see was already there. In fact, almost everybody he knew in Coventry, with the exception of Jacqui and a few coworkers, was sitting in his living room.

The guys were focused on the TV. He set his laptop aside and headed for the front door.

Nothing could have prepared him for the woman standing on his stoop. The sounds of the game, the guys yelling... They all faded to background noise.

Carly's eyes were wide. She blinked, stepped back on the concrete stoop. "Your mom didn't tell you?"

He could hardly hear her through the glass storm door and pushed it open.

She took another step back, out of its way.

"What are you doing here?"

"She was going to..." Carly started to take another step back.

Braden gripped her arm an instant before her foot met air. The stoop wasn't that big. When she was steady on her feet, he asked, "You all right?"

"I'm sorry. I would never... I didn't want to come here, but they insisted. Your mom said she'd warn you."

He tapped his pockets for his phone. Not there. Where had he left it? It wasn't like him to ignore it, but he'd been doing just that for hours, focused on his friends and the ideas firing in his brain for the proposal he hoped to have ready the next day. "I haven't checked my phone in a while."

"Oh."

He waited for Carly to add more to the single syllable, some words that would explain what she was doing at his house at nine thirty on a Monday night.

The very last thing Braden needed was Carly and all the drama that would surely come with her. What could she possibly want? How did she even...?

He spotted it then, his old Monte Carlo parked half in the snow-covered yard, half on the road.

Everything in him wanted to send her away. She'd lost her right to ask anything of him when she'd rejected his proposal. He'd spent years getting over her, and the last thing he needed was for her to needle her way back into his life.

But his parents had sent her. He had to at least find out what was going on. She'd probably ask for money. He'd gladly give her whatever she needed and send her on her way.

"Come on in." He directed her through the dark, empty dining room and into the kitchen, avoiding the guys in the living room. They yelled as the buzzer sounded on the TV. The game was over, and based on their unhappy remarks, the Celtics had lost.

Fitting end to a good night turned bad.

Carly stepped into Braden's small eat-in kitchen and looked around, assessing it. "This is yours?" Was that wonder in her voice?

"Real estate's more affordable here."

"Sure. But still... Wow."

"Have a seat. I'll be right—"

"Hey. Who was at the...?" Reid stepped into the kitchen and smiled at Carly, sticking out his hand. "Hi. I'm Reid Cote."

"Carly Garcia."

As they shook hands, the other guys filed in, carrying their cups and plates and dropping them on the counter. They all introduced themselves. They all gave Braden questioning looks.

Normally, they'd hang out for a while, help him pick up and fill the dishwasher. But tonight, they grabbed their keys and called their good-byes within minutes of the end of the game, shooting him looks over their shoulders.

When the rest had gone, Reid lingered at the front door, lowering his voice. "What's going on?"

"No idea. She just showed up."

"Can I help?"

Braden shrugged. "She probably needs money."

"Want me to stay until—?"

"No, no. Get home to Ella. We'll be fine."

Reid gripped Braden's shoulder and squeezed. "You need anything, anything at all, just call."

"I will. Thanks."

When Reid was gone, Braden closed the door and pressed his forehead against it. He shot up a quick prayer for wisdom before returning to the kitchen.

Carly was still standing in the middle of the space, arms crossed, jacket on. "I didn't mean to interrupt."

"It's fine."

Her gaze flicked around the room, looking at everything but him. "Can I use your bathroom?"

"Oh. Sure." He directed her to the one between the kitchen and the living room. "Help yourself."

She removed a backpack he hadn't noticed and her bright red parka, the same one she'd worn years before, leaving them both on a kitchen chair, then disappeared into the bathroom.

He dumped the remains of the bowl of chips into the trash, stowed the leftover cold cuts in a zipper bag, and tossed out the container they'd come in. He covered the dip and slipped it into the fridge, then loaded the dishwasher and wiped down the counters.

What was Carly doing in there? He checked his phone, but the texts and voicemails from his mother only offered warnings that Carly was on her way. He shot off a quick *She's here. What's going on?*

Mom's response was immediate. *Glad she made it. I'm sure she'll tell you. Be nice.*

Be nice. Like he was in kindergarten.

He shoved the phone into his pocket, grabbed the kitchen chair from the living room, and put it where it belonged.

His house was back to normal. Except that Carly was there.

Finally, the bathroom door opened, and she stepped into the room.

He hated the way his heart rate still kicked up at the sight of her. But that was only physical, a perfectly reasonable reaction to a beautiful woman. And Carly was that and more. Hair and eyes dark as night, skin pale and clear. Full lips. Very kissable lips.

Though she'd hidden her body beneath an oversize sweatshirt, there'd been a time when he'd been intimately acquainted with every curve. There'd been a time when he'd thought he'd spend the rest of his life—

*Stop it.*

She was gazing around his house and hadn't noticed his staring. Good thing. The last thing he wanted was to start anything with Carly. He'd been there and had the scars to prove it.

He forced his gaze off her and saw his kitchen fresh from her eyes. He hadn't done much to the house since he bought it a few months before. The walls had already been painted beige. The kitchen and bathrooms had been updated—new tile, new granite countertops. He'd bought the black square kitchen table in Concord not long after he'd moved in—along with the sofa and chairs in the living room and all the other furniture he'd needed. When Mom had come up, she'd added a few decorating touches in here—a centerpiece, some new kitchen towels. But mostly it was sparse and utilitarian, just like he liked it.

Based on Carly's assessment, she was impressed.

Not that he cared. "Are you going to tell me why you're here?"

She gestured to the table. "Mind if I—?"

"Go ahead."

She collapsed into a chair, propped her elbows on the wood,

and dropped her head into her hands. When she did, her sweat-shirt slid down her arms, revealing a black-and-blue smudge that covered the back of her wrist.

He sat beside her and tapped her hand. "What happened?

She looked at the bruise as if she'd never seen it before. "Oh. I fell. My bike skidded on the gravel."

"You never fall."

She shrugged. "I wasn't paying attention to where I was going."

Also something Carly rarely did. The woman had been riding the streets of Boston for as long as he'd known her. Back in high school, she'd had a delivery job and had whipped all around the city on that thing, weaving through traffic, taking all the shortcuts. She made a lot of money at that job because she was fast and reliable.

That she'd fallen surprised him.

That she was here, in New Hampshire... That she'd driven his old car—he hadn't even known she had a license—all the way to his house.

All of it surprised him.

"What's wrong, Carly? What happened?"

When she looked at him again, he noticed her red-rimmed eyes, the black smudges beneath them. He wasn't sure how he'd missed them before. He'd been imagining the girl he'd once known, not the one here tonight. "It's sort of a long story."

"You drove all the way up here. Surely you can spare a few minutes to tell me why."

She pulled in a long breath, then blew it out. "I had to get out of town for a while. Your parents let me use their car, and they insisted I come here."

"Why?"

"I guess they thought you'd—"

"No. I mean..." He forced a patient tone. "I understand why my parents would send you to me." They loved Carly like a daugh-ter, despite the fact that she'd broken his heart. It wasn't that they'd taken Carly's side when she'd rejected his proposal, but they'd understood.

He hadn't, not at all. All he'd wanted was to take care of her, to keep her safe. And she'd rejected him, using her family as an excuse. Why would she give up life with a man she supposedly loved in order to look after three girls who weren't even related to her?

Because she didn't love him, not enough.

"Why did you have to get out of town?" he prompted.

She sat back, lowered her hands to her lap. Started to speak, but the words were cut off by a yawn.

It was a few minutes shy of ten o'clock, but she looked exhausted.

Though part of him was tempted to send her on her way, his parents had urged her to go to his house. They must know what was going on. He wasn't sure he trusted Carly, but he did trust them.

And the fear in Carly's eyes...?

He couldn't send her away.

But he had stuff to do. He didn't have to have all the answers right then. Frankly, he didn't have to have the answers ever. If she just needed a place to crash, he could provide one. If she wanted to leave without telling him her story, he wouldn't stop her. What did he care?

He did care, idiot that he was, but he shouldn't.

"It's all right," he said. "I assume you need a bed?"

"I know it's a lot to ask. Like I said, I wouldn't have come, but your parents made me promise. I can leave tomorrow, but tonight, I'm so tired. I filled up the car, so there's plenty of gas to keep me warm. I could sleep—"

"You're not sleeping in the car." He hadn't meant the words to sound so harsh, but as the reality of what was about to happen hit him, he felt unsettled. He forced a gentle tone. "Do you need anything to eat? Drink?"

"No. I'm..." The words were cut off by another yawn.

"Why don't you go upstairs? Turn left at the top, the guest room is on the right. There's only one bathroom up there, but I can use the one down here tonight. I'll need to shower tomorrow, but otherwise... Did you lock the car? I'll go get your suitcase."

Her gaze flicked to his but didn't hold. "I don't have a suitcase. Just..." She indicated the clothes she was wearing.

Odd. Fishy, even. He allowed a moment to process that information, then said, "Okay. I have an extra toothbrush. Do you want to borrow a T-shirt, maybe a pair of sweatpants?" Not that they'd fit her, but they'd keep her warm.

"If you don't mind."

He minded, but she was there, and she clearly needed a place to regroup. He could provide that place for one night, anyway. "Come on."

# CHAPTER FIVE

THE EVENTS of the day had invaded her rest. All night, she'd pedaled on her bicycle, desperate to flee from faceless, nameless killers. She saw her sisters, only they weren't seated but slouched over and lifeless on the couch. She gasped awake at the sound of phantom gunshots.

She didn't know when the nightmares finally gave way to sleep, but last she remembered before she fell asleep, the sun had been brightening the sky outside the window. Now, she stretched in the queen-sized bed and listened for signs of life.

Aside from a low hum—she guessed the furnace—the world was silent. No cars on the street outside. No squabbling of sisters. No voices carrying from the neighborhood.

In the city, there was always noise. Always light too. Even in the middle of the night, lights from homes and apartments and stores and offices spilled onto sidewalks. Floodlights, headlights, streetlights... there were always lights.

But as soon as Carly had exited the interstate the night before, she'd been in total darkness. She'd never seen such darkness. The fear that had plagued her all day threatened to do her in on that long drive from the highway, so much so that by the time she had arrived at Braden's, she'd been downright terrified. She'd had to force herself to walk up his plowed driveway and not bolt through the snow to his front door. Intellectually, she'd known nobody was behind her—she'd surely have seen headlights cutting through all that blackness. But fear came from deep in the belly, from memories and notions not rooted in logical thought.

When Braden had opened the door and ushered her inside, despite the suspicion in his eyes and the reluctance in his voice, she'd felt safe. For the first time since she'd taken that pregnancy test, she'd felt safe.

Maybe for the first time since Braden left her.

Maybe for the first time since her mother died.

Not that the feeling with Braden had lasted.

Now, she glanced at the time on her phone—after nine in the morning. She stood, paused through a wave of nausea, and slipped into the sweatpants Braden had given her, cinching the drawstring waist tight. She opened the blinds, and the dull winter sunshine illuminated the pretty blue comforter as she made the bed. The headboard matched the end tables on both sides and the bureau. They all looked brand new. Braden had called this a guest room. It was a decent size and bland—beige walls, no pictures, no decorations. Who'd slept there before her? His parents? Siblings? Friends, maybe? She tiptoed to the door and opened it, wincing at the creak in the hinge. But the house was silent.

After visiting the restroom, she crept along the hallway and down the long flight of stairs, half afraid of seeing Braden, half eager to do so. At the bottom, she glanced at the dining room, which she'd walked through the night before. She knew it was a dining room because of the chandelier hanging from the center of the ceiling. But aside from the light fixture, the room was empty.

She turned to take in the living room, which she hadn't gotten more than a glance of when she'd arrived. Hardwood floors. A brown leather couch with a matching love seat on one side, a chair on the other, all angled toward a big-screen TV. No pictures on the walls. No area rug. No decor of any kind.

Had he recently moved in, or was he not the decorating type?

The second, probably. Maybe the first too.

There were a couple of photographs in frames on the coffee table. She sat on the cool sofa and studied them. Braden's parents and siblings and nieces.

No unidentified women. Maybe no girlfriend? Certainly no wife, or else his parents would have warned Carly.

Which meant Braden lived in this very family-friendly house all alone. If she'd said yes to him three years before, would this be her home? Her life?

But she'd had to say no. As much as it had broken her heart, she hadn't had a choice. Braden hadn't understood, and that had been the end of their relationship, the beginning of her descent into...

She didn't know how to classify the years since Braden left. Suffice it to say, they'd been bad. Very, very bad.

What would it be like to have so much space to herself? Even Ian, for all his income, didn't live this well. He had a new townhouse with nice furniture, but his place was nothing like this.

Except Ian didn't have any of those things anymore. He didn't even have breath in his lungs, life in his body.

She shuddered at the memory. Poor Ian. No matter what he'd done, he hadn't deserved to be murdered.

Carly couldn't think about him. Not here in Braden's house, not now. Because she should feel all sorts of things. She should feel sadness and grief and pain at his loss. But what she felt more than anything was relief.

And guilt, because what kind of person did that make her? She patted her abdomen, thought of the child she carried. Ian wouldn't have been a good father. He might have tried, but in the end, unless he'd surrendered his life to Christ—and she'd been praying since she'd become a Christian that he would—he would have been a terrible father. Awful as it was, her child had been spared that, at least.

Carly had sworn, sworn she would never bring a child into the world until she had a man by her side. She'd been raised without a father, and she never wanted to put her child through that. And yet, here she was, following in Mama's footsteps, the ones Mama had tried so hard to get her to avoid.

She continued through the living room. She couldn't imagine being able to afford a house and new furniture and a car. How did Braden do it?

He'd left a note beside a key on the kitchen table. *Off to work. Be home about five thirty. Help yourself to whatever you want. Sorry there isn't more to eat. Don't leave without letting me know. —B*

Below the words, he'd jotted his phone number, as if she wouldn't remember it. As if she hadn't called him and texted him a million times in their former lives.

She reread the note. She wasn't supposed to leave without telling him? What did he mean? She couldn't go to the store without his permission? What if she did? Was there an *or else* attached to that? Memories of similar threats had nausea churning again, but no, Braden wasn't like that. Braden wasn't like Ian at all. Surely, he only wanted to know what she was up to. He wanted to know if he'd be coming home to her or an empty house. He'd probably prefer the second, but she had nowhere else to go.

Her stomach bubbled and churned. She'd gotten a burger and fries at a drive-through on her way north the night before, but she was starving now. She opened his cabinets, spying glasses and plates and cookware. Not helpful. A door caught her eye, and she pulled it open. A pantry.

"Jackpot."

Her word sounded too loud in the silence, but it wasn't as if there were anyone there to hear. She snatched a box of crackers, freed a couple from their sleeve, and munched. After she ate a few more, the nausea settled, and she looked for something more substantial.

After a thorough search of Braden's pantry, refrigerator, and freezer, she concluded that he must eat a lot of take-out.

The man didn't even have eggs.

She toasted two pieces of bread, buttered them, and added a glass of water.

Not coffee, though she did gaze longingly at his Keurig.

Toast in hand, she stood at the sliding glass door that led out the back. The house must have been built onto a hillside because, though she was on the first floor, the deck was quite a distance from the ground below. The snow had melted in Boston, but obviously it was much colder here in the mountains. How did Braden stand it? Even as she asked the question, though, her gaze lifted to the woods behind his house.

Dark brown trunks rose to needles and bare branches. The pines and oaks and maples were interspersed with white birch trees. She'd never realized how starkly beautiful a winter forest could be. Of course, she'd never been this far from home. In fact, she'd never even left the city, except for a field trip to visit Plymouth Plantation when she was a kid. The only nature she'd ever experienced had been in the parks near her house. She'd never skied. She'd never visited a lake. She'd never been to the beach.

Her entire life had been lived in Boston, most of it in her Dorchester neighborhood. There'd been no money for a car when she was a kid, much less vacations. And she and her mother hadn't needed to go anywhere to have fun. Mama had made the world fun every day. They'd had barbecues and invited the whole neighborhood. Every Fourth of July, Mama orchestrated scavenger hunts for the kids on the block. At Thanksgiving, she invited people who had no place else to go. At Christmas, she decorated every surface and hosted cookie exchanges and organized caroling. Mama had made life fun.

But had Mama wanted to get out of Boston? Had she longed to visit the beach, the mountains, the lakes? Had she longed to see Puerto Rico, where her parents had been born?

Carly had never thought to ask those questions, and now it was too late.

Grow up, get married, stay in Boston forever. That was what Mama had done—well, except the marriage part, not until Carly was eighteen—and that was what Carly had planned. If not for Ian's having insisted, she'd never have learned to drive or gotten her license. Who needed a car when there were buses and trains and bicycles?

Who needed to leave the city when everything a person needed was right there?

As Carly took in the beauty all around her, she wondered what else she'd missed. Because this was amazing. She'd seen pictures of nature, of course. She'd watched TV and seen movies. But this was like nothing she'd ever imagined.

She munched her toast and sipped her water. Yes, she could see why Braden liked it here. Carly had always been a city dweller. Braden had always been so much more.

After she ate, she found a hairbrush and brushed her hair and slipped back into the clothes she'd worn the day before. She powered up the no-contract phone she'd bought at the service station the night before and called her work, explaining she wouldn't be in for the rest of the week, citing an emergency.

Her supervisor had been unimpressed, even threatening to fire her. As if she'd risk her life to save her crappy customer service job.

In the end, he'd huffed a long breath and said, "Fine. See you next Monday."

Part of her was sorry she hadn't lost the job she hated.

What next?

She'd need a plan, soon. But for now, she felt safe in Coventry. Nobody in the world would guess where she was. Surely the police would arrest the people responsible for Ian's murder soon, and she could go home. If Braden would let her stay until then, she'd be safe.

If she was going to stay, then she'd need to make herself useful. She sent Braden a quick text. *Off to the store. Need anything?*

She started the Monte Carlo and let it warm up, then searched her phone for the closest grocery store, figuring she'd call Braden if he didn't respond soon. But Braden's answer came as she pulled into the parking lot. *Get whatever you want. I'll pay you back.*

Kind of him, but she could afford food. The money Mr. Reilly had handed her, plus what she'd withdrawn from an ATM machine the night before, could last weeks.

She wasn't going to think about the paper sack filled with cash. She wasn't going to touch it, not unless she had no choice. She didn't know what she'd do with it, but for now, it would stay hidden in her backpack.

She grabbed the ingredients for a couple of meals along with a few staples Braden's kitchen had lacked, then added toothpaste and other toiletries to her basket and checked out, paying with the money Mrs. Reilly had given her the night before. When she left, she found a small clothing store—an overpriced shop aimed, no doubt, at tourists—and grabbed a few days' worth of necessities—underwear, socks, a few T-shirts, and a sweatshirt with one of those front pouches. The black fabric was emblazoned with the words *Lake Ayasha. The "Little One" with the Big Fun.*

Whatever that meant.

Back at Braden's, she unloaded the car, showered, and changed her clothes, feeling normal for the first time since she'd taken the pregnancy test. Had it only been one day? Seemed like she'd lived a year since then.

She settled in to wait for Braden to come home. When he did, he'd surely want an explanation. The thought of telling him what had happened set her stomach to churning again. She could drive away and avoid that unpleasant conversation. Avoid admitting she was carrying another man's child, and avoid the judgment she'd surely see in his expression.

She would leave to avoid all of that.

If she had anywhere else to go.

## CHAPTER SIX

Braden waited for the copies to print, sending up a quick prayer asking for God's blessing on his plans, and then headed for Jacqui's desk. He skirted the machines, where other researchers were busy working on their latest project. He'd been the first to join Jacqui here, but they'd brought more on board since she'd relocated the company from Boston to Plymouth. His desk was nearest hers—not across from it, as Don's had been at their lab back in the city, but close enough. He'd been her confidant at BNB since Don left, and he liked it. He liked knowing he mattered, knowing he was more than just another employee.

Not that there was anything wrong with being a researcher. He loved his job. He was doing exactly what he'd dreamed of doing ever since he learned about the medical device industry back in high school. He'd worked hard and been offered a scholarship to MIT—no easy feat, that. And then he'd gone on to earn his master's and probably would have continued with his studies until he'd earned a doctorate if Don and Jacqui hadn't recruited him. So, it wasn't that he wasn't happy with his job, but he wanted more. He needed more. He needed to know he was indispensable, that, no matter what ups and downs the medical research development community faced, he would always have a job.

He could still remember the day Dad had told the family that he'd been "let go." Braden had been seven years old and hadn't immediately understood what that meant. Dad had been fired—fired because he'd refused to tell an elderly customer on a fixed income that her car required repairs it didn't really need. The boss had told Dad that he wasn't a team player, that the company needed guys they could count on.

Not count on to be honest, though. Count on to swindle little old ladies.

Dad had believed the Lord would bless him for his obedience, and He had. But that blessing had come after a lot of hardship. Dad had gotten another job quickly, but the money he earned changing oil at a quickie drive-through place was nothing like what he'd earned as a master mechanic. Braden's parents had fallen behind on the rent on their dingy little apartment and been evicted. They'd lived in a homeless shelter for months while Dad worked at the shop and Mom did her best to keep the kids fed and protected from other homeless people, many of whom were mentally ill or addicts or both. Even after they'd put away the money to secure another apartment, if not for food stamps, they wouldn't have had enough to eat.

Braden would never go through that again. He'd worked hard in school, secured scholarships, excelled at MIT, and been awarded a fellowship to continue his studies, all with the goal of ultimately getting a stable job so he could support himself and his future family. He needed Jacqui to make him the business manager at BNB. Researchers, though not exactly a dime a dozen, were replaceable, but if he were the business manager, he'd always have a job with BNB. Considering Jacqui's considerable intelligence—he'd never known anyone as bright as she—her company would be successful only if she had somebody with business acumen to steer it in the right direction. Reid, her soon-to-be husband, could play that role, but he had a business of his own. No, Jacqui needed somebody who understood the R and D world, somebody who worked for her full time.

Braden wanted to be that somebody.

He left the research area that made up the front of the facility and peered across the desks to Jacqui's. She wasn't there. She had been a moment before, though. He checked the break room. Empty except for the counter, sink, and small refrigerator. Someone had left a platter of cookies on the counter, and he snatched one, biting it as he walked away. He poked his head into the conference room and found Jacqui seated at the far end of the long table. He'd been with her when she'd picked it out and the twenty chairs that went with it. Their entire operation consisted of only eight people, but it was just a matter of time before they would have enough employees to fill all the chairs and more.

She was bent over a stack of papers, so he knocked on the doorjamb. "Sorry to bother you."

She looked up and smiled. "Not a bother at all. What's up?"

"Do you mind if I...?" He nodded to the seat beside her.

She pushed her papers out of the way. "Please."

Tamping down his nerves, he settled in the chair beside her. "I've been thinking about our difficulties attracting talented researchers to Plymouth."

She leaned back in her chair and pushed her long red hair away from her face. She used to always wear it in a ponytail, but she'd adopted a softer look since she'd moved to New Hampshire. Back in Boston, he'd thought of her as brilliant and insightful and unique in an industry where uniqueness and outside-the-box thinking were rewarded. He still saw her as all those things, but now he also saw her as a woman, an attractive, joyful woman. "Definitely an issue. When whatshername turned us down, the one who wrote that brilliant dissertation on nanotech in cancer diagnostics, the one from Stanford... You know who I mean..."

Typical of Jacqui to remember what the woman studied but not her name. "Amber Cho."

"Right. Her. That was a blow."

"That's why I put this together." He laid the papers in front of her. "Last night, I was brainstorming ideas for how we could attract researchers to Plymouth. I thought we could..."

Jacqui lifted a finger in the universal sign for *give me a minute* and perused his proposal.

Braden did everything in his power not to shift nervously while she read. He was proud of the ideas he'd come up with. Among others, he thought they should develop a glossy brochure highlighting all the benefits of central New Hampshire and put together an annual event inviting future graduates from the best schools in the area to visit Plymouth for the weekend. The candidates would meet Jacqui—a draw in itself for anybody who knew anything about their industry—and get to tour the facility. There would be plenty of time to explore the lakes and mountains. They could have a seminar on local real estate and schools. After people got a look at New Hampshire, they wouldn't want to leave. He knew he didn't.

Finally, Jacqui looked up, eyes bright. "This is excellent." She slid the papers she'd been studying earlier to Braden. "Great minds think alike, I guess. I've been mulling over the problem myself, which is why I asked Andrew to come up with some ideas."

Braden's nerves formed a ball and settled in his gut. He glanced at the colorful papers, Andrew's proposal to solve the exact same problem. Only his included statistics and research, bar graphs and maps. It had everything Braden's proposal had and much, much more. As Braden flipped the pages, the lump in his stomach expanded.

"I love your idea of the open house weekend." Tapping the paper, Jacqui didn't sound defensive or apologetic. She sounded as relaxed as she'd been when he'd first walked in. She was brilliant, but she missed social cues most first graders would pick up, a fact he was thankful for at that moment. He certainly wouldn't want his boss to discern his disappointment. "Let's see what Andrew thinks."

"Sure. Good idea."

"He suggested we work with a publicist to get the word out about BNB's new location."

Just one of many ideas Braden hadn't thought of.

"Maybe the publicist could tell us how to promote the open house weekend." Jacqui pushed Braden's proposal away. "I think you're right. Once people come up here and see the area, a lot of them won't want to leave. Maybe we could..." Her attention shifted to the doorway. "Oh, good. Come in."

Braden turned as Andrew rounded the table and sat on Jacqui's other side, across from Braden. The new guy's dark brown hair was cut short, his thick beard trimmed close to his face. He was tall—over six feet. It was February, but somehow, the guy had a tan. Probably went to a tanning salon. Most of the researchers wore jeans and T-shirts. Jacqui dressed nicer than that, and Braden wore slacks and a golf shirt most days. But Andrew... It was one thing to wear a suit on day one—he hadn't known the company's culture yet. But here he was again, dress shirt and tie. What was he trying to prove?

"Braden was thinking along the same lines as us," Jacqui said.

Andrew glanced at the pathetic little proposal Braden had lost sleep putting together, then looked up with a grin as honest as a gossip rag's headline. He tapped the paper. "Good ideas." His attention shifted to Jacqui. "A whole weekend. I love that. But maybe, rather than inviting anyone graduating in the field, we make it exclusive. We handpick the people we invite. Then we know we're focusing on the best and not wasting money on people we wouldn't consider, and we're also creating scarcity, which gives students bragging rights. You know—only the very best get invited to visit BNB."

Jacqui leaned back, eyes bright and excited. "Such a good idea, Andrew." She shifted to Braden. "Isn't he amazing?"

Braden hoped his smile didn't look as tight as it felt. "Amazing."

～

BRADEN STEWED all afternoon about the Amazing Andrew and his Perfect Proposal. The guy was a jerk, but Jacqui didn't see it. Hopefully, she'd figure it out before she promoted him to the job that should already be Braden's.

It had been a lousy day, and it wasn't about to get any better. As he turned from the state highway onto the narrow streets of his neighborhood, he thought about his houseguest. Not that Carly hadn't been hovering at the back of his mind since she'd shown up on his doorstep the night before, but unlike when he was at work, he couldn't just shove thoughts of her away and not deal with them. In just a few minutes, he'd see her again.

He slowed to a crawl. He wasn't ready. At least he wouldn't be blindsided this time. He'd called his mom that morning to find out what she knew, but she hadn't said much, only that Braden would need to ask Carly what was going on. "It's not my place."

Seemed it should be her place, considering she'd foisted Carly on him, but he knew how fruitless it was to argue with Anna Beth Reilly.

Braden hadn't heard from Carly since she texted that she was going to the grocery store that morning. Maybe she'd decided to leave. Maybe he'd arrive home to an empty house.

The thought didn't bring the relief it should have. Instead, his heart beat faster, and he pressed down on the accelerator. So, fine. He wanted Carly to still be there. He wanted to see her one more time, to have a chance to find out what was going on. He wanted his curiosity satisfied. Nothing else.

He refused to be attracted to her. He refused to fall for her. He'd made that mistake once, and he wasn't going to do it again. Which was why it would be better if she'd just move along, go somewhere else to... to do whatever it was she'd come to Coventry to do.

But when he rounded the corner and saw the familiar gold Monte Carlo, he blew out a relieved breath.

No matter what his stupid heart thought, he was going to send her on her way as soon as possible. He had a plan in Coventry, a plan with BNB, and he wasn't going to let Carly screw it up.

He parked in the garage and killed his pickup's engine, allowing the silence to wrap around him. Normally, that silence filled him with peace, but anxiety wouldn't be put off today. He closed his eyes. *I need Your help, Lord. I fell for her once. Please, help me not to fall for her again. Protect my heart. I don't know what she needs, but You do. Make her path clear and help me know my part in it. I trust You.*

Mostly, he trusted God. Tried to, anyway. But with Carly just up those stairs, he feared what might happen between them. Getting over her was the hardest thing he'd ever done. He hadn't dated since, preferring to focus on his career and not get side-tracked by dating.

Ha. Dating would be a piece of cake compared to having the love of his life—*former* love of his life—under his roof.

The February chill seeped into the cab of his truck. He couldn't sit in the garage all night. He got out and slammed the door, words playing in his mind on repeat. *Help, Lord. Help.*

As Braden climbed the steps from the combination basement-garage, the scents of garlic and onions hit him, as did the sound of music. What was Carly up to?

He opened the door and stepped into his kitchen, where the radio his father had given him for emergencies, which he'd never used, was playing oldies. More delectable scents reached his nose. Carly wasn't there, but the evidence of her afternoon was spread across every surface.

She hadn't changed a bit. Carly was a great cook—she and her mother had loved creating meals together—but nobody would ever accuse her of being tidy. Eight empty cans of crushed tomatoes littered the counter. Onion and garlic skins, along with something

—were those sausage casings?—had been left atop his rarely used cutting board. Two empty disposable meat trays had been shoved in a grocery sack but hadn't made it into the trash yet. He crossed to the stove, where tomato sauce bubbled in an enormous pot he'd never seen before. A smaller pot held more simmering sauce, only this one also had browned meat. A third pot held water just coming to a boil.

A door opened, and Carly hurried into the room, freezing when she saw him, eyes wide, almost fearful. "You're early."

He was usually careful to be the last to leave work, but he'd been eager to get out of there after the proposal debacle. And maybe, if he were honest, to get home to see Carly. "You've been busy."

"I hope you don't mind."

He chuckled. "I think I'll find it in my heart to forgive you."

Her smile was shy as she shooed him away. "Go do... whatever you have to do. It'll be ready at five thirty."

Much as he'd like to stay and help... Help. Right. He wanted to stay and watch her work. She'd pulled her long hair into a ponytail that hung over one shoulder. She wore no makeup but didn't need any—those big brown eyes were already mesmerizing. He wanted more than anything to stay and watch her in those skinny jeans and the pink T-shirt she must have bought that day. It was fitted enough that it showed off all her curves. She'd found the apron Mom had bought him, the one that read *Mr. Good Looking is Cooking*, which, of course, he'd never donned. It hung nearly to her knees and looked a little ridiculous and a lot... sexy.

When he managed to return his gaze to her face, he realized she was watching him, eyebrows hiked. He shook himself out of his stupor. "Yeah, okay. I'll go..." Anywhere. Anywhere away from there.

He took the steps upstairs two at a time, telling himself to slow down as he hurried to change his clothes and get back to the kitchen, to that delicious meal he couldn't wait to eat, and to the woman preparing it.

He visited the bathroom, washed his hands, and lectured the idiot in the mirror. "Stop it. Just... stop it."

But seconds later, he was headed back downstairs.

His little table was set. She'd even used the placemats Mom had insisted he needed to protect the wood. Also never used until now.

Carly didn't turn when he walked in, probably didn't hear him over the stove's low fan and the music. She was sort of swaying to the beat as she stirred the smaller pot of sauce and turned off the burner. Then, she poured the spaghetti into the colander in the sink. Steam rose, warming the room and explaining the heat he felt all over his body.

Sure. It was the spaghetti.

A timer dinged, and she grabbed an oven mitt, bent beautifully, and pulled something from the oven.

She'd cut a loaf of bread longways, and the two halves bubbled with butter and garlic.

When she turned to set it on the counter, she spotted him. "Oh. Hey."

Caught, but she didn't seem to realize he'd been standing there, watching her like some kind of peeping Tom. His mouth was too dry to form words.

She asked, "Will you slice this?"

Uh... His only cutting board was covered with stuff. She dumped the garbage into his trash can and flipped it over to the clean—cleaner, anyway—side on the only empty space on the counter. She handed him a long, serrated knife as if he didn't know where they were in his own kitchen, or maybe didn't know which one to use. Which would be true. She pushed the bread onto the board. "Careful, it's hot."

He sliced it slowly, trying not to burn himself on the steaming bread, telling himself to cool off. Because the heat he felt had nothing to do with the bread and burners and oven and everything to do with the gorgeous creature who'd fixed him dinner.

*She broke your heart. She turned you down. She didn't want you.*

But he'd wanted her. And a part of him still did. A big part, a part he'd been ignoring for three long and lonely years.

"There's no room on the table for serving dishes," Carly said.

He finished cutting duty and turned to see her holding out a plate for him. "I guess we can just serve ourselves."

"Ladies first."

"Oh. Okay." She put a tiny portion of spaghetti on her plate, added some sauce, and then snatched a piece of bread.

He followed, though his spaghetti was piled inches high—he should have gotten a bowl. He added two pieces of bread and joined her at the table.

She sat across from him, hands in her lap. He'd been so focused on the cook that he hadn't noticed the salads before, but there was a bowl at each place setting. Caesar, it looked like, complete with Parmesan and croutons and cherry tomatoes. There was a glass of ice water in front of his plate, a glass of milk in front of hers.

Milk? With spaghetti? Yuck, but he wouldn't say so.

He couldn't wait to dig in. He was reaching for his fork when she cleared her throat.

"Do you want to say grace?" she asked.

Grace. Right. Since when did Carly say grace? But he didn't argue, just bowed his head and uttered a quick prayer, thanking God for the food and the woman who'd prepared it. After the amens, he dug in.

The first bite elicited a moan. Al dente pasta, tangy sauce, spicy sausage accompanying the ground beef. He should have complemented her, but instead, he went for a second bite. Then tried the salad—cool, crisp. The tomatoes added a burst of sweetness. The bread was soft and salty and garlicky.

He'd eaten half his food before he looked up to find her watching him.

He wiped his mouth with his napkin, suddenly self-conscious. "Sorry. I haven't eaten this well in a long time."

"You always did like spaghetti."

"My favorite. And this is outstanding. Don't tell my mother, but your sauce beats hers hands down."

Carly's cheeks turned pink, and she focused on her plate, forking a small bite. "It's the hot sausage. Gives it great flavor."

"What did you do today besides cook?"

She shrugged. "Picked up a few things. I had to go back out when I realized you didn't have a stock pot. I grabbed that at Walmart. I got some plastic containers too. I didn't know if you'd have enough for the sauce. I made a bunch so you can freeze some."

"Thank you. Let me know what I owe you."

"You don't have to pay me. Just letting me stay here..." Her words trailed, and she grabbed a piece of bread and tore it into smaller pieces.

He set his fork down. "You want to tell me what's going on?"

Still picking at her bread, she said, "I guess I should."

"I guess so."

"Did you talk to your mom?"

"She didn't tell me anything. Said it's your story."

Carly popped a tiny bite of bread into her mouth.

He reached for another slice from the cutting board on the counter and dipped it in his sauce. He ate the bite, determined not to push. If she needed time, he could give her time.

But she didn't say anything, just stood and dumped what was left on her plate into the trash. When she turned on the spigot, he said, "I'll do that. You cooked."

But she ignored him and started cleaning the kitchen. He would probably have lingered over the meal, but guilt had him scarfing down what was left on his plate—no sense wasting such a good meal—and joining her at the sink. "Let me do these, please."

She shrugged and stepped back but didn't sit. Instead, she put the leftovers away, including the sauce in the giant pot, which she poured into five smaller containers and stowed in his freezer. That sauce had no meat in it, but he could fry up some hamburger or sausage, or even get some of those frozen meatballs. He could cook spaghetti or even make meatball subs. It would be nice to have a decent meal once in a while.

When they were finished, she pulled a plastic container he hadn't seen before from the pantry and held it out to him.

Chocolate chip cookies.

He was full, but apparently there was room for one. Two, because he didn't want to be rude. He took a bite. "You should be a cook. Seriously. What a meal."

She blushed, shrugged. Reached for a cookie, then seemed to change her mind. She put the top on the container and moved it across his now clean countertop, then leaned back and crossed her arms.

Apparently, she'd done everything she could think of to stall.

He tipped his head toward the living room. "We'll be more comfortable."

She walked past him and sat on the end of the sofa, pulling her knees to her chest.

"You cold?" He glanced at the fireplace on the far wall. He'd never bothered with a fire, but he could do that.

Just what they needed—a romantic fire crackling in the corner. Bad idea.

"You need me to turn up the heat?"

"I'm fine."

He sat in his chair and leaned toward her. "How've you been?"

Maybe if he started her talking, she'd get around to her reason for being there.

But she only shrugged again. "You know."

"I don't, actually. I haven't seen you in years." Not since the day he'd gotten down on one knee. The day she'd shaken her head and cried and run.

She said, "Busy, I guess."

He blew out a long breath. *Patience.* Something was going on with her, something that had her fleeing the city without packing a bag and rushing to New Hampshire. If she had to work herself up to telling him what that something was, then he would wait.

"Obviously, I moved here," he said. "After I earned my master's, I was recruited by an R and D company in Boston. BNB. Maybe you've heard of them?"

She shook her head. Apparently, Mom hadn't kept Carly abreast of his life. He was glad of that.

"Anyway, the company went through a rather strange transition last year."

Her eyebrows lifted, the first sign that she cared about what he was saying.

"Sort of a long story," he said. "Maybe I'll tell you about it one of these days. Didn't really affect me, except for a few months of paid time off, but the owner... Anyway, she came up here for a couple of months and met someone. She decided to relocate here, and that's why I moved."

"You like it?"

"Love it. Love everything about it."

"It's so... quiet." Her gaze found the window. "And dark."

"Yes. To both. But also beautiful and peaceful." He glanced around his home and added, "And affordable."

"I like your house."

"Thank you."

When a full minute of silence had passed, he said, "I don't think you understand how conversation works. I talk, and then you talk."

Her lips quirked up at the corner as if they might, if given a little more incentive, actually break into a smile.

But the look faded fast.

"Carly, I need to know—"

"I witnessed a murder."

A *murder?*

He felt frozen. Couldn't think of a single thing to say.

Of all the things he'd imagined, he had never... would never have guessed that. Before he could put all the questions bouncing around in his brain to words, she continued as if, having broken the seal, she couldn't help but gush out the rest of the story.

"I mean, I didn't witness it, but I heard it, which is maybe the same thing. But I don't know who did it. I got away on my bike. They followed me, and I lost them, but they must've seen me because when I went home, there were men in my... in Pete's house, and the girls were there. I didn't see their faces. Not the girls—I saw them. The men. I don't know who they were. Pete and the girls must know, but I'm afraid to call them. I didn't know what to do, so I called your mom, and she and your dad met me at the bus station and gave me your car and told me to come here."

Braden sat back in his chair. Gulped.

A murder? She'd witnessed a murder? She'd been chased. By murderers.

The food he'd eaten churned in his stomach, and he swallowed one more time to keep it from coming up.

"They saw your face?" he asked.

"Maybe. I mean, how else would they know who I was? I didn't go home for hours, and they were there before me, so they didn't follow me. But I can't figure out when they could have seen me. Unless they just recognized me somehow. Maybe they're people I've met. Maybe they know about my..."

When she didn't finish, he said, "Your what? Know about your what?"

She hugged her knees as if clinging to the only lifesaver in a raging sea.

The fear in her eyes was unmistakable. He wanted to sit beside her, to hold her and assure her that she was safe there. But he needed the whole story.

"Where did this happen?"

"At a machine shop about a block from Upham's."

One of the busier business districts in Dorchester. "When?"

"Yesterday morning. Maybe ten o'clock."

"You need to call the police."

"I did! Right after it happened, and they said they'd check it out. I called again when I saw the men in Pete's house, and the police showed up, but they didn't arrest anybody. Maybe the bad guys took off out the back or... I don't know. The police left after a few minutes, so Pete must not have told them anything."

"Or maybe you misinterpreted—"

"No. I saw them through the window. Even Pete looked scared, and Laurie warned me off. I could see it in her eyes. They were bad people. They were—"

"Okay, okay. I believe you."

She swiped at her eyes, at tears he hadn't noticed.

Maybe he should back off. But he wanted to get the whole story at once so they wouldn't have to go through this again. "Was anybody else there, at the machine shop?"

She shook her head.

"Just you and the killers and the man who was killed? No employees or customers?"

"I think it was closed."

Closed? But then... "Why were you there, if it was closed? What were you doing at a machine shop anyway?"

Her gaze dropped to her knees. "I went to see the owner. The man who was murdered."

"Who is...?"

"Ian Murphy."

The name rang a bell. Braden closed his eyes, and an image formed. Big, muscular Irish guy who'd been a few years ahead of Braden in school. Braden remembered girls talking about how he was *so cute*. Whatever. Braden hadn't been impressed. He'd seen the guy in action at a party once. Ian had been charming with the ladies—in the deceitful sense of the word.

Carly still hadn't looked up.

Braden didn't want to know, but he forced the words out. "Were you seeing him?"

"Not anymore. For a while, after you and me..."

Braden hadn't dated anyone since Carly had refused him, but apparently, she'd found a new guy and never looked back. It was stupid, the surge of anger. Braden and Carly had broken up, and she could see anybody she wanted, even a lying, *so cute* charmer who'd probably charmed her right into his bed.

But it was fine.

Fine.

He clenched his fists and told himself he wasn't jealous. That he had no right to be jealous. Carly wasn't his anymore. And Ian was...

If Carly was right, then Ian was dead.

Braden refused to be jealous of a dead guy.

The anger cleared from his vision. "So, you went to see your boyfriend, and—"

"Not anymore."

"Huh?"

"He's not my boyfriend. He was, before. But we broke up."

"I don't care." The lie slipped out and almost sounded true.

"Just saying."

But why would she bother to *just say*? They weren't together. She'd made sure of that. Dumped him so she could take up with the likes of...

"If you weren't together," he said, "then why did you go see him?"

"I needed to talk to him about something."

Vague much? He blew out a long breath. "Okay. And then...?"

"And he was acting weird, almost nervous. You have to know him. Ian's never nervous." Her voice hitched. "*Was* never nervous. He was always calm. Totally unflappable. But yesterday, he was sort of... frantic. He pulled a bag out of the very back of the filing cabinet. Another was in the ceiling."

"In the—?"

"You know, those white ceilings with all the little holes with the metal bars holding them up."

"Acoustic tiles. He'd hidden something above them?" At her nod, he said, "Any idea what?"

She stood, jogged up the stairs, and came back down carrying a paper bag. She tossed it to him before dropping onto the sofa again.

He caught it and peered inside.

And stifled the swear word that almost escaped.

He dumped the cash onto the coffee table. Silently, he sorted it. Stacked it. Counted it.

"Ten grand and change." He looked up to find her watching him, wary.

"The guy who killed him claimed he was running a protection scheme, and Ian didn't deny it. I had no idea."

"Did you steal this?" He gestured to the cash on the coffee table. "Or, was he looking for it to give to you? I don't understand."

"He just shoved that bag into my hands. I didn't even know what it was. When the men showed up, he told me to hide, so I did, under the desk." She described what she heard, the voices, the words. The gunshot.

And then she described what happened after, how the men got a tarp—probably to wrap the body in. How they talked about searching the place, and how she'd run then, knowing they'd find her.

While she talked, Braden imagined the scene, his heart rate kicking up as if he were the one being chased, hiding out, afraid for his life. As if he were looking into his family's picture window and seeing his loved ones on a couch, threatened.

He couldn't stand the distance between them. Maybe it was stupid. Maybe he'd regret it. But he launched himself off his chair and settled in beside Carly on the couch and pulled her close, absorbing her tremors and feeling her sobs. Poor, sweet Carly. For all the heartbreak she'd caused him, she was still that, still the same tenderhearted girl she'd always been.

"You're safe now." He stroked her hair, her back, trying not to think about how well she still fit in his arms. Hating himself for the memories that filled him, memories of far more intimate moments. "You're safe here. You can stay as long as you need to."

He'd regret that tomorrow, no maybe about it. But for now, what else could he do but promise to protect her? Not that long ago, he'd hoped to love her and provide for her and protect her all his life, and it seemed those hopes hadn't been buried as deep as he'd once believed.

# CHAPTER SEVEN

CARLY COULD STAY on Braden's sofa, in Braden's arms, for the rest of her life. She'd forgotten—how could she have forgotten?—what it felt like to truly be loved by a man. Not a man like Ian, who used affection as a weapon, but a man like Braden, whose touch held tenderness and care. Whose words weren't flattery when he wanted something and hateful when he was angry, but a man whose words were kind and honest.

She'd forgotten how it felt to be loved by Braden.

She shouldn't revel in his touch. She shouldn't allow herself to enjoy it quite so much. It wouldn't last—she knew that. She had known when she refused his proposal that she would lose him forever, and as hard as it was, she'd accepted that. What choice had she had?

He leaned away to look down at her. "What now? What's your plan?"

"I don't have a plan. I guess I can use that"—she gestured to the money on the table—"to find someplace to stay until the murderers are caught. Except it's not my money. It's stolen money. I really need to turn it over to the police."

"Why didn't you already?"

"I was afraid."

Braden scooted away and turned to face her, leaving nothing but cold air behind him. "Of what?"

"At first, just the murderers finding me. The police station was the most obvious place for me to go, so if they were searching for me, why not stake it out? And what would the police do? Take my statement and send me on my way. I mean... I don't know, but do they protect witnesses in those kinds of situations? Ian wasn't high-profile or anything, just a regular guy. I just... I didn't think they'd keep me safe. But it's more than that." She felt foolish adding this last part, but Braden needed the whole story. "I'm probably way off, but I really don't believe the killers saw my face. Maybe they know that Ian and I used to date, but we broke up a year ago."

Braden's eyes narrowed, and his head dipped slightly to the side. Before he could ask whatever question was forming in his head, she barreled forward.

"So I wouldn't think they'd immediately believe it was me. I mean, I don't exactly stand out. Ordinary women with long brown hair—we're a dime a dozen in Dorchester."

"You're not ordinary, Carly. Nothing about you is—"

"You know what I mean." She couldn't let herself be drawn in by Braden's kindness. "I wore that puffy parka, so they wouldn't have gotten a sense of my size. It just seems unlikely that they'd figure out it was me so quickly."

"Were you and Ian still friends? Maybe they'd seen you go to the shop other times."

"I hadn't been there since we broke up."

"You went yesterday because...?"

She didn't want to say. Braden had hoped she would someday carry his child. He'd told her that more than once. That she was carrying Ian's...

She couldn't tell him. She didn't want to hurt him. She didn't want to see his disappointment. Maybe, if the murderers were caught quickly, she could return to Dorchester, and Braden would never have to know.

The thought brought not peace but sadness. She hadn't realized how much she'd missed Braden, but tonight, the way he held her, the way he listened to her, she remembered how they used to be—remembered all they'd lost when she refused him.

"If you don't want to tell me—"

"I needed to tell him something, but it's..." She didn't know how to finish the sentence without lying, and she didn't want to lie.

"Were you two going to get back together?"

"No. Never. It was over."

"Since it seems he was a criminal, I'm glad to hear that."

Silence settled between them. They'd been talking about something, but she'd lost the thread of conversation.

After a minute, he said, "You were telling me why you were afraid—"

"Right. The police. I told them my name when I reported Ian's murder. It's stupid, right? How would the killers get that information from the police? But at the time... I don't know. I was nervous."

"It's not stupid. It's a good hypothesis."

She nearly chuckled at the word. Typical of Braden.

"On the other hand," he said, "maybe if you talk to the police, you can help them narrow down who the killers are."

"How? I didn't see their faces."

"Anything unique about their voices?"

"One of them was really high-pitched, but otherwise, no."

"Accents?"

She closed her eyes, tried to remember what she'd heard. "Southie, mostly. But the high-pitched guy—he was the one in charge—his was a little more refined."

"Interesting. What else?"

She racked her brain. "They were following me in a black SUV. I don't know what kind."

"Didn't get a look at the driver?"

"I was frantically biking in the opposite direction."

Braden nodded slowly. "Okay. Okay. I don't know what you should do. Maybe the police can't be trusted. Maybe somebody's— what do they call it? On the take."

"I'm probably just being paranoid."

"Better paranoid than sorry."

She started to respond to that twisted cliche, but her words were cut off by a yawn. It was barely seven o'clock, but she was exhausted.

"Maybe that's enough for tonight," he said. "Let's think about it. I'll pray about it, if you don't mind."

She reached out, almost touched him, then changed her mind and settled her hands on her lap. "I'll pray too. I gave my life to Christ about a year ago."

His eyebrows lifted, and his face transformed into an expression of pure joy, an expression she'd seen often when they were together, an expression she loved. "You did? You really did?"

"I really did. I'm still learning, but—"

Her words were cut short when he wrapped her in a hug. "I'm so glad, Carly. I can't even tell you... I've been praying you would for so long."

"Maybe I should have told you so you wouldn't waste your time praying for me anymore."

He leaned back, and she saw that the joy had faded from his face. Now, his lips were pressed together. "Not a waste. Praying for you has been my honor."

Oh.

She didn't know what to say to that.

Braden scooted to the far side of the couch, snatching the TV remote on his way. "We can't solve anything tonight. Let's sleep on it and pray about it. Tonight, we'll find something to watch and just relax. Okay?"

She blew out a relieved breath. She'd gotten through it. Most of it, anyway. With luck, she'd never have to tell him about the baby.

With luck, the killers would be brought to justice, and she could go back to Dorchester and never see Braden again.

She wasn't even surprised by the sadness that rose at the thought of it.

## CHAPTER EIGHT

BRADEN FOUND a romantic comedy they'd watched when they were still dating. He remembered that Carly had liked it and wasn't surprised to hear her snickering beside him. It seemed that telling him what had brought her to Coventry had released her tension.

It had added to his.

And having the woman he'd once loved on the other end of the sofa was only making that tension worse.

The movie was half-finished when she said, "Mind if we pause it? I need a bathroom break."

He hit the button, and she scurried toward the stairs.

"You can use the one down here," he called, but she was already halfway up.

He wandered into the kitchen and grabbed a Fresca from the fridge, then took another before snatching the container of cookies. Seated on the sofa again, he was munching on a cookie when Carly returned, carrying a phone.

He lifted the soda. "Still like Fresca?"

"Does it have caffeine?"

He shrugged. "I don't think so. Does caffeine keep you awake?

You used to be able to drink coffee all day." He read the can. "No caffeine."

She reached for it, but he opened it for her before holding it out. "Here you go."

When she took it, their fingers brushed, causing a familiar spark. He shouldn't still be so affected by her. It had been three years. Three years, and she could still make his heart race like he was a schoolboy with his first crush.

To cover his reaction, he said, "You'd better eat a cookie. Keep your strength up."

"I'm fine."

"What are you, watching your weight? You're as slim as ever." Not that he should comment. Or notice, for that matter.

Ignoring him, she focused on the phone's screen. She'd always used Apple products, but that looked like a cheapie.

"That a good phone?"

She shrugged. "It'll do. I shut mine down. I heard somewhere that the phone still tracks you, even if you shut the locator off. Probably not true, but I didn't want..." She shrugged. "Maybe I'm being paranoid."

"It's not paranoia if people are actually out to get you."

She glanced up at him with a half-smile playing at her lips. "Go ahead and restart the movie."

He did, but the antics on the screen couldn't hold his attention. He kept glancing at Carly—beside him, in his house. Alone. At night.

He snatched another cookie. But food wasn't going to satisfy the hunger he was feeling. This was why God commanded people to wait until marriage. Because once a person had been there and done that, the body remembered it. His did, anyway, very well.

The screen showed the requisite big break-up scene. Beside him, Carly was scrolling through Instagram. Would that track her?

He grabbed his own phone to search for the answer. When he found it, he said, "Did you turn off your location on the app?"

"Of course."

He should have known she'd think of that.

"I'm just checking on my sisters. I'll message them, let them know I'm fine and make sure they're all right."

Her sisters. Of course she had to check on *them*. He wasn't proud of the wave of frustration her words brought.

As long as she wasn't watching the movie, either, he didn't have to pretend. He searched his phone for news of Ian Murphy's murder. Surely there'd be an article, and he could learn what the police were saying.

But there was no news about any murder in Dorchester the day before, not even an un-named victim.

Weird.

Did Carly have it wrong? Not if she'd described what she'd heard accurately. Gunshot. Talk of moving a body. Unless Carly had lost her mind—and she seemed perfectly sane to him—the murderers had covered their tracks well. Or the police were keeping it quiet.

Maybe both.

He needed to find out. If the police weren't investigating the man's murder, then they obviously wouldn't find the murderers. Would that make Carly more or less safe?

There was no way to find out the answer to that question.

Maybe he hadn't put the right terms into his browser. He was continuing the search when Carly gasped beside him.

"What happened?"

She turned the screen. On it, Carly's sister Sophia. Wow, she'd grown up since he'd seen her last. Did her stepfather allow her to wear clothes like that? Painted-on jeans, a top that didn't reach her belly button. She was holding hands with an older guy. Not just older than Sophia—was she seventeen now, eighteen?—but older than Braden and Carly. The guy had to be thirty, maybe thirty-five.

The caption read *Dinner at Roxanne's with my beau.*

Braden lifted his gaze to Carly. Her brown eyes were wide with worry.

"Is she dating that guy?" he asked.

"I didn't think she was seeing anybody. She didn't tell me…" She took the phone back and started typing.

"What are you doing?"

"Asking her what's going on."

Braden waited, half watching the stupid movie, mostly watching Carly as she typed, read, typed some more.

"She met him last night, after the men came to the house."

"What does she say about those men?"

"They were scary and looking for me, but then they left. I asked if they threatened them, and she said no, of course not. Like it was a stupid question."

Sophia wasn't the brightest bulb in the chandelier, though. Maybe Danielle or Laurie could offer more information. Better yet, Pete, but Carly hadn't mentioned contacting him. Apparently, their relationship hadn't improved.

"She went with some friends to see a movie and met this guy. He walked her home and took her to dinner tonight." Carly blew out a breath. "She thinks she's in love. She's known the guy approximately twenty-four hours, and she thinks she's in love." She dropped the phone to her lap and faced him.

"I'm sure she'll be fine."

"Ha. She'll be sleeping with him by the end of the week, if she isn't already. If she doesn't smarten up…" She shook her head. "This is such a lovely little fantasy, that I could just stay here until everything sorts itself out. But I have to go back. They need me."

Anger, the same anger that had been simmering for three years, bubbled up and overflowed.

He launched himself from the couch and rounded to face her. "Your life is in danger, but you're going to go back to take care of *them?*"

"I don't mean—"

"They're not your responsibility!" He hadn't meant to shout. He couldn't seem to calm his temper. "They're not your daughters. They're not even really your sisters. They're Pete's kids."

"But my mother—"

"I know!" He marched into the kitchen, stood in the middle of the floor to breathe. To think.

Because those girls, those stupid, vapid girls, had been Carly's excuse for refusing his proposal. She claimed she couldn't marry him because the girls needed her. He'd asked her to move with him to Cambridge, *Cambridge*, just across the Charles River from Boston. She could enroll in college, maybe even get back the scholarship she'd given up when her mother'd gotten sick. She'd always dreamed of going to Boston University. Together, they could make that happen.

He'd even planned to buy her a car and teach her to drive so she could get back to Dorchester easily.

But she wouldn't do it.

The ridiculous fantasy that had been brewing in the back of his mind puffed and dissipated like smoke from a chimney. For a moment, he'd been able to picture it, Carly in his house, in his life, forever. She fit so well beside him. They went so well together.

But her almost-family had always come before him. Always would.

If she'd refused to move as close as Cambridge, she'd never consider a move to New Hampshire. And he wasn't leaving. Not for her. Not for a woman who'd put her stepsisters, whom she hadn't even met until she'd been nearly out of high school, above him. Ever since Carly's mother had married that useless sack of cells and brought those three girls into their lives, they'd been more important than Braden.

When was he going to get it through his thick skull that Carly didn't love him like he loved her?

*Had* loved her. Not anymore.

When he turned to go back to the living room, Carly was in the entry. "I'm sorry."

"Nope." The word was curt, and he worked to sound rational. "I'm sorry. That's old news." He brushed past her and snatched the cookies and his Fresca from the coffee table. "You need anything else?"

"It wasn't just the girls. It was... all of it."

He ignored her, returning to the kitchen to dump his soda. Barely past nine o'clock, but he was finished with the conversation, the company, and the ideas his stupid brain couldn't seem to put away. He started the dishwasher and turned to face her. "I'm going to bed."

"Okay."

He stepped into the dining room to avoid brushing by her again but stopped when a thought occurred to him. He turned just enough to see her out of the corner of his eye. "You're not going back tomorrow, right? Even though your"—he managed to edit out the word *stupid*—"sister needs you?"

"I can't until I know more. But I can find someplace else if—"

"You're fine here. I can handle it if you can." At her nod, he stalked away, not sure if he felt more relieved or frustrated.

The last thing he needed was to drag this... whatever it was... out longer.

# CHAPTER NINE

CARLY PULLED into the lot of the Concord bus station the next morning, stifling a yawn. Thanks to the unpleasant way the previous evening had ended, she'd had another terrible night's sleep. If she could have, she'd have stayed in bed all day long, but she needed to make a couple of calls, and she was afraid to make them from Braden's house. Paranoia again, but maybe somebody could track her location on her new cheapie phone. She was afraid to reveal the phone number. Afraid to reveal her location. Just... afraid.

That morning, she'd decided Concord was her best bet, and then she'd searched for pay phones and discovered there were some at the bus station. If anybody did trace the call, they'd assume she'd taken the bus to Concord, and maybe they'd assume it was a stop on a longer trip north. In any event, Concord was an hour from Braden's home in Coventry. Nobody should be able to figure out where she was.

Better too cautious than not cautious enough.

She probably should have made this call the day before. Maybe it was ridiculous that she hadn't, but she hadn't been thinking straight. Easier to focus on shopping and fixing a nice meal than the horror of a murder. Now, she had to face it. Much as she'd like to stay at Braden's, dawdle in New Hampshire, and wait for everything to blow over, she had to get back to Dorchester. Her sisters needed somebody to look after them, and heaven knew Pete wasn't going to do it.

Carly spotted the pay phones in the back of the small station, looked up the number on her cell, and made the first call.

"Boston Police Department," a woman answered.

Carly looked around, but the station was nearly empty. Nobody would be able to hear her. "I need to talk to the detective investigating Ian Murphy's murder."

"Hold please."

A minute later, a man said, "Homicide. Klein."

"My name is Carly Garcia. I called Monday morning to report a murder—Ian Murphy's murder. I was hoping you could give me an update on your investigation."

"We've been looking for you, Miss Garcia." His voice was deep and gentle. "When can you come down to the station? We need to get your statement to close this up."

"Close it? You found the murderers?"

"We need to speak with you in person."

"I can't do that. The people who did it, they were at my stepfather's house Monday night." At least, she thought so. It was a good… hypothesis, as Braden would say.

Fingers tapped on a keyboard, then, "Peter Lancaster? Is that your stepfather?"

"That's him." She described what she'd seen through the picture window.

"Uniforms checked it out. Your father explained—"

"Stepfather."

"Sorry. Stepfather. He explained that some men had come by looking for you, that he'd told them he didn't know where you were, and they left."

"If they did, they went out the back door. I was watching the house, and they didn't leave through the front."

"Well, that is odd. But unless Lancaster tells us differently, there's no reason—"

"A man was murdered!" She hadn't meant to raise her voice. An older man behind the counter peered at her, then returned his attention to his work.

She lowered her voice. "They killed Ian Murphy."

"Did you see the murder?"

"No, but I heard it."

"Did you see who did it?"

"Not their faces, but—"

"The problem, Miss Garcia, is that Ian Murphy isn't dead. I spoke to him myself."

"What? How? I heard the whole thing. I heard..." She stopped, took a deep breath, and started over. "That doesn't make sense."

"It took us a couple of hours to get ahold of him. After you called Monday, we sent uniforms to the address you gave us, but there was no body, no blood. The lock looked as if it might have been jimmied, but we couldn't tell for sure. I didn't have a cell number for him, but his dad's phone number was listed, so I called him. He gave me Ian's cell and told me Ian had texted that he was headed to Florida for a few days. The dad says he goes down there a lot."

A couple of times a year, but never on the spur of the moment. Carly worked hard to keep her voice even. The last thing she needed was to sound hysterical. "He wasn't in Florida, Detective. I saw him Monday."

"He must've gone straight to the airport. I called the number his dad gave me, but it went to voice mail. Ian called me that afternoon. Said he was sorry he'd missed my call, but his phone was off because he was on the plane. So, whatever you think you heard, you didn't. Your friend is fine."

Could that be true?

No. No. She knew what she heard.

"He's *not* fine. I'm not crazy, Detective. We were in his office. He heard someone come in, and he told me to hide. I ducked under his desk. Men confronted him. There was a gunshot, and then they talked about what to do with his body. When I ran, the men followed me. He's dead." She couldn't help the way her voice cracked on that last word. How could he not believe her?

"Okay." Klein's single word was patient, which only annoyed her more.

"I'm not crazy."

"I'm sure you're not." He took a breath and blew it out. "I'm only suggesting that you didn't hear what you think you heard."

"I'm not stupid either. Did you ask around, see if anybody else heard the gunshot?"

"We don't investigate murders that didn't happen, Miss Garcia. The man's not—"

"Have you ever spoken to Ian Murphy before?"

After a pause, the detective sounded resigned when he said, "No."

"Then how do you know the man you spoke to was him? It could have been anybody. Obviously, the killers took his phone."

"His father assures me he's alive."

"Did Mr. Murphy speak to him or just read his text message?"

"All right, look," Klein said, "I'll follow up with the dad, see if he's spoken to him. And I'll have someone canvass the neighbors to find out if anybody else heard gunshots. If you want to come down and give your statement—"

"I'm not coming in until the murderers are caught. I'm the only person who knows what they did."

"All right, all right." If he followed up those placating words with *calm down,* she'd scream. "I hear what you're saying. I'll keep the case open until I confirm that Ian Murphy is alive. Meanwhile, stay out of sight. Where can I reach you?"

She considered giving him her phone number but thought better of it. Maybe she should mention her fear that somebody at the station had told the killers her name. But Klein already thought she was imagining things. The last thing she needed was to give him more reason to think she was nuts. "I'll call you back tomorrow."

"That'll work. I'm going to give you my direct line." He rattled off a number, and she typed it into her phone.

"Thank you."

"Miss Garcia? I'm not saying I believe you. At this point, I don't know what to think, but if what you're saying is true... Just stay out of sight until we can figure this out."

"That's the plan." Carly hung up the phone and forced a deep breath as a wave of nausea hit. She pulled a sleeve of crackers from her backpack and munched until her stomach settled.

The nausea had been rough that morning—part of the reason she hadn't slept well. She'd awakened before dawn and run to the bathroom to throw up.

Would the detective do what he'd promised? If he did, eventually he'd figure out that Ian was dead. And he'd investigate and find the killers. Maybe.

Without a body, though? Without any evidence? How would they figure out who did it?

And if they didn't, how could she ever go home?

Did she even want to?

She shook her head hard enough that it throbbed, the dull ache she'd awakened with reminding her of its presence, no doubt a result of avoiding caffeine.

Of course she wanted to go home. She had to. She had to take care of her sisters. If she didn't, who would? And she'd promised Mama.

So, the killers had to be found. They simply had to. If Carly was right and they'd gone to Pete's house...

She returned to the phone and called the hardware store where Pete worked as a manager. A woman answered, and Carly asked for him.

He came on the line a moment later, his voice gruff and angry. "What the devil is going on?"

"Hello to you too."

"Don't start with me. When I let you move back in, you promised to take care of the house. There're dishes piled to the flippin' ceiling, and there's no food in the fridge. Either you—"

"Ian was murdered."

That shut him up. A moment passed before he said, "What are you talking about?"

"I was at his shop." She gave her stepfather the short version of what she'd heard. "Problem is, by the time the cops got there, Ian's body was gone. They think he's in Florida."

"Hold on. Don't hang up!" The store's on-hold music started to play, and Carly leaned against the wall, cursing the man who cared so little about her that he'd decide, at that exact moment, to help a customer.

When he picked up again, he said, "Sorry. I wanted to get somewhere nobody could overhear. I'm in the office now."

Oh. She was still processing that when he said, "Are you all right?"

In all the years she'd known Pete, he'd never once asked her that. Never once. Not even after Mama's diagnosis. Not after Mama's death. Carly was so shocked, she didn't know how to answer.

"Are you still there?"

And was that concern in Pete's voice?

"Yeah. Yeah. I'm here. I'm okay. I got out of town."

"Smart."

"So you believe me?"

His short laugh was anything but amused. "Why wouldn't I? You've never lied to me. You're trustworthy, like your mother. You say you heard his murder, then you heard it."

Her eyes stung at Pete's words. All she'd ever wanted was to be like her mother. She was following in Mama's footsteps, though, in all the wrong ways.

"I'm not gonna ask you where you are," Pete said. "Better I don't know. A couple of thugs came to talk to you Monday night, told me about some protection scheme Murphy's been running. I'd heard about it from Stan down at the bar, but I didn't know Murphy was behind it. If I had, I'd have told you the guy was bad news. Never did like him. Anyway, he never bothered our store. We're not in the neighborhood, though, and Murphy probably knew I wouldn't put up with that crap. Anyway, those guys Monday told me you were a part of it. Like I'd believe that."

She processed that information, then asked, "Did they tell you their names?"

"Not that I remember."

"What did they say exactly?"

"That you were involved in Murphy's criminal activity, and they wanted to persuade you to turn against him so they could catch him. Claimed to be local business owners, but they didn't look like they could count to a hundred, much less run their own businesses. They were thugs, through and through. They asked me to let them search your room."

"My room? Why?"

"Beats me. I refused, of course. Then, they asked me to let them know when you got home."

"Did they give you a number to call?"

"Uh. Yeah. I wrote it down at the house. Maybe it's still there."

If Carly had to guess, the paper he'd written it on hadn't moved from wherever he'd set it at the time. It wasn't as if anybody would have thrown it out.

"Did one of them have a high voice?" she asked.

"Uh, no, not that I remember. They were both pretty gruff."

Pete would have remembered the voice. Which meant the one who'd sounded like the ringleader hadn't been there.

She asked, "Why didn't you tell the cops about them?"

"How'd you—?"

She explained how she'd seen them through the window and called the police.

"You were there?"

"Laurie didn't tell you? She spotted me outside the window."

"Not a word. Glad you saw 'em before you came in. When the

cops pulled up, the thugs said they didn't want to have to tell the police what was going on, that they didn't want to get you in trouble. I knew you didn't do anything wrong, but I didn't want you to get wrapped up in Murphy's crap."

"So you told the police—?"

"That some friends had stopped by. I was trying to protect you."

Again, tears pricked her eyes. She and Pete had never been close. They'd never been more than distant roommates. That he cared enough to even try... it meant something.

Sometimes, it was easy for her to forget that this man had loved her mother. And Mama had loved him.

And Mama had loved his girls.

But Pete hadn't become the father figure Carly had craved her whole life. She didn't blame him. He was barely a father to his own children.

But it seemed he cared, in his own paltry way.

"Thank you for that," she said. "It would help me out if you'd call Detective Klein at the Boston PD and tell him what you told me. I'll give you his number."

"I don't want to get involved. I have the girls, and—"

"Just this one call. You don't have to make an official statement or anything. Just tell him what you told me and what the guys looked like."

Pete didn't answer right away. She waited, praying he'd do it. If he reported this to Klein, the detective would be more inclined to believe Carly's story.

Finally, Pete said, "Yeah. Okay. I guess I can do that."

"Thank you."

"But you gotta stay away from the house. Don't come back till this is cleared up. Don't want to put the girls in danger."

"Of course. But Pete, you've got to keep an eye on them."

"I'll make a grocery run tonight. We'll survive."

"I'm not talking about that. Not just that, anyway. Have you seen Sophia's Instagram?"

"I don't have time to check—"

"She's seeing a guy who's closer to your age than hers. You have to figure out what's going on with her. She's going to get herself in deep trouble if she's not careful."

"Nothing I can do about her. She's an adult now."

Barely eighteen, and being a legal adult didn't make her mature or wise. "She's a high-school girl, and she needs direction. She needs a father."

"I don't have any influence over that girl. Never did."

"You could try to—"

"Listen, it's all I can do to put food on the table. Sophia's just like her mother. I can't control that."

The girls' mother had run off when they were young with some man. She came by every so often, but she was even less of a mother than Pete was a father.

"Only one who ever had any influence over Sophia was your mama."

"If you'd try—"

"I gotta get back to work. Stay safe, and don't come home till this is over."

# CHAPTER TEN

Braden sat back at his desk and covered a yawn. Having Carly at his house was wreaking havoc on his sleep. How was a guy supposed to rest after he found out the woman he'd once loved had almost been killed? Had run for her life?

And still didn't want him.

That last part... He wished he didn't care. Why did he, after three years? Why couldn't he just let her go?

He hadn't fallen asleep until after midnight, and then he'd been awakened before dawn to hear her retching in the bathroom. A stomach bug would explain why she'd eaten so little of the meal she'd prepared. He'd reach out to her in a few hours and see how she was, but he didn't want to call and wake her if she was sick.

At his office, he'd been focused on his work for a couple of hours and needed to move. He stretched out the kinks in his back and headed toward the break room, offering Jacqui what he hoped was a genuine smile as he walked by, though thoughts of the new guy and his sparkly MBA weren't far from his mind.

Jacqui said, "I can't remember the last time you hadn't already started the coffee by the time I got here."

"Overslept," he said. "I'm on my way to grab a cup. Did you make it today?"

"Tried to."

He faked a shudder. "Should have hit Cuppa Josie's."

Jacqui laughed. "Sometimes I think you forget who signs your paychecks."

He chuckled, enjoying the banter. His boss used to be so focused and driven. She still was, but she had more time for the people in her life than before. She was aware of others and their needs in a way she hadn't been before. She'd always cared, but she hadn't been great about showing it. Being with Reid had softened her, changed her in good ways.

That was what being in love was supposed to look like. A man loves a woman, a woman loves him back, and they both love God. They grow together, making each other a priority. They respect each other. They value each other. And, over time, they grow closer to God and become better versions of themselves. Jacqui and Reid were modeling exactly the kind of relationship Braden wanted. The kind of relationship he could never have with Carly, even if she had given her life to Christ. Carly would never put him first. She would always put her sisters before him.

Why would he love a woman like that?

"You coming to the potluck tonight?" Jacqui called as he stepped into the break room.

He popped his head back out. He'd forgotten all about the monthly potluck at their church. He hadn't missed one since he'd lived there, mostly because he usually had nothing better to do. But with Carly in town, he figured he'd better skip this time. He'd opened his mouth to say so when Jacqui spoke again.

"Andrew's going. He's still looking for a house, so I figured I'd give him a tour of Coventry."

If Andrew was going to be there, then Braden would too. "I may have a friend with me."

Jacqui's eyebrows rose. "Any chance it's the woman Reid told me about? The one who showed up at your house Monday night? I've been waiting for you to tell me about her."

Not that they generally sat around chitchatting, but he appreciated that Jacqui wanted to know about his life.

"An old friend from Boston," he said. "She needed a place to stay."

"She's still with you, then?"

"For a few more days, I think."

"I look forward to meeting her." Jacqui turned her attention to her screen, and Braden poured a cup of coffee.

When he left the break room, he spotted Andrew leaning a hip against Braden's desk and considered retreating until the man moved on. But Andrew lifted a hand.

Braden crossed the space and forced a cordial tone. "What's up?"

"What is it you love about living here?"

"It's a great place." Braden couldn't help but be offended on behalf of his new rural home. "If you can't see that, I'm sure—"

"No." Andrew seemed perfectly at ease. "I love it. Jacqui asked me to come up with some points for that brochure you suggested—great idea, by the way. I'm going to add the information to a page on the website as well."

Braden should have thought of that.

"I thought I should start by canvassing the employees," Andrew said. "See what they think. Nobody knows the benefits of working here better than those of us who already do."

"You've worked here, what, twenty hours?" Braden's voice sounded accusing. He needed to dial back his frustration.

Andrew's easy smile stiffened. "That's why I'm asking you. And everybody else."

Braden wanted to hate this guy, but it wasn't easy. Asking around to get others' input... Braden hadn't thought to do that. Andrew was coming off as humble and honest and competent.

The man was easily qualified to manage BNB. Braden wasn't. Maybe he should just give up that dream.

But he wasn't willing to do that. For now, he needed to show he was a team player. "I'll think about it and send you an email."

"I'd love your initial reaction to the question now, if you can—"

"Fine. I grew up in Boston." Braden took a breath and tried to make his voice sound more conversational, less aggressive. "Not exactly a nature-lovers paradise."

Andrew started typing into his phone. "Go on. I'm taking notes."

Not that Braden was offering anything earth-shattering, but whatever. "We went camping every summer, and it was always my favorite time of the year. I love the outdoors, always have, and the parks near my house didn't exactly satisfy. With what I wanted to do, I figured I'd always live in Boston or the suburbs. I never thought I'd get to live anywhere like this. I love the woods, the mountains, the lakes. There's so much to explore. When people talk about living in the city, they always focus on the culture—the museums and the shows—but let's be real. How often do people actually go to those things? Truth is, I never cared for museums or watching people dance and sing onstage. That's not exactly my favorite way to spend an evening. But up here, I've been cross-country skiing on trails near my house, and I'm planning to take up fishing this summer. Might even buy myself a boat. Next winter, I'm determined to learn how to downhill ski."

Andrew looked up. "Good, good. And BNB?"

Braden told him all the things he enjoyed about working there while Andrew continued to take notes. Weird, considering Braden wasn't saying anything all that surprising. But maybe this guy with his suit and his MBA knew something Braden didn't.

When he was finished, Andrew pocketed the phone. "Great stuff. The more I talk to employees, the more thankful I am for this job. I hope you'll help me once I get a rough draft."

"Sure, sure."

Andrew wandered away, leaving Braden feeling... unsettled.

Not because the guy wasn't great but because he *was*. It never would have occurred to Braden to ask the employees for help putting that brochure together. He'd have done it himself, and probably missed a lot of good insights. It seemed Jacqui'd been right to hire the guy.

Much as Braden hated to admit it, Andrew seemed perfect to manage BNB. The thought made Braden's stomach clench. Had he picked up whatever had caused Carly to vomit that morning?

*Lord, You know how much I've enjoyed my role here. Are You going to take that away from me too?*

Too.

As if God had taken Carly away from him. But no, she'd done that all by herself.

Speaking of Carly... It was after ten, so he dialed her phone, hoping he wouldn't wake her.

"Hey." Her voice sounded strong, not at all ill. He could hear the rumble of his old Monte Carlo's engine in the background.

"I heard you getting sick this morning, but I guess you're feeling better if you're out."

"Oh, I'm sorry you heard that. I'll go downstairs next time."

Next time? Did she throw up often?

She wasn't bulimic, was she? No, he couldn't imagine that. And anyway, if she were, she'd have binged on spaghetti and then made herself sick after dinner, not eaten like a bird and waited twelve hours to purge.

She said, "I hope I didn't wake you."

"It's fine. I went back to sleep." And then overslept, but he wouldn't put that on her. "Where you headed?"

"Back to your place. I went to Concord to make some phone calls."

"Why all the way there?"

"Trying to keep this cell from being traced. I found a payphone."

He was glad she was being careful. "What'd you learn?"

"I'll tell you tonight. Since we had Italian last night, I was thinking for dinner—"

"Actually, there's a potluck at my church that I need to go to. Do you want to join me?"

"Oh. Uh... You think it'll be safe?"

"You think the murderers might randomly show up at a church potluck in Coventry, New Hampshire?"

Her laugh was short-lived. "I'm more worried about my face on social media."

"I think it'll be fine. I've never been tagged in a post or anything. But you can stay home if you'd rather."

"Well." She drew the word out as if she were considering her options. "I'd like to get out of the house, if you don't mind me being there. What are you planning to take?"

"I usually grab a box of pastries from the bakery in town."

"I'll make something. It'll give me something to do this afternoon."

"You're sure you're feeling well enough? No stomach issues?"

"I think that was just... nerves or something. I'm fine."

The last time he'd picked up a stomach bug, he'd stayed in bed for two days. Seemed Carly was more resilient than he was. He hoped that whatever had made her sick wasn't contagious. He couldn't afford to be away from work, especially not now, not with Andrew so intent on stealing the job Braden had set his sights on.

BRADEN SPENT MUCH of the afternoon helping the newer researchers with their tasks, guiding them when they got off track and helping them to use the information they were gathering to draw conclusions and come up with their next steps. Of all the researchers, he'd been with BNB the longest, so he was the most logical person to ask for guidance, and he didn't mind offering it, except that it kept him from his own to-do list. Fortunately, he wasn't on any tight deadlines at the moment.

Meanwhile, he watched, often listened, as Andrew made the rounds, gathering information and making friends along the way.

Jacqui hadn't announced it, but it was obvious by the way she dealt with Andrew that she had a lot of respect for his opinions. It was obvious by the way she neglected to ask Braden's opinion about a business matter that came up that afternoon that she no longer saw him as her confidant. She had Andrew now.

Braden's stomach turned as he watched the two disappear into the conference room near the end of the day.

He hated seeing the role he'd so enjoyed slipping through his fingers. He hated knowing he was, indeed, just another researcher now.

Mostly, he hated admitting that Jacqui'd found a better manager than he could have ever been.

But she had, and that was that.

He'd just have to let that dream go.

Why did he ever bother with dreams, anyway? They always managed to crumble, leaving him standing in the wreckage, covered in dust.

Whatever.

He finished his work, barely looking up when Jacqui and Andrew left the conference room, both wearing confident expressions. They'd decided something, and they hadn't needed his input at all.

A bitter wind slapped Braden when he stepped outside at just after five o'clock. He'd stayed a little later than everybody else, even Jacqui. Old habits, not that it mattered now. Who was he trying to impress?

He locked up and headed for his pickup. An SUV was idling on the far side, though he couldn't see much of it, just the white exhaust pumping into the cold air. Who was still there?

He was just about to circle his truck to the driver's side when he heard a voice.

Andrew.

"Don't even think about coming up here."

Braden froze.

It was probably wrong to eavesdrop. But there was something in the other man's angry tone—a tone so loud it carried through the car's closed doors and over the low hum of its engine, that kept Braden from making his presence known.

"Listen, I don't care what you think you know," Andrew said. "I will not be blackmailed."

Blackmailed?

Andrew was quiet a moment, most likely listening to whomever he was talking to.

Then, "Just keep your mouth shut."

Braden heard the thud of the car shifting into gear, and Andrew drove away, turning the opposite direction.

Andrew would never know Braden had overheard.

What had that been about? It sounded like Andrew was in some sort of trouble. Did Jacqui know about that trouble? Would it come back to harm them?

As much as Braden wanted the manager job, he was more concerned about the company. If Andrew brought baggage or, heaven forbid, danger, Jacqui needed to know.

And if whatever was in Andrew's past might cast him in a bad light, it could damage BNB's reputation in the industry.

A little voice in the back of Braden's mind told him this was about more than the company's reputation, though. Maybe the manager job wasn't really out of his reach.

When the sound of Andrew's car faded, Braden climbed into his pickup and started the engine.

He needed to protect Jacqui and BNB. And if it helped him secure the job he'd been working so hard to get...

That'd just be icing on the cake.

# CHAPTER ELEVEN

Carly checked her reflection in the bathroom mirror. She'd purchased a few essentials at Walmart, including a little makeup, which she'd applied that afternoon. She'd also bought a new sweater, but now that she had it on, she wasn't so sure. It was snugger than she'd thought it would be, hugging her curves rather than hiding them. Not only that, but she'd chosen the dark red one, though there'd been both blue and green. As she turned this way and that to see how she looked, she realized why she'd chosen it.

Braden had once told her she looked pretty in red.

Maybe she should change.

But into what? The T-shirt she'd worn the day before? She'd splattered spaghetti sauce on it, and anyway, it was too cold for a T-shirt. Her only other option was the sweatshirt she'd bought, and that probably wasn't dressy enough for a church potluck.

Not that she'd ever been to one.

She heard an engine and hurried back to her bedroom to look out the window. Braden's pickup was pulling into the driveway. Too late to change now, not that she had any other choices.

She slipped on her sneakers, wishing she had a better choice of footwear. Short boots would look cute with the outfit, but she hadn't thought to buy any. And really, did she want to spend the money? She had plenty of clothes at home.

Maybe Sophia would mail them to her. Except then Carly would have to tell her where she was, and she couldn't do that. She wouldn't put her sister in danger.

Certainly not for the sake of vanity.

It was fine. She looked fine. She just hoped she wouldn't embarrass Braden too much. She'd try to keep her mouth shut and smile a lot. She could do that.

Why had she agreed to this? And why was she so nervous to go to a church potluck? She was being ridiculous.

Braden's heavy footsteps on the stairs told her he was on his way up. "Carly?"

She snagged her backpack—no purse, unfortunately—and stepped into the hallway. "I'm ready."

His eyebrows lifted, and his jaw slacked just a tiny bit. "You look good."

"Oh." Her heart floated a little at the compliment. "Thank you."

He stared at her another moment, then swallowed and stepped back. "Let me just throw on some jeans."

Five minutes later, she walked through the garage beneath his house and out to the driveway, amazed anew at how dark the world around her was. It was only five thirty, but the sun had long set. If not for the floodlights over Braden's garage door, she wouldn't be able to see her feet on the ground.

She shoved her backpack onto the floor and climbed into his passenger seat, then balanced the dessert she'd made on her lap.

Braden climbed in the other side, only then noticing in the dim overhead light what she'd brought. "Is that pound cake?"

"Mama's recipe. I remember how much you used to like it."

"You'd better leave that here."

The heart that had floated earlier now sank to the ground. "Is it not appropriate? I wasn't sure what to make, and I don't have any recipes with me. I remembered this one because Mama and I made it so often. But if it's not acceptable..."

He chuckled. "It's too good for that crowd. I'd rather keep it to myself."

"Oh." She relaxed and put on her seatbelt. "If they eat it all, I'll make you another one."

"I'll hold you to that. Tell me what you found out."

The lighthearted moment melted like April snow. While Braden drove through the darkness as if he knew every curve of the road, she gave him a rundown on what she'd learned. By the time she was finished, his smile had turned to a scowl.

"So you're saying they're not even investigating?" he clarified.

"They don't believe he's been murdered, but it's just a matter of time before they figure it out, right? Except, whoever has his phone knows him well enough to be posting pictures. There were a few today from Florida, so somebody is there at his place."

At Braden's raised eyebrows, she rushed to clarify. "Not that I've ever been to Ian's condo in Florida, but he's always posting pictures, and it looks familiar."

"He's kind of a bragger, I guess."

*Was* a bragger, no question. She shrugged rather than voice her agreement, but Braden wasn't wrong.

"I scrolled through his social media contacts to see if I could figure out who those guys were at his shop."

Braden maneuvered through the little downtown area, which was lit by old-fashioned black lampposts. The storefronts spilled light onto the sidewalks outside. There were people window-shopping, some cradling cups of coffee or cocoa in their mittened hands.

"Tourists," Braden said, following her line of sight. "There are a few ski areas close by, so we have them all year long."

"Do they get annoying?"

He shrugged. "Not to me. The traffic gets old, but otherwise, I don't mind them like the locals do, the locals who don't count on them for their income, anyway. James—you'll meet him tonight. He'll shut down anybody who complains about them because he understands that it's the tourists who keep his restaurant open, and many of the other businesses in town."

Coventry was so charming. She could imagine how lovely it would be in the summertime, when the lake wasn't frozen, when the world was green and blue and dotted with brightly colored flowers.

And in the fall when the trees changed color. How gorgeous it must look. Of course, the trees in Boston were pretty in October, but there weren't nearly as many of them there as here. She'd love to see it. Someday.

"I thought you didn't see their faces," Braden said, pulling her back to the conversation.

"I thought maybe something would trigger a memory."

"And?"

"Nothing. But... did you know Richard Lynch? Ian posted a lot of things about him, though I never knew him to care about politics."

"I never met Lynch, but of course I've heard about him. Remember Geoffrey Stuart?"

"Student council, right?"

"Yeah. We had a lot of classes together. He works on Lynch's campaign."

"Have you and Geoff stayed in touch?"

"No, no. Just on social media, but he posts all the time. And everybody has an opinion. Lynch seems to be one of those guys people either love or hate."

"Seems like the nature of politics these days. Friend or enemy—there's no in-between." Carly had never been that interested in politics, and the vitriolic nature of the debates over the previous few years did not entice her to get involved. "Ian wasn't into politics, but he seemed to be following the campaign a lot lately, posting and reposting things. What surprises me is that he didn't like Lynch."

"You think he should have?"

"Ian had pretty strong views on politics, and Lynch's positions seem to line right up with them."

"Did they know each other?"

She considered his question. "Not as far as I know. And really, if they did, he'd have told me."

"Because he's a name dropper—and a bragger."

"*Was*," she said. "He *was* those things."

"Good point. I should be more respectful of the dead."

Braden's words sounded forced. Because Ian was a name-dropping bragger? Because he'd turned out to be a criminal?

Or because she'd been with him?

Maybe all of the above.

"So, he didn't know Lynch," Braden prompted.

"Not as far as I know. It's just weird he seemed to be following his campaign so closely when he wasn't into politics and didn't like the guy."

"Maybe... Ian was running a protection scheme, right? Does Lynch own any businesses in town?"

"Not the kind you're thinking of. He's a real estate developer."

"Huh. There's probably no connection there."

"There's probably no connection at all," she said. "I'm just trying to figure it out, but that thread leads nowhere." There was something else she needed to say to Braden, though she feared his reaction. To be fair, her idea was a little crazy. But she could do it. She thought so, anyway. And she would do it without telling Braden in advance, except she knew he wouldn't like that, and he'd been so good to her. And maybe he'd see a hole in her plan she missed.

"I've been thinking." He glanced her way, and she prayed for wisdom and words. "I told you Pete said the bad guys wanted to search my room."

"Yeah." The single word was dragged out, dripping with suspicion. Or maybe worry.

"I don't have anything of Ian's. We'd been broken up for months before I moved home, and he never went to my house after that. There's no way he could have hidden anything in my stuff. But he had hiding places in his apartment."

Braden's jaw hardened. He didn't look her way, but his hands tightened on the steering wheel.

She continued as if she hadn't noticed. "I saw him getting into one once. I doubt anybody would find it. I was thinking that maybe I should go and look for whatever it is the bad guys are looking for. Maybe that would shine a light—"

"Absolutely not." His words were spoken as if he had authority over her. As if they carried weight.

"I know it makes you nervous, but—"

"No." He stopped too hard at a stop sign, and the cake almost came loose from her hands.

"Look," she said, "I appreciate your input, but you can't actually forbid—"

"You're using my home as a refuge. And my old car. I'd say that gives me at least some say in what you do."

"Fine. It's your father's car. I'll move to a hotel." Not that she could afford to. Not that she wanted to leave the haven she'd found at Braden's. Maybe she should just shut up and let the police handle it. Except they weren't handling it. And meanwhile, her sisters had nobody looking after them. When she'd moved out the year before, she'd continued to check on them, make sure they did their homework, make sure they were keeping up in school. If Pete were doing those things, then Carly wouldn't have to, but based on their social media posts, Pete wasn't keeping as close an eye on them as he should.

Sophia had posted more photos of herself with the man she'd started seeing. Carly had done some internet snooping but couldn't figure out who he was.

No way his motives were anything but... gross.

She'd messaged her sister on Instagram, but Sophia had brushed her off. *He's a sweet guy. What is age anyway?*

Sophia needed somebody to steer her in the right direction, and Pete obviously wasn't going to do it.

Beside her, Braden's jaw worked, and his Adam's apple bobbed. He'd said nothing for miles.

"Getting into Ian's will be easy," she said. "In and out. I still have a key."

That information only elicited a glare.

"I tried to give it back to him when we broke up, but he wouldn't—"

"I don't need to know, Carly."

"I'll get in fast, check his hiding places, and get out. I could wear a disguise."

He took a long breath. "I'm trying to keep you alive."

"I know."

"Just tell the detective you talked to today. He can search for it."

"He doesn't even think Ian was killed. How could he search the home of a guy who isn't officially the victim of a crime?"

"Give it time."

"And give the killers a chance to find... whatever it is they're looking for? That seems risky."

Braden was quiet as he pulled into the parking lot of a pretty white church complete with a steeple. There were plenty of churches back in Boston, but this one was nestled among tall pines and oaks and birches. Not that she could see anything well in the darkness, but she guessed it was gorgeous in the daytime.

He killed the engine but didn't move.

"I'm not trying to make you mad. But if the murderers aren't found, I'm never going to be safe."

He turned her way, and she leaned back, afraid of the words that would follow that angry scowl. But his expression shifted. His eyes softened. "I understand what you're saying, but it doesn't seem necessary for you to put your life in danger to solve this mystery. Just stay here where you're safe and let the police sort it out."

"But they aren't sorting it out. And meanwhile, my sisters need me."

Braden turned away, but not in time to hide the frustration her words brought. He'd never understood her need to look after them.

"We'll talk about it later." Before she could respond, Braden climbed out of the truck.

She pulled her cell from her backpack at her feet, shoved it in her pocket, and reached for the handle.

The door opened, and Braden took the cake. "I can get this."

"Oh. Thanks."

She climbed out, and he closed the door behind her, just like he used to.

How could she have forgotten how good and kind he was? How courteous? How gentle? Even angry with her, he was all those things and more.

He was also off-limits. Because he lived here, and she lived there, and she had responsibilities. She'd do well to keep that in mind before she got too comfortable with Braden. Of course, if he kicked her out for going back to Dorchester, that wouldn't be an issue.

Assuming she made it out alive.

CARLY'S ANXIETY ramped up as Braden led her inside, up a short staircase, and into a room that spanned the width and almost the length of the building—probably forty feet by fifty. The floor was hardwood, the walls pale blue. Round tables were interspersed and surrounded by folding chairs, and people of all ages and shapes and sizes milled around, chatting. Their conversation bounced off all the hard surfaces, creating a low hum—or maybe not so low. The scents of so many foods filled the space that she couldn't differentiate any of them.

"Hey, Braden."

One of the men she'd seen Monday night approached, hand held out. Braden shifted the plate with her cake into his left and shook, then turned to her. "Reid, this is an old friend, Carly Garcia."

"It's a pleasure to officially meet you," Reid said.

Carly took his outstretched hand, which was as warm as his voice. "I was a little overwhelmed the other night."

"I'm sure you didn't anticipate walking into a houseful of guys."

A woman with dark red hair joined Reid but focused on Carly. "I'm Jacqui Beal."

"Hi. Carly."

Jacqui took the cake from Braden's hands but kept her focus on Carly. "Let's take this to the kitchen."

"Oh. Okay." With a glance at Braden, whose expression had shifted from friendly to concerned, she walked with Jacqui to a kitchen at the far end of the room. Inside, women and men were preparing food and setting it on a long counter that separated the big room from the workspace.

"We should cut this." Jacqui set the plate with the cake on a counter and grabbed a knife from a drawer. "If we don't, nobody will cut it when they're in the line. Is that okay?"

"Whatever you think," Carly said.

Jacqui held out the knife. "Do you want to, or shall I?"

Carly took it and started slicing.

Behind her Jacqui called, "Hey, Cassidy, come meet Braden's friend."

A moment later, a woman with the most unusual blue-green eyes Carly had ever seen stopped in front of her. Her hair was dark brown, her smile genuine. "Hi. Cassidy Sullivan. I'm married to James, who's Reid's oldest friend. Reid is Jacqui's fiancé."

Carly glanced at the redhead's left hand and saw the ring. "Congratulations. When's the wedding?"

"This summer. We're very excited."

"Enough about her, though," Cassidy said. "Tell us about you."

"Maybe we should let her get some food before we grill her," Jacqui said.

Cassidy shrugged. "I guess I can wait." She winked and led the way out of the kitchen.

A line was already forming. Braden, Reid, and two other men she didn't recognize were in line, talking to one another.

Cassidy walked to the one who sort of looked like the handsome king in the *Lord of the Rings* movies and kissed his cheek.

Carly was tempted to go stand beside—behind, maybe—Braden. There were too many people. Too many strangers. But none of them was out to get her, and Mama had taught her to never shrink in social situations. Mama had said that Carly would always be just as valuable as anybody else in the room, even if she was in a room with royalty. So she grinned at the unknown man Cassidy had kissed and said, "Let me guess. You're James?"

"Guilty. And you're Carly."

She nodded and turned to the other one she hadn't met. He wore a suit and tie and had tanned skin and a trimmed beard.

"This is Andrew Middleton," Braden said. "He just started at BNB." He added, "Where I work," as an afterthought.

"Pleasure," she said.

Andrew gave her an appraising look. "The pleasure is all mine."

Braden scowled and took Carly's hand as if to claim her, surprising her into silence. She'd have yanked it away if she didn't enjoy the touch so much.

James took in their joined hands, an amused expression on his face. "What brings you to Coventry?"

"Oh, that's sort of a long story."

James's gaze flicked to Braden, who steered the conversation away from her by bringing up the Celtics and their chances to make the playoffs.

It was a good night. A crazy night. Braden seemed to have shaken off their discussion in the car and looked like he was having fun. She picked up on more than a little tension between him and Andrew, though most of it seemed to be on Braden's side. She'd have to remember to ask him about that later.

They sat at one of the round tables, joined eventually by two latecomers, Dylan and Chelsea. Chelsea had an English accent, which Braden hadn't explained. She seemed a little standoffish, but also very kind, a weird combination that Carly couldn't quite figure out.

Reid's daughter Ella finally responded to her father's request that she join them and eat instead of playing with her friends. She sat between him and Jacqui and talked nonstop. She was adorable, reminding Carly of Danielle when Carly had first met her.

Not once did Carly see anybody snap a photo. Not once did she feel unsafe or unprotected. There was something about this place and these people that made her feel secure.

The grilling Cassidy had alluded to in the kitchen never came. She, Jacqui, and Chelsea asked Carly polite questions, but nothing probing, which she appreciated.

Jacqui spent much of the meal telling them all about Andrew, who had earned both a master's in some science degree or other and an MBA. These people with their degrees and professions were so far out of her league, she'd be lucky to serve them dinner, much less eat with them.

When an hour or more had passed, James and Cassidy started clearing paper plates. Chelsea grabbed her own and her husband's as he walked away to join a group of men folding chairs in the corner.

Carly pushed her chair back, intending to help, but Chelsea waved her off. "We take turns. And anyway, you're a guest tonight." Her English was so refined that it made Carly almost too self-conscious to answer in her Southie accent, with its nasally tone and dropped Rs.

"Okay, thanks."

James gathered her plate. "Jacqui tells me you brought the pound cake. It was outstanding. I'd love that recipe."

James was the one who owned a restaurant in town, so she was more than flattered by his words. "It was my mother's. I'll write it down for you."

After they left, Jacqui and Reid stood to leave with talk of bath time and bedtime for little Ella. "It was nice to meet you," Reid said.

"Maybe we can get together for dinner one night while you're here. We're free tomorrow"—Jacqui turned to Reid —"right?"

"Think so. We could meet at The Patriot."

"Let's do it," Braden said, barely looking at her. But she knew what he was doing. They'd known each other long enough that she could see through his false cheer. He was trying to make sure she stayed in town.

"Actually, I'm not going to be around tomorrow," Carly said. "I've got to make a quick trip back to the city."

"Oh, no." Jacqui seemed genuinely distressed, her gaze flicking from her to Braden and back. "You'll return, I hope."

Carly didn't look at Braden, though she was tempted to. "I'm not sure. Maybe." *If I'm welcome.*

Braden's sigh was loud enough to carry over the conversation all around them. "She'll be back. It's just for a day. Assuming I can't talk her out of it."

She faced him, trying to keep a pleasant expression on her face. "I'm pretty determined."

He didn't even bother to fake a happy expression. "I'm getting that impression."

"Why don't you go with her?" Jacqui said. "Keep her company. BNB will survive without you for one day, and then she won't have to make the trip all by herself."

Braden's gaze flicked from Jacqui to Carly, and everything on his face told her he hated that idea.

"That's okay," Carly said. "I can handle it myself."

Jacqui looked confused.

Reid looked concerned.

And Braden blew out another sigh. "Actually, I'd like that, if you really don't mind."

Jacqui seemed to relax, as if she'd been nervous or something. "Great. I'll see you Friday then. You two have fun."

Ella gave Carly a good-bye hug as if they'd known each other for years.

Andrew followed them out with barely a *see you later*.

Braden pushed back in his chair.

Carly started to follow, thinking they were leaving, but he walked to the corner, where he cornered Dylan. The two men had a hushed conversation.

Fine, then.

Carly went to the kitchen to retrieve Braden's plate and the leftover cake. There was only one slice, and just as she was about to cover it with plastic wrap, an older woman shuffled in and saw it. "Is that all that's left of the pound cake? I heard it was really good." Her eyes flicked from the cake to Carly's face. "Do you mind if I...?"

Carly held the plate toward her, and the woman snatched the last piece and popped a bite into her mouth. Her eyes closed, she said, "Totally worth the calories." When her eyes opened again, she asked, "It's fat free and sugar free, right?"

Perhaps the woman didn't understand why it was called pound cake—because even the fat was measured in pounds. "Uh..."

The woman laughed. "Too much to hope, I suppose." She grabbed a casserole dish and stepped out, tossing a "Thanks again" over her shoulder.

Ten minutes later, Braden ushered Carly from the building and back to his cold pickup. As kind and cordial as he'd been during dinner and that awkward conversation afterward, it was clear he wasn't happy. Frustration wafted off him like the exhaust pumping into the frigid night.

They were through the cheerily lit town and back on the pitch-black roads before he finally spoke. "Dylan used to be a police detective."

The redheaded guy. Nothing about him had screamed *cop* to her.

"He wants to reach out to your Detective Klein, find out what he can. If that's okay with you."

"Does he think he can learn something I didn't?"

Braden's shoulders lifted, then fell. "Maybe. One of those cop-to-cop things."

"But he's not a cop anymore."

"True. I've never met Klein, but Jacqui and Reid worked with him before. He wasn't in homicide then, so he must be new to the role. They think he's a good detective, and a good guy. If Dylan can get through to him... I think we should wait to hear what he learns before we go to Dorchester. Maybe they're investigating the murder now. Maybe they can search Ian's place."

"When will he hear?"

"You said Klein gave you his direct line."

"He did."

"If you'll give it to me, I'll pass it along to Dylan, and he can make the call tonight."

"Will he tell Klein where I am? I don't want anybody to know, not even the cops."

"He understands the importance of keeping your whereabouts secret. He'll be careful."

She considered the implications of waiting. The longer she waited before going back, the better the chances the killers would find whatever they were looking for in Ian's place. On the other hand, if Klein could search the place, then she wouldn't have to leave the safe haven she'd found at Braden's.

At the end of the day, she really didn't want to put herself at risk.

She didn't want to die.

And it wasn't just about her anymore.

Her hand shifted almost of its own accord to rest on her abdomen, but she snatched it away, thankful Braden's gaze was on the road. "We'll wait to hear from your friend. But if he finds out the police still aren't investigating, then I'm going back. I'll wear a disguise. I'll get in and out of his place in minutes. It'll be fine."

"Unless the bad guys are watching. In which case, it'll be anything but fine."

Braden was right. Maybe her plan was a bad one. But she couldn't hide out for the rest of her life, no matter how much she liked this little town and the people she'd met here. She could see herself getting to know them better, even maybe eventually fitting in here.

But this wasn't her home. She was a city girl, through and through. She'd never wanted to be anything else. Besides, she had a family back in Dorchester, a family that needed her.

She had to go back.

# CHAPTER TWELVE

THERE WAS no way Braden was going to stand by and let Carly go to Ian's apartment alone. He couldn't believe she was even considering it. She would risk her safety, risk her very life, in order to solve the murder of a man she claimed she no longer loved so she could go back to taking care of girls who weren't even related to her.

If Braden had half a brain, he'd just let her go. The last thing he needed was to take a day off from work and give Andrew more opportunity to worm his way into Braden's job.

That night at dinner, Jacqui, clueless about his feelings, had gushed to the whole table about Andrew and the *insightful contributions* he'd already made to BNB.

Braden had done his very best to keep his feelings on the matter to himself, and Jacqui never picked up on them. But Reid, far more insightful than his future wife, had studied him with narrowed eyes.

Maybe Reid would keep his thoughts to himself. Or maybe he'd discuss the situation with Jacqui. Just what Braden needed, his boss's fiancé taking up for him—assuming he would. As if Braden couldn't manage his work life all by himself.

Not that he could.

He pulled into his garage and parked and was rounding the car to open Carly's door when she pushed it open herself. Just as well. They weren't together anymore, and he needed to stop treating her as if they were.

And noticing things like how beautiful she looked in her new sweater and those skinny jeans. Everybody had noticed Carly, not that she was the type to fade into the background. But when Andrew had given her that look, it'd taken all of Braden's self-control not to punch the guy.

He probably shouldn't have grabbed her hand as if they were together, but he'd already lost—or almost lost, anyway—his job as manager to Andrew. He sure as heck wasn't going to lose Carly, especially not to him.

Not that she was his to lose.

"What's wrong?"

They were in the kitchen, though he barely remembered having climbed the steps from his garage. She'd flipped on the light and turned to look at him.

"Nothing."

"That scowl on your face says otherwise."

He snatched the plate out of Carly's hands and shoved it into the dishwasher, surprised by how full it was. But Carly had been home all day, and she'd baked.

"I owe you another one."

He had no idea what she was talking about. He closed the dishwasher and turned to her. His confusion must've shown, because she added, "Cake. I'll bake one—"

"Forget it."

"Look, I know you're not happy—"

"Can you text me the detective's number?"

She pulled her phone from her pocket, tapped the screen, and a moment later, his dinged.

"Thank you." He swiveled and stalked to the living room, where he texted the information to Dylan. He got an immediate reply.

*Calling now. Stand by.*

Braden plopped into his chair, exhausted and irritated and frustrated.

In the other room, the water ran, then stopped. He heard ice clinking into a glass, then the sound of filtered water coming from his fridge.

Carly came in, glass in hand, and perched on the arm of the sofa. "I guess I'll just go up."

"Wait until Dylan responds. Maybe he'll have good news."

She slid all the way onto the couch, staring at the blank TV screen.

They didn't speak. She sipped her water, and he wished he'd gotten himself some, but he didn't have it in him to move.

She pulled out her phone and scrolled through something. Social media, he assumed. He had a Facebook account that he checked every week or so, but no more. Certainly not nightly, like Carly did.

Was she on Facebook, or did she focus more on Instagram? Maybe, if he joined that site, he could see pictures of her all the time.

Right. Just what he needed—a constant reminder of the one who got away.

Never mind that she was sitting a few feet from him.

Her soft gasp had him turning toward her. Even in the dim light, he could see the distress on her features. "What?"

She turned the phone and leaned toward him so he could see.

A photograph of her younger sisters, Laurie and Danielle. They'd both changed a lot since the last time he'd seen them. They carried backpacks that looked heavy with books. Based on the time stamp on the photo, it'd been posted that morning, so the girls were probably walking to school.

There was nothing nefarious about the photograph itself. It hadn't been posted on the site but in a private message to Carly. And the caption...

*Dangerous to walk the streets alone. I sure hope nothing happens to them.*

The message came from someone calling himself John Smith. His profile picture was the image of a tiger crouched behind a bush as if stalking prey.

Braden lifted his gaze to Carly to find her face had paled.

"Are they okay right now?"

She pulled the phone back to herself and started typing. A moment later, she said, "Yes, they're both home. Sophia's out with her new boyfriend."

"Can you get Pete to make sure they get to and from school safely?"

"I'll try. I don't want to freak out the girls, but I don't see that I have any option. The problem is, Pete doesn't do social media, so the only way to contact him is by phone or text, and I don't want to use this one."

"You could use mine."

"But if somebody's checking his call logs... It just makes me nervous."

"You should tell Klein about that. Maybe that'll make him realize—"

Braden's phone rang, and he swiped to answer and put it on speaker. "Dylan," he said so Carly would know who was on the phone. "What'd you learn?"

"I had a chat with Detective Klein." He blew out a long breath. "He seems like a good detective, but he just moved over into homicide this week. Apparently, they had a detective up and quit."

"We got the newbie?" Braden couldn't keep frustration from his voice. "That figures."

"Don't make assumptions. The guy's a veteran, he's just new to homicide. He still isn't convinced Murphy was murdered, which makes sense since Murphy's family claims to have heard from him. Plus, they're seeing his posts all over social media."

"The killers have his phone," Carly said. "I know what I heard."

Dylan's voice was kind when he said, "I believe you. They're smart. The longer the police wait before they start investigating, the colder the case will get. The problem is, until they have solid evidence that your friend was murdered, there's nothing they can do. Right now, Klein has no body, no murder weapon, no signs of a struggle, no proof Murphy's place had been broken into, and two parents telling him their son is fine."

"But he's not." Carly's voice broke, and she hunched over on the sofa.

Before Braden could talk himself out of it, he moved to sit beside her, and she cuddled into his side. Just what he needed. He said, "Carly got a threat in her Instagram today."

"What kind of a threat?"

Braden explained the photo of her sisters and the message that went along with it.

"It's not nothing. Tell Klein about it, but I doubt it'll change anything. Truth is, they're stretched thin right now. They can't investigate a crime that might not've happened."

"What if we get proof?" Braden asked. "Or something to point to who might've done it, so that when they finally figure out he's dead, they'll have a place to start."

"What are you thinking of doing?"

He explained Carly's plan to search Ian's apartment.

"It's not a good idea. Breaking and entering—"

"She has a key," Braden said.

"Still, it wouldn't be safe."

Braden nodded along with Dylan's words. Of course it was a terrible idea.

"You're better off letting the police find what's there and take it as evidence."

Carly pushed herself forward and leaned toward the phone on the coffee table. "The police aren't investigating. You just said that. By the time they do, the killers could find any evidence and destroy it."

Braden wasn't about to say so, but she was probably right.

Dylan sighed. "I understand you want to do something, Carly, but your best bet is just to stay out of sight until—"

"Until they kill one of my sisters?"

That silenced Dylan.

She wouldn't appreciate Braden's answer to that. Carly's sisters weren't her responsibility, but saying so wouldn't change anything. It would just make her angry.

"I can't just sit here in safety while my sisters are in danger."

"Maybe you should get them out of town too," Dylan suggested.

Braden managed to stifle his groan. The last thing he needed was three more females in his house. Of course, if those females' lives were in danger, he'd make room.

"I can try," Carly said. "But I don't know if Pete'll go for it."

"Pete is...?" Dylan asked.

"Her former stepfather," Braden said, instantly sorry he'd put the emphasis on *former*. "And the girls are her stepsisters."

"But they're important to you, Carly," Dylan guessed. "And even if they weren't, the killers think they are. They're innocent in all of this. I recommend you see if you can get them out of town until this is all over."

"But if the police never investigate Ian's murder, it'll never be over."

"Eventually they'll realize something's wrong. I mean, if the guy's dead, then he's never going to come home. The killers are only putting off the inevitable."

"By then," she said, "all the evidence of his murder will be gone. I'll be the only person left who can recognize the killers' voices. I'll be the only loose end they have to tie up."

Her words made too much sense. Braden could see all his and Dylan's arguments crumbling like dust.

"That's a good point," Dylan said, "but surely it won't come to that."

Braden took Carly's hand. "We're going to have to trust God to figure this out."

"I should trust Him to fix everything while I hide here?" Her gaze flicked from the phone to him. "But I shouldn't trust Him to keep me safe while I try to do the right thing?"

Dylan said nothing.

Braden swallowed the fear rising in his throat. Because no matter what he said, Carly was intent on this course. "The police will—"

"The police will do nothing." Carly launched herself from the sofa and stalked away before turning to face him. "And my sisters' lives are in danger, and probably so is Pete's. I know you don't care about them, but they're the only family I have in the world."

Braden started to argue, but Carly wasn't finished.

"Even if I could convince them to get out of town, how long can that last? What happens if, by waiting, all the clues are wiped away? What happens if the police never catch the killers because they waited too long? My life—all of our lives—will be in danger until this is over. I'm not willing to risk it."

Braden didn't know what to say.

From the speaker, Dylan said, "Just be careful. Both of you. And let me know if there's anything else I can do."

Dylan rang off, and Carly leaned against the wall, arms crossed, satisfied that she'd made her point. And she had.

Fine, then. She wasn't going to Ian's apartment the next day. He'd do it. He'd figure out what the man had hidden, and he'd get it to Klein.

But he'd make sure Carly was safe first. That was nonnegotiable.

# CHAPTER THIRTEEN

IT WASN'T OFTEN that Carly purposefully wore a glare, but she was aiming one at Braden across the kitchen the next morning.

"If you stay here where you're safe—"

"I'm going, Braden. Either with you or separately, but I'm going."

He blew out a long-suffering breath. "Carly, you'll be safe here. Nobody will suspect me, but if somebody sees you—"

"I'll sit in the truck and keep an eye on the building. But you're not going by yourself. I appreciate that you're trying to keep me safe, but this is my battle, not yours. I need to be there. I'll shove my hair into a hat, maybe throw on some sunglasses. If I keep my head down, nobody will recognize me."

"Unless they're looking for you."

"I'll be in your truck. It'll be fine."

"There's a reason you left the city."

"And there's a reason I have to go back."

She'd messaged her sisters the night before and told them to get Pete to drive them to and from school. Then, she'd asked Dylan to call Detective Klein and ask him—maybe demand was the better word—to call Pete and tell him about the threats aimed at his girls.

Dylan did, and Klein had agreed the photograph and message seemed threatening. He made the call.

Her fear was probably unnecessary. She felt ridiculous even thinking about the roundabout way she'd gone about warning Pete. But if the goal was to remain hidden, then she'd accomplished that.

Hopefully, Pete would keep the girls safe until Carly could figure this out.

On the far side of the kitchen, Braden rubbed his temples.

Behind Carly, the coffee gurgled. The early morning sun was bright, though her weather app told her it was just over twenty degrees outside.

"I heard you getting sick again this morning. What is that? Nerves, or..." His eyes narrowed. "You're not bulimic, are you?"

"Of course not." She'd planned to come downstairs if the morning sickness hit again, but she'd barely made it to the upstairs toilet. "It's not every day a person's life is in danger."

"So, nerves."

She felt bad for deceiving him, but she couldn't tell him the truth, not yet. Maybe not ever.

"Because someone's trying to kill you. Which is why you should stay here."

"I can't, Braden." Why couldn't he understand? "This is *my* family in danger. This is *my* ex who was murdered." The father of my child, though she didn't add that. "This is *my* problem. I'd go by myself to keep from involving you—"

"Absolutely not."

"—if I thought you'd let me. I hate that I've put my sisters in danger. The last thing I want is to put you in their crosshairs too." Her voice cracked with emotion, with the thought of endangering Braden. She swallowed the lump forming in her throat. "I'm definitely not going to do that while I sit here and sip cocoa. I'm going. End of story."

Braden growled as he swiveled and stomped out of the room.

Hands shaking—partly because of the argument and partly

because she was still feeling hungry and sick—she bit the cold toast on the counter. While she chewed, she found an insulated travel cup and filled it with coffee. She doctored it, hoping Braden hadn't changed the way he took his coffee since they'd broken up. Then she found a second travel cup and filled it with water. She'd need to pick up some decaf. It would be better than tepid water with breakfast.

Ready to leave, she finished her toast.

She listened to his footsteps above her, footsteps not on the other side of the house in the master bedroom, but straight above the kitchen—in her room. She pictured him searching her backpack.

She was pretty sure that, if he'd had the key to Ian's apartment, he'd have left her at home this morning, possibly even taking the Monte Carlo keys with him in order to trap her at his house. He didn't know Ian's address, but his friend could probably get that information for him.

She was fairly certain Braden was looking for those keys now.

He wouldn't find them, though. They were tucked deep in her pockets.

His footsteps were loud and fast as he came down the stairs. He stomped through the dining room and froze in the kitchen. "You have them, don't you?"

"I do."

He glared. "Carly—"

"Can we just get past this and go? The sooner we leave, the sooner we'll get it over with." She held out his coffee, and he snatched it.

After a moment, he mumbled, "Thank you."

"You need breakfast, or—"

"No. I'm ready."

It was a long, tense drive south. Carly tried a couple of times to draw Braden out, to start a conversation, but he wasn't interested. Finally, she gave in and settled back to listen to the music on his playlist. They'd always agreed on music, and though Braden now played Christian songs, it seemed they still had similar tastes.

What had taken less than two hours Monday night took closer to two and a half Thursday morning, thanks to traffic. By the time they reached Dorchester, it was after nine.

Carly directed Braden to Ian's place. The closer they got, the more Braden scowled, which she wouldn't have guessed possible.

"What's wrong?"

"I wish you weren't here."

"Golly, you sure know how to make a girl feel special."

When he turned her direction, she wasn't surprised to see anger in his expression. She was surprised at the fear lingering beneath it.

She said, "I know this makes you nervous."

"If anything happens to you on my watch..."

"I'll be safe in your truck."

He'd brought her a ski cap, and he gestured to it now.

She leaned forward and shoved her hair into the cap, then sat back up. It was sunny, so the sunglasses she'd bought at the drug store on the way made sense.

He stopped at a light and faced her.

"What do you think?" she asked.

"You still look like you."

"From two feet away, sure. But from a distance?"

He shrugged. "Which way?"

"Straight here. Left at the next light."

"Left?" His eyebrows rose, and he gazed that direction. "Toward the harbor?"

His surprise made sense. Ian's background wasn't so different from hers. Though he'd had both his parents, they'd never had a lot of money. But Ian had moved from his dingy apartment to a new townhouse by the harbor not long after Carly had started dating him. This was the gentrified part of the neighborhood, attracting young professionals who appreciated the short T ride into the city. They probably didn't tell people they lived in Dorchester, assuming they even knew that was where their new yuppie apartments were located.

"I guess the protection racket pays," Braden said, the sardonic tone not lost on her.

She'd been such a fool to believe Ian's machine shop had been so successful that he could afford his new place. That was what she got for trusting a man like Ian.

Seemed like many men were like Ian or Pete or Carly's absent father. She'd thought Ian was different. Kind, gentle, and dependable. She'd quickly learned that his kindness always came with expectations. His gentleness could morph to anger in a second. Until Monday, though, she'd believed him dependable.

What a fool she was.

Braden followed her directions until she pointed out Ian's building. Braden passed it and took a right a few blocks down and parked.

"There're spaces—"

"I don't want you to be seen."

She gestured to the cap and glasses. "Even if I am, I won't be recognized."

"What am I looking for?"

"I'll tell you when you get back to the building. Park across from the townhouse, and I'll watch the front door, let you know if anybody comes."

Braden studied her a long moment, then leaned against the headrest and closed his eyes. A moment passed before he blew out a breath. "Fine." He got out of the car, and for a moment she thought he might walk away. But to where, she didn't know, since he still didn't have the key to Ian's townhouse. But Braden rounded the car and opened her door. "I want you behind the wheel and ready to drive away, okay? If anybody sees you, you get out of here. Promise?"

The last thing she wanted was to leave Braden alone at Ian's if the killers were nearby, but getting herself killed wouldn't do anybody any good. "I promise."

She hopped the console and slid into the driver's seat. Adjusting it so she could reach the pedals, she explained to Braden the hiding space she'd caught him checking and the other she'd happened upon while cleaning.

"Why were you cleaning his house?" Braden shook his head quickly. "Never mind. If you lived here—"

"We didn't live together." Not that he hadn't asked her to move in more than once. She shifted into Drive. "His cleaning lady had to cancel. I was doing him a favor." She drove back to Ian's townhouse slowly, unaccustomed to such a big vehicle. She found a spot on the shady side of the street about a block away from the front door. Hopefully, nobody would be able to see into the pickup without making it obvious they were looking.

Braden dug into the drugstore bag on the floor at his feet and pulled out the box of medical gloves they'd bought. He shoved a pair into his pocket and put on a second pair, then held out his hand.

She slipped the key into his palm. "Call me if you have any trouble."

"You do the same. And if you think somebody sees you, or you see anybody suspicious, or... anything, just drive away. I can take care of myself."

He reached for the door, but she grabbed his hand before he could open it.

"I'll be praying for you."

"Ditto." He held eye contact a long moment, then climbed from the car and jogged across the street. After he went inside, she did exactly what she'd promised.

# CHAPTER FOURTEEN

BRADEN LET himself into the townhouse and closed and locked the door behind him.

It was toasty warm inside, warmer than a person would leave it if he were headed to Florida for a week.

He had no doubt this townhouse complex dubbed itself as *luxury*. Granite countertops, tile that looked like hardwood on the floor. Fancy crown molding. The furniture looked standard-issue, though, bland and tasteless. Maybe it'd come with the apartment. Surely Carly hadn't helped him pick it out. She had better taste than what he was seeing.

Not that Braden should criticize. His place could use a woman's touch.

He glanced at the view of Boston Harbor through the windows that made up the bulk of the back wall. Was it worth it to extort money from your neighbors to have a couple of bedrooms and a view? Braden would never understand that level of greed.

He was a little surprised that the place didn't look as if it had been searched. If it had, the killers had done a good job of covering up their presence. Of course, their goal was to make it seem as if Ian were alive and well, and tossing his townhouse would certainly send the wrong message.

A few dishes sat in the sink. The coffee pot was half full—again, backing up the theory that he'd planned to return soon.

Nothing seemed glaringly out of place.

Braden took the steps to the second floor two at a time, trying not to think of Carly climbing these same stairs with Ian, of the intimacy they must have shared for her to have caught Ian digging into the hiding spot she'd told Braden about. He didn't linger when he reached the master bedroom, where he found a neatly made bed. He moved the end table out of the way, then lifted the mattress and nudged it off the box spring until it was propped against the floor and the frame.

The box spring looked new, the flimsy fabric pulled taut, but Braden found the spot Carly had insisted would be there. Ian had ripped the fabric back to expose the wood beneath, then reattached it with Velcro so it would look as if nothing had changed. Braden pulled it away. Sure enough, inside he found an oversize manila envelope.

He snapped a picture of the envelope where it lay in the box spring to show to Klein, then backed up and got a shot that encompassed the whole room. After he tossed the envelope on the floor, he put everything back as he'd found it, even straightening the bedspread, then glanced at his watch. He'd been inside about five minutes. No call from Carly. So far, so good.

He checked the other hiding place Carly had stumbled upon, this one in the master bathroom. He felt behind the tank and, sure enough, touched something plastic. No easy task getting a photo of that, but he removed the top of the tank to get a better angle and managed to catch the top edge of the plastic bag in the picture. He carefully pulled the zipper bag away and found a thin notebook inside. He was putting the top back on the tank when his phone dinged with an incoming text.

He read the message—*Someone's coming!*—just as the door downstairs opened, a man's voice carrying upstairs. "...here now. I'll let you know."

Stifling a curse word, Braden looked for a place to hide. In the shower, under the bed, in the closet... None of them would be good enough if the man downstairs knew Braden was there.

*Crap, crap, crap.*

Envelope and notebook in hand, he shoved his phone deep in his pocket and crept across the bedroom.

Downstairs, doors opened and slammed, footsteps pounded on the tile floor. Sounded like one man, but one would be enough if he was armed. And Braden had no doubt he was.

Was Carly all right? Surely she'd driven away. *Please, God...*

Braden reached the windows and unlocked one, his hands trembling with adrenaline. The window stuck, and he had to crouch and push with the flat of his palms to get it to slide up. The storm window behind it scraped up on its runner. Braden latched it out of the way, praying the intruder hadn't heard.

But the footsteps were coming fast now, closer. He must be on the stairs.

Braden climbed onto the sill, only then looking down. The wooden deck below wouldn't be as soft a landing as grass, but there was no other option.

He lowered his legs outside and hung from his fingertips, praying he wouldn't break a leg on the landing.

Inside, he heard a door slam against a wall.

He dropped to the deck with a thud.

"Hey!"

Braden didn't look up at the voice, just sprinted off the deck and across the lawn, heading for another row of townhouses.

A gunshot rang out. A few feet in front of him, a pot of flowers on a deck railing exploded.

Sprinting around a corner and away from the street where he'd left Carly, Braden yanked his phone from his pocket. Another gunshot rang out, this from farther away.

*Carly. God, protect her!*

He slowed just long enough to dial, then took off running again.

Carly didn't answer.

# CHAPTER FIFTEEN

CARLY CALLED 911 and reported an intruder at Ian's townhouse. *Please let Braden be okay. Please, Lord.*

She kept her gaze trained on the front door. Where was he? What should she do?

How long would it take the police to get there?

She glanced at the phone in her hand, then at the clock on the dash.

Something in the rearview mirror caught her eye.

Two men were walking toward the truck, one on the sidewalk, the other on the street. Not dressed for exercise. Walking slowly, close to the cars, slightly crouched.

Light glinted off something in one of their hands. A gun.

She yanked the gear shift into Drive and hit the gas. The truck lurched forward.

Behind her, the men ran after her.

A gunshot rang out, though not from behind her. It came from far away.

*Dear God, Braden!*

A sedan pulling away from the curb jutted in front of the pickup. She jabbed the horn and angled around it.

Another gunshot, this one closer.

In her rearview, she saw the sedan's back window shatter.

*Oh God oh God oh God. Help!*

She blasted through a stop sign, praying she could leave the two men on foot behind. Then caught sight of a familiar black SUV, gaining fast.

They were coming for her.

Again.

# CHAPTER SIXTEEN

Braden didn't want to think about that second gunshot.

He didn't want to think about how he'd left Carly alone and unprotected.

He didn't want to think about how stupid, how incredibly stupid, he'd been to bring her back here.

He'd escaped the townhouse development, skirted a construction zone, and headed onto the UMASS Boston campus, yanking off the gloves. He shoved them in the first trash can he found and continued at a slower pace, trying to blend in with the students. But it was no use. There weren't many wandering around on that chilly morning.

He veered off Columbus Avenue, sprinting between campus buildings, trying to keep out of sight of the main road, making his way south and putting as much distance as he could between himself and whoever had taken that shot.

He needed to get inside, off the street. When he spotted a familiar building, he called Carly again.

She didn't answer.

His heart, already racing, stuttered. Where was she? Where *was* she?

*Lord, please. Please.*

But she didn't answer.

He shot off a quick text. *I'm at the JFK Library.*

It was a good place to wait for her. There'd be security and cameras everywhere. Even if the guy caught up with Braden, surely he wouldn't do anything there.

Braden stepped inside the lobby, breathing heavily, and watched through the windows. And prayed.

# CHAPTER SEVENTEEN

Carly gunned the engine and raced through a red light, barely making it before the cross traffic started.

The SUV tried to follow. Carly didn't see everything, but she heard a horn blaring, the screech of tires, the crash of metal on metal.

Her hands were trembling. Her heart racing. Her mind... confused.

She dialed 911 again.

When the operator answered, she said, "There was an accident at the corner of..." She tried to think where she was. "Columbia and... Dorchester, I think. The black SUV in that accident... the guy inside was following me. He had a gun." Her voice was high, hysterical. "He shot at me."

"All right," the too-calm woman said. "Are you safe now?"

"No! I'm not safe. Somebody is trying to kill me!"

Her phone buzzed with an incoming call.

"Ma'am, where are you—?"

"Get in touch with Detective Klein. Tell him I called."

"What's your na—?"

"Carly Garcia. He'll know. Tell him what happened. Tell him

this is related to the break-in at Harbor Point. And Ian Murphy's murder." She ended the call.

She swiped to answer the one incoming, but she'd missed it.

One glance at the screen, and she blew out a relieved breath. Braden. Thank God.

CARLY SLOWED the truck near the entrance to the John F. Kennedy Presidential Library, afraid to come to a stop. She should have called Braden back, confirmed it had indeed been he who'd texted. Because these killers could have gotten his phone and sent the text themselves. If that was what happened, that would mean Braden was...

She couldn't even bring herself to consider it.

She was about to hit the gas and get out of there when the doors opened.

Braden stepped outside.

Alive and well. *Thank God.* The most beautiful sight she'd ever seen.

He jogged across the blocked-off circle drive and yanked open the passenger door. As soon as he'd launched himself inside, he said, "Go. Go."

She hit the gas. "You're okay?"

"Yeah." He tossed something onto the floor. "What happened to you?"

She gave him a quick rundown, not bothering to look at his reaction. She could feel the fear and fury wafting off him like the scent of the harbor.

When she was done, she said, "What happened to you?"

He described jumping out a second-story window and running, dodging bullets and barely escaping with his life.

She didn't want to think about what he'd gone through, about the price he'd almost paid for helping her.

"I'm so sorry." Her voice was high-pitched again, only not with fear but regret. "It was stupid. You were right—it was stupid, and I almost got you—"

"I'm fine." His low tenor, the calm tone, helped soothe her nerves. "Head for the highway."

She did. When she saw it, she shifted into the right lane to get on the northbound onramp.

"No. Go south."

"Why? What's south?" She glanced his way, saw his eyes closed, his fingers rubbing circles on his temples.

She trusted his judgment better than she trusted her own at that moment. She angled back to the left and turned at the light. A moment later, she blended into the traffic on I-93 headed toward the Cape and Rhode Island. "Are you all right?"

"Yeah. Just trying to think, to figure out what we should do."

"Why are we—?"

"They saw my truck." Frustration tinged his words as his hands dropped to his lap. "They must've noted the New Hampshire plates."

And the number, but she didn't state the obvious. Braden had surely figured that out on his own.

"They'll expect us to go north."

Carly swallowed hard and focused on driving. Focused on not collapsing in a puddle of sobs.

Braden's hand touched hers on the steering wheel, which she was gripping with white-knuckled intensity. "It's okay. We're okay."

"I should have gone alone. I almost got you killed."

"Honey, you didn't force me to do anything. I wouldn't have let you go alone. And if you had..." He didn't finish the thought as he urged her hand off the wheel and held it in his. "God protected us."

God had now protected Carly twice. No, three times, because if she hadn't seen the killers through the window in Pete's house, she'd have been murdered Monday night.

How many more chances would He give her before He threw

up His divine hands and let her suffer the consequences of her own stupid decisions?

Would Braden have to suffer those consequences too? Braden, who'd done nothing but help her?

"Why don't you pull off at the next exit, and we'll switch places?"

"Yeah. Okay." Because she couldn't think straight, couldn't focus on anything but the sound of gunshots still ringing in her ears.

She found a gas station and parked behind the small building, out of sight of the highway and the main road. Beside her, Braden climbed out, but she couldn't seem to make herself move. Her whole body shook. Her mind felt unfocused. Confused.

The door opened beside her, and Braden reached into the truck and undid her seatbelt. He took her hand, helped her from the car, and then folded her into a hug.

A sob bubbled up from deep, deep in her heart. She clung to him and wept.

"We're okay, honey." His words were soothing, gentle. "We're okay."

But nothing felt okay. Nothing would ever be okay again. Somebody had *shot* at them. Not one somebody, but multiple somebodies. And Carly had no idea who they were.

And now... now, they wouldn't just be after Carly, but they'd be after Braden.

What had she done?

One of Braden's hands held her head against his shoulder. The other rubbed circles on her back. Comforting her, when she'd caused all this trouble for him. How could he be so kind?

She deserved none of his kindness. She deserved...

She didn't want to think about what she deserved. She definitely didn't want to *get* what she deserved.

But Braden deserved only good things. Beauty and wonder and happiness.

He deserved so much better than her.

"I think we should get in the truck." His voice was low in her ear. "You're trembling."

She would be much colder when Braden let her go, but she stepped away, angling up to face him. "I am so, so sorry."

He kissed her forehead. "None of this is your fault."

He was wrong. All of it was her fault.

If only she hadn't gone to Ian's on Monday, she wouldn't have seen his murder.

If only she hadn't given him a key to her apartment, she wouldn't be expecting his baby.

If only she hadn't dated him in the first place, settling for a poor substitute for the man she really loved.

If only she'd accepted Braden's proposal.

Her life had been on a downward spiral ever since that moment.

If only she'd had another choice.

If only she could have another chance.

He kept his arm around her back as he urged her to the passenger door and back inside the truck.

Two minutes later, they were on the interstate again. But where could they go now?

# CHAPTER EIGHTEEN

BRADEN FOLLOWED 93 south to 95 north and exited on Route 1 in Norwood, a place he'd never been. It was a more urban than rural suburb not far from Boston. He doubted Carly had ever been there, either. He suspected she'd hardly left Boston until that week.

She seemed to have calmed down some. Good thing. For a minute there, he feared he was going to have to have her treated for shock, and the last thing they needed was to end up at the ER.

Though, maybe they'd be safe at a hospital. How could Braden know? It wasn't as if they'd taught *Evading Killers 101* at MIT.

He was way out of his depth.

He found a Ninety-Nine, a local chain restaurant, and cruised by the entrance to see what time they opened. Ten thirty. A glance at the dashboard clock told him it was twenty till eleven.

Perfect.

"Hungry?" he asked.

"Not really."

He glanced at her but looked away fast. Spending time in her presence was one thing. But having her in his arms... She'd fit so well there. And the way she'd gripped his sweater beneath his jacket and held on as if he were her only link to safety. The way she still smelled like she used to, like strawberries and happiness and...

They weren't together. He had to remind himself again that they weren't together.

But he'd come so close to losing her. It was one thing for her to leave him, to choose her family over him, even to choose another man. It was one thing to be separated from her. But the idea that she might no longer exist on the planet... He couldn't fathom it. It would mean the death of her beauty, her kindness, her gifts.

And the death of Braden's hope. Because, though he'd hardly admitted it to himself, he still wanted her. God help him, he still loved her. Maybe the feeling had been packed away, but it had never gone far.

He parked and rounded to Carly's side, but she'd climbed out already. Not that she needed his help, but he wouldn't have minded the excuse to take her hand.

Did he need an excuse? Probably, but he didn't care.

He pulled her close again.

She came willingly, wrapped her arms around him, and pressed her cheek to his chest.

"I can't believe..." Her words were muffled against his jacket. "I can't believe I almost lost you."

Her words echoed his thoughts. Could it be that, after three years, she still had feelings for him as well?

He had to know. Because... because if she loved him still...

Backing up just enough to look down at the top of her head, he whispered, "Carly."

Her gaze came up to meet his, and his answers were shining in her eyes. His hope, which had been caged in some dark corner of his mind, escaped and soared.

He pulled off her ski cap, and her hair fell down over his hand, soft and gentle and setting off a surge of emotions he could no longer deny.

Eyes wide, her lips parted, and he took it as an invitation. But he lowered his chin and waited. He wouldn't take what wasn't offered freely. He wouldn't assume.

Carly slipped her hands over his shoulders, pulled him closer, and pressed her lips to his.

And every craving he'd ever had for her, every memory he'd locked away, swirled in his mind. He pulled her against him and deepened the kiss, riding the wave of desire.

This. This was what his life had lacked. This was the missing ingredient that would make it all come together. The house in the woods would feel like home, if only she were there.

He would give her... everything. Anything to make her happy.

When he felt the gentle pressure on his chest, he knew he had to stop. Against his will, he ended the kiss and stepped away, expecting regret or, even worse, censure, in her expression.

But her eyes were wide and filled with wonder, perhaps mirroring what was in his own. "We probably shouldn't be standing in public, what with the killers—"

"Right. Right." His brain had taken a backseat. All rational thought had taken a backseat. He forced a deep breath and yanked off his jacket, suddenly far too warm for the thirty-degree day. After shoving Ian's things into his backpack, he said, "Let's get inside."

As they made their way to the front door, she slipped her hand into his, and his heart stuttered again.

He glanced down at her to find her looking up at him. She averted her gaze, but not before he caught the slight smile.

He could get lost in that smile, in her.

He pulled the heavy door open and followed Carly inside.

The host said, "Two for lunch?"

He glanced around the dark space. Nearly empty. "In the back, if you don't mind."

There were a lot of these restaurants in the area, and he was glad to see that this one was similar to others he'd been to. It was dimly lit, and high-backed booths lined the walls. They should be well hidden here. They slid into the benches at the secluded table.

"What sounds good?" he asked, suddenly feeling like an idiot. They'd almost died, and here he was acting like this was a lunch date.

"My stomach's a little off again," she said. "I could use some crackers."

The server had been approaching the table but must have heard Carly's remark because he turned around before he reached them.

"Have you seen a doctor about that?" Braden asked.

"Not yet."

"Has it lasted long? Stomach bugs usually pass quickly. It doesn't seem normal, the way you get sick so often."

"It's been a pretty... not normal day," she said.

"Point taken."

The server returned with two glasses of water, set a couple of bags of oyster crackers on the table, and took their drink orders. Carly ordered a Coke, and Braden said, "Same."

This was all a little surreal. How had he ended up having lunch with Carly Garcia in Norwood, Massachusetts, on a Thursday?

After being chased and shot at?

And kissing her.

He'd kissed her, and she'd kissed him back. Awful as the rest of it was, if it brought them back together...

He was getting ahead of himself. Way ahead. Which was exactly what he'd done before when he'd scared her away. He needed to slow down, to play it cool.

He might have been elected president of the robotics club, but he'd never been anywhere near *cool*.

"Did you find anything at Ian's?" She opened the bag of crackers and popped one in her mouth.

He set down the menu and grabbed the manila envelope and zipper bag he'd shoved into his backpack. "These are what I found." He upended the envelope, and a small notebook and a handful of newspaper clippings fell out. "This was in the box spring." He set the clippings aside and angled so both he and Carly could see the notebook. It wasn't exactly comfortable trying to lean over the table to look.

"Why don't I...?" He tipped his head toward the space next to her.

She scooted over, and he sat on her side of the booth, careful not to get so close that they touched. That would definitely not help the focusing situation. He opened the notebook.

Carly leaned closer. "It's Ian's handwriting. What is it?"

The words were in cursive, just legible enough to make them out. The first line had an address. Below it, a date and a dollar amount in the hundreds of thousands. Then, another dollar amount followed a hyphen. Or maybe a minus sign.

Ian had skipped a line, and on the next two lines he'd written a different address and date. The dollar amounts were similar—first the big number, then the hyphen or minus sign and a smaller number.

The second date was a few weeks later than the first, both a few years past.

Another skipped line, and the pattern repeated.

It was a small notebook, maybe six by eight, so each page held... He quickly counted. Six addresses. Only six, but the larger dollar amounts totaled over four million dollars.

"What is it?" Carly asked.

Braden didn't know yet. He flipped through the next five pages. The first two seemed to have been written at the same time. Same pen, same chicken-scratch cursive. On the third page, the lines weren't as consistent. Different colors of pens. Some printed, others cursive. But every line held the same kind of information. The dates became more recent, the last one just six weeks before.

When the server returned, Carly ordered a bowl of broccoli cheddar soup. Braden ordered the steak tip and chicken finger combo. "Extra fries," he said, guessing Carly would have a few. She always had, back when they were dating.

The server left, and Braden pulled his laptop from his bag and typed the last address in the search bar.

"It's a restaurant," he said.

Carly tapped the screen. "They're going out of business. I saw the sign a couple of weeks ago that they'd be closing."

"Not relocating?" Braden asked.

"Maybe they're retiring. It's one of those old buildings not far off the highway. The strip close to where Sandy used to live."

An old mutual friend. Braden knew exactly where Carly was talking about. A rundown area that catered to the people in that neighborhood and nobody else. It wasn't exactly a destination, more like the kind of place a person was unlucky enough to happen upon.

Braden marked the address as a favorite on his map app and looked up the second.

It was just a block from the first. Interesting. He kept it up and found that the most recent addresses were all in a cluster. They'd all been sold in the previous year for the price Ian had listed beside them.

What was the smaller number?

Braden was working backwards in the notebook. He marked twelve addresses, all in the same area.

Carly tapped the notebook on the next line up. "Look at the date. There's a big gap. The others after this were just a few weeks, maybe within a couple of months of each other. But now we have—"

"Almost a year." He hadn't noticed before. He typed in the address. It was in a different area entirely, farther north and near a T stop.

"That's where that new development is going," she said. "This must be one of the buildings that was razed."

Oh. *Oh.* "Is there going to be a new development down here?" He tapped the map further south, where they'd already plotted the other addresses.

She shrugged. "I don't know. I haven't heard anything, but it's not as if I'm up on my real estate news."

He considered what they'd learned. "So maybe... maybe Ian was just keeping an eye on the properties being bought and sold. Maybe he was studying the real estate market. Maybe he wanted to become a developer?"

But Carly was shaking her head. "Not as far as I know. And if that were the case, why hide the notebook?"

"Right. Good point."

The server delivered their lunches, and Braden pushed the laptop away and shifted to the other side of the booth. After the server left, Braden put ketchup on his plate and turned it so the mound of fries was closer to her. "Help yourself."

Her grin was wide and beautiful and could have stopped hearts. His, anyway. "You know me so well."

"I recall many a meal when I felt french-fry deprived."

"I don't eat *that* many."

He cast a pointed glance at the handful she'd already taken, but she only shrugged and put one in her mouth.

Some things, often the best things, never changed.

He glanced at the second notebook, expecting to find the same kinds of information as in the first, but he was wrong. This one contained names, dollar amounts, dates. "Probably related to the protection scheme." He snapped the notebooks closed and stored both in the manila envelope with the newspaper clippings, then shoved that and the laptop back in his bag. It was one thing to take what might be evidence from Ian's townhouse. It was an entirely different thing to turn it over to the police with french-fry grease all over it.

Carly lifted a sip of her thick soup to her mouth, and Braden sampled the chicken, then the steak tips. The chicken was good, but the steak was outstanding. Tender and covered in a salty gravy.

"All this is fascinating," Carly said, waving to his closed bag, "but we're skirting the more immediate problem here."

"Which is...?"

"They saw your truck."

Braden hadn't let himself contemplate the ramifications of that yet.

"If they saw your truck, Braden, then they'll be able to figure out who you are."

"Not necessarily. I mean, license plate numbers and who they belong to—that isn't exactly public information, right?"

"But you have to assume... And if they figure out who you are, then they can figure out where you live."

She was right, of course. All this time, he'd imagined going back to Coventry and holing up in his house in the woods. But would his house be safe now?

If he couldn't go home, then he couldn't go back to work.

If he couldn't go back to work...

Andrew was already a shoo-in for the manager job, but Braden still hoped he could change Jacqui's mind about that. How could he do that if he couldn't even show up?

How long would it take to catch Ian's killers? If it didn't happen fast... Would Jacqui hold his job for him? Could he work remotely for a little while?

If Andrew was going to be his new boss, did Braden even want to stay at BNB?

Across the table, Carly was looking at him with wide, frightened eyes. Frightened for herself? For him?

Of him?

Surely not the last. He attempted a smile, though he could feel how unnatural the stretch felt on his lips. "We'll figure it out. Don't worry. God's got it."

Braden needed to tell himself the same thing. Because it seemed that, by helping Carly, he was letting his own dreams slip through his fingers.

～

BRADEN FINISHED the steak tips but asked for a box for the chicken fingers. On any other day, he'd have had no trouble finishing the whole plate, but his stomach felt too full or too nervous to eat them. Or maybe he'd picked up whatever illness had Carly feeling nauseated. If the feeling persisted, he'd have to ask her about her other symptoms.

Oddly, Carly'd eaten all her soup and scarfed down about half his fries. Plus, she'd nabbed one of his chicken fingers. It was a very strange day indeed when he was the one asking for a doggie bag.

The sooner they could figure out who'd killed Ian and get the man behind bars, the sooner Carly would be safe and Braden could go back to work. He opened his bag and pulled out the newspaper clippings.

Carly shifted the dishes to her side of the table and scooted in beside him. She wasn't as careful to keep her distance as he'd been, and their arms brushed against each other.

"Oh, sorry," she said.

He scooted away, shooting her an apologetic look. "I need to focus." And having her so close wouldn't help.

They studied the first clipping, a kitchen fire in a restaurant. Though the article didn't mention the exact address, it did reference one of the streets Ian had noted in the notebook.

The next article was about a brutal assault. Was that related to one of the properties as well? It was impossible to know.

Each article noted some crime or destructive incident in Dorchester—a fire, a broken water line, an explosion from a gas leak—though they seemed unrelated to each other. But Braden was starting to form a theory.

"Ian wasn't into real estate development at all, right?" Braden asked.

"Not as far as I know, and if he had been, he'd have told me."

Because the guy was a bragger. And of course he would have wanted to impress Carly. Braden scoffed at the first thought, but the second he could understand. "What if the developers were incentivizing, if you will, the owners of those properties to sell?"

She was nodding before he finished the line. "That's the only thing that makes sense. I mean, we'll have to look up the people and the properties to be sure, but that's a good guess."

"And Ian figured it out. Somehow. Maybe he was putting together a case against the developers."

"Why would he do that?" Carly asked. "He was a criminal himself. Why bother with other...? Oh."

Braden shifted to face her and waited.

"That day, at Ian's shop. Ian said he was trying to protect his neighbors. The other guy said he was only trying to protect his income. Whatever the reason—"

"Ian realized his... clients, for lack of a better term, were being targeted. He was trying to figure out why."

"He did figure it out. He must have. I mean, *that*"—she gestured to the manila envelope on the table—"paints a pretty clear picture. If we're right about those crimes being related, anyway."

"I think we are," Braden said. "We'll need to confirm it, but it's a solid theory."

When the server dropped the check, Braden realized that the restaurant had filled for lunch. Too many people around. He and Carly shouldn't stay there. Could they go back to Coventry?

He had no idea. It was time to enlist some help.

Back in the truck, Braden navigated the streets of Norwood. He stopped at a gas station to buy himself a burner phone. He got it working, then turned his own off.

He never considered himself cell-phone addicted, but it was strange cutting off all contact with his friends and family. He could understand why Carly had spent so much time on social media the last few days, trying to keep in contact with her sisters.

He drove randomly until he pulled over in a quiet residential area. They should be safe there. He called Dylan and told him what happened at Ian's place. "Can they figure out where I live from my license plate?"

"Not easily, but yeah. If they're connected or hire the right investigator."

Dylan's words carried through the Bluetooth speakers, and Carly's face fell. She mouthed *I'm sorry*.

Braden focused on the dash—away from her very distracting presence beside him.

"So, we can't go home," Braden clarified.

"I wouldn't, not right away. Not until we know if they know who you are."

"How can we—?"

"Why don't I install a couple of cameras to record who drives on the street in front of your house?" Dylan had been an occasional guest for Monday Night Football back in the fall. "That way, if anybody unusual passes your house, we'll get a record of their plates. That'll do two things. First, it'll tell us if anybody's looking for you, and second, it'll help us identify them."

Braden lived halfway down a very quiet road that had only four other houses on it, all on two-acre lots. A stranger's car would stand out, especially one with out-of-state plates. "That's a good idea. Thanks."

If the killers could figure out Braden's name, then figuring out where he worked would be a simple next step. He was listed on the company website. He doubted that BNB would be targeted, though. And Jacqui had top-notch security at the building, including cameras covering all the exits and the parking lot.

But maybe the place would be watched. He definitely couldn't go back to work.

A serious problem.

"And I can probably find you a place to hole up," Dylan said, "if you don't have something in mind already."

He'd considered and discarded friends and family. The last thing he wanted was to put anybody else in danger. "I was thinking I'd rent us a couple of rooms."

"Don't do that yet. I've got some friends who own a bed-and-breakfast in Nutfield. They closed up this winter, but I think they're in town. Let me give them a call."

"I'm not sure I want to pay for anything that fancy. It might take some time to get this sorted out."

"I doubt they'll let you pay them, not when I give them the rundown on what's going on. That is, if you don't mind me telling them your story. The short version, anyway."

He glanced at Carly, who shrugged. "We don't, but I hate to take advantage."

"Angel and Donovan will be happy to help."

Braden couldn't think of a good reason to refuse the offer. A bed-and-breakfast, one not even open in a town he'd never visited owned by people he'd never met. Nobody would look for them there. It'd be the perfect place to hide. "I'm really gonna owe you after this."

Dylan scoffed. "This is what friends do. I'll get back to you."

Friends. He liked that he'd made friends in Coventry. For the first time since he'd finished grad school, he had a life apart from work. He had a church and people he could count on.

People like Dylan, who'd go out of their way to help him just because they liked him.

It was a new and comfortable feeling. The very last thing he wanted was to lose what he'd gained.

Which was why he had to learn everything he could about Andrew. To protect his job at BNB. To regain the position he'd worked so hard for. And then, God willing, talk Carly into joining him in New Hampshire.

When Braden finished the call with Dylan, Carly said, "I thought you were going to ask about the addresses and clippings. Isn't he a PI?"

"Yeah, but his specialty is finding missing people. I'm sure he could do the work, but he'd insist on doing it for nothing, and I'm not willing to take any more advantage of our friendship than I already have." Not that Dylan couldn't afford to work for free. As the owner of Hamilton Clothiers, his wife was the richest woman in the state. But unlimited money didn't give a person unlimited time, and Dylan ran a nonprofit that reunited runaways with their parents all over New England. The work kept him very busy. "Besides, I have someone else in mind, a local. You remember Ronnie Brazos?"

Her nose scrunched up adorably. "That geeky kid who got suspended for breaking into the school's database and changing people's grades?"

"Exactly."

"How can he help?"

"He's got skills. Trust me, he can help."

Braden had met many intelligent and talented people at MIT, but none of them would do what he needed now. Sure, any investigator could help with the addresses and clippings, but Braden had another job for an investigator to do. For that, Braden had to go back farther than MIT and his professional life, back to his Dorchester roots, to find somebody capable of doing what needed to be done. And willing to do it.

"Long time, no hear," Ronny said after Braden's greeting.

"You still got the PI business?"

"Pays the rent and car payment." Ronnie's Southie accent was even thicker than Carly's. *Caah payment.* Braden had worked hard to lose that accent, at least the blue-collar aspects of it, but most people from the city figured everybody else talked wrong.

"I've got a job for you." Braden explained the information he'd gathered from Ian's townhouse. "We need to figure out everything we can about those addresses, the numbers noted beside them, and if they're related to the newspaper clippings. I could probably do the work myself—"

"But you wanna help your old friend Ronnie, eh? Support local business and all that."

"Exactly." Braden gave Carly an apologetic smile and stepped out of the car. "One sec, Ron." After he shut the door, ignoring the confused expression on Carly's face, he disconnected his phone from his truck's Bluetooth and walked a few car lengths away. "I have one more thing."

"A twofer. Don't think I'm runnin' any bulk discount specials."

Braden chuckled. "There's this new guy at my work. Name's Andrew Middleton. I overheard a troubling conversation. I think he's being blackmailed."

"Why not just talk to the person who hired him? He probably did a background check."

"If I know the boss, she might've run one of those cursory internet searches, but I doubt she did any real digging. I just want to make sure there's nothing troubling in his past that could harm the company."

There was a short pause before Ronny spoke again. "You know I got this super sensitive BS meter. And something don't smell right. People don't check up on other employees without a lot more than an overheard conversation, and they sure don't do it on their own dime. Why not just tell your boss what you heard?"

"I'd rather not go to her unless I know for certain there's a problem."

"In other words, you want to dig up the dirt and present it to her. And if you don't find any, you don't want anyone to know you were looking."

"My motives aren't nefarious here, Ron."

"Nefarious? What are you, a flippin' dictionary? Maybe they're not *nefarious*, but I'd put money on 'em being *mercenary*. See, I can use five-dollar words too."

In the years since he'd seen him, Ron hadn't changed a bit. "Not... exactly."

"Think of me like a lawyer." *Law-yah.* "My mind's like a steel flippin' trap. I need to know what I'm looking for and why."

Braden wasn't comfortable spelling it out. But he wanted that manager job, badly. "Fine. I'm looking for dirt. Anything that'll cast the guy in a bad light. I mean, if there's no dirt to be had, then I haven't lost anything. But if it's there—"

"I'll find it. What's my priority?"

"The addresses and clippings. I'll take pictures and email those images to you now."

"I'll get back to you as soon as I know something. Tonight, tomorrow latest."

Braden ended the call and took a long, slow breath of the chilly air. Guilt tried to press in, but he pushed it away. If there was nothing questionable in Andrew's past, then Braden would accept that BNB would be under Andrew's management. He might not like it... He might not stay, but he'd accept it. And if he did find something, then Jacqui would be grateful he'd looked.

Wouldn't she?

# CHAPTER NINETEEN

Carly focused on the passing landscape as Braden navigated a winding country road. As promised, his friend Dylan had found them a place to stay, and they were on their way there. She could hardly keep her eyes open. Evading killers and solving mysteries was proving exhausting. Doing all that while her body grew a baby...

According to the GPS, they were still twenty minutes away. She could close her eyes for a little catnap, but the scenery was so pretty. It was different here from Coventry. Braden's town was nestled between two mountains. Nutfield was closer to the coast, where the landscape had rolling hills but nothing taller. There wasn't as much snow on the ground, and some of last summer's grass peeked through where the sun made it past the trees to warm the ground. But the forests were just as thick as they had been up north. The sky was bright blue, dotted with fluffy white clouds. The town, complete with a little park flanked by two white-steepled churches, was charming.

All her life, she'd thought Boston had everything she needed. All the stores and services, trade schools and universities, businesses and hospitals. Not to mention museums, parks, and entertainment. She supposed Boston offered as much as anybody could need. Not that she often availed herself of those things. Not that she ever left her little Dorchester neighborhood.

But this...

Once again, she was struck by how big the world was, how small her itty-bitty corner of it.

What else had she missed?

An hour earlier, after Dylan had called and given them the address, she'd connected her phone to the truck's Bluetooth and dialed Detective Klein while Braden took photos of the notebook pages and newspaper articles.

Klein told her that, by the time the police had arrived at the traffic accident—no more than a fender bender—that morning, the black SUV had taken off. The other driver involved in the accident had made note of the license plate, but the plate had been stolen. The SUV, a newer model Honda CR-V, was one of the most common models in America.

Nobody had gotten a good look at the people inside.

Dead ends, all.

Carly told Klein that both she and Braden had been chased and shot at when they'd gone to Ian's house.

"You shouldn't have done that," Klein said. As if she didn't know already that she'd almost gotten Braden killed. "That was dangerous and stupid."

Braden shot her a look, lips pressed together. It was clear he wanted to say something, so she nodded for him to go ahead.

"We wouldn't have had to if you people had done your jobs." His voice had a hard edge to it.

"We have rules and procedures and—"

"Well, we don't," Braden snapped. "And anyway, it was only stupid if we're right about Murphy's murder. If the man's really partying it up in Florida, then it shouldn't have mattered at all. No harm, no foul."

"Harm and foul if you broke into a man's house," Klein said.

"Carly has a key. Nobody broke into anything, unless you

count the guy who shot at me. And we had to do something, considering you're obviously not. They're trying to kill her."

There was a long pause. When Klein spoke again, his voice was as calm as ever. "I understand what you're saying."

"I don't think you do. I don't think you…"

Carly grabbed his hand to quiet him, and he mashed his lips closed.

"We survived," she said. "Did anybody report the shots fired?"

"Besides you two? No."

"How can that be?" Braden asked. "Surely gunshots aren't that common—"

"Lots of construction in that area," Klein said. "Lots of traffic. Most people are at work. Those who're home, they drown out the noises."

"Now that you know a break-in has occurred," Carly said, "you could search his place."

"I'll have to get Ian's permission or a warrant."

Beside her, Braden banged his forehead on the steering wheel. She felt exactly the same way.

She said, "Ian is dead, Detective."

"I understand what you think. Even if that's true, it's not official. Look, I'll reach out and—"

"And nothing," Braden said. "The person who has his phone will tell you no, you may not search. They were firing shots from his bedroom, and you're telling me—"

"I don't think I have enough to get a warrant, but I'll try," Klein said. "Meanwhile, you need to give me the information you got there. If you don't want to drop it off, you can—"

"No," Braden snapped. "Not unless you're going to investigate."

"I can only do what I can do. For now—"

"We can get pictures of it and email it to you." Carly squeezed Braden's hand.

"I need the originals," Klein said.

"When you start investigating," Braden shot back, "then you can have them."

Klein exhaled a loud sigh. "Fine. Email copies. I'll have a look as soon as I'm back at my desk."

In other words, he was in no hurry. In other words, he still wasn't convinced.

She ended the call and leaned back against the seat.

"This is ridiculous," Braden said. "A man was murdered, and that guy acts like it's about as important as not enough jelly in his donut."

She tried to consider it from Klein's perspective. "He thinks I overreacted, that I didn't hear what I claim to have heard. And he has rules he has to follow. And other crimes to investigate. And, I mean... What Dylan said last night makes sense. I'm the only person who even knows Ian's dead. There is exactly zero evidence to back me up. We claim gunshots today, but nobody else reported them. We claim we were being chased, but by the time the police got there, there was no SUV. What's he supposed to do?"

"His job." Braden's voice was low and furious as he shifted into Drive and headed for the highway. Aside from a quick call to his boss explaining that he wouldn't be in the following day—Jacqui was gracious, much more so than Carly's boss had been—they'd made the bulk of the trip to Nutfield in silence.

Now, Braden turned off the road that led through town. She caught glimpses of a lake through the trees. They passed two restaurants situated right on the water that were probably packed in the summertime, and then Braden turned onto a narrow driveway with an unobtrusive wooden sign that read *Clearwater Hideaway*.

The driveway wound among the trees and opened to a clearing and small parking area.

And a three-story... castle.

Maybe not a castle, but close enough. It was fancy, with its detailed trim work and a round room at the corner. But the wrap-around front porch made it welcoming.

Braden whistled beside her. "Nicer than the Motel 6 I was planning on."

"You really know how to spoil a girl."

He chuckled as he shifted into Park, and she was thankful to see his mood had improved. With nothing but their two backpacks, they made their way up the steps and knocked on the oversize front door.

A moment later, it opened, and a petite brunette smiled at them. "Welcome."

Braden stepped forward, arm outstretched. "Braden Reilly, and this is Carly Garcia."

The woman shook their hands. "Angelica Gilcreast. My friends call me Angel." She ushered them inside.

Carly froze in the entry.

Holy smoke. The place was... gorgeous. High ceilings with ornate crown molding. Refinished hardwood floors. Gleaming white woodwork, and a rug that probably cost more than a year's rent.

She peeked into the first room, saw a grand piano. Across the hall, built-in shelves held hundreds of books. The chairs and tables looked antique. A stone fireplace gave the room a rustic feel.

Carly wouldn't have felt more out of place if she'd landed on the moon.

"Come on back," Angel said. "I'll give you a quick tour and then show you to your rooms. Rooms, right? Plural?"

"Yeah," Braden said. "We're not..."

She wondered how he'd planned to finish that statement, but the words just trailed off.

"That's what Dylan said, but I wanted to confirm." She headed down the wide hallway past a staircase that wound up two stories.

"Thanks so much for letting us stay here," Braden said. "I know you're closed for business."

"We're always open for friends. And friends of friends, especially when they're in need." Angel led them around a corner and stopped in a room with three sofas all facing a huge TV hung above an oversize fireplace. Unlike the formal rooms at the front of the house, this one felt homey, cozy. The kind of place where a person could slip off her shoes and cuddle under a throw blanket. And sure enough, a basket of blankets had been nestled beside one of the sofas. "Media room," Angel said. "If you want to watch a movie. The bedrooms don't have TVs. We try to foster community around here."

She pointed at a door on the back wall of the house beside a wall of windows. Beyond the windows, she glimpsed a long narrow room surrounded by glass on three sides. An easel stood in the corner with an unfinished painting on it "Sunroom's closed for the season. Donovan's using it as a studio right now. He's an artist." She said the last words with pride as she continued through a door and into the kitchen. This room screamed high-tech and efficient. It was tidy but obviously well-used. Clean pots were drying beside the sink, and a couple of dishes were resting inside. The glowing light on a crock pot explained the delicious scent of roasting meat and spices. A round table large enough for six sat in front of bay windows that looked out over the lake.

"Usually," Angel said, "we don't invite guests into the kitchen. I serve breakfast in the dining room"—she pointed to a door on the far side—"when we're open for business. But since you're the only guests, just make yourselves at home. There're snacks in here." She opened a tall cabinet door, and Carly glimpsed bread and chips and crackers and plastic containers of who-knew-what. "I'm making roast beef for supper, if that sounds good."

"You don't have to feed us," Carly said. "We can go out for sandwiches or—"

"Don't be silly. We love having guests. We're only closed because it's so slow in the winter anyway, and Donovan's remodeling the basement."

"More guest rooms?" Braden asked.

"Actually, he's building a game room. Once he finishes out the walls and ceilings and adds all the electrical, we'll add a pool table and a ping pong table, an air hockey game, and I think we're going to get some vintage video games. I found a Ms. Pac Man on—"

Her words were cut off by a squawk coming from the other room. The squawk came again, only this time it sounded more like a laugh.

A baby's laugh.

Angel grinned. "Be right back." She disappeared through a swinging door into the dining room and returned a moment later with a bundle in a blue blanket.

Carly stepped closer and peered at the baby, who looked at Carly with big brown eyes and a gummy smile. "Oh, wow. He's gorgeous."

Angel lowered the blanket and took the tiny fist that popped out. "This is William. We call him Billy. He's the other reason we're closed for the winter."

Carly glanced at Braden, who was looking at the baby with wide eyes. Nervous? Did he not like babies?

She turned back to Angel. "How old is he?"

"Four months. We keep a cradle in the dining room because the nursery is on the third floor with our bedroom, and it's a heckuva walk for me to check on him." She shook Billy's little hand and switched to a baby-talk voice. "Which I do about a hundred times a day. Don't I, peanut?" She tickled his tummy, and he let out one of those baby laughs that makes even the grumpiest Gus chuckle.

Carly was itching to hold him, but Angel brushed past her. "Let me show you to your rooms. Dylan said this was a last-minute thing, so I put essentials in both your baths—toothbrushes, toothpaste, deodorant, razors, and shaving cream. And of course the bathrooms already have soap and shampoo. There're hair dryers under the sinks. We have robes for all the guests, and I can get you both something to sleep in, if you want to wash your clothes. Carly, you're about the same size I was before this little fellow destroyed my figure."

Angel was thin and petite. "I think *destroyed* is a pretty strong term."

She just laughed as she turned and looked Braden up and down. "Some of Donovan's sleep pants and Ts will probably fit you."

Angel showed them to two rooms on the second floor, each with its own bathroom, explaining along the way how Donovan had fixed the place up for the owner—Angel's brother—and then bought it because Angel loved it so much. All the while, she gushed about her husband's immense talent, pointing out his paintings along the way.

Carly didn't know much about art, but the man was clearly gifted. Even she could see that.

Angel left to feed the baby, telling them to yell if they needed anything. Everything she'd need had already been provided. The furniture looked antique, as if it'd come with the house. And maybe it had. The queen-size four-poster bed was covered in a thick blue-and-white comforter that contrasted well with the pale-yellow walls. Other blue-and-white things were scattered about the space—a bowl, a couple of fancy figurines. Even the clock had that same blue-and-white pattern.

Yawning, she turned to Braden, who lingered in the doorway. He said, "I think you could use a nap."

She didn't bother to disagree.

"Why don't you rest?" he said. "I'll see you at dinner, and we'll talk after."

They should probably have a look at the second notebook, but she could hardly think straight. She glanced at the bed, then back at Braden. "If you think it's okay..."

He grasped her doorknob. "I'll knock a little before six so we're not late."

As soon as the door closed, she collapsed on the bed and closed her eyes.

They were safe.

For now.

~

REFRESHED AFTER HER SHORT NAP, Carly joined Braden in the hallway.

"Sleep well?"

"I crashed. I was exhausted."

He took her hand as if it were the most normal thing in the world and started for the staircase.

She couldn't quite figure out how everything in her life could be so screwed up, yet she could feel so happy just holding Braden's hand.

As if their relationship were back to normal. As if it ever could be.

But her slight nausea was a nearly constant reminder that nothing would be normal between them. She was carrying another man's child, and as soon as she told Braden, then this—whatever it was—would be over.

Tomorrow. She'd tell him everything tomorrow.

Today, she'd just enjoy holding his hand.

They stepped into the kitchen as Angel set a bowl of steaming gravy on the table. Beside it, the roast beef was resting on a serving dish. Green beans with almonds, a tossed salad, and a basket of rolls rounded out the meal.

The baby babbled and bounced in one of those little seats on the counter, a brightly colored teether in his fist.

"Come in, come in," Angel said. "Have a seat. This is Donovan."

The quintessential tall, dark, and handsome man pushed off from where he'd leaned against the counter and held out his hand to Braden, who introduced himself and Carly. Donovan looked to be in his mid-thirties, a little older than his wife, Carly guessed, but his thin T-shirt proved he kept himself in great shape. Maybe all that remodeling was good for the muscles.

They weren't as nice as Braden's, but they were nice.

Carly turned to Angel. "I should have come down to help. I took a nap and just woke up."

Angel brushed the words off with a wave. "It was no trouble. This is what I do."

"And she does it very well." Donovan motioned to the table.

Carly sat, but the men waited until Angel had taken her seat before they settled in their chairs.

So polite. She remembered Braden's father'd always done the same. At her house, Pete had no problem sitting at the table, waiting to be served. Expecting it.

Better than her so-called father. At least Pete had been there.

The meal was delicious, which prompted conversation about favorite foods. It seemed Angel liked to cook as much as Carly did, and they traded recipes and tips and laughed throughout the meal.

Donovan didn't say much, seeming content to let his wife carry the conversation, occasionally glancing at his son on the counter.

They were the perfect little family. Mom, dad, baby. Exactly how it was supposed to be done.

Exactly how Carly had always wanted to do it.

She'd messed that up. Big time.

The thought of it must have shown on her face, because Angel stopped in the middle of sharing her favorite chicken recipe. "You okay?"

Carly forced herself back to the moment. "Yeah. Great." She forked another bite of the salty, spicy roast. "This is so good."

Donovan focused on Braden. "Dylan told us you're new to New Hampshire."

"I am. I love it. Not sure it's going to last, but it's a great job for now."

The men settled into talk about all the outdoorsy things to do in the state. As far as she could tell, Braden enjoyed his new job and his new life. So why would he add that last remark—*for now*?

She'd ask him about it later. Not that it was her business, but she was curious.

A little part of her, a tiny, silly little part, hoped maybe he was thinking of leaving New Hampshire for her. But why would he? She wasn't that important to him. Now that Mama was dead, she wasn't that important to anybody—except as the cook and housekeeper and minder of teenage girls. She did her job at work, but it wasn't as if she were irreplaceable. Anybody with a modicum of patience could answer the phone and calm down irate customers.

Carly was imminently... irrelevant in the world.

Except... She squelched the urge to pat her belly, touch the one person who'd someday find her incredibly important, and instead lifted her gaze to the baby on the counter. Angel and Donovan were the most important people in the world to that child. And that made them incredibly important.

Carly would be for her child too. She would be her—she was already thinking of the child as a girl—most valuable person. Together, they'd make their way.

What that would look like, she had no idea.

"Carly?"

Her attention snapped from the baby to Angel, who smiled. "We lost you there."

"Your Billy is mesmerizing."

"That he is. Are you finished?"

She glanced down at her plate. She'd eaten every morsel and gone back for a second roll. She couldn't seem to get enough to eat these days.

Either growing babies needed a whole lot of calories, or Carly was on her way to gaining a whole lot of weight.

"It was delicious."

She and Braden helped clear the table, and she insisted on doing the dishes, practically having to shove Angel away from the sink. "It's the least I can do."

Braden wet a couple of paper towels. "I'll wipe down the surfaces. You two... three," he added, glancing at the baby, "go relax. Let this be our thank-you for dinner. And for letting us stay here."

Angel glanced at Donovan. "I'm not dumb enough to refuse that offer."

Donovan lifted the baby, grabbed her hand, and said, "Hurry, before they change their minds."

Angel's laughter followed them into the media room.

## CHAPTER TWENTY

WHEN EVERYTHING WAS LOADED in the dishwasher or drying on the rack, Carly dried her hands on a paper towel.

"Donovan said we could use the library," Braden said. "I figure we'd better look at Ian's other notebook tonight."

"Lead the way."

A few minutes later, Braden was seated at a small antique table in one of the rooms nearest the front door.

Donovan had lit a fire in the stone fireplace, and Carly warmed her hands, watching the flames dance.

If they were there for any other reason, she'd say it was romantic.

Maybe it was romantic anyway.

She turned to Braden. "That was nice of Donovan."

"I asked him earlier if we could use the room. He said it gets cold in here."

She couldn't argue with that as she stepped away from the fire and sat across from Braden. Fortunately, the fireplace was close enough that she could still feel its heat.

"First." Braden set his hand on top of the notebook lying between them, drawing her gaze to his face. It was so weird, being there with him. After yearning for him for years, to be in his presence, to feel comfortable...

He squinted. "You with me?"

"Yeah." She needed to focus. "Sorry."

"Ronnie called and confirmed what we thought. Each of those newspaper clippings catalogues an event related to one of the businesses or an owner of one of the businesses in the box spring notebook."

"The real estate notebook."

"Yeah." His smile was boyish, sweet. "That name makes more sense. Which means Ian was putting it together. Not just putting it together, but collecting information."

"What did he plan to do with it, though?" She couldn't imagine him passing it along to the police. On the other hand, she couldn't imagine him involved in any of this stuff. Before she'd gotten to know him better, she wouldn't have been able to imagine him hurting her, either. Or letting himself into her apartment without her permission.

Ian was full of surprises.

*Had been* full of surprises.

"Whatever his plan, whoever did that stuff"—Braden tapped the manila envelope that held the clippings—"figured out what he was doing."

"How, though?"

Braden shrugged. "You said yourself the guy was a bragger."

She was pretty sure it was Braden who'd used that term, not her. But she didn't say so.

"You two hadn't seen each other in a while, so he hadn't told you. But I'm guessing he did tell someone. Did he have a new girlfriend?"

"Not as far as I know."

"Then a friend, maybe. Or... was he a drinker?"

"Yes." She must've said the word too emphatically, because Braden's eyebrows lifted. He studied her a moment, seemed to be waiting for her to supply more information about that. She didn't.

"So maybe he went to a bar," Braden guessed, "got drunk, and started shooting his mouth off."

That, she could imagine. "And the wrong person overheard."

"Exactly." Braden lifted his hand from the second notebook. "The toilet notebook."

She chuckled. "Let's find another way to describe it."

Their eyes met and held for a moment. Bizarre to have a romantic notion while discussing toilet notebooks, but there it was.

He looked away, perhaps thinking the same thing. "I have a guess, but I wanted to get your take on it before drawing any conclusions."

She studied the information she'd barely glanced at before. Each page had the name of a business on the top. She recognized a few of them—bars and restaurants in the neighborhood where she grew up. Below each business, the page was separated into two columns. The first had a date, each separated by about a month, the second a dollar amount in the thousands. All round numbers. She skimmed down the page. Twelve hundred, eleven hundred, thirteen hundred, twelve again.

She said, "Looks like twelve hundred is the goal. They didn't have it here"—Carly tapped the eleven hundred number—"and made up for it the next month."

"Exactly what I was thinking." Braden beamed at her as if she'd solved a complex mystery. "I did some research this afternoon on protection schemes and how they work."

"Amazing what you can find on the internet."

"Seriously. It was practically a how-to. There are two aspects to it. The first... Basically, it's extortion. A business pays them, and they protect that business from their wrath."

She couldn't imagine Ian threatening people. "Ian was a lot of things, but he wasn't a thug."

"I'm guessing he ran the operation and hired thugs to do the dirty work. I doubt any of these business owners knew he was behind it."

That made sense, especially considering Ian's favorite bar was listed in the notebook.

"The other part, though, is trickier," Braden said. "The protector is promising, well... protection. Obviously. People running protection schemes are generally, to use a term I read on Google today, *mobbed up*. They're connected to some big crime syndicate, and they're basically saying, look, we'll leave you alone and protect you from anybody who tries to mess with you if you pay us."

"Ian involved with mobsters?" She shook her head. "I don't know about that."

"It's possible he wasn't, but the business owners wouldn't have known that. Remember, they didn't know who they were dealing with. They figured, pay these guys, and we'll be safer than if we don't. Which they probably were, even if only from Ian's... thugs, to use your word." He pointed to the first date on the first page. "Seems like it worked for a couple of years."

"Until somebody else started threatening the businesses."

"Exactly. Ian had promised protection, and suddenly, he couldn't deliver. If you'll turn the page..."

She did and noticed the payments from the first business becoming sporadic until they stopped entirely a few months before. "Looks like they decided that, if he wasn't going to protect them, why pay?"

"I think so." Braden's head was bent over the paperwork. "Maybe, at first, he used the other business owners' misfortune to his advantage. Maybe the message was, 'They quit paying, and look what happened to them.' But..." He looked up to face her. "My dad owns his own shop now. He knows lots of business owners in the area. Not just other mechanics, but owners of all kinds of businesses. They're in Rotary Club and the Chamber of Commerce. They work together on nonprofits sometimes. They talk."

"You're saying they figured it out. They knew who was paying and who wasn't."

"Maybe." Braden shrugged. "It's just a theory."

"It's a good one." Carly flipped through the pages and discovered that many of the businesses had quit paying. "So they figured out their protector wasn't able to protect. They decided to take their chances. Are any of these businesses related to the newspaper clippings?"

"A few." He flipped through the sheets of newsprint and pulled out one. "This place, Mama Mia's. Didn't you work there once?"

"My first job." She couldn't believe Braden remembered. She'd waited tables one summer but had quit when school started back again. "I heard when it caught fire. The owner was kind to me."

"Dark-haired lady, right? Marie something?"

"Mariana Aquino."

Braden's focus returned to the page. "She'd paid Ian eighteen thousand dollars over the course of a couple of years, and then"—he tapped the article—"poof, her place goes up in smoke."

"She was all right, though, right?"

"Nobody was injured, but the place burned to the ground. Ronnie said they took the insurance money and sold the property."

"We could talk to her, see if our theory is correct."

"Not a bad idea, but let's have Ronnie do it. I don't want to go anywhere near Dorchester until the killers are put away."

Thinking of the morning they'd had, she couldn't agree more.

Braden shot off a quick email to Ronnie about talking to the restaurant owner.

When he was finished, she asked, "Did you forward the images of the protection notebook to Klein?"

Braden's expression morphed from a half-smile to a scowl. "For all the good it'll do."

"Maybe we can tell him what we learned. He hasn't found Ian's body, but maybe if we give him the motive..."

"Do his job for him, you mean."

She lifted one shoulder, let it drop. "I'm frustrated, too, but the sooner we get the police investigating—"

"I know. You're right. I'll email him now." He tapped on his computer, and she stood and perused the bookshelves. Stacks and stacks of every genre one could imagine. Everything from classic literature to art history. Some volumes looked as old as the house, others with brightly colored dust jackets were obviously new. She tipped out one with an intriguing title. A romance. She shoved it back in. She didn't read romance. Those stories made her wish for things she'd never have.

Except...

She'd worked hard all day not to think about that kiss.

If she started thinking about it, she'd think of little else.

Her mother'd given up on romance, or so she'd claimed, but she'd found her love story with Pete. As much as Carly wasn't the guy's biggest fan, he'd adored Mama. Before she died, he'd actually been happy. He'd come home for dinner, help in the kitchen, compliment the food, and kiss the cook.

Carly had thought Mama was happy, but when Pete and the girls moved in, Mama had gone from content to joyful. Her grin had been brighter, her laugh richer. She'd finally gotten her love story.

Nobody could have guessed that cancer would end it so quickly.

Maybe that explained why Carly was afraid to hope for her own love story. She'd rarely seen one with a happy ending.

"It's done." Behind her, Braden snapped his laptop closed. "Maybe Klein will take us seriously now."

She turned and grinned at him. "Look at us. We're like... Sherlock Holmes and Dr. Watson."

From his chair, Braden reached out and snagged her hand, then pulled her closer. "You're a lot better looking than any Dr. Watson I've ever seen."

She giggled. "That's because I'm Sherlock."

He wrapped his arm around her middle. "You think so, do you?"

How easy it would be to settle right there on his lap and kiss him senseless. It's what she would have done back when they were together. Back before Braden became a Christian and declared they either needed to marry or stop seeing each other. Because he knew he wouldn't be able to keep up his vow to wait until marriage to be intimate again if they were still together. At the time, she'd thought him cruel and demanding. Now she understood.

She twisted away and sat on her chair opposite him.

His expression looked pained, as if his mind had gone to the same place hers had. To the thing they'd both done so easily when they were together. The thing neither of them would do today.

Or maybe he was remembering, just like she was, how things used to be. How they'd loved each other. Made promises to each other. But he'd wanted their future to happen so much faster than she was prepared for. Marriage? She'd been twenty-one, still grieving her mother and trying to keep her promise to take care of her family. How could she have considered a move to Cambridge?

How could he have asked her to?

And now he lived hours away.

Neither of them spoke, and the tension pulled tight.

Remembering his remark from dinner and desperate to change the subject she'd only broached in her heart, she said, "I thought you loved your job. Why don't you think it'll last?"

He stood, stretched, and settled on the little settee in front of the windows. "That chair isn't exactly comfortable." He shifted, grimaced. "Not that this is much better. It's not built for grown-ups."

It did look comically small for his six-foot frame. "People used to be shorter."

"I think people used to like slow torture." He stood and poked at the fire, sending a spray of sparks up the chimney. "I don't know how much you know about what I do."

"Um... something with science and computers, right?"

He glanced at her over his shoulder. "BNB is a medical research and development company. Jacqui is brilliant, smarter than anyone I've ever known."

"That's saying something, coming from you."

He returned the poker and turned. "I have a decent IQ, but mostly I just work really hard. She's next level. Mensa level."

"Okay."

"But she's like... like the prototypical absentminded scientist." He settled back in the chair across from Carly's. "She gets into her work and forgets to eat. She can figure out how to design the most complex things you've ever heard of, but she has eight employees and probably doesn't remember three of their names."

Carly laughed. "That's pretty sad."

"And she has no instinct for business."

"How'd she build a successful company then?"

"Her former partner managed that end of it, and she managed the research. It was perfect until the former partner... Well, that's a long story. Suffice it to say, he's in prison now."

"Oh, no."

"Yeah, so there was a vacuum in the business, and when she moved the company to New Hampshire, it was worse. I'm the only employee who came with her. I did my best to step into that vacuum, and with some help from Jacqui's future husband—"

"Reid, right?"

"Right. He has a great mind for business, but mostly, I've been managing BNB's finances and hiring and marketing. I thought I was doing a good job."

Carly put the pieces together. "And then she hired Andrew."

"The guy's got a master's in biochemistry and an MBA. He's pushing me aside."

Carly understood what he was saying, but... "You never wanted to be in business management before. Why do you care?"

Braden launched himself out of the chair and paced. "I was doing it. I was managing the back office, helping with hiring, dealing with the website. I thought I had it under control. I did have it under control."

"So your feelings are—"

"It's not about my feelings." He stopped and stared down at

her. "It's about... It's not that people who do what I do are a dime a dozen. I have specific skills, and there's a limited number of people who have those skills. But there are enough of us. I'm very replaceable. And not only that, but if the company..." He seemed to be trying to gather his words. "Things are good right now. We sold patent licenses last year for an artificial neuron. As those businesses develop products, the money should keep us going. But it won't last forever. We have to develop things to sell, consistently, and if we don't, then we won't be able to maintain all the employees' salaries. As a researcher, I can be replaced. But if I were also managing—"

"You could still be replaced," Carly said. "Andrew is proof of that."

Braden's glare could have sparked a flame. "Thanks. Very helpful."

"I don't mean that in a bad way. I'm just saying..." She sighed, started over. "Let's say you found a different job. Would you not be replaceable there too?"

"The thing is, there are no other jobs doing what I do in the area. If something happens to my job at BNB, then I don't just lose it, but I lose everything. My house, my church... I'll have to start all over."

"Isn't that what life is about? Sometimes, things happen and we have to regroup."

"You don't understand."

Her short burst of laughter was anything but amused. "Don't I? Don't I understand how a person's life can shift in an instant? Gee, Braden, I feel like maybe I've got a little experience with that. Mom died. The man I thought I'd spend my life with left me." She hadn't meant to say that.

Shouldn't have said it.

The anger slid off his face, replaced by defeat that almost felt palpable. "I know." He perched on the chair across from her, shoulders lowered. "That's the point, though. I want... I want a secure life. I want to know I can provide for myself and a family. I wish things had been different with you. I wish I'd been stronger. The timing was off. I was trying to move too fast. I just... I didn't know what to do." His hand inched over hers. "I like my job, I do. But you're in Boston. If you and I—"

"Don't." She snatched her hand back. "Don't do that."

*Don't make promises you won't keep.*

Again.

"I'm sorry." He leaned back, took a breath. "Too fast. Too far, too fast. Always my problem."

If things were different, she'd throw herself into his arms. But she was pregnant with Ian's baby.

And someone was trying to kill her.

"I understand what you're saying." She folded her hands on her lap to keep from reaching out to him. "That desperate need for security. That fear of—"

"It's not fear. It's... I just don't want to get comfortable in Coventry if it's not going to last. I'd rather return to Boston now, while I'm young and unattached, where there are more opportunities."

It *was* fear. She recognized it in Braden because she saw it in the mirror every single day. But it would be pointless to argue. "After Mama died and you..."

"I never meant to hurt you."

"I never meant to hurt *you.*"

His grimace confirmed that she had hurt him when she'd refused his proposal. "I wanted to say yes. I just wasn't ready. I couldn't leave my family. And... Braden, my mother had only been gone a few months. You were asking me to leave my home to create a future life with you. I couldn't see it. I couldn't fathom ever being happy again. It wasn't my need to care for sisters that had me refusing your proposal—at least, it wasn't only that. It was... it was all of it. I couldn't do it."

After a moment, he said, "I didn't get it at the time. Maybe I never will."

"I didn't know how to put it into words. I'm sorry I made you think I chose the girls over you."

"You were grieving." His eyes softened, filled with compassion. "And you were trying to figure out how to manage your family and their needs."

She had been. Three years later, she still was.

"I'm sorry." He laid his hand, palm up, on the table between them. She set hers in it, and he squeezed. "I didn't have any idea what you were going through. I was arrogant. I thought I could solve all your problems. As if grief can be solved. As if leaving your family would have been the answer. It was stupid on my part."

"It was sweet and romantic."

"But also stupid, I realize now." He took a long breath. "And if I'd just tried to understand instead of leaving, we could have tried to continue the relationship."

"We would have failed, though."

In the years since Braden left, she'd come to understand his point. When he became a Christian, his values changed. Their very intimate past would have called them back again and again. He would have compromised. She would have felt guilty. There would have been conflict, tension that hadn't existed before.

Nothing about their relationship would have been healthy.

Marriage wouldn't have been the right choice, either. Maybe Braden had been ready, but she hadn't been, not even close. There was the crushing grief. And she hadn't been a believer yet. Maybe she needed to go through the hard years without Braden in order to find salvation. Because, back then, she'd thought Braden was her savior.

And no man deserved that kind of pressure.

Maybe Braden's leaving, in a weird way, had been good for her.

"Anyway." She needed to steer the conversation away from her and Braden and their romantic past. "I felt alone, more alone than I'd ever felt in my life. Without Mama... it was terrifying. She was my foundation. Pete didn't kick me out, of course, but I couldn't rely on him. Or confide in him. And the girls were looking to me as if I were their new mother. I could barely function, but suddenly I had to figure out how to take care of three grieving girls and stay out of the way of their grieving father, who barely tolerated me. It was lonely."

At Braden's pained expression, she squeezed his hand. "I'm okay now. But at the time—"

"I should have been there for you."

"You couldn't have solved it, Braden. You weren't my answer. And neither was Ian, though I thought he was at the time. Having someone who seemed to cherish me. He protected me. He took care of me, bought me gifts, worried about me. He was charming and generous and gentle. At first. It was a short-term dream that turned into a long-term nightmare."

Braden's eyebrows lowered. "What do you mean by that? What did he do?"

She didn't need to give Braden all the gory details of their relationship. "He was... controlling. It didn't take long before I knew I needed to get out of that relationship, which quickly turned destructive and unhealthy. But without Ian, I would be alone, and that was a terrifying thought. I'd break up with him, and then he'd worm his way back into my life, and I'd give in because I was just... I was pathetic."

"You were lonely."

She shrugged. It was a sad excuse. "I'd gotten the job I have now by then and moved in with a woman I worked with, Kelly. I was trying to extricate myself from Ian and from my family, but it was harder than I thought it would be. Almost all the time I was with Ian, Kelly would talk about Jesus. It wasn't like she was just trying to save me, though. She talked about Jesus like He was her very best friend. He came up in conversation all the time, as if she'd just hung up the phone with Him, and she wanted to tell me about their conversation. It was weird, honestly. But she was kind and happy and secure. She was generous and gentle. She was filled with joy. And then one day, it was like... like the light went on, and

I realized Kelly had something I wanted. Something I desperately needed."

Carly could still remember how she'd felt that morning, waking up with bruises on her arms from her most recent fight with Ian. The night before, she'd started to storm out of his townhouse. He'd grabbed her. *"You're mine. Mine. And you always will be."*

He'd felt guilty for hurting her, as he always did after the fact, and finally let her leave.

The next morning, she'd told herself for the thousandth time that she needed to break it off with him for good. But there was a snide voice in the back of her mind telling her she'd never have the courage to do it. That voice told her that Ian was right—she belonged to him.

And then, a whisper. A gentle whisper. *Daughter. You were never his. You will always and forever be Mine. Come home to Me.*

"That day, I asked Kelly to tell me about Jesus again, and she did. And I gave myself to Him."

Braden patted her hand. "I am so glad."

"But there was always that pull, Ian promising security. When I was with him, if I had trouble making the rent, he paid it. If I needed something, he bought it. Without him, I had to make my own way. It was scary. But I was reading the Bible, and I found this great verse. It comes from one of the books of Samuel, I think. 'They confronted me in the day of my calamity, but the Lord was my support. He brought me out into a broad place; He rescued me because He delighted in me.'"

"I've never heard that one," Braden said. "I'll have to look it up."

"Ian had taken advantage of me in my calamity, right? In my grief and need, Ian stepped in and made everything worse. But God was my support."

"He rescued you because He delights in you."

Carly fought tears that stung her eyes. When she could speak again, she said, "I held onto that promise, and I ended things with Ian for good. And even though it hasn't been easy, and there've been times when I wondered where God was…" She shrugged. "If not for the Lord looking out for me, I'd have been killed Monday morning."

Braden swallowed hard. "I'm grateful He protected you."

"But my point, Braden, is that… I mean, you've known Him longer than I have, so maybe I'm missing something here. But I don't think your job is your support. Your security. Doesn't that come from God? Shouldn't you just… just trust Him with the details? Or, does He not get involved in things like that? I mean, I don't know. I'm just figuring this stuff out."

Braden's hand lifted off hers, and he sat back. "No, you're right. I do trust Him. I'm just…"

"Hedging your bets?"

He shrugged. "Yeah. Maybe. Which, when you say it that way, seems pretty stupid. I mean, He is God." Braden gripped her hand and rubbed his thumb along her wrist. "You know what? You're pretty smart."

She giggled. "Not compared to you, college boy."

He stood and pulled her to her feet. "You have your own brand of smarts, and it happens to be my favorite kind." His amusement faded as he looked into her eyes. His were warm and held a question that had her lips tingling. "Do you think I could kiss you again?"

When she told him the rest of her story, he'd want nothing to do with her. She should push him away, but to kiss him one last time… She rose to her tiptoes and pressed her lips to his.

And everything else faded into the background.

# CHAPTER TWENTY-ONE

Braden's phone vibrated in his pocket, and he silently cursed the stupid thing.

And thanked God for it as Carly ended the kiss, looking up at him with an expression on her face he was afraid to name. Looked too much like love.

Back in the day, that kiss would have been the first course. Now, if he wanted to remain faithful to the One who'd saved him, the kiss would have to serve as the entire meal. He wished he didn't so vividly remember the main dish.

The phone rang again, and Carly smiled. "You going to answer that?"

Right. He yanked it from his pocket and glanced at the number before swiping to answer. "Ronnie. What's up?"

Carly's eyebrows lifted, and she settled back into her chair.

Braden tapped the screen and set the phone on the table. "You're on speaker. Carly's here."

"Hey, Carly," Ronnie said. "Long time."

"Thanks for helping us out," she said.

"Did a little more digging." Ronnie's voice took on its no-nonsense tone. "I thought you'd want to know right away what I found out."

"Which was?"

"The first rash of crimes were linked to the addresses where that new condo development is, right off the highway. The current developer didn't own the property at the time, though. The land was being bought up by a company called Abecedarian Properties. You know what Abecedarian means?"

Braden glanced at Carly, who shrugged. He said, "Never heard the word in my life."

"Means elementary or rudimentary," Ronnie said. "Also, arranged alphabetically. Sometimes, it's used to refer to students of the alphabet. Like first graders."

Braden had to work to keep his patience in place. "Why do I care what the name means?"

"Just thought it was interesting. It's kind of a hoity-toity word, right? You're in that hoity-toity world. I thought maybe you'd see a connection."

Braden's world was far from hoity-toity, but he didn't bother to say so. "I don't."

"If you're trying to think up a name for a company... Basically, they called it ABC Construction."

"Still not sure why I care," Braden said.

"You care 'cause it's not real. They got a website and an EIN number, but if you dig around, they don't actually build anything. No projects under their belts. They buy property then unload it immediately."

"So it's a front company."

"Exactly."

"Owned by whom?"

"Haven't figured that out yet, but I'm working on it. Abecedarian is the name they use when they're buying up the property. It's bought cheap, sometimes under market value. That's the meaning of the minus sign and the smaller number in Ian's notebook—an estimate of how much under market value each property sold for. Then it's unloaded to the developer."

Braden said, "They make a profit, I assume."

"Yeah, a good profit, but if it's a front company, then it's just shifting money from one account to another. Smoke and mirrors."

"And the developer is...?"

"Richard M. Lynch Properties."

Carly's eyes widened. "Lynch? As in, the guy running for Congress?"

"One and the same," Ronnie said. "Looks like our hometown hero has some explaining to do."

Braden settled in the chair across from Carly. "You don't think he's actually behind the crimes and Ian's murder?"

"Far as I can tell, he's got a pretty sizable operation," Ronnie said. "He's currently building four developments in the Boston area with a few on schedule to begin next year. It's possible somebody in his operation is behind the crimes, and he's not aware of them. But it don't look good."

Carly pulled Braden's laptop from his backpack and looked at him with lifted eyebrows.

"Go ahead," he said.

She opened it and started typing.

"Would any of this hold up in court?" Braden asked Ronnie.

"I didn't exactly ask permission before I started digging around. Cops would have to find it for themselves, but they could get a warrant. About the other thing..."

"Hold up." Braden snatched the phone and took it off speaker, earning a confused look from Carly.

He stepped across the hall into the dark music room and lowered his voice. "I'm thinking I should let that go."

"I wouldn't if I were you. There's definitely something there."

Braden tried to deny the surge of excitement Ronnie's words elicited.

He shouldn't ask. But what if Andrew really was bad news for BNB? Braden had come this far. What would it hurt to learn what Ronnie had found out?

"Go on," he said.

"Did you know the guy spent time in prison?"

"*Prison?* Not jail, but actual prison?"

"Six months for embezzlement."

"I don't understand. Jacqui always does background checks, so why—?"

"His record was expunged."

Expunged.

More importantly... embezzlement. Braden was almost too shocked to reply. He finally asked the obvious. "Why was it expunged? Was he not guilty?"

"Haven't figured that out yet," Ronnie said. "Best guess—he made a deal, turned state's evidence or maybe overheard another con shooting off his mouth about a crime and used the info to save himself. I guess it's possible he wasn't guilty in the first place, but I haven't turned up anything that points to that."

"How long was his sentence supposed to be?"

"Three years."

Braden whistled. This was not nothing.

Did Jacqui know? Surely not. Surely she wouldn't be considering turning her company over to a man she knew was guilty of stealing from a former employer.

This could do it. This could be the information that saved Braden's position at BNB.

A soft knock had Braden turning. Carly was standing in the open door. "I'm going up."

"Oh. Hold on." He turned his back to her and spoke into the phone. "Find out what you can."

"On it. Call you tomorrow."

Braden shoved his phone back into his pocket and spun to her. "Sorry. Business."

"Business with BNB?" At his nod, she added, "With Ronnie?"

"Nothing to worry about." He crossed into the library and made sure the fireplace screen was firmly in place. The fire was dying anyway. He snatched his bag. She'd already placed the laptop and all the other materials back into it. "I'll walk you up."

"You don't have to. It's only nine thirty."

It wasn't as if he was going to go intrude on the family in the media room. He held out his hand, and she slid hers into it. After he flipped off the light, they climbed to the second floor. He paused outside her door, which she'd left open. No reason to close and lock it when they were the only guests in the house. Her bed was unmade, conjuring too many ideas in his too-busy mind.

"I checked on my sisters," she said, "and then I was looking for familiar faces on the Lynch Development website."

"I thought you said you didn't see the people who killed Ian."

"I didn't. But I did get a glimpse of the guys who were creeping up to your truck this morning. I thought maybe—"

"Any luck?"

She shook her head. "But I'm so tired. I'll be fresher in the morning."

"Yeah. We need to talk about what Ronnie learned, but I've had my fill of mystery-solving tonight. How're your sisters?"

"The girls are all safe and well. Laurie was complaining about her father hovering, so I think he's taking it seriously."

"Good news, then."

"Except that Sophia is with that guy again tonight."

"The pervert." Braden couldn't think of a better term for a thirty-something guy who dated a teenage girl.

"Yeah." She pulled her hand away from his and pushed her hair out of her face. "There's something really... off about it. The timing. Everything."

He agreed, though he didn't say so. Carly seemed worried enough already. "Today was a hard day, but we learned a lot. Let's get a good night's sleep and figure out the rest tomorrow. Maybe by the end of the day, we'll be able to present everything we've learned to Klein. Maybe then he'll take us seriously."

She yawned. "I didn't hear anything after 'sleep.'"

He grinned at her. "It's been a good day, too, I think. You and me and..." He shrugged, telling himself to shut up. But despite his best efforts, he couldn't seem to keep himself from adding, "I've missed you. It feels... right to be with you again."

He expected her to smile at his remark, but a look he couldn't quite decipher crossed her features, gone too quickly to analyze.

She dropped her gaze to the floor. When she looked up again, she said, "I've missed you too."

He leaned down and kissed her cheek, not trusting himself to do more. "Good night, beautiful."

She blushed and stepped into her room.

He walked away before her door closed, needing the distance. The moment to think.

Carly was back, and he was more in love with her than ever.

And because one mystery was close to being solved, but a new one had presented itself with Andrew.

It seemed that, if Braden played his cards right, he might just get everything he'd ever wanted.

BRADEN HAD BEEN awake for an hour, trying to go back to sleep despite the weird dreams and memories that had replayed themselves all night. Gunshots and running and the news about Andrew and kissing Carly...

Despite the drama of the rest of it, kissing Carly kept floating to the top.

Three years since they'd broken up. He'd tried for three years to convince himself he didn't love her, didn't need her, didn't want her.

He'd been lying to himself. Now that she was back, he could admit the truth. Carly was the only woman he'd ever loved. He'd compared every other woman since then to her, and they'd all fallen short. She was no angel—he knew that. He knew she'd been intimate with another man. He knew she'd been lost for years. But so had he before he came to Christ. God had redeemed Braden's life, and He'd redeemed Carly's.

They could go into their future together on equal footing.

But how would it work? Would she relocate to Coventry? He

loved his job there, and it seemed he'd retain his management role, if what Ronnie had said was true, but for Carly, he'd give it up and find a job back in Boston. He hadn't been willing years before, but he'd learned a lot since then. One lesson had presented itself over and over.

*It's not about me.*

Christ sacrificed everything to save Braden. Braden could sacrifice the job he loved to be with Carly. He would, too, if that was what it took.

But he'd prefer to have them both—the job he loved and the girl he loved in the house he loved and the town he loved.

Could that dream come true?

Contemplating that all night... It was no wonder he'd hardly slept. It was almost dawn, but he could use another hour or three of sleep.

The faint sound coming from the room next door never would have woken him. But thanks to the thin wall that separated his room from Carly's and the fact that he was already awake, planning a future with the woman he loved, he heard it.

She was throwing up. Again.

In the morning. Again.

The truth slammed into his midsection like a fist. He pushed himself up in the bed, nearly breathless with the realization.

She wasn't sick. It wasn't nerves or fear or bad fish.

Carly was pregnant.

Braden let himself into the house after an hour-long jog in the frigid morning air wearing nothing but Donovan's too-long pajama pants, a T-shirt, and his sneakers, not one bit less angry than he'd been when he left. He'd tried praying through it, but God had felt too far away to reach. He'd hoped the physical exertion would calm him, but with every footfall, the truth pounded into his brain.

She was pregnant. Pregnant with another man's baby.

She'd come to Braden for help to solve her lover's murder.

She'd used him. Pretended to care about him because she needed shelter and help figuring out who'd killed the man she really loved.

Now, furious but dehydrated, he headed for the kitchen.

Carly was sitting at the table, sipping from a glass of water. A plate with a couple of crackers sat in front of her.

She smiled when she saw him, but the look faded quickly. "What happened?"

"Why don't you tell me?"

She must've picked up on his anger because she stood and crossed her arms. "I don't know—"

"It was all a lie, wasn't it? All of it."

"What are you—?"

"You and Murphy. You were still with him."

"We broke up a year ago, Braden." She backed up, swallowed. "I told you—"

"I know what you told me." He stepped closer, and she moved back again, bumping into the wall. "I also know it's all a lie. You're *pregnant*."

Her face paled. "I-I was going to tell—"

"So if you and Ian weren't together, then whose kid is it? Do you even know?"

She gasped. He couldn't tell if she was honestly shocked by his question or just a fantastic actor. Based on the week they'd spent together, he'd guess the second.

She lifted her chin. "It's Ian's."

"But you weren't dating anymore." He could hear the scornful tone but didn't temper it. "What, was it some sort of friends-with-benefits—?"

"It wasn't like that."

He moved closer still, close enough that less than a foot separated them. He needed to see in her eyes, discern lies from truth. He needed to *understand*. "What was it then, huh? Couldn't help yourself? Couldn't keep your hands off each other?"

A deep voice came from behind him. "Step away. Now."

Donovan. And the words didn't sound like a suggestion.

Braden blinked. Suddenly, he saw the situation the way Donovan did.

Carly looked terrified, as if Braden might hit her. Never, never would he hurt her. No matter how angry he was.

But nobody in the room seemed to realize that.

He stepped back, hands lifted. "I'm sorry. I didn't mean..." To what? Frighten her? Maybe that was exactly what he'd wanted. What was wrong with him?

The terror on Carly's face didn't fade.

How could she ever, ever believe he would hurt her?

Donovan said, "Walk away, Braden."

He needed answers, but Carly wasn't talking. And he wasn't in the state of mind to encourage her to share.

Donovan was right behind him, poised to step in.

Braden couldn't think of anything to say.

He turned and walked past the man, bumping his shoulder. Through the house and out the front door.

Another jog might help to calm him down. But it wouldn't change anything.

# CHAPTER TWENTY-TWO

THE DOOR at the front of the house slammed.

Carly collapsed back in her chair, unable to force herself to meet Donovan's eyes.

He swiveled and headed for the door. "Sit tight."

Sit tight? Where could she go? Not home, where killers were trying to find her. But she couldn't stay there with Braden. Not now that he knew the truth.

She should have told him sooner. Right away.

Before he'd kissed her. Definitely before then.

Before she'd let herself fall in love with him again.

"Carly?"

She looked up at the soft voice. Angel stepped into the room wearing pajamas, her hair in a messy ponytail.

"Is everything okay?"

"You didn't need to get up. I'm fine."

She rounded the bar and lifted the carafe of coffee. "Billy just finished eating. You need some?"

"I'm fine." She couldn't drink it anyway, pregnancy notwithstanding, not with her stomach churning like it was.

Angel filled herself a mug, then perched on the chair.

"Donovan was in the sunroom painting. He gets his best work done early in the mornings. He didn't mean to overhear, but—"

"So you know."

"It's true then? You're pregnant?" At Carly's nod, Angel added, "And it's not Braden's?"

"We just reconnected this week."

When Carly said nothing else, Angel asked, "Do you want to talk about it? You don't have to, but it might make you feel better."

Would telling somebody the whole truth enable Carly to put it into perspective? If nothing else, maybe Angel could help her figure out what to do next. She started with the easy part. "We were broken up, Ian and I. For a year. He was one of those guys... When I started dating him, he was charming and attentive, but he became... I don't want to use the word 'abusive.' He never hit me. But..." She thought back on the bruises he'd left on her arms, the times she'd fallen because he'd lost his temper and pushed her. "Maybe 'abusive' is the right word. He hurt me. He was controlling and manipulative, and our relationship was... destructive."

Angel laid her hand over Carly's. "I've met my share of men like that."

Met them, but she probably hadn't been stupid enough to get involved with them. Angel seemed much wiser than Carly had ever been. "It was hard to end things. I kept breaking it off, and he kept begging me to come back. I have no real family. My mom died. I never knew my father. My stepfather and stepsisters aren't exactly supportive. I thought Ian was the only person in the world who really cared about me. But he didn't. Care about me, that is. He cared about controlling me and manipulating me." The weird thing was, Carly was pretty sure he'd thought he loved her. He simply didn't understand real love. Maybe he couldn't comprehend what real love should look like. That it should be sacrificial, not demanding. That it should be kind, not controlling. Ian had tried to be a boyfriend, and if she'd let him, he would have tried to be a good husband. Without Christ, he would have failed, over and over. But he would have tried.

Might Ian have become a believer someday? If he'd lived long enough?

Now, it was too late for him.

She didn't want to think about the man Ian could have been, the father God had created him to be. He'd never have the chance to grow into that person. He'd never meet his child.

She didn't grieve him, not after what he'd done to her. But she grieved. She grieved what had been lost when Ian had chosen badly so many times. She grieved all he'd missed because of the way he'd chosen to live his life.

Beside her at the table, Angel waited patiently. Carly wiped her eyes and swallowed the sadness. "When I became a Christian, God gave me the courage to end things with him. I blocked his number. When he sent me gifts, I sent them back."

"Good for you."

"After a few months, he gave up. I didn't see him or hear from him. I thought it was over, finally. And then..."

Carly closed her eyes against the pressure building there. Her throat swelled. "When we were dating, I gave him a key to my apartment." Her voice was high and tight. She swallowed and tried again. "I asked for my key when we broke up the first time, and he gave it back to me. But he must have made a copy. A couple of months ago... I was asleep, and he was just... there. My roommate was out of town. I tried to make him stop..."

Carly couldn't bear to open her eyes, too embarrassed or ashamed or... She didn't know what she felt.

Angel's chair scraped against the floor, and her arms wrapped around Carly's shoulders. "I'm so sorry. I'm so, so sorry that happened to you."

Carly leaned against the shoulder of this woman she barely knew and accepted the comfort. When she could force words past her tight throat, she backed away and continued. "After, he apologized. Not a real apology, though. More like, 'Sorry you made me do that.' And then he made it clear I shouldn't call the police. It was my word against his, he said, and we used to date, so nobody would believe it wasn't consensual. I don't know if he was right."

"You didn't report it?"

Carly shrugged. "I should have. I just... It was over. I thought I could put it out of my mind. Pretend it didn't happen. I moved back to my stepfather's house, thinking I'd be safe there. Ian wouldn't dare bother me with Pete around. I tried not to think about it, but the memory plagues my nightmares. And then I found out I'm pregnant."

And then Braden found out. And he hated her for it. And she couldn't even blame him.

There was nothing else to say. Carly's ugliness was out there, and she had to live with it. She allowed Angel to draw her into a hug again, thankful for the arms around her and feeling pathetic for how badly she needed them.

Angel kept up a stream of encouraging words, slipping into prayer after a moment, asking God to give Carly peace.

Maybe He did. Maybe a measure of peace invaded the hurricane of thoughts swirling through her mind. Just Angel's gentle presence beside her provided some of that. That this woman, this virtual stranger, would pray for her...

God was with Carly. Through this whole mess, He'd proved His presence, His protection, and His care over and over.

Carly wasn't alone. She didn't have Braden, but she had God. God would pull her through.

Her tears dried, and she felt stronger than she had since she'd discovered the news Monday morning.

Angel backed away and sat in the chair again. "Have you told Braden all of that?"

"He didn't exactly give me the chance to explain."

"You need to tell him the truth." Angel spoke the words as if they were the most obvious solution.

But Carly wasn't sure. "What if he doesn't believe me?"

"Then he's a jerk. Better to find that out now."

Braden wasn't a jerk, though. He was a kind, gentle soul who felt hurt and betrayed.

Carly could understand that. She didn't blame him for his anger. "I don't want him to be with me because he feels sorry for me. I don't need him to take care of me."

She almost added the biggest lie in the world—that she could take care of herself. She couldn't. If this week had proved anything, it had proved that she needed people in her life. She needed help.

But she had God. And He would provide the right people, the people He chose.

Angel only smiled. "I'm pretty good at reading people, and if my read on Braden is correct, the strongest feeling he has for you is nowhere on the scale near pity. That man loves you."

But Carly could only shake her head. "Maybe he did once. But after this... I should have told him sooner. About the baby and what happened with Ian. I'm afraid it's too late now. And even if he could forgive me for lying to him, why would he want another man's child?"

With another squeeze to Carly's hand, Angel said, "I've seen relationships weather worse, my friend. Give him a chance."

CARLY NEEDED to tell Braden the truth. Angel was right about that. But the longer Carly waited to talk to him, the more frustrated she became. She showered, dressed in her clothes from the day before, and braided her long hair, all the while remembering the accusations and insults Braden had launched her way.

How could a man who'd been so tender and loving the night before suddenly become so scornful and cruel?

Maybe Braden was more like Ian than she'd realized. Maybe Carly had a type of man she was attracted to, and her type was *that*. Men who could turn on a dime. Men who hid their wrath behind a thin coating of charm.

Cruel men.

Abusive men.

Maybe, deep down, that described all men.

No. She refused to believe that.

She heard the door open downstairs when Braden returned from wherever he'd gone. Heard his shower turn on and, a few minutes later, turn back off. She heard him pacing in his room.

While she paced in hers.

They needed to have a conversation. But where would she and Braden go from there? Not back to where they'd been the night before. Even if Braden could overlook the fact that she was carrying Ian's child, she couldn't overlook the fact that he'd so quickly assumed the worst about her.

And then launched accusations like missiles.

No. She couldn't overlook that. She wouldn't. Not again.

She stepped out of her room, walked the few steps down the hallway, and knocked on his door.

His hair was still wet, the scent of shampoo and soap and Braden wafting into the hallway. Her resolve wobbled, but she straightened her back. "Do you want to know what really happened, or do you prefer your sick little fantasy?"

His eyebrows rose. He opened his mouth, shut it again. Crossed his arms. "I'm listening."

"He raped me."

She hadn't meant the words to come out like that. She'd meant to work into it. Tell about the key and her roommate being out of town. Tell it how she'd told Angel. But anger and frustration had her brain misfiring and her mouth misbehaving.

Braden's jaw dropped. His arms dropped. His whole countenance dropped. "Oh, honey, I'm sorry. I'm so..." He reached out, but Carly stepped back.

"You don't get to comfort me. After the things you said to me, the way you treated me? I told your mother it was a bad idea to go to you. I told her, but I was desperate, and she made me promise."

"She knew?"

"About the baby, yes. About the... other?" Carly shook her head. "It's not exactly an easy thing to explain over coffee."

"I would never have... if I'd known. I'm so sorry."

"Me too. You know what else I'm sorry about? That you immediately assumed the worst about me. That you have so little regard for me." She turned and marched back to her room and closed the door.

She didn't know where to go from there. She didn't know what to do next.

She only knew that she couldn't stand to see Braden looking at her like that, expression full of pity and sadness and regret. As if he really cared.

She crawled beneath the covers and curled into a ball, arms protecting the tiny life inside her. "It's just you and me, sweetheart. Just you and me and God."

~

CARLY WANTED nothing more than to stay in her bed all day long, praying and crying and licking her wounds.

But an hour after she'd left Braden, she opened Instagram, and another photo of Sophia and her new *boyfriend* popped up, this one posted well after Sophia's midnight curfew. Perhaps she'd posted it after she got home, but Carly doubted it.

There'd been no more threats from the Instagram profile called John Smith. She didn't take comfort in that, though. Rather, it made her wonder if perhaps whoever'd been behind those threats had found another way to get to her.

The images of Sophia and the pervert... She had a very bad feeling about that.

She had to get back to Dorchester. Her family needed her. They were the only family she had left in the world, after all. The little glimmer of hope for a family of her own, the one that had sparked the day before in Braden's arms, had been doused in an ice bath of reality.

She needed to put this little fantasy with Braden in her past so she could figure out what her future was going to look like. She'd gone to Ian's to tell him about the baby hoping he'd help provide financially for the child his evil behavior had produced. Though she wasn't sorry she wouldn't have to deal with Ian for the rest of her life, now that he was dead, she would have to provide for her child alone. No easy feat in a city as expensive as Boston.

Maybe she could find a job in a cheaper area and move. She could find online classes and work on her degree at night. Once she earned her paralegal certificate, she could get a better job, provide for her child all by herself. Maybe even continue for her bachelor's. Once upon a time, she'd wanted to be a lawyer. She'd given up that dream when she relinquished her scholarship to stay home and care for Mom. But she could revive it. She could do it.

First, she'd need a job she could do now.

Were there customer service jobs in New Hampshire?

No. That was her stupid hope—apparently not completely extinguished yet—invading her reason. The last thing she needed was to be closer to the man who'd broken her heart. Twice.

Florida, then. Or North Carolina. She'd once heard there were lots of jobs there. Or... she had a customer in Oklahoma City who'd claimed it was a very affordable place to live. Maybe she could go there. The University of Oklahoma was supposed to have a good law school. If she established residency in the state...

She tried to see herself in Oklahoma, but the picture wouldn't come. She might as well have been trying to imagine moving to Saturn.

Because she couldn't leave the city, not until her sisters were grown. Maybe they'd help her with the baby.

That picture wouldn't come either. She couldn't trust them to run a load of laundry. Would she really trust them with her child?

Not likely.

Carly had no idea what her future was going to look like. She did know that if she didn't figure out who killed Ian and then convince the police, she wasn't going to have a future at all.

And, though she'd prefer to avoid Braden indefinitely, she had gotten him into this. He was in danger now because of her.

She huffed out an exasperated breath, flung back the covers, and climbed out of bed.

Five minutes later, she found Braden sipping coffee at the kitchen table. Though the scents of sausage and pancakes hung in the air, Angel and Donovan were nowhere in sight.

Braden jumped up when she came in and rounded the island into the kitchen. "Angel saved you a plate. Bobby had a doctor's appointment."

"Billy. The baby's name is Billy."

"Oh. That's what I meant. Anyway, then they're going to run some errands and go to lunch." He tapped a square sticky note on the counter. "Angel left her number, if you need her."

As Carly pocketed the note, Braden donned a bright pink mitt. He pulled a foil-covered plate from the oven and settled it onto a placemat on the table. "The butter's here, and there's syrup." He indicated the items as if she might not recognize them. "Can I get you some coffee? Or... no. I get why you haven't been... Water then."

He filled a glass and set it beside the plate.

Carly was still standing in the doorway, dumbfounded at Braden's behavior. Was he suddenly worried about her because she was pregnant? Did he think her that fragile? Or was this his guilt in action?

Either way, she tried very hard not to let his kindness soften her feelings. She was right not to entertain romantic notions. She didn't know what Braden was thinking, but once his guilt faded and his worry proved unfounded, he'd be thankful for the distance she placed between them. "I'm not that hungry."

"You should eat though, right? I mean, not that I'm telling you what to do. I don't know anything about..." He blinked, his ice-blue eyes somehow both warm and fearful as he backed away. "I can leave, if you want me to. I thought we should talk, but if you'd rather—"

"It's fine." She sat in front of the plate, her rumbling stomach defying the lie she'd uttered seconds before. "We need to figure this out and tell Klein. The sooner we do that, the sooner we can go back to our own lives."

The look on his face shifted so quickly, she could hardly discern what she saw there. Maybe hurt. Maybe sadness. She had no idea what he was thinking. She'd once thought she knew Braden so well, but it seemed she didn't know him at all.

He didn't know her either.

They were practically strangers. Strangers with a past, but with no future.

"You can sit," she said.

He chose the chair across from her. "I really am sorry for the things I said. It never occurred to me that you were..." His eyes hardened, his lips tightened. "If Ian were still alive, I'd kill him myself."

Her heart thrilled at the protective remark. It wasn't true, though. If Ian were alive, Braden wouldn't know anything about what he'd done. And probably wouldn't care. "It's fine. I'm fine." Another untruth she didn't correct. She buttered her pancakes and added syrup and took a bite. They'd probably been delicious when Angel served them, but now they felt rubbery and tasted bland, despite the accouterments. One bite of sausage turned her stomach.

Braden said, "Honey, would you—?"

"Don't call me that." She looked up from her plate and tried to soften her expression, wondering what Braden saw there. "It's been fun, pretending you and I could be together again. But we both know it wouldn't work. I'm going to have another man's child. I'm not leaving the city. You have a job in Coventry. Let's not make this any harder than it'll already be."

"We can—"

"No. We can't."

She wouldn't let herself consider it. What was left of her broken and trampled heart would not survive another stomping.

His head dropped, and he rubbed the back of his neck.

She returned to her breakfast but couldn't force it down, despite her hunger. She stood, dumped the food, and snatched crackers from the cabinet Angel had showed them the day before.

Back at the table, she ate a few and sipped her water. "I looked at Lynch's construction company's website last night, but there are no photographs of employees there."

Braden looked up and leaned toward her. "I'm not willing to give up on us that easily."

"There is no *us*, Braden. There hasn't been for a long time."

He didn't lean back. Didn't move. Just held her gaze.

She told herself to look away but couldn't seem to make it happen.

His lips quirked. "That's not true. You know it as well as I do. There's always been an *us*. Since we were fifteen years old, there's been an *us*, and there always will be. You can pretend if it makes you feel better today, but—"

"I get to decide my life. Not you."

He blinked, sat back. "I know that. I'm just saying—"

"I've had enough of being controlled by men. Pete making me pay rent and do all the housework as if I'm a servant, not a member of the family. Ian telling me where to live, how to live. Telling me I belong to him. Threatening me. Hurting me, then telling me it was my fault."

Braden's back stiffened, but she wasn't finished.

"I never belonged to him. And I don't belong to you."

"I'm not Ian." The words were low and angry. "I would never hurt you. And I didn't mean it that way."

"Whatever you meant, you can keep your thoughts to yourself. You've made it very clear what you think of me, what kind of a person you think I am."

"I'm sorry for—"

"It's over, Braden. Just... let it go."

He turned to stare out the window at the overcast day. The

lake had a film of ice in the center. The landscape was stark and cold and lifeless.

He pushed back his chair, stood, and walked out of the kitchen.

Fine then. Apparently, he'd gotten the message.

Just like she'd wanted.

So why did she feel so... sad?

A moment later, he returned with his backpack and plopped it on the table. "I guess we should see if we can figure this out. You said you got a look at the guys in the rearview mirror?"

She tried to shift her thinking back to the more important issue. "Just a glance. I was so scared, I didn't think to take a closer look."

"Maybe it'll be enough. What about the guy going into Ian's townhouse? You must've..."

His words faded when she shook her head. "He wore a baseball cap. I didn't get a look at his face."

"That's okay. You saw the other two. That's a place to start." He took out his laptop and tapped the keyboard. "You checked the real estate development website."

"There aren't any pictures of employees on there, though."

"Maybe this one..." He angled it so she could see the screen. This site was all about Lynch, the candidate.

Carly studied the image on the home page. Richard Lynch had light brown hair cut short on the sides but a little longer on top. He had perfectly sculpted eyebrows over hazel eyes and a wide smile. He was attractive, but not overly so. Everything about him projected *trust me*.

Richard's arm was around his wife—brown hair, brown eyes, girl-next-door good looks. Their two darling children—a boy about seven years old in a golf shirt and khakis and a girl about five in a frilly dress—rounded out the photo. All they needed was a golden retriever and they'd make the perfect American family.

The rest of the page held Lynch's biography. No help there. She clicked through other pages. Photographs everywhere. Based on the captions, the images were of donors, people he'd worked with, other politicians, business owners, and local community activists.

Braden tapped a photograph on the screen. "There's Geoff."

She recognized him, though the skinny, geeky kid from high school had grown taller and filled out. He'd traded his black-rimmed glasses for stylish frames, his plaid button-downs for a designer suit. "Your old friend."

He shrugged. "We didn't hang out or anything. We took a lot of the same classes, but he was more straightlaced. A little geeky, really."

"They're the ones who'll run the world."

"True, that. Not that I was cool or anything."

She couldn't help the grin. "You were cool for a smart kid."

"So slightly less nerdy than Geoff."

"Slightly."

They continued clicking through the *Lynch for Congress* site. Near the bottom of one page, a photograph of a crowd of people caught her eye. They were in what looked like a warehouse, though long banquet-style tables filled the space. The people were crowded around Lynch, all smiling for the camera. They wore jeans and T-shirts emblazoned with the name of a Boston homeless shelter. The caption read, "Richard Lynch and his team didn't just raise money for the homeless, they served them lunch too."

It wasn't the posing people who caught Carly's eye, though.

A man stood behind and to the right, near the door. Obviously, he'd not planned to be in the photograph. He had too-long blond hair, a little scraggly, and was glaring at somebody off camera.

Acid filled Carly's empty stomach.

She tapped the screen. "Him. That was one of the guys I saw creeping up behind the truck yesterday."

Braden shifted the screen to better see the image. "You're sure?"

She closed her eyes, remembered the moment. She could picture him in the rearview, the determination in his expression. She opened her eyes. "That was him."

Braden took a screenshot and pasted it in an email to Ronnie. She watched as he typed.

*Can you figure out who this is? We think he's one of the guys who shot at Carly.* Braden added the URL for the website and sent it.

Braden sat back. "I didn't want to believe it."

Seriously? Braden had been quick to believe the worst about Carly, but about Lynch, a total stranger...

She swallowed the thought. It tasted bitter going down. "Maybe you should reach out to Geoff. Unless you think he'd have something to do with Ian's murder."

"I can't imagine. Of course, all of this feels unimaginable. But Geoff was idealistic to a fault."

"Now he's in politics," she said. "You suppose his ideals have lasted?"

Braden stared beyond her a minute, then shrugged. "Either way, why would I contact him? What would the endgame be?"

"Lynch needs to know we're putting it together, that the...the jig is almost up."

"The jig?" Braden's lips quirked at the corners.

She shrugged, fighting her own smile. Crazy how she could be so angry with Braden one minute, so comfortable with him the next.

That was the weird thing about love. True love didn't grip offenses tightly. True love held its palm open. Its heart.

Which was why she needed to get over it. Because her heart felt like an errant grape rolling around underfoot. Braden had already kicked it a couple of times. If she didn't stow it away, he was sure to squish it.

She tried to shove her heart back deep in her chest where it belonged. "Maybe if Lynch understands we're putting it together and passing along the information to the police, he'll back off, leave me alone."

"Why would he? He's already killed your... killed Ian."

"My what?"

Braden's Adam's apple bobbed. "Sorry. I don't mean…"

She sighed as that tender little grape shot across the floor.

"If Geoff hasn't changed his cell phone number," Braden continued quickly, "then I can get in touch with him."

"But the number would be on your phone, and we're trying not to turn that on."

He tapped his skull. "Freakish memory."

She rolled her eyes. The man never forgot anything. "What will you say? You can't just come out and accuse his boss of murder."

"No." He stared beyond her, then shrugged. "I don't know. I'll need to think about it. But it does seem like a good idea. I doubt Geoff is involved, but whether he is or he isn't, he seems like a safe avenue to communicate with Lynch."

An unread email popped up on Braden's screen. It was from Ronnie promising to get right on it.

They returned their attention to the candidate's website. She hadn't gotten as good a look at the second man creeping up on her the day before, but maybe an image would jar her memory.

Braden scrolled through snapshots of Lynch at various functions, fundraisers, and fancy events while Carly studied them.

Nothing interesting until…

"Stop."

Braden did, and Carly leaned closer to the screen.

Her blood ran cold.

She tapped the image of a thirty-something man standing beside Lynch.

Braden swore under his breath.

Nausea crept up Carly's throat.

"It's him," Braden said. "No doubt about it. That's the pervert who's dating your sister."

# CHAPTER TWENTY-THREE

Fighting fury, fighting to think straight, Braden took a screenshot of the man's image and forwarded it to Ronnie, along with the URL. Hopefully, Ronnie could ID the guy.

If not him, then maybe Geoff.

He composed an email to Detective Klein detailing all they'd learned and attaching the photographs. He received a response almost immediately.

*Got it. On it.*

Sure he was. Frustration had Braden slamming his laptop closed. He breathed a prayer for patience and peace and studied Carly.

She wasn't okay. Her skin had paled. She was trembling, inhaling sharp breaths.

He grabbed the seat of her chair on either side of her legs and shifted it so she was facing him. He took her hands. "Just breathe."

Carly's eyes were wide, terrified. "He's going to kill her."

"No. He's going to try to use her to get to you. But now we know—"

"I have to go." Carly pushed back her chair and stood, but Braden didn't relinquish his hold on her hands. "I have to—"

"Sit. And think. Getting yourself killed isn't going to help your sister."

"But—"

"If she suspects what's going on and you reveal yourself to them, will they have any reason to keep her alive?"

Carly blinked. "But I have to warn her."

"The less Sophia knows, the safer she'll be. Right?"

Slowly, Carly sat back down.

"At this point, she thinks she's found a new boyfriend. She has no idea this is about you. There's no reason to believe he's harmed her. There'd be nothing to be gained by harming her."

"I'm supposed to just... just ignore it?" Braden would have expected Carly to sound frantic, maybe hysterical. But her voice was flat, almost emotionless. Maybe she'd had as much as she could take.

"Of course not. We need to let Pete know, see if he'll get the girls out of the city."

"He wouldn't before. I mean, Dylan told Klein to tell him... I have no idea what they talked about. I should have called myself. I shouldn't have trusted Klein—"

"Let's don't do that. There's no reason to believe Pete would have listened to you. If you tell him what you've learned, he might do it now."

She closed her eyes, swallowed. Tears escaped between her eyelids. "If anything happens to her, it'll be my fault."

"None of this is your fault." Braden squeezed her hands. "Your pregnancy isn't your fault. Being at Ian's when those murderers showed up—not your fault. Your sister's behavior, taking up with a man twice her age..." He swallowed his frustration with the stupid girl, and his fear for her. "Not your fault."

Braden thought of the stepsisters he'd met when Carly's mom married Pete. Sophia had been twelve at the time, sweet and innocent and eager to impress. Even then she'd been pretty. The images Carly had shown him this week proved she'd learned to use her looks to her advantage.

Or, considering what those looks led to, perhaps to her disadvantage.

Not that her beauty or lack thereof would have made a difference in this case. The pervert had targeted Sophia to get to Carly.

And now, somehow, they had to figure out how to protect Sophia and keep Carly safe at the same time.

She gently pulled her hands away from his. "Pete's at work. I'll call him there."

"Hold on." He snatched his phone off the table. "Use mine. Actually, what's the number? I'll call and ask for him so nobody suspects it's you."

She rattled off the number, and he dialed. A woman answered.

"I need to speak with Peter Lancaster please."

"Just a sec," the woman said.

Braden offered what he hoped looked like a compassionate expression while he listened to the on-hold music. Then, "This is Pete Lancaster."

"Temper your reaction, please," Braden said. "We're trying to keep this quiet."

"What? Who is this?"

He handed Carly the phone.

"Pete, it's me."

Braden listened for the man's raised voice but heard nothing through the phone, proving Pete had indeed tempered his reaction. He wasn't surprised. Pete was a lousy father, but he wasn't stupid.

As Carly explained what they'd learned, Braden grabbed her phone from the table and, taking his laptop, wandered into the media room. He sat on the sofa and leaned forward, propping his elbows on his knees.

He prayed for direction and guidance, for wisdom and discernment. Because the deeper he got into this mess, the less he knew how to handle it.

Was contacting Geoff a good idea? Or would it only cause more trouble in the long run?

He tossed the question up in prayer. Maybe calling Geoff

would help. If nothing else, Braden couldn't figure out how it could hurt. Lynch already had Carly in his crosshairs, and probably Braden, if his goons had ID'd his pickup. Even if they hadn't connected Braden to Carly yet, it didn't matter. It wasn't as if he was going to abandon her to figure this out by herself. He was in this with Carly, and he'd stay in it with her until she was safe again.

God willing, safe in his arms.

He tried to rid his mind of the thought. *In Your arms, Lord. That's her safe place. But I wouldn't refuse the other, if You were to soften her toward me.*

*Assuming we survive.*

As he prayed, he waited for some warning, some shift in his thought process.

He got neither. In fact, the longer he prayed, the more confident he was that calling Geoff was the right move.

*All right, then. Guide me.*

He leaned back and dialed Geoff's cell from memory. He waited for the call to go to voice mail and rehearsed the message he'd leave. Who answered calls when they didn't recognize the number? But two rings in, the call connected.

"Geoffrey Stuart."

Braden launched himself off the couch. "Geoff, it's Braden Reilly."

If Geoff were in the know, Braden would've expected him to sound concerned or angry or even defensive, but his old acquaintance surprised him with a laugh. "Reilly, dude. What have you been up to? It's been a hot minute."

*A hot minute?* The serious, nerdy student Braden had known in high school had loosened up.

More to the point, Geoff sounded genuinely surprised to hear from him. Which lent credence to the idea that Braden's name hadn't come up in Geoff's presence. Maybe that meant the goons hadn't ID'd his truck. More likely, it meant Geoff wasn't involved in Lynch's illegal activities, which was what Braden had believed all along.

"You've been taking the R and D world by storm," Geoff said. "I read all about your artificial neuron last year."

"I was just one of the researchers on that project. I'm surprised you even knew I was involved."

"Oh, I keep up with my old rivals."

Braden laughed at that. "Rivals? You wish. I remember smoking you in the science fair. How many times in a row was it?"

"All of them." But Geoff admitted it good-naturedly. "You were the science and math star."

"You were the star of all our other classes."

"Some things never change." Geoff's amused tone shifted when he said, "I assume you're calling for a reason. I also assume you know I'm working for Richard Lynch's campaign. Since BNB's no longer in the state, I'm struggling to figure out what I can do for you."

The man really had kept abreast of Braden's activities. Or maybe he'd been keeping an eye on BNB after the trouble they'd had the previous year.

"I'm not calling about my company," Braden said. "It's about your boss."

"He's always willing to listen to future constituents, though with you in New Hampshire—"

"How much do you know about his real estate business?"

That garnered a pause. "I work for the campaign. I can get you a number for—"

"I know you're a man of ideals, Geoff. Despite the fact that you went into politics, you were always honest."

"I went into politics because we need honest people in Washington."

"And you think Lynch fits the bill?"

"I've never met a man with higher ideals."

"So you don't know about his real estate business?"

"Just that it's successful." Geoff sounded truly baffled. "That he's reviving rundown neighborhoods and providing livable housing in communities that desperately need it. Every one of his developments benefits the—"

"Spare me the campaign rhetoric. At what cost, those developments?"

"I don't know what you mean."

In the other room, Carly's voice rose in volume and pitch. And did he hear tears in her voice? He wanted to check on her, but this conversation took precedence. And anyway, she wouldn't welcome his comforting arms.

He walked into the hallway by the staircase, needing to focus. "Maybe you're ignorant of Lynch's business practices," Braden said. "Maybe you're not."

"Richard Lynch is an honest businessman."

"I hope you really believe that because I can't imagine the Geoff I knew would willingly work for a murderer."

Silence greeted that statement.

Braden waited it out.

Finally, Geoff said, "What are you talking about?" His voice was lower, nearly a whisper.

"Have you ever heard of Abecedarian Construction?"

"I've seen the name," Geoff said. "One of Lynch's donors owns it."

"And that is...?"

"Hold on."

Braden waited, listening to the background noise through the phone, trying not to eavesdrop on Carly's conversation in the other room. She sounded scared. He'd figure out why when he was finished. He paced down the hallway toward the front door.

Geoff called to someone, "Going for a coffee." A moment later, the sounds of traffic carried through the speaker before Geoff snapped, "What's going on?"

"Who owns Abecedarian?"

He exhaled loudly enough for Braden to pick up the frustration in the sound. "His name's Oscar Shaw. He's kind of a... Back in the day, I guess he wanted to run for office himself. But he doesn't have what it takes."

Braden hurried back to the media room and typed the man's name into the browser on his laptop, saying nothing and leaving silence he hoped Geoff would fill.

"His height is a problem," Geoff said, "but he could have overcome that. Dukakis did, right? If not for that stupid stunt in the tank..." He laughed, but it died fast.

Braden found the right Oscar Shaw, the Boston businessman and real estate developer, according to a website about Boston's who's who. The name of the holding company, Abecedarian, wasn't listed, but another company was, a remodeling company. Braden clicked the man's image. Forties, maybe fifties, balding, and the hair he had left was gray and clipped short. He had narrow shoulders and a slight paunch around the middle.

"The bigger issue," Geoff continued, "is that Oscar's got this voice... high for a man, and really annoying. It's unfair, but people tend to trust taller people more than short ones. And deeper voices more than high ones."

Something twinged in Braden's memory. Carly had said something about one of the guys who murdered Ian having a high voice.

"To tell you the truth," Geoff added, "Oscar doesn't have the character to be a politician. Or maybe I should say, to be an *honest* politician."

"Meaning?"

"Just a feeling. I don't like the guy. Never have. Your turn. Tell me what's going on."

"Before I do, I want you to know that I've already forwarded all this information to the police. It's just a matter of time before indictments are handed out. Adding more bodies to the count isn't going to help Lynch or anybody else."

"Bodies? Tell me you're being metaphorical."

"I'm trying to keep my friend alive here. If something happens to her, or to me, the police are going to know exactly who did it."

"And you're saying Oscar Shaw—"

"I'm saying Richard Lynch. He's the head of the real estate operation. He's the one responsible."

Geoff's voice sounded unnaturally calm when he said, "Explain."

So Braden did, pacing the long hallway past the staircase and library and music room to the front door and back, beginning with Ian's murder and ending with the information they'd uncovered about Abecedarian Construction and its connection to Richard M. Lynch Properties.

"We just discovered that one of Lynch's supporters, a thirty-something man, has been *dating*"—he infused the word with a heavy dose of sarcasm—"the eighteen-year-old sister of my friend."

"Whoa. Who?"

"Still trying to get a name. All I have right now is his photo."

"Email it to me." He gave his email address, and Braden memorized it.

"As soon as I hang up, I'll do that. We believe this man plans to use the girl to lure my friend out of hiding. And then kill her. And maybe her sister too."

When he was finished, he waited for a reaction.

A good thirty seconds, maybe even a minute, passed before Geoff said, "I guarantee Richard knows nothing about any of this."

"That's a heckuva guarantee, my friend."

"The man I know—"

"Maybe isn't the man you think you know." Braden leaned against the entry to the library, registering the scent of last night's fire, familiar and cozy and conjuring memories of Carly in his arms, memories that were not at all appropriate in that moment.

"Okay," Geoff said. "Okay, this is bad. This is—"

"Are you thinking about the election?" He pushed off the wall. "Because that's the least of your boss's worries."

"I'm paid to think about that. But... Yeah, you're right. Even if he doesn't know—"

"I don't care about any of that. I don't care about the election or the condo developments. I don't even care about putting anybody behind bars for Murphy's murder." Not at that moment, anyway, though he trusted justice would be done. "I'm not out for blood here. Ian Murphy was no friend of mine. I'm just trying to protect someone."

"Carly Garcia. That's who you're trying to protect, right? You two back together?"

How did Geoff…?

"My family's still in the neighborhood," he explained before Braden could ask. "I heard you and Carly broke up and she started seeing Murphy. Seemed to me she traded sirloin for day-old meatloaf."

"Sirloin. I'm flattered."

"Don't be. I'm filet mignon."

Despite the tension, or maybe because of it, Braden laughed. "You wish."

"So that's who we're talking about here, right? Carly?"

Braden's amusement faded. "She was there when they murdered him, Geoff. She heard the shot. They chased her. They went to her house and threatened her family. They tried to kill her." The words sent acid to his stomach. "So I don't care about your boss's political aspirations or the tax dollars his developments bring into a community or any of his so-called good deeds. These people are murderers, and I'm gonna bring them down. You can help me, or you can crash right along with them."

AFTER SECURING Geoff's promise to help in any way he could, Braden ended the phone call and returned to his laptop in the living room, trying not to overhear Carly's conversation.

She was standing at the window, looking out at the stark winter day, phone pressed to her ear. He guessed she was no longer talking with Pete. Her gentler tone told him one of her sisters was on the other end of the line. Sophia, he hoped.

He settled on a couch where he could keep his eye on her,

opened his computer, and found the screenshot of the man who'd shot at Carly and the one of the pervert dating Sophia. He forwarded both to Geoff. *Name and any other information you have on them, ASAP.*

Then, he sat back and tried to think through everything they'd learned.

Carly massaged her temples. Watching her, everything that had happened that week—that day—came back to him.

Braden had lived twenty-five years. They hadn't been particularly difficult years. They'd held poverty when he was young, heartache when Carly refused his proposal. For the most part, though, his life had been blessed. He'd been blessed.

Which was probably why he'd never before felt such rage. Though he was trying to tamp it down, to focus, it had been rising and gathering force ever since Carly had blurted those terrible words, the words that wouldn't stop replaying in Braden's head.

*He raped me.*

Not that Braden would have doubted her otherwise, but the way her skin flushed when she said it, from fear or pain or what, he didn't know, testified to the truth. No, he didn't doubt her. Wouldn't doubt her.

Somehow, he found himself in the position of trying to bring down the person who'd murdered the man who'd assaulted the woman Braden loved.

He didn't care about justice for Ian's murder. He should, but he didn't. As far as he was concerned, Ian had gotten what he deserved. Braden only wished he'd been the one to deliver the death blow.

None of that was helping him focus.

And articulating it to Carly wouldn't do any good.

He was somehow managing to think logically, but the rage was flowing like lava too close to the surface, threatening to break through and destroy everything in its path.

He closed his eyes, blocking his view of Carly, which wasn't helping anything.

*Someday, let her share the whole story with me. Someday, let her allow me to hold her close and comfort her and tell her she's precious and loved and infinitely valuable.*

No matter what Carly said, Braden wasn't going to accept her foolish notion that they couldn't be together. Unlike the man who'd proposed to her three years prior, the Braden he'd matured into understood that love meant sacrifice. If being with Carly meant sacrificing the job he loved, the home he'd built, the ambitions he'd entertained, so be it. For Carly, he'd sacrifice it all.

But today, he'd keep his thoughts on the subject to himself. And his hands. And his lips.

If they lived to see tomorrow, then he'd confess his feelings—and his hopes for their future.

In the kitchen, Carly slumped in the chair and set his phone on the table.

When he stepped through the door, she looked up with red eyes and wet cheeks.

He crouched beside her. "What is it?"

She sat up straight. "I told Pete about Sophia's new boyfriend, and he freaked out. I've never heard him like that before. Earlier in the week when I called, he was mad. But this was something different. He sounded terrified."

"Did he agree to get the girls out of town?"

"Yeah. He hung up to call his boss, and I called Sophia to let her know they needed to start packing."

That was good news. But nothing in Carly's countenance showed relief.

"I know I shouldn't have used your phone," she said, voice dull, almost numb, "but it was an emergency."

As if he cared about his stupid disposable cell. "What'd she say?"

"She didn't answer. So I called Laurie. She told me Sophia never came home last night."

"She had a sleepover at a friend's, or...?" Based on Carly's expression, that wasn't the case.

"Pete sometimes falls asleep watching TV. I guess he did that last night. When he woke up, he didn't bother to check to make sure Sophia was home. Didn't look this morning. Wouldn't have known if Laurie hadn't realized it and told me. I called him back and told him."

A fresh dose of rage heated Braden's blood. Along with a fresh dose of compassion for Sophia. No wonder the girl was desperate for a man to love her. Her own father couldn't be bothered. "How does God give a man like that daughters?"

"He used to be a good dad. When Mama died…"

Grief was no excuse to check out of parenting your kids.

"Does Laurie have any idea where she is?" Braden asked.

"Nobody's heard from her. I've been watching her on social media, but the last thing she posted was from last night."

Wherever Sophia was now, she was about to be used as bait.

And Carly was the fish they were trying to hook.

An hour later, Braden sat in the passenger seat of his pickup wishing they were driving anywhere else. But Carly, fearing for her sister, insisted they head back toward Boston. "To be close, in case Sophia needs me."

He knew what Carly meant. She'd risk her life to save her sister.

Braden would risk his life to save Carly. But he'd prefer to keep her away from danger altogether.

Since his crappy disposable cell was fairly useless—though at least its hotspot worked, sort of—he was checking his email on his computer, which he'd laid across his lap. His phone rang, connecting to the truck's Bluetooth. Dylan's name showed on the display, and Braden hit the button to answer. "You're on speaker with Carly."

"The camera picked up a suspicious sedan on your street,"

Dylan said. "Guy drove by your house more than once but never pulled in the driveway."

Carly cut a glance to Braden.

He said, "He didn't try to break in?"

"We got a few more inches of snow last night," Dylan explained. "With no tracks on the driveway, it's pretty obvious no one's there."

"You get a name from the plate?" Braden asked.

"Wiley Cuthrow."

"Did you say *Wiley*?" Braden asked.

"That's a new one to me too. I take it you've never heard of him."

"Nope."

Carly said, "Never."

"I did a quick search but haven't come up with much," Dylan said. "He's in his early twenties. Driver's license address shows an apartment in South Boston."

Not far from Dorchester. Could be a connection.

"That's a great start," Braden said. "I'll pass his name on to Klein."

"I did already. Talked to him this morning. I think he's coming around to believing your story, Carly."

"Took him long enough," she said.

"He said the detective he replaced left a pile of unfinished work. Klein's doing his best to wade through it. With all the funding cuts, they're understaffed and overworked."

"It's great they want to solve murders that already happened," Braden said, "but it'd sure be nice if they tried to prevent new ones."

"There's a good point." Dylan let that hang in the air, then said, "The cameras are still on at your place, so if anybody else cruises by, we'll know."

Braden thanked him and ended the call as he typed the name into his browser. The disposable phone's hotspot was slow as sludge, though. Seconds passed, and nothing came up.

His phone dinged with a text. "It's Ronnie. He's got some information for us. I'll just call him back."

Carly barely acknowledged the words. She'd insisted on driving so Braden could focus on the information they'd learned and what was still coming in, provided he kept an eye on her phone for social media messages. They figured eventually Sophie's pervert boyfriend would contact them.

Anybody else might think Carly was doing fine, but he could see the worry in the tightness of her eyes, the pallor of her skin. What Carly needed was a good night's sleep and a decent meal. She needed pampering and protecting.

She needed to feel safe. She needed to *be* safe.

He was doing his best to get her there.

He dialed, and Ronnie answered on the first ring. "Blond guy's name is Wiley Cuthrow. Lives in—"

"Southie." Braden explained the information he'd just received.

"Well, well, well, look who's playing Magnum, P.I."

"The Tom Selleck version," Braden said. "Obviously. Except that's all I know."

"Proving I'm the best in the biz. Cuthrow works for Abecedarian, which is owned by—"

"Oscar Shaw."

"What the frick, dude? Why are you paying me if you're gonna do all the legwork yourself?"

Braden chuckled, glancing at Carly. Her focus didn't shift from the road, and her expression remained unchanged.

He forced his gaze to the dashboard speaker. "This time, that's really all I know."

"Good. And don't think you're getting a discount on my rate."

"Never crossed my mind."

Ronnie *humphed*. "Shaw's a longtime political advisor. Used to be a Democrat but switched sides when Lynch threw his hat in the ring. Maybe his ideals changed."

"Maybe he never had any in the first place."

"Prob'ly that," Ronnie said. "Seemed Shaw had political aspirations himself, serving on a school board fifteen, twenty years ago, then in the state legislature."

*Commonwealth,* but Braden didn't correct him.

"He ran for other offices back in the day," Ronnie said, "but he couldn't seem to rise further. Eventually got voted out of that position."

Braden had forgotten to talk to Carly about her mention of a man with a high voice. Now, he said to Ronnie, "Any chance you could find an audio recording of him?"

Carly cut her gaze to Braden, eyebrows raised.

Ronnie said, "Sure. I'll see what I can find and send it to you. There's gotta be something out there. If not, I'll just call the guy, record the conversation. What are you thinking?"

"Carly didn't see the murderers' faces, but she heard their voices. Maybe—"

"Yeah," Ronnie said. "Good idea."

Carly said, "You think Shaw was one of them?"

"Just a hunch." Braden didn't want to tell her what Geoff had said. He'd rather she hear the voice without any suggestions coloring her reaction.

"Tell me how you figured out Shaw's name," Ronnie said.

Braden explained how he'd contacted Geoff. He was barely through the explanation before Ronnie swore. Loudly.

"You trying to get yourself killed?"

Braden kept his tone even, though his heart pounded. "They're already trying to kill us. How could it hurt?" He feared Ronnie would explain exactly how. Had calling Geoff been a tactical error?

"Now they know for sure who you are and that you're on to them."

"They already did. Drove by my house. That's how I got Wiley's name."

"Still, you've tipped 'em off. They're prob'ly shredding evidence as we speak."

"Only if Geoff told Lynch, which he swore he wouldn't."

"You really think that weaselly kid has an ounce of courage in him?"

Braden's stomach clenched, but he said, "We're not in high school anymore, Ronnie. Geoff has courage." Braden hoped, prayed, he was right about his old acquaintance. "More than that, he has convictions."

Ronnie's *pfft* expressed how highly he valued those.

"It's done." Braden wouldn't regret his actions, not when it was too late to change them. "Move on."

"You told Klein all this stuff?"

"Emailed him before we left with all the information and asked him to call me. He hasn't yet."

"Sounds like you're in a car. Where you headed?"

He glanced at Carly, but she didn't take her gaze off the road. He said, "South," and left it at that.

"Any chance you'll be near Londonderry?"

Braden checked their location. They were north of Manchester on I-93. "We'll drive through in about twenty minutes."

"You asked me to talk to the owner of that restaurant that burned, Mama Mia's. Mariana something."

"Aquino," Braden said.

"Yeah. Her. She relocated up there, opened a café. Figured you guys could stop by, talk to her yourself."

For the first time during their ride, Carly reacted, shaking her head. She was desperate to get back to Dorchester as soon as possible.

He was desperate to keep her away as long as he could. "We'll do it. Send the address."

# CHAPTER TWENTY-FOUR

"This is pointless." When Braden didn't respond, Carly glared at him. Not that it did any good, since he was focused on the map on his phone.

"Take a left there, before the light." He pointed, and she did what he said.

They'd been so close to Massachusetts when he'd directed her off the highway and into this little suburban town—just ten, maybe twelve miles north of the border. Everything looked new here in Londonderry, at least compared to her neighborhood. The buildings, the roads, the stoplights. Even the cars looked newer, all despite the sign that claimed the town had been established three hundred years ago.

Carly weaved through the parking lot. "Mariana's not going to tell us anything we haven't already learned."

She saw the café. Unlike the old building that housed Mama Mia's back in Dorchester, this restaurant was tucked between a fabric shop and a travel agency in a shiny new strip mall. Plenty of parking, plenty of space. There was a little covered outdoor area where Carly assumed people sat in the warmer months, though it was deserted in February.

"We don't know what Mariana knows." Braden pointed to a spot. "It won't hurt to talk to her."

Carly wanted to drive right by it and get back on the road, but conceding that she might not be thinking clearly, she swung into a parking space.

When she turned off the car, Braden took her hand. "I know you're frightened for Sophia."

The thin veneer of anger slipped, and tears filled her eyes. "She's just a kid. I know she's been making stupid decisions. I know she shouldn't have taken up with that guy to begin with. But she's a child. Her mom abandoned her. She was just starting to trust my mom when she died, and Pete doesn't bother to take care of her. She has nobody but her sisters and me."

Braden's grip firmed, and Carly held on tight. Everything was falling to pieces. Her family. Her future. Braden seemed like her only link to sanity. She shouldn't depend on him, but if she let him go, she feared she might crumble.

"We can be in the city in an hour," he said. "Once we get there, we'll have nowhere to go and nothing to do until they contact us. If they contact us. This stop isn't going to hurt anything. And it might give us insight we don't have."

She pulled in a deep breath, blew it out, and made herself hear what Braden was saying. Maybe he was right.

He must've seen the agreement on her face because he released her hand and climbed out of the truck.

A moment later, her door opened. She didn't need his help out, but she accepted it anyway.

And she shouldn't have stepped into the arms he opened, but she accepted the hug too.

She gripped his jacket in her fists and leaned into his chest, wanting nothing more than to stay there, in that safe spot, for the rest of the day. Or her life.

As much as she told herself to, she couldn't banish that thought.

"Father," Braden said, "we need You like we've never needed You before. Lead us now, in this conversation. Lead us beyond it. Give us wisdom. Open Klein's eyes to what's going on. Open all of our eyes. Pull Sophia under the shelter of Your wings. Let no harm come to her." He settled his cheek against Carly's head and rubbed her back. "And please, protect this precious woman and her precious child. Please..." That word hitched, and Braden didn't continue for a long time. Finally, he said, "We trust You, Jesus. With Sophia, with Carly, with her child, we trust You to guide and protect us."

Carly's tears soaked Braden's jacket, but she couldn't temper them.

This man. Oh, this man. If only things could be different.

It was possible things could be different. It was possible...

*Lord, if we survive...*

No. She would trust like Braden trusted.

*When we survive, Lord, lead us forward. If You want Braden and me to be together, then...* The thought of it filled and expanded in her heart. Maybe, maybe it could work. *But You're going to have to do it. You're going to have to work it all out. Without You, we'll just screw it up.*

Not the most articulate prayer, but God knew her heart.

He knew it all.

Braden held her another moment before he backed away.

Wiping her tears on the sleeve of her jacket, she walked beside him to the café's entrance.

The scents hit her first. The decor was completely different from the place in Dorchester—pale gray walls with pretty landscapes and fancy knickknacks on display shelves, shiny round tables surrounded by upholstered chairs. But the scents took her right back to her first job. Huevos rancheros, burritos with eggs and chorizo sausage, chilaquiles and, of course, typical American breakfast and lunch fare. Mariana had changed locations, but it seemed she hadn't changed the menu.

A twenty-something server said, "Grab any table you like."

"Actually," Braden said, "we're here to see Mariana. Is she here?"

"I'll get her." The woman disappeared through a swinging door. A moment later, Mariana exited the same door. Her long brown-black hair was pulled back in a ponytail that swung nearly to her ample waist. A white apron that would probably meet at Carly's backbone barely covered the front of Maria's generous girth. She'd aged more than Carly would've expected, considering it had been less than ten years since she'd seen the older woman. She had laugh lines fanning out from her eyes and framing her mouth, which spread into a smile when she saw who waited at the door.

"*Amiguita.*" Mariana's arms opened.

Carly stepped into them, reveling in the nickname. *Little friend.* Mariana had called Carly that the whole time she worked for her.

"What are you doing here?" She spoke excellent English, but the Spanish accent held on despite the years she'd been in the States.

Carly wasn't ready to answer that question. She wasn't ready for the hug to end. Just like with Braden, she reveled in the closeness.

But Mariana stepped back, surveyed Carly tip to toe, and then focused on Braden. "I remember you. You're the old boyfriend, no? Are you the new boyfriend as well?" Her eyes twinkled with the question.

"I'm working on it." He shot Carly a wink.

She looked away, but not before his words penetrated.

Was he serious or just trying to charm information out of Mariana?

Before either of them could respond, Braden said, "Is there somewhere we could talk? We have some questions about the fire."

The kindness in Mariana's expression dissipated like steam from the coffee carafes. "What about it?"

Braden stepped in and lowered his voice. "Let's go somewhere private."

She swiveled and marched through the restaurant.

Braden held out his arm, and Carly followed Mariana through the kitchen, past the cooks, who barely looked up from their work, and into a cluttered room with just enough space for a desk and chairs.

Mariana rounded to the far side but didn't sit.

Behind Carly, Braden stepped in and closed the door.

"It was just a fire," Mariana said. "An accident."

Braden stood beside Carly, the desk separating them from her now defensive old friend. He said, "We know about the protection money you were paying."

"Ah." Her lips quirked at the corners. "I hope Ian isn't in too much trouble. He tried to make good on his promises, but..." She focused on Carly. "You knew nothing, yes? When he came to me... I knew you two had been together. I hated to think you were involved. He swore you weren't. That you had no idea where he made his money."

Carly was struggling to take in everything Mariana had said. "You knew it was Ian all along?"

"Not all along. After the dry cleaner down the street was smashed up, Ian came to me. He told me he was trying to figure out what was going on and asked for my help."

"Had you already quit paying him?"

"*Sí.* Months before, but he didn't hurt me or my business. It was always only threats." Lips pursed, she shook her head. "That boy getting rich off the backs of his neighbors. But in the end, he was trying to figure out who was behind all the crime. He was trying to help. Are you working with him now?"

Carly cut a glance at Braden, who was watching Mariana with narrowed eyes. "I'm sorry to tell you this," she said. "Ian was murdered this week."

Maria's eyes widened? "No. Who... What happened?"

Braden said, "That's what we're trying to figure out. We think it was related to the crimes."

"That construction company." Mariana said the words with complete confidence, no hesitation. "They got what they wanted after the fire and all the rest."

"Abecedarian?"

Her eyes widened as if she were surprised he knew the name. "They were behind it, not that anybody cared."

"Did they threaten you?"

She shrugged her sturdy shoulders. "Not in so many words. About once a week, a man would come and offer to buy the building. He was not the owner, I think. Just a punk in a suit."

Braden took out his phone and tapped the screen, then turned it to face Mariana. "Is that the man?"

Her nod confirmed it.

"Wiley Cuthrow."

"Appropriate name," she said. "Over and over for months, I refused to sell. They were arm-stronging me and the other businesses on the block."

Strong-arming, but neither Carly nor Braden corrected her.

"My family, they put up with too much of powerful people hurting the weak for profit. We thought America would be different. The other owners and I got together and decided to stand up to them. Then the trouble started. First, it was little. Broken pipes, break-ins. Then one landlord was beaten up badly. He caved, sold his place, and kicked out the businesses renting from him. Another, his family was in a hit-and-run. His child landed in the hospital on one of those"—she tapped her chest—"machines that makes you breathe. He survived but..." Her lips flattened into a grimace. "That man sold. One by one, all of them sold. I was ready to give in myself—what was the point in holding out? And then..."

The fire, but she didn't speak the words.

"Did you report the threats to the police?" Braden asked.

"Bah." Her hands flew up as if to toss the question away. "They did nothing. They had one of their cars patrol the area a couple of times a night, as if that would stop anyone."

"After the fire, though," Braden pressed, "did they investigate?"

"They said so, yes. The *policía* in charge, he explained it all away, said the crimes weren't connected. One fire, one assault, one hit-and-run. There were break-ins, vandalism. All reported to different departments. The one in charge, he never believed us. Or..." She crossed thick arms. "I think America is not so different from my country. I think the company paid him better than the taxpayers, no?"

Carly looked at Braden, whose lips were pressed in a white line. He said, "I'm sorry that happened to you and your friends. What was his name?"

"O'Malley. Detective Aaron O'Malley. I heard he was transferred into homicide not long after all that happened. A reward for the incompetent."

"Or the crooked," Braden said.

"Perhaps crooked, yes." Her eyes narrowed and focused on Carly. "You shouldn't be asking these questions. If they want your property, just sell and get out." She looked around her office, and her lips shifted into a grin. "This place is good, Londonderry. The people are nice. My kids are happy. We have a condo of our own with four bedrooms. Four! You should come here. I have a job for you always."

Carly reached across the desk and took her old friend's hand. "Thank you. I appreciate that."

But the older woman's smile faded. She leaned forward, squeezing Carly's fingers. "Trust me. No good comes from these questions. You can't fight these people. If they are threatening you, just go away and don't look back."

Carly hurried through saying good-bye to her friend, promising to keep in touch. She rushed outside the restaurant, stepped onto a grassy area out of sight of the diners beyond the windows, and vomited.

Braden held her braid back, murmuring kind words while she expelled her paltry breakfast.

Ian.

She didn't want to think about Ian, but he'd sidled up in her memories and leaned against the wall of her mind, arms crossed, smirk in place.

The man she'd thought she loved. The man who'd raped her. The man who'd also tried to protect the very people he'd been extorting.

Since that night two months before, she'd thought of him as evil, only evil.

But after what Mariana said, knowing that Ian died not because he was trying to protect his income but because he was trying to protect his neighbors...

There'd been virtue there. A trace, nothing more. But maybe, someday, if given the chance, Ian would have come to know the Lord. Maybe, he'd have been saved and redeemed.

If he hadn't been murdered.

She wanted to hate him. It was easier to hate him after all he'd done to her.

But other memories came to mind. His kindness, when he wanted to show it. His generosity. She thought of his smile, his laugh.

He could have been so much more than he'd become.

She hated that she grieved him. He didn't deserve her grief. He didn't deserve a single mention in her thoughts. But... but. He'd been created in love and crafted by the Lord's hand.

And he was gone, all hope extinguished on that cold cement floor in a building that smelled like machine oil and gasoline and now, death.

Stomach empty, she stood and stepped back, bumping into Braden.

"I got you." His words were low and gentle. "What can I do? What do you need?"

She leaned against him, allowed him to support her while she caught her breath and tried to process what she was feeling. It was too much. It was all too much.

"Food, I think," he guessed. "Should we go back inside? We can eat here."

She shook her head. "The smells. I need something less...fragrant."

"There were a couple of fast-food places. We passed a Dunkin' Donuts."

"Yeah. Okay."

That morning, she'd insisted on driving, telling him she wanted him to continue the work he'd begun, putting together the information they'd received. Truth was, she'd driven because she'd needed to *do* something, even if only follow a map and stay within the lines on the road.

But now, she didn't think she could even manage that and didn't argue when Braden helped her into the passenger seat.

Ten minutes later, they found a parking spot on the far side of the donut shop's lot facing away from the busy road and into the thick forest. She nibbled her bagel sandwich and sipped her Sprite and prayed her stomach would settle. Beside her, Braden ate his lunch. Every time she looked his way, his gaze, filled with concern and care, was on her.

When she'd finished half, she folded the sandwich back in its wrapper.

"You're full?"

"I need to let it settle."

He gathered the trash and jogged to the garbage can. Rather than come right back, he took out his phone and dialed.

She watched him talk. She should be curious, but she didn't have it in her. She was wrung out.

Less than a minute later, he jogged back to the truck and opened the door, letting in the cool air. "Do you want to drive?"

She shook her head. "I don't think I can. Who'd you call?"

"Klein." He climbed in but didn't shift gears. "I left him a message." He faced her, concern on his face. "I should have known Ian wasn't all bad. You wouldn't have been attracted to him if he had been."

Ian. Of course Braden knew where her thoughts were focused.

Earlier that day, she'd concluded that Braden didn't know her at all, nor she him. What a liar she was.

The worst lies she'd ever fallen for were the ones she'd told herself. Or maybe... Her old roommate had told her once that Carly had an enemy that whispered deceptive words into her heart, that she'd need to learn to differentiate his voice from her own.

The deceiver had been busy that morning.

He'd been busy for months, years, in Carly's life. What other lies did she believe?

Braden's fingers trailed down her arm until their palms connected. He held her hand and squeezed gently. "You with me?"

"I'm sorry. I'm just... it's been a long day already."

"I'm afraid it's just getting started," he said. "Do you want to talk about it? Him?"

"It was easier to think of him as a monster."

Braden's lips parted, then sealed shut. After a minute, he said, "I'm sure."

She wondered what he was thinking and not saying. And then, she knew. She voiced what he wanted to say. "He was a monster."

Braden nodded but said nothing.

"But he wasn't *only* a monster."

Braden didn't respond, didn't move.

"I guess Ian was like the rest of us, to a degree." She was trying to figure out how to articulate what she was thinking. "Some good, some bad. He let the bad win too often. He let himself be motivated by greed. He always wanted more—more than he could earn, more than he could handle. Money, liquor."

"More than he deserved," Braden added. "You."

She gazed into the woods. She wasn't sure she'd been *more* when she and Ian were together. Lost, desperate, looking to fill her own emptiness with all the wrong things. She'd been just as messy and ugly as he. But God had rescued her. He'd put someone in her life to tell her the truth. He'd pulled her out of the pit she'd dug for herself. He'd redeemed her.

And then Ian had sought to yank her right back into the filth. He'd tried to charm her and, when that didn't work, he'd forced his way into her bed.

Motivated by greed and lust? Probably. Motivated by the enemy whispering in his ear?

Definitely.

"Carly?"

She turned back to Braden. "I'm sorry. I'm just..." She shook her head. "I never loved him, not like...you. But we were together for a while."

"You haven't had a lot of time to process what happened. I understand that."

"Even after what he did to me? I should hate him."

"You do. Like you said, good and bad. Love and hate. These things somehow all exist at the same time, in the same space." He shifted her hand so the back was facing up and traced the little veins beneath the skin. "This is just a hand. You use it a million times a day for everything from scratching your nose to gripping a sandwich to... to stroking a baby's tender skin. And yet, this one small part of your body is made up of twenty-seven bones, thirty-four muscles, and two major arteries. The skin covering it has countless cells serving various purposes, each one an organism that grows and reproduces and dies." Gently, he lifted her wrist and kissed her palm, sending tingles up her arm and throughout her body. "Those little nerves pick up the lightest touch."

His brief smile told her he knew exactly what he'd done as he set their hands on the console between them. "It's just a hand, one tiny little part of you, but its complexity is astounding." He gazed into her eyes. "That's basic anatomy. As complex as it is, it's nothing compared with your mind, your soul, your spirit. What you're feeling... It's okay. It's okay to not know how to feel about a man you once cared for, a man who hurt you, a man who died trying to do the right thing. You can feel all that. You can hate him and love his child. You can grieve him and care for me. It's okay."

Tears burned her eyes. She didn't know what to say and didn't think she'd be able to force words past her swollen throat if she did.

Braden seemed to understand. He kept her hand in his but faced forward while she processed all he'd said, all she was feeling.

She'd hated Ian. And before that, she'd cared for him. And he was gone. But this man beside her... What she felt for Braden was so far beyond anything she'd ever felt for Ian. Yes, she'd need to process his death. Not that she grieved him, but she grieved the man he could have been, and her own foolish choices that led her to him. She'd probably see Ian in her child. Because she carried that part of him, she'd never be able to forget him completely.

But she didn't have to let Ian's memory get in the way of her future. Ian was gone, his soul in the hands of the God who loved him.

Braden was here—a good man, a godly man, who cared for her and always had.

She lifted his hand and kissed his knuckles. "Thank you."

He turned her way. "I suppose I can't talk you into going back to Donovan and Angel's?"

She shook her head. "I would, but—"

"Sophia."

"Sophia."

He studied her through narrowed eyes. "You know I'm not going to let you put yourself in danger for her sake."

"She's just a kid. She doesn't deserve any of this."

Very gently, Braden shifted their hands and settled hers on her abdomen. "I know you feel protective of your stepsister. But don't tell me you don't feel protective of this little one."

She looked down at their hands, linked there.

"Others can protect Sophia," he said. "Only you can protect this one. God gave him—"

"Her, I think."

Braden smiled as if he liked the thought of it, but the expression didn't last. "Her, then. God gave her to you. She's the one He's called you to protect. We will do everything we can to help the police rescue Sophia, but ultimately, Sophia is Pete's responsibility. She's her own responsibility. She's God's. She's not yours."

Braden's words were so similar to what he'd said to Carly when she'd refused his proposal three years before. Though he hadn't spoken as gently or kindly at that time, he'd voiced the same ideas. Her stepsisters were not her responsibility. No matter the promise she'd made to her mother.

As if hearing her thoughts, he added, "If your mother were here, who would she want you to protect? Sophia, or her grandchild?"

"I know you're right. But Sophia—"

"Is in God's hands. We'll do what we can, but you're not putting yourself in danger. Okay?"

She closed her eyes, imagined releasing Sophia into the Lord's care. His arms, larger, stronger, wrapped around Carly's sister. *She's Yours. Protect her. Protect all of them.*

Peace like she hadn't felt since before her mother's eyes closed for the last time filled her heart. Whatever happened, God was with them.

# CHAPTER TWENTY-FIVE

Twenty minutes had passed since Braden had gotten them back onto the road when his phone rang. He recognized the number on the display and hit the button to connect. "You're on with Carly and me."

"Where are you two?" Detective Klein's deep voice was too loud in the small cab.

Braden lowered the volume a little. "We just passed into Massachusetts on our way back to the city."

"I want you to come here, BPD headquarters. I need to get a full accounting of everything that's happened this week, beginning Monday morning."

Braden glanced at Carly, whose eyebrows lifted in surprise.

"Do you believe me?" she asked.

The man's sigh was audible. "I got a call from Murphy's father this morning. He admitted that he didn't actually speak to Ian this week, just got text messages from him. He's tried to call a few times but said Ian never picks up. I guess they weren't close, so that's not unusual, but when he left the messages and Ian didn't call back... He admitted it was possible something had happened to his son."

Another blue-star father. Braden thanked God for the man who'd raised him.

"Took him long enough," Carly said.

"We used his call and all the information you've given us as evidence for a judge, who issued a search warrant for both Ian's home and place of business. Went to his house this morning. It had been tossed. The place was a wreck. If anything was there, it's long gone. Machine shop looked about the same. Someone searched both thoroughly."

"Good thing we got the notebooks." Braden managed to keep smugness out of his voice. Surprising, considering how Klein had lectured them about that.

Of course, they'd almost been killed getting those notebooks.

"I'm gonna need those ASAP," Klein said. "We've been studying the pics you sent of them, but we'll need the originals to build a case."

Braden had left them in his room at the B and B with a note on top for Angel and Donovan that directed them to send the notebooks to Klein if anything should happen to Braden and Carly. "We can get them to you."

Carly asked, "At the machine shop, did you find any evidence—?"

"Blood spatters," Klein said. "Just a couple of drops the killers must've missed when they cleaned up. Forensics is there now."

The display showed another call coming in. Braden rejected it. He'd call Ronnie back. "Guess it's a problem you didn't believe Carly when she first told you about the murder." This time, Braden couldn't keep his anger out of his voice. "Maybe if you had—"

"Water over the dam," Klein said. "Let's not rehash everything we've done wrong."

"That would take all day," Braden said.

Rather than get irritated, Klein chuckled. "Not disagreeing, son." The amusement was gone when he said, "You said in your message that you wanted to talk about O'Malley. Where'd you get his name?"

"He was the detective the business owners in Dorchester reported all the crimes to. We spoke to one of them today. They tried to convince him they were being targeted, but he blew them off, claimed the incidents were unrelated."

Klein didn't say anything for a few seconds. Then, "He's the guy I replaced. He's the reason..." His words faded. Then, "I can't say much. There's an internal investigation, which is probably going to turn into more. The problem is, O'Malley's gone. He quit out of the blue Monday. I got sent to homicide because they were desperate. I've been playing catch-up all week. I've tried to contact him a few times this week, but he's not answering. After I got your call, I went over to his house. No answer. Car's gone. For-sale sign in the yard. I went to see his ex. She hasn't heard from him either."

"He took off right after the murder." Carly's words were hurled, high-pitched and angry. "He knew. He was involved."

"Maybe," Klein said. "Maybe not. Either way—"

"Either way nothing." Braden angled off the highway, hands shaking with rage. He needed to find a place to stop for this conversation. "A detective in your department was working with crooks and killers."

"We'll get to the bottom of it." Unlike Braden and Carly, Klein remained unflappable. "Meanwhile, we need those notebooks. And Carly, we need a statement from you."

"What about Sophia?" she asked. "Have you had any luck finding her?"

"We're on the lookout. We spoke to the man you think she's with."

"Name?" Braden parked in a gas station parking lot.

"Preston Shaw."

Carly's eyes widened. "Wait... Shaw, as in—?"

"He's Oscar Shaw's nephew. He's a lobbyist here in the city, doing a lot of work for the construction industry. We called him this morning, and he came right down. Admitted he'd taken Sophia on a few dates but said he hasn't seen her since he dropped her off at home last night."

"That's a lie," Carly said.

"Yeah." Klein seemed as frustrated as she. "But we have no

evidence a crime's been committed. We're watching him. Hopefully, he'll lead us to your sister."

"What do we do in the meantime?" Carly asked.

"Come in, give your statement, get us those notebooks, and then let us do our jobs."

"We need to find Sophia now," Carly said. "She needs—"

"Young lady." Klein's words brooked no argument. "I understand you love your sister. The best thing you can do for her is trust the department to handle this."

Braden considered the fact that someone in that same department had been involved with the criminals from the start, but he didn't say that. He was one hundred percent on Klein's side in this one.

Carly wasn't convinced. "Because you've done such a good job *handling* it so far."

Klein didn't rise to her bait but continued in his calm voice. "We figure one of the Shaw men will contact you. If that happens, we'll put together a team to get your sister back. At this point, recovering Sophia is our first priority. We've got a whole team looking for her. They're going through her social media accounts, talking to her friends. Your father... stepfather, I mean, and stepsisters are with one of our detectives right now."

Carly's eyebrows hiked, and she glanced at Braden. "They're there?"

"Of course. Where else would they be?" Klein sounded genuinely perplexed. "Look, Carly. I know the department's been slow to the party on this one, but we're definitely in the ballroom now."

She said nothing. Braden took her hand but didn't interject. Instead, he prayed she'd agree to do what Klein asked, to go to the police department and wait it out with the rest of her family.

That she'd trust the police, trust the Lord, with her sister. That, for once, she'd put her own safety first.

Klein said, "You hear what I'm saying, Carly? Are you with me?"

It was clear from the look on her face that she wasn't comfortable turning over her sister's care to Klein or anybody else. Her hands went to her abdomen and held there. After a minute, she said, "Okay. We're on our way."

Klein ended the call, and the truck's cab filled with silence.

Sophia wasn't out of danger, but maybe Carly was. Braden didn't give voice to the relief that filled him.

He prayed Sophia would be rescued. He prayed that, whether Sophia was or wasn't returned to her father and sisters, Carly would be safe.

Braden was reaching for the gear shift when Carly stopped him with a hand on his forearm. "As long as we're here, I'm going to run in and use the bathroom."

Call him paranoid, but he walked her inside. He wasn't comfortable letting her out of his sight for even a minute. As she disappeared into the restroom, he returned the call that had come in earlier.

Ronnie said, "Got a recording of Shaw's voice."

"Carly's not with me. I can call you back—"

"Also got the scoop on your friend Andrew."

Braden should let it go. Maybe the Lord was leading him to give up BNB altogether and move back to the city to be closer to Carly. But even as he had the thought, it didn't feel right. God had led him to Jacqui's company, led him to move to New Hampshire.

He didn't know what God had planned, but whatever his future held, Braden wanted to protect BNB.

And, admittedly, his own professional aspirations. Now that Carly was back in his life, expecting a baby no less, he needed security more than ever.

"What did you learn?"

"I talked to the prosecutor, the one who ultimately recommended he be released from prison. He told me Andrew was just twenty, working his way through college, when he got arrested. He'd confided to his supervisor that he'd gotten himself in trouble betting on sports and owed his bookie a couple grand. A lot for a kid barely scraping by."

Braden had assumed Andrew was more like Jacqui than himself, that he'd come from wealth. But that didn't seem to be the case. If not for the scholarships, Braden would have been in a similar situation. Except for the gambling—that had never been one of his vices.

Ronnie continued. "His supervisor told him he had a side job for him *adjusting* some of the numbers in their bookkeeping records. Andrew swears he didn't understand what he was doing and trusted his boss, though why he thought he'd get paid so much for a weekend of work, I got no idea."

"So you're saying the adjustments he was making enabled the supervisor to steal from their employer?"

"Exactly. And since Andrew kept three grand, he was considered an accomplice. Nobody believed a guy studying to be a doctor was dumb enough not to understand those books."

Braden scoffed. "They've obviously never met my boss. The woman's brilliant but couldn't correct a balance sheet on a bet."

"Yeah. It's a whole different ballgame."

"He was in medical school?"

"Premed at the time," Ronnie said. "I guess going to prison got him kicked out of the program."

Carly stepped out of the bathroom, saw that Braden was on the phone, and headed for the drink cooler. He tracked her progress but didn't move closer. "Why was he released from prison?"

"The owner of the company had second thoughts. He went to the prosecutor and asked for leniency. Between that and the supervisor's admission that he lied to Andrew—"

"And the prosecutor, he believes Andrew's story?"

"I guess he always did, only prosecuted because the owner and the DA are friends, and the DA *strongly encouraged* him to prosecute both of 'em."

"Does that happen often, people's records being expunged?"

"It's rare, but I'm guessing it goes back to that friendship thing. Owner, DA, judge—they probably all belong to the same club, sip martinis at lunchtime or whatever the heck rich people do. They were probably all self-congratulatory for not ruining the kid's life for being stupid."

On the far side of the gas station, Carly lifted a bottle of water from the cooler and looked at him with raised eyebrows.

He nodded, and she reached for a second, then moved behind a tall display, out of his view.

Braden headed her way, slowed by a bunch of kids filling cups with slushy drinks at the spigots.

"So that's the story," Ronnie said.

He made it to the far side of the tall display, but Carly was gone.

"You there?" Ronnie asked.

"Yeah. Thanks for the info. Can you hold on about two minutes?" He spun, searching. "We're almost finished here, and you can play that recording for Carly."

"Nah. I'll text you the link."

Braden ended the call and shoved his phone into his jacket pocket, heart pounding.

How had he lost her in such a small store?

He hadn't heard the exterior door open—the bells above would have alerted him. But he'd been distracted. Maybe he'd missed the sound. Was she out there?

He walked across the front of the small station, peering down every aisle, ready to call the police and report her missing.

And then she stepped from behind an end cap and spotted him. She lifted a small bag of peanuts as he walked her direction. "You want some?"

She was fine. Perfectly fine. He forced a calm tone. "I'm good. Thanks, though."

He stayed with her in line, paid for their drinks and her

peanuts, despite her objection, thanking God that nothing had happened to her.

He couldn't lose her now. He'd lived without her for three years, but he'd only been living half a life. Now that Carly was back, he wasn't going to let her go.

Could he have her and the job? Would she consider New Hampshire?

He didn't want to lose the position he'd worked so hard for.

But Andrew wasn't a thief. Did he have a gambling problem? Perhaps. He certainly had at one point. Had he lied on his job application? Technically, maybe, if he said he'd never been convicted of a felony, because he *had* been convicted.

If Braden chose, he could present only part of the evidence and let Andrew explain himself. Jacqui trusted Braden enough that she might just let Andrew go, if Braden framed it right. The thought of it didn't sit right. The man had been stupid, and he'd paid a heavy toll already for that stupidity.

Braden wasn't in any position to make a decision that day. He'd think on it, pray on it, and deal with it when Carly was safe.

They were settled in the truck—her in the driver's seat again—when she asked, "That was Ronnie on the phone?" At his nod, she said, "I figured, since you waited until you were alone to call him back. Are you going to tell me what that's about?"

"He sent us a link to hear Oscar Shaw's voice."

"And?"

"What do you mean?" Guilt pricked his conscience. He knew exactly what she meant.

"So... you're not going to tell me."

He opened his mouth to argue, then shut it again.

The fact that he didn't want to tell Carly what he'd been up to regarding his coworker was probably all the answer he needed. He was ashamed of what he'd done.

Her eyebrows hiked.

"Sorry."

"Whatever."

"It has nothing to do with you."

She twisted the cap off her water. Sipped. "Go ahead then."

He must've looked confused because she added, "Play the recording."

Right. He clicked on the link Ronnie had sent, and a voice came through the truck's speaker. The voice was high enough to belong to a woman, not pretty but scratchy, almost hollow-sounding.

They were only seconds into it when the color drained from Carly's face. Her jaw dropped, and she leaned away from the speaker as if the man were standing right there.

Braden clicked to stop it and dialed.

Klein answered on the second ring. "You almost here?"

"Map says we'll be there in a half hour or so. Carly just heard a recording of Oscar Shaw's voice." He looked at her, inviting her to jump in.

"It was definitely him." She swallowed hard. "He was the man in charge, the man who killed Ian."

The detective's deep sigh was followed by, "I wish you'd let us direct this investigation. We have policies and procedures for—"

"Until today," Braden snapped, "you haven't done a"—he swallowed the curse word that tried to come out—"single thing. So don't lecture us. We're trying to keep Carly alive here."

As always, Klein's voice was calm when he responded. "I understand how you feel."

Braden didn't want the man's *understanding*. He wanted him to do his job. If Braden could, he'd reach through the phone and punch the guy. "Are you going to arrest him?"

"We're building a case. And we're watching him, hoping he'll—"

"He's a murderer. On the loose."

"I'm aware of the situ—"

"The *situation* is that Oscar Shaw murdered Ian Murphy, and now he's trying to kill Carly. You want us to come back to the city, put her in danger, so you can follow your policies and..." He quieted when Carly's hand curled around his arm.

"He's working on it." Carly's voice was calm, just like Klein's. It irritated him, but he clamped his lips shut.

"If you're not comfortable coming to Boston," Klein said, "I can meet you somewhere outside the city. Just tell me where."

Braden said, "That would be—"

"We'll come to you." Carly spoke over him. "We'll be there soon."

Before Braden could unleash more anger, Carly ended the call.

"Incompetent idiot," he said.

Carly's head tipped from side to side. "I don't think so. I think he's just getting up to speed. And maybe he doesn't want to tip Shaw off that they're on to him. Maybe they're hoping one of the Shaw men will lead them to Sophia."

Carly was probably right, but Braden was too angry to think rationally.

The very last thing he wanted was to return Carly to Boston. The chances of one of the Shaw men spotting them in a metro area of more than four million people were slim. Still, if it were up to Braden, they wouldn't go anywhere near the city.

If it were up to Braden, he'd still be the manager of the company he loved.

If it were up to Braden, Carly would be tucked safely in his house in Coventry, where no bad guys knew Braden's name or address. Where she would be safe.

Truth be told, if it were up to Braden, he and Carly would have married years before, the child in her womb would be his, and none of this would have happened.

None of this was up to Braden, though.

Despite the worry churning in his gut, Carly shifted into Drive and headed back toward the highway that would take them to Boston.

# CHAPTER TWENTY-SIX

Carly had just exited Storrow Drive toward Fenway when her phone rang. But it wasn't the normal ringtone. An Instagram call was coming through. Her heart leapt when she saw the name. "It's Sophia."

She stopped at a red light and clicked to connect. Her sister's image filled the tiny screen. She was in a dark room. In the dimness, Carly saw that Sophia's blond hair was mussed, her mascara smudged beneath her eyes.

"Soph, are you—?"

"Omygosh, Carly. Where are you?"

"In the city. The police are—"

"You have to help me." Her voice was barely more than a whisper. "I don't know what's going on." She sounded frantic, eyes darting away from the screen in multiple directions.

"Where are you exactly?" Carly asked.

"Preston's place. He's the guy—"

"I know who he is." The light turned green, and Carly pulled forward and parked alongside the curb. "Can you send us your location?"

"Yeah, I can—"

"You need to call the police." Braden leaned toward the phone.

"Hang up and call the police."

"No, no!" Sophia said. "I will, after. Carly, you have to come get me."

"Of course, just—"

"Absolutely not!" Braden glared at Carly, then at the screen. "We'll call the police. Send us your loc—"

"He told me he'd kill me if I got the police involved. Me and Laurie and Danielle, he'll kill us all." Sophia's eyes were wide, terrified. "Please, sis. I need your help. Just come, please."

An address popped up in their private message thread.

Carly clicked it, and Sophia's image disappeared. The address was in the Back Bay, less than a mile from where they were. She navigated to the directions, speaking to her sister. "You still there?"

"You're gonna have to get me out of here. I'm in the basement, but all the doors are locked. I can't get out."

Carly pulled into traffic. "We're on our—"

"What are you doing?" Braden sounded both angry and terrified. "The police can get her."

She lowered her cell and whispered, "Call them on your phone. I don't want to freak her out." She pulled back into traffic and followed the directions on the screen.

"Carly, stop." Braden had dialed, and the phone was pressed to his ear. He'd obviously taken it off Bluetooth, a good thing to keep Sophia from hearing him call the authorities and panicking.

Carly muted the conversation. "I'm just going to get close so I can be there when they rescue her."

"Stop. Don't get any..." Someone must've come on because he said, "Klein, they've got Sophia. She's at"—he snatched the phone from Carly's hand and read the Marlborough Street address. Before he handed the phone back, he closed the map app.

As if she couldn't find it again.

But she didn't have to. She'd seen enough of the directions to know where she was going. She didn't plan to go all the way to Preston's apartment anyway.

"Don't worry," Braden said to Klein. "We won't get anywhere near her."

Through the phone in Carly's hand, Sophia asked, "Are you coming? Are you on your way?"

She unmuted herself. "Of course. I'll be there any minute. Which unit is Preston's?"

"Third floor, apartment five, but he's not in there. He's searching for me."

Carly looked at Braden, who related the information to the detective.

"I don't understand. How'd you get away?" Carly asked Sophia.

"I don't know. I was just... He was taking me somewhere, and he got a call. I started running and yanked open this door and scrambled down here. I thought it would lead outside, but..."

Carly tried to picture what Sophia described. "How did he not see you?"

"I don't know. He's gonna find me. I don't know what he's into. Maybe he's gonna sell me into slavery or..." Sophia's whisper got louder, vehement. "You gotta come, Carly. I need you."

Beside her, Braden said, "Stop here. At the corner."

"Where are you?" Sophia hissed the words. "Please...?"

Carly parallel parked near where Braden directed, somehow managing the task despite how huge his truck was, the small space, and her nerves. She peered at the street signs. "We're at the corner of Marlborough and Dartmouth, right down the street." They were about a block from where Sophia was hiding.

The dim light that had lit Sophia's image went out. "He's coming." The words were barely a whisper. "Omigosh, he's gonna find me."

Carly reached for the door handle. "We're on—"

"No." Braden gripped her arm. "Stay here. Keep the doors locked. Do not, under any circumstances, get out of this car. Do you understand me?"

"I need to—"

"You promised me, Carly. When I agreed to bring you into the city, you promised me. That baby comes first."

Through the phone, she heard, "What?" The word was hissed. "Are you pregnant?"

Carly glared at Braden and whispered at her sister, "Mute the call." Carly lifted the screen and put her fingers to her lips to emphasize the point. For such a smart girl, Sophia could be dumb as a box of rocks.

But she got the message and didn't say anything else. If any expression showed on her face, Carly couldn't see it in the darkness. "Did you mute?"

Sophia didn't answer, which was answer enough.

Braden was still glaring at Carly. "I'll do my best to get to her. But you have to promise me you're going to stay here."

Carly didn't want Braden harmed either. But Sophia was just a teenager, a vulnerable teenager.

She gripped his hand and kissed his cheek. "I promise to stay here if you promise to come back to me, safe and sound."

"I intend to." He slipped out of the car and headed toward danger.

Sophia fell silent, and Carly was glad. Talking would only draw Preston her way. Her image remained on the screen, though only her blond hair and the whites of her eyes were visible in the dim light.

Carly kept her gaze there, ensuring herself Sophia was safe for now.

*Please, God, please protect my sister. And Braden. Don't let any harm come to them. Get them both out of there without a confrontation with Preston. Bring the police fast.*

She kept it up, begging God for His help. This could be it, the end to the nightmare. If the police came and arrested Preston, surely they'd also arrest his uncle, the mastermind behind this whole thing. And the other guy... the Wiley guy. And maybe even Lynch. Maybe they were all in on it together.

Carly didn't know and didn't need to know. God knew exactly what was going on. He had it in hand. She had to believe that. She would believe it.

Six, seven minutes went by. A police car passed her and stopped a couple hundred feet ahead of her in front of the building that had to be Preston Shaw's.

Thank God. Thank God, it was almost over.

A shadow crossed over Carly, and she glanced out her window.

Wiley Cuthrow, stringy blond hair hanging down either side of his ugly face, held a pistol aimed at her head. A slow smile spread across his lips as he tapped the glass with the weapon. "Open sesame."

Panic froze her in place. Would he shoot her? Right there, with the police less than a block away?

The look in his eyes told her he would, in a heartbeat. She spoke into the phone, hoping maybe Sophia had unmuted or could read her lips. "Call the police. They're going to take me."

But when she looked at the screen, Sophia was gone.

# CHAPTER TWENTY-SEVEN

THIS WAS DEFINITELY the right address.

Braden hadn't been able to find any exterior entry to the basement, though he was sure Sophia had said there was a door, and it was locked.

Maybe she'd found a door and assumed it led outside.

Braden had gained entry through the front door when a resident exited the converted brownstone. So much for security. He'd gone down the stairs and now stood outside two basement apartments.

There were no other doors. Sophia must've given them the wrong address.

He dialed 911 and updated the dispatcher on what he'd found. "Must be one of the nearby buildings," he said. It was the only thing that made sense.

When the 911 operator started lecturing him about waiting outside until the authorities arrived, he hung up on him and dialed Klein. It went to voice mail.

"Preston has Sophia in his building. She gave us an address"—he rattled it off—"but I think she has the number wrong. If you know his address, let the police know. They should be on their way."

He ended the call and shoved his phone back in his pocket.

*Sophia, where are you?*

And why was he looking for her? He should go back to his pickup, let the cops do their job. Except the fear in Carly's eyes—and the admiration when he'd said he'd find her—had spurred him on to this apparently fruitless task.

He'd go back to Carly, ask Sophia if she could send a pin from her current location, and then update the 911 operator.

He pushed out the front door and saw a police cruiser idling at the curb. One officer was standing outside, talking into the radio on his shoulder. Another was just disappearing around the end of the block.

He approached the one in front of him. "I'm the guy who made the call."

The man spoke into the radio, and then said, "Name?"

"Braden Reilly. I've already looked—"

"Sir, you need to step away and let us do our jobs."

"I don't think this is the right building."

The cop pointed to the sidewalk on the opposite side of the street. "Wait there."

Fine. He'd let them waste their time while he went back to question Sophia. Maybe she could describe the building if she couldn't remember the number.

He was nearing the pickup when his heart started racing. It took a moment for his brain to register what he'd seen.

Something was wrong.

He didn't see Carly through the glass.

She must be hunched over or lying down or... something.

The closer he got, the more his eyes told him what his heart didn't want to believe.

He yanked on the driver's door handle, praying she was hiding. Maybe she'd spotted Preston or Oscar. Maybe she didn't want to be seen.

The door was unlocked.

The keys were dangling from the ignition.

But Carly was gone.

~

"She was right there!" Braden shouted. "She can't have been gone more than two, three minutes. You need—"

"Step back, sir." The uniformed police officer, who'd already told him to wait, lifted his hand as if to stave off an attack. "We were called here to find—"

"I know!" He forced himself to lower his voice. "I'm the one who called it in. I just told you that. The girl isn't there. The basement has two apartments in it and nothing else. She must've..." He tried to rid his mind of a suspicion that occurred to him. "I don't know where Sophia is, but a woman was just taken, right there." He pointed to where his truck was parked. "I think it was a trap. Call Klein, Detective—"

"Sir, if you don't step back"—the officer laid a hand on his holstered firearm—"I'm going to place you under arrest."

Barely stifling a roar of frustration, Braden did what the man asked, yanking out his phone. He dialed Klein's number and he walked across the quiet street. "Answer, answer," he mumbled.

"Detective Kl—"

"Carly's been taken. She's gone."

"Who is... Braden? What happened?"

Fast as he could, Braden related the events.

"And you're sure she didn't go looking on her own?" Klein asked.

"She promised me. She swore she'd wait. They've got her, Klein. They've got her." The truth of it was just soaking in. Braden sat on the stoop across from the building where Sophia wasn't and propped his head on his hand. "I don't know what to do."

"What's the name of the officer on-site?"

Braden glared at the cop on the other side of the street as he related the man's name.

"I'll call him. I'm on it. Don't do anything."

The phone disconnected.

Don't do anything... As if he might go on a rescue mission of his own. He would if he had any idea where to go.

He should never have left Carly. He should have known. He should have stayed with her and let the police handle Sophia.

Where was that girl? Did she just have the address wrong, as Braden had first thought? Was it much worse than that? Had Sophia been coerced into leading her sister here? Or... surely Sophia hadn't willingly led her sister into a trap.

*Please, God, let it not be that.*

But he remembered Sophia's reaction on the phone, her not-at-all-quiet-or-scared reaction to the news that Carly was pregnant. For that one moment, she'd forgotten she was in danger and hiding.

Or perhaps, for that one moment, she'd forgotten to act as if she were.

He hated himself for his suspicions, but the longer he lingered, the more convinced he was.

Carly had risked her life for a girl who'd betrayed her.

And because of that, she likely wouldn't survive.

# CHAPTER TWENTY-EIGHT

IF CARLY HADN'T PARALLEL PARKED, she would have taken off the minute Wiley appeared in the pickup's window. But there was no way she'd have been able to get out of that parking spot faster than Wiley could fire his weapon. And then another figure had appeared, this one at the passenger window, wielding a second gun aimed at her head. With shaking fingers, ducking as if she could escape a flying bullet, she'd opened the door.

Wiley hadn't been gentle when he'd taken her phone and smashed it under his boot, then kicked it beneath the pickup. He hadn't been gentle when he'd grabbed her upper arm, spun her around, and stuck his gun in her back, leaning down to whisper, "Got a new silencer, and I'm itching to try it. Give me a reason."

He hadn't been gentle when he'd pushed her to the black SUV double-parked a few spaces behind her. If she'd been paying attention to her surroundings instead of watching the screen for Sophia, she might've seen the familiar vehicle pull up. Wiley shoved her onto the floor between the rows in the backseat.

Another minute had passed before the other man climbed into the driver's seat, though she couldn't imagine what had kept him.

Would the police find Sophia in time? Had Preston let her

escape with a phone so she would lead Carly there? Had it all been a setup?

Why would Preston and Oscar let Sophia live now?

Why would they let Carly live?

Carly's tears hadn't only been for her sister and herself. Her innocent, unborn child didn't deserve to have her life cut off before it even began.

And Braden. Now that he was back in her life, she didn't want to lose him again. She didn't know what that would look like, what it could look like. She didn't know if he could love Ian's child. But she thought he could. She wanted to know how that story played out.

Wiley had sat on the seat above her and rested his feet on her hip. He nudged her shoulder with his boot. "Don't move. And keep your head down. I'd hate to have to stomp that pretty face."

The SUV had lurched into traffic.

Carly had shifted over the hump between the seats on the scratchy floor, wishing she'd donned her padded parka, which was behind the front seats in Braden's pickup.

And she prayed. For herself. For Sophia. For Braden. For justice.

The verse she'd recited to Braden the night before replayed in her mind.

*He rescued me because He delights in me.*

Would He rescue her one more time?

After what she guessed was fifteen minutes of stops and starts and turns, the dull afternoon light faded to darkness. The SUV angled downward and parked.

Wiley yanked Carly out into an empty underground garage. She and her two abductors—the other was younger than Wiley with a shaved head and black eyes, also not hiding his identity— rode an elevator to the fourth floor. She prayed a bystander would see her in there with those two men, that she'd be able to signal that she needed help.

But the elevator didn't stop. And, considering they were in a city where parking spots were often bought and sold as investment properties, the empty parking garage did not bode well.

Like the garage and the elevator, the floor where they exited seemed deserted as her abductors escorted her across a mostly empty space about the size of a classroom. Open doors revealed deserted offices with furniture piled in one of them. Dismantled cubicle walls and accessories had been stacked in the center of the space. Fresh lumber leaned against a far wall.

Dark hallways leading to darker offices led away from the large room to either side, another at the back.

Before she could get more of a sense of the building, Wiley yanked her to a small windowless room, pushed her inside, and stepped back out. "Be good or I'll tie you up"—he winked—"and won't that be fun."

The door slammed behind him.

She was alone. She thanked God for that small favor.

A single fluorescent bulb buzzed overhead. It barely cut through the dimness in the room, but it was enough for her to get a sense of her prison. She crossed her arms in the chilly air. It was cooler than she'd consider room temperature, but if there were no heat, she'd probably be able to see her breath.

More small—very small—favors.

After Wiley and his buddy's footsteps faded, she tried the door, hoping futilely they'd forgotten to lock it. Of course it didn't budge. The door itself looked brand new—raw, unstained wood. The brushed nickel knob and lock felt secure.

She turned to the rest of the room. Three of the walls surrounding her were unprimed sheetrock with chalky white lines of joint compound breaking up the dull brown. She could kick through the drywall, but not before somebody heard and discovered what she was doing. Bad enough to be trapped, but she really didn't want to be bound as well.

The exterior wall was aged red brick. In the corner, a closet had been framed out, but the lack of drywall revealed that the small space stored nothing. She walked that way anyway, hoping somebody had left a spare tool lying around. A hammer would be nice.

A nail gun even better.

But her initial assessment had been correct. No tools, not even a stray screw.

The scents of sawdust and joint compound filled her nostrils. The garage had seemed old and dingy, as did the faded carpet beneath her, which had been pulled up around the edges but remained affixed in the center. Eventually, it would be replaced, all evidence that she'd been there piled in a dump somewhere, nobody the wiser.

She settled onto the floor against the brick wall and kept her eyes trained on the door, worrying a spot where the carpet was still glued down, pulling it, yanking it. Telling herself to relax.

She squeezed her hands into fists, then forced them together and, eyes wide open, prayed.

Thirty minutes, maybe an hour had passed when faraway voices came closer, one of them familiar enough to send Carly's heartbeat racing.

The people stopped nearby. It sounded like they were just beyond the door.

"You promised me!"

The words were nearly shrieked.

Sophia.

The truth hit, the blow more painful than any Ian had hurled.

Sophia hadn't been kidnapped. She'd been working with the kidnappers.

She'd lured Carly to that street corner. Sophia had probably never been there at all.

The fact that the girl now seemed utterly dumbfounded to discover that the kidnappers weren't keeping their promises didn't change anything.

Carly's own sister had betrayed her.

For what, Carly wondered. Money? Affection? Love?

After everything Carly had done for her, how cheaply had she sold her out?

"My dear Sophie." The man's voice was oily smooth. Sophia had demanded people stop using that nickname when she hit fifteen, but she didn't correct him. "We haven't hurt her. Your sister is fine. Would you like to see?"

"No! No, I don't want her to know—"

The man *tsked*. "Oh, dear. I'm afraid that cat has clawed its way out of the bag. You see, your sister is right"—a knock sounded on Carly's door—"in here. Perhaps if you'd learn to keep your voice down."

Clearly, the man had brought Sophia to that spot for a reason.

Carly stood and crossed to the door to better hear them.

"Preston, baby." Sophia's voice, lower but still audible, was no longer frantic or angry. Now, she sounded... seductive.

*Oh, sister. It's too late for that.*

"You said you just needed to get some information and then you'd let her go. Could you just, please, ask her your questions? And then we'll get out of your hair."

"We?" He sounded truly surprised, the liar. "Are you leaving me, darling?"

Darling. Carly resisted an urge to throw up that had nothing to do with morning sickness.

"I just need to make sure she gets home okay," Sophia said. "You know what she said on the phone."

"That she's expecting a little blessing. Yes, I remember."

The man's smooth voice sent a shudder down Carly's back, and she crossed her arms over her abdomen.

"I'm sure she'll be shaken up," Sophia said. "I'll just get her home and come right back."

Did Carly pick up fear in Sophia's voice? Maybe her sister was realizing she was involved in something much bigger and more dangerous than she'd imagined.

It was equally plausible that Carly was only hearing what she wanted to hear.

"Hmm," Preston said. "I see what you mean. We're not ready to question her yet. Why don't you keep her company for me until we are?"

The knob jiggled, and Carly scrambled to the far side of the room, then pressed her back against the brick.

The door pushed open.

Preston, looking as suave and put-together as he had in Sophia's photos, filled the space. In person, he didn't look as old as he had in photos. He was handsome, no question, more so thanks to the perfectly cut suit and stylish tie. When he met Carly's gaze, his smile was conciliatory, a deceptive look that she didn't believe for a second. "Ah, and you must be Carly."

"Preston."

If she'd expected surprise that she knew his name, she'd have been disappointed. He reached back to beyond Carly's view in the other room and pulled Sophia in front of him.

The mussed blond hair Carly'd seen in the video had been brushed, her face scrubbed clean of the mascara that had been smeared below her eyes. She wore a skimpy top beneath a cardigan over too-tight jeans—the outfit she'd had on in the photos she'd posted the night before. With no makeup, she looked young and fresh, like the girl she'd been when Carly had first met her.

"Don't be shy, darling." Preston's voice nearly purred. "It's too late for all that. Come on, now." He urged her into the room before releasing her. "You can wait in here with your sister."

Sophia didn't meet Carly's eyes before she turned to face him.

But Preston focused on Carly. "So nice to finally meet you face-to-face."

"I'd have preferred different circumstances."

His smile morphed into one of pure delight. "Oh, I'm sure you would have. I'll just let you two catch up."

He was pulling the door closed when Sophia crossed to where he stood, sidling up close. "Baby, can I have my phone back now?"

He seemed as if he were considering it. "Ah... I don't think so. Not quite yet. We'll discuss it with my uncle when he arrives."

His uncle. Oscar was coming?

Klein had said the police were watching Preston, but he'd obviously slipped their surveillance. Would Oscar as well, or would he lead them to this building?

Maybe she and Sophia would be rescued after all.

Preston closed the door behind himself.

A moment passed before Sophia turned to Carly. "I'm sorry. I had no idea—"

"Don't." Anger rose up from a place deep inside, a place Carly had tried her best for years to keep closed.

When Sophia didn't help cook or clean, Carly did it without complaint.

When Sophia couldn't be bothered to put her dirty clothes in the basket, Carly gathered them and washed them with the rest of the laundry.

When Sophia disobeyed the rules her father set, ignored Carly's suggestions, rolled her eyes when Carly told her about the Lord, she forgave her easily and prayed for her harder.

All for what? Betrayal?

Maybe Carly would live long enough to forgive Sophia, but all things considered, she wouldn't put money on it.

She resumed her seat on the floor, her back against the wall.

"If I'd known..." Sophia crouched in front of her. "I didn't know about the baby. Whose is it? Is it Ian's? Was that Braden on the phone today? Is it his?"

Carly tried to ignore her sister's words.

"Oh, Carly, I didn't mean for any of this to happen. Preston said he had a question for you and that you were avoiding him. He's been so nice to me. I'm sure once he asks you his questions, everything will be fine."

Carly closed her eyes. Nothing that came out of her mouth would be kind or merciful. Better not to say anything.

And better that Sophia continue in her ignorance. Maybe, if she didn't understand what Preston and Oscar had done, didn't understand how dangerous they were, maybe they wouldn't hurt her.

"He's gonna pay for me to go to college." Sophia's voice was pleading, as if that would excuse her behavior. "I'm gonna go, just like you said I should. And he bought me the nicest things. Look."

Carly opened her eyes, and Sophia stuck out her arm, where a ruby-and-diamond tennis bracelet dangled. "Isn't it pretty? My birthstone. He loves me. He just asked me to do this one thing for—"

"Stop it." Carly looked up into the face of the girl she'd loved. One of the girls she'd given up everything to care for.

And here she was, thinking Sophia was the idiot.

Carly was the dimwitted one.

"Has it not occurred to you, *Sophie,* that Preston said all those things and did all those things to get you to trust him? That he's using you? That he's been using you all along to get to me? That you sold me out for a *bracelet?*" Carly's voice rose at the end, the anger and disbelief pitching the words high.

Sophia had the gall to look surprised. "No. It was an accident, me and Preston meeting. It was—"

"Just stop talking."

"Carly, you gotta—"

"I'm serious, Sophia. Shut. Up. I need to think."

"Fine. Be that way. Whatever." Sophia backed away and sat against the adjacent wall, pout firmly in place.

Thank heavens.

Not that there was anything for Carly to think about. Not that there was any way to escape. They were trapped. Their only hope was that Oscar would lead the police to them, and that he'd do it in time.

# CHAPTER TWENTY-NINE



Braden had to do something.

If only the kidnappers had taken his laptop. Though the bag had been emptied, its contents scattered on the passenger seat, his laptop was still there.

If they'd taken it, he could have tracked it.

Obviously, they knew that.

Crime scene investigators were all over his pickup, dusting for prints, looking for evidence. They'd found Carly's phone on the pavement beneath it but, as far as he could tell, nothing else.

He got a ride from the Back Bay neighborhood, where the cops had obviously not found Sophia, to police headquarters in the backseat of a cruiser.

Ignoring the two uniformed officers in the front, he called Geoff.

His friend answered with, "I talked to Lynch. He knows nothing about—"

"Carly's been kidnapped."

Geoff's pause was short. Then, his tone was confident. "I swear, man, Lynch had nothing to do with it."

"I don't care." Braden's voice sounded unnaturally calm, considering the fury simmering beneath it. He ignored the cops in the front seat and focused on the call. "I don't care what you say. I don't care what you think. I don't care about Lynch's career or political aspirations or construction projects or any of it. I'll bring him down and you right along with him if anything happens to Carly."

The officer in the passenger seat turned his way, warning in his expression.

Braden looked out the window. "I'll take what I've learned to every news outlet from here to Washington, D.C." He let those words simmer, then added, "The media will gut him. It won't matter if Lynch is guilty or not. If he knows—"

"He doesn't know anything." Geoff's confidence was faltering, based on the undertone of pleading in the words.

"You tell him," Braden said. "You tell him, if she's harmed, I will destroy him."

Before Geoff could say another word, Braden hung up, hands trembling with rage and worry.

At the station, he climbed from the cruiser, waited for the cops to go inside, and stood on the sidewalk outside to breathe and pray, allowing the winter air to cool his temper. He texted Reid and Dylan and asked them to pray. When he thought he could at least sound rational, he called his parents. He only wanted to alert them to the situation, desperate for as many people as possible to be interceding on Carly's behalf. He shouldn't have been surprised by Dad's response.

"We're on our way. We'll wait with you."

Braden hung up, thinking he should feel thankful his parents were coming. But any gratitude that might've existed was eaten away by all the other emotions churning in his gut.

He pushed inside the building and was ushered upstairs. After a brief meeting with Klein to tell him what had happened—as if he hadn't explained it repeatedly to the cops at the scene—he was ushered into a claustrophobic room and told to wait.

Pete was there already, his younger daughters on either side of him. Braden hadn't seen the man since Carly's mother's funeral.

His light brown hair was thinning on top, and it looked as if he hadn't trimmed his beard in weeks. He'd aged, a lot. Wrinkles fanned out from his eyes and surrounded his lips. His skin was pale, his eyes red.

If Pete had done a better job of protecting Sophia, they wouldn't be in this mess.

Maybe.

But Pete's oldest daughter had always had a mind of her own. They couldn't possibly know what would have happened in another scenario. Rather than consider the what-ifs, Braden needed to focus on the what-nows.

He'd been polite to the older man. Pete's failures as a father were on display for the world to see. It wasn't Braden's job to point them out, nor did he think he needed to. The equally terrified and guilty look in Pete's expression told Braden he was beating himself up enough for both of them.

Danielle and Laurie had grown up since Braden had last seen them, but in that moment, they seemed barely more than girls, their frightened faces tracking Braden's movements.

He couldn't sit. He prowled the space, desperate to do something.

Pete said, "Son, why don't you—"

"Don't call me that." Braden froze and glared at the man. He had a father, a good father. He sure didn't need this one trying to step in as a surrogate.

He also didn't need to make this already tense situation worse.

The walls were closing in.

He yanked open the door and stalked to where Klein and a few other detectives were huddled around a monitor. One was tapping on a keyboard, another talking on the phone.

Klein looked up and stepped away. Fifties, he guessed, with black skin, very short black hair graying on the sides, and blue eyes. The man seemed to have felt his approach more than heard it.

"Have you found—?"

"When we learn something," Klein said, "I'll let you know."

"What are you doing over there?"

"Shaw owns property all over the metro. We've got a list, and we're trying to narrow it down so we can start searching. We're crossing off occupied condos and office space."

"Any luck?"

"We'll get there."

Braden took in the information, tried to let the fact that they were working on it encourage him. But despair had seeped into his skin, his every cell. "She's pregnant. Did she tell you that?"

Klein's eyebrows lifted. "Carly?"

"Ian's kid." When the raised eyebrows only went higher, Braden couldn't help himself and added, "The monster broke into her apartment one night." He swallowed a fresh wave of fury. "The baby was his parting gift after she dumped him."

Braden shouldn't have told Klein that. He was losing control of his mouth. His thoughts.

They might as well join everything else in this crazy situation.

Klein gripped his shoulder and squeezed. "We're doing everything—"

"Can I help narrow down the properties?"

"We're on it, son."

If one more person called him "son," he was going to punch him. "You have to give me something to do or I'll go crazy."

Dropping his arm, Klein said, "The best thing you can do is stay out of our way and pray."

Pray. He'd been doing that, constantly.

Klein stepped closer and lowered his voice. "We have Oscar in our sights. If he goes to where she is—"

"And if he doesn't—?"

Klein stepped back. "Then we'll bring him in and get him to talk."

"Why not just do that now? Why wait?"

"We believe Oscar will lead us to Carly and Sophia. That's our best shot of finding them fast. You just need to trust us." He returned to his desk, leaving Braden standing in the giant room surrounded by detectives and desks and chairs and phones and still, somehow, utterly alone.

The elevator dinged, and he watched his parents step off. He crossed to them and hugged his mom, then his dad, allowing Dad's strength to hold him up for just a minute.

When he stepped away, Mom laid a hand on his arm. "Any news?"

"Maybe. Soon."

But the police were supposed to have been surveilling Preston, yet somehow, nobody knew where the younger Shaw was. Braden had been waiting to talk to Klein when a uniformed officer delivered that news. The detective's dark skin had turned nearly purple, his hands white where he clenched them into fists. It seemed that, since Preston had willingly come to the police that morning, the higher-ups had decided their resources could be better utilized elsewhere, and they'd reassigned the cops who'd been tailing him. Klein had sworn under his breath, muttering something about defunding and budget cuts and morons in brass.

Now, Mom was talking about prayer, and Dad was encouraging Braden that God had it under control. Maybe, but he couldn't handle the words, which only felt like platitudes.

"Come on down here." He'd cut his father off mid-sentence and walked away. He'd have to apologize for that when this was over. "You can sit with Pete and the girls. I'm sure they'd appreciate the company."

After leading them to the door that opened to the small room, he stepped aside for them to enter and then walked away.

He was glad his parents were there. He wanted them there. But he needed...

To be somewhere else.

To be doing *something*.

A loud cheer drew his attention back to Klein and the bevy of detectives.

Klein said, "Quiet!" and snatched up a phone receiver. While he talked, he shuffled another detective away from the computer screen and sat in front of it. "So, south on..." He wrote something on a notepad. "Got it. I'll get backup headed that way. Don't do anything until they get there. This guy's killed at least one..." Another pause to listen. "See that you do. Two lives are at stake here."

*Three,* Braden silently corrected.

Because Klein and the rest assumed Sophia was with the kidnappers, either as their captive or as their accomplice. Either way, her life was in danger.

But the lives Braden cared about were Carly's and that of the child she carried.

*Protect them, Lord. Please, protect them.*

While another detective marched to the elevator, Klein scanned the room until his gaze hooked on Braden's. "Oscar's on the move, and we're on his tail."

"Where?"

"Headed south out of the city. He owns more than one property in Quincy. My guess is, he's going to one of those places. If he doesn't lead us to Carly, we'll bring him in and question him. Either way, we'll find her."

A lump of emotion rose in Braden's throat. Gratitude, hope, terror.

Klein spun and hurried to the elevator.

Braden watched until the men disappeared behind the closing doors.

*Please, go with them. Save the ones I love.*

Because there was no doubt he loved Carly. He'd never quit loving her.

And the child she carried... Braden loved that innocent life as well. How could he not love Carly's child? The facts of the baby's conception were not his fault. Or *her* fault, if Carly was right.

Braden imagined a tiny face like Carly's, fuzzy brown hair, beautiful brown eyes.

But if the child had Ian's coloring, Ian's face...?

It wouldn't matter. Braden would love him just the same.

# CHAPTER THIRTY

When the door opened, Carly looked up from her frantic prayers.

Preston stepped inside, and Wiley filled the doorway behind him.

Sophia scrambled to her feet and lunged toward Preston. "Baby, you locked us in. I knocked, but you must not have heard."

Carly stood as well but kept her back firmly pressed to the wall.

Sophia had tried a few more times to engage Carly in conversation, but Carly had ignored her, focusing on prayer. She should have been kind. She knew that. Considering they probably wouldn't survive the day, she should have been forgiving. But since she hadn't believed she could manage either, she'd decided her time was better spent talking to God than attempting conversation with her stepsister.

Preston's smile was tight at the corners, as if Sophia's stupidity wore thin on him too. "You were supposed to keep your sister company." His gaze flicked between them. "Did you have a nice chat?"

Sophia glanced at Carly, fear in her expression. Maybe Sophia knew more than she was letting on. If nothing else, it seemed the truth was at least starting to filter past the blond highlights and into her brain. Pout in place, she trailed her hand up his arm. "She wouldn't even talk to me. Do I have to stay in here? Can I have my phone back?"

Sophia was laying it on thick now, and Preston's eyes narrowed. He covered his suspicion quickly. "I'd hoped you could repair your relationship, but it seems that hasn't happened."

Repair it? They hardly *had* a relationship. They certainly weren't sisters to each other, never had been. Carly had tried to be a friend, but Sophia had rebuffed her every attempt. She'd tried to be a mentor, but Sophia had only scoffed at her counsel.

Maybe Sophia had wished for more, as Carly always had.

Unfortunately, it was too late.

"Hard to have a conversation with someone who hates you." Sophia hung on Preston's arm. "Are there any more donuts left? I'm starving."

Preston patted her hand and gently removed it from his arm. "Go on with Wiley. I need to talk to Carly for a few minutes."

"Oh, good. When she answers your questions, you can send her home, and you and I can go back to your place."

He leaned down and kissed her cheek. "I'll look forward to that."

Carly closed her eyes to the disgusting display. Preston was only playing a part, but she had no doubt he'd been happily playing it all the way into the bedroom.

The click of the door closing had Carly's eyes popping open.

Preston stood in front of it, lying grin beneath predatory eyes.

"Your sister is something."

Carly crossed her arms over her ugly sweatshirt and said nothing.

"Though she puts on a good show, I think she's figured me out."

Carly hoped so but said, "I doubt it."

"By now, surely, you've told her everything."

"I told her nothing. Nothing about Ian's murder. Nothing about how you tried to kill me the other day. I told her nothing."

He studied her a long moment, finally saying, "Why?"

"She's still my stepsister, even after this. If she knows nothing, then you have no reason to hurt her. And she won't figure anything out on her own. For all her intelligence, when it comes to common sense, she's not the sharpest tool in the shed."

"Are you, though?" He took a step toward her. "Are you one of the sharper tools, Carly Garcia?"

"I used to think so. I'm beginning to wonder, to tell you the truth."

His eyebrows hiked, inviting her to expand on her remark. She didn't.

He walked closer, stopping when just a few feet separated them. "You don't have to be afraid of me. You only have to tell me exactly what you told the police."

"Everything."

Maybe she should have kept quiet. Maybe she should have taken more time before answering the question. But she could see no reason not to be honest with him. He needed to understand that, no matter what he and his uncle did, they were going down.

They needed to believe that killing Carly and Sophia would only lengthen their prison sentences.

Though one life sentence or three... Did it matter, at the end of the day?

Again, he didn't speak, just waited for her to fill in the blanks. So she did.

"They know about you and your uncle Oscar. They know about how his company used thugs to force business owners and landlords to sell so Abecedarian could turn the properties over to Lynch's company—earning a nice profit. They know how you seduced my sister. They know about Ian's murder. They know everything."

Preston's expression hadn't shifted, though he'd moved closer.

No more than a foot separated them now. She could feel the heat of his skin against hers.

He asked, "And the notebooks?"

They were still at Angel and Donovan's B and B.

But she couldn't tell Preston that. He needed to believe he was going down, no matter what. And she wouldn't put those kind people and their precious child in danger.

"The police have them, of course."

Squinting, Preston leaned toward her, his gaze flicking from one of her eyes to the other. "Interesting. When did you turn them over?"

She swallowed, scrambling for an answer. "Yesterday. Right after we found them. We went straight to the police."

His eyes stayed fixed on her face, burning her skin. She could feel a flush rising to her cheeks.

When she said nothing else, he said, "We had someone watching police headquarters. You never went there."

"We went..." She scrambled for a believable story. "We met the detective at a restaurant."

"What restaurant?"

"I don't remember—"

"In the city?"

"Um, no." *The truth. Stick as close to the truth as much as possible.* "At the Ninety-Nine in Norwood."

"I thought you couldn't—"

"I just remembered. You're making me nervous."

"Ah." His grin was so satisfied, she could practically see the canary feathers sticking out of his mouth. "Because you find me so attractive?"

"Because you're a pervert and a kidnapper. And an accomplice to murder."

The words didn't affect him at all. "You really are a terrible liar, Carly Garcia."

"I'm not lying. I had broccoli cheddar soup. Braden had steak tips and chicken fingers."

"And the detective? What's his name?"

"Klein. Detective Kl—"

"What did he eat?"

"He didn't..." She swallowed, scrambled. Preston was right—Carly was a terrible liar. Always had been. "He wasn't hungry. He ate some of our fries. Braden's fries."

Preston stepped back. "The notebooks weren't in your friend's pickup. It was searched thoroughly."

"That's because we already turned them over."

He brushed off her comment with a flick of his wrist and paced to the far side of the room, where he leaned against the wall. "I recommend you tell me where they are before my uncle arrives."

She crossed her arms and glared. "What difference does it make? The police know everything. You'll go to prison. Do you need to add to the body count? You'd be better off turning yourself in now."

"It doesn't matter what the police *know*." Preston said the words as if they were the most obvious in the world. "It matters what they can *prove*. And without Murphy's notebooks, they can't prove anything."

Surely they could. They had images of the notebooks. Would that be enough, though?

"My uncle," Preston said. "How much do you know about him?"

"Enough. I know he's a killer. I know he's a greedy, scheming crook. I know he wanted to go into politics but didn't have what it took. Seems like the perfect profession for someone like him."

"The thing about Oscar is that he comes off as meek and mild. I assure you, he is anything but."

After what she'd heard at Ian's shop on Monday, Carly already knew that.

"Ever heard of enhanced interrogation techniques?"

The expression was familiar enough to send cold fear dripping down her spine.

"He was never in the military, but he's a student of such things."

"Sounds like a warm guy. I can see why you're close. Nothing like a little *torture* to unite a family."

Preston's eyes shrank as if he found the word offensive. Maybe he found the action offensive, not that it would change anything.

"He's had some opportunities to practice what he's learned. He's become very good. Very good. I know you want justice for your dead boyfriend."

"He wasn't—"

"Dead *ex*-boyfriend." He conceded the point with a slight nod. "But really, is it worth all that? Worth the pain Oscar's going to inflict on you? Worth the risk to your unborn child?"

She considered the man's words. Was justice worth all that?

Maybe it was. It wasn't her place to weigh justice against lives, innocent or otherwise. That was God's job.

But the bigger issue was one the smooth-talking Preston wouldn't bring up. If she told him where the notebooks were, there'd be no reason to keep her alive. She was the only witness to Ian's murder. If she were dead, it was possible Oscar and his band of accomplices would walk away, scot-free.

"Yes," Preston said. "I realize you've seen past me. You are definitely one of the sharper tools in that shed, Carly Garcia." He rushed her so fast that she backed against the wall, her head hitting the brick. The jolt of pain was the least of her worries.

Preston stopped just short of her. "I suppose you realize how this ends for you. The problem is, everybody talks eventually. You'll beg for death. And for what? Even if we don't get the notebooks, with Murphy out of the way, without the only witness to testify to what happened Monday morning, what can the police prove?" He shrugged, his cold eyes not leaving hers. "You're going to end up exactly how you should have ended up Monday morning, but it doesn't have to end like that for your sister. She's witnessed nothing, knows nothing. She doesn't need to die for you.

Her little sisters—Laurie and Danielle. They don't need to die for you."

Nausea churned, climbed to Carly's throat.

"Your stepfather doesn't need to die for you. Braden Reilly doesn't need to die for you. We can end it all right here, right now. Just tell me where the notebooks are."

She swallowed. Swallowed again. Closed her eyes against the cruel man and his evil threats. But behind her lids, she imagined it, her family and the man she loved, dead.

*Help me. What do I do?*

There was no answer. No glimmer of light. No flash of insight.

But... but if the police were on Oscar's tail, then they'd know where she was.

*He rescued me because He delighted in me.*

God had rescued Carly from so much. From the destructive relationship with Ian. From being discovered Monday morning at his shop. From Wiley and his buddy on Thursday. He hadn't kept her from being taken today, but it wasn't over yet.

She opened her eyes and glared.

"I know what you're thinking." He *tsked*. "I see hope in your eyes. You're convinced the police are going to find you. Even if they were to surround the building, you wouldn't be safe. You see, my uncle is smart. He always has a way of escape. In this case, he's devised a way to get from the roof of this building to the one next door. That one's connected to the next, which is connected to the next, an apartment building he happens to own." Preston's eyes twinkled. "At that point, it's simply a matter of getting into the stairwell and going out the back door. That's all assuming the police trail him here at all. But he knows he's being watched, and he's made arrangements. Nobody's coming to save you, Carly. Nobody knows where you are."

God knew where she was.

If this was how it would end for her, then so be it. She trusted God with her life on earth, and she knew where she was going in the next one.

No matter what, she wouldn't give up hope. Another verse flitted through her memory. *Hope does not disappoint.*

Preston leaned closer, whispering in her ear. "Tell me where the notebooks are, and I'll make sure your sister gets home safely. I'll protect the rest of your family and your boyfriend. I'll protect you from my uncle. I'll make it quick and painless. Just tell me."

She didn't move, didn't breathe, didn't speak.

But, despite Preston's words, she did hope.

When she'd gone to Ian's shop Monday morning, she'd done so to secure a future for her child. She'd failed, and in the process, put herself and her baby at risk. Maybe Oscar and his crew hadn't killed her that day, but it was possible her escape had only delayed the inevitable.

Now, she had to hold off, hold off and pray the police found them in time. Or they secured the notebooks before Oscar got the evidence's whereabouts out of her. If it would be her last act, then she'd make it a good one. If it would lead to justice, then it would be worth it.

It was all she had left to offer.

# CHAPTER THIRTY-ONE

Braden updated Pete, the girls, and his parents about Klein's hope that Oscar would lead them to Carly. He was desperate for fresh air but afraid to walk away, even for a minute, hoping and praying for good news.

But not expecting it.

Though Klein had seemed confident, Braden wasn't convinced.

The department had done nothing but bungle this investigation from the very beginning. Yes, there'd been budget cuts. Yes, there'd been increased crime. Those things played a part.

A crooked detective had played a part.

The fact that Klein had been recently assigned to homicide, catching up on other cases all week. That played a part.

He knew all that, but it didn't change anything. They'd been more than a step behind since Murphy's murder, and unless they caught up fast...

They were doing everything they could. He knew that.

But would it be enough?

Could it?

His phone rang, and he glanced at the screen, then shot to his feet.

Carly's family and his folks looked his way.

"I gotta take this. Be right out here." He hurried from the tiny room and closed the door behind him. The detective's bullpen was filled with men and women bent over reports and taking victims' statements and talking on the phone. None of them looked up when he walked past. "Geoff, did you learn something?"

"Braden Reilly?" It wasn't Geoff, despite the fact that his number had shown on Braden's screen. The vaguely familiar voice was smooth and deep, tinged with concern Braden didn't trust.

He said, "Speaking."

"It's Richard Lynch. Geoffrey told me what's going on."

"I don't care about anything but getting her back. I'll keep my mouth shut. You just have to tell me where she is."

"The things you told Geoff," Richard said. "I had no idea. Oscar's a contributor, a volunteer with the campaign. Our companies have done business with each other. But if the things you've learned about Abecedarian are true, I can assure you, I wasn't involved." The candidate's response sounded believable, but then, he was a politician. He'd probably perfected the art of lying. And since he had nothing to offer but excuses...

"Then you don't mind if I go to the press," Braden said.

"That's not why I'm calling. I just wanted you to know that I have no reason to protect Shaw. I don't know where your girlfriend is, but I have a theory."

"Okay." Braden tried to keep the doubt out of his tone. "Let's hear it."

"Shaw was at our campaign offices about a month ago. I overheard him telling somebody on the phone that he'd meet him at the Deerfield Building offices."

"The police have a list of all—"

"Let me finish. I know the Deerfield Building. It's on the same block as the law office where I worked when I was in college. I read the building's name every day for a whole school year. It's an old, beautiful brick building that I always loved. So, his remark piqued my interest. I know where his company's office is, and it's nowhere near the Deerfield. I asked him about it, thinking maybe he'd bought the old place. He brushed me off, said his company didn't own it but had been hired to remodel it."

Braden's heart raced. "You're saying he has access." But it wouldn't be on the list Klein and the others had studied earlier.

"Exactly. It seemed weird at the time that he called it his office. I figured it was an inside joke or something. But now that I know what he's been up to, it makes me wonder—"

"Maybe they're doing more than construction there. Any chance the building's south of the city?" Where had Klein guessed they were going? "Maybe in Quincy?"

"Quincy? No. It's right here, downtown. Just a few blocks from the Common."

In Boston? If Lynch was right...

Then the police were going in the wrong direction.

# CHAPTER THIRTY-TWO

WHEN PRESTON LEFT, Carly searched the space again. There had to be something she could use to defend herself. Maybe even escape.

She tried to force the pins from the door's hinges, but she couldn't budge them. She needed a hammer at the very least.

Could she pick the lock? Interior door locks were usually easy to pick, but this one had a keyhole. If only she were one of those women who used bobby pins or barrettes. An underwire bra would have come in handy, but she wasn't wearing one of those either.

What if she found a nail?

She spun to the framed-out closet. She'd seen no stray nails, but maybe she could work one out of the wood. She chose a small two-by-four and tried to jimmy it loose from the others. She needed a pry bar.

As long as she was wishing for things she didn't have, she'd add *gun* and *cell phone* to the list. Maybe even *SWAT team*.

Okay, she could do this. *Lord, make me strong.*

She leaned her back on the vertical stud that the short one was nailed to and pushed her weight against it, trying to create separation between the two boards.

No movement. At all.

She checked the other boards. One of them had to be loose or...

There. One short two-by-four had been added to gird up a corner at the floor, forming a triangle. She worked it up from the bottom, felt it give just a smidge. She turned and used the heel of her sneaker to kick at it.

Voices rose from down the hall and set her heart racing.

Her time was running out.

But the board was coming... coming.

Yes! She separated it from the others. Not even twelve inches long, it had miter cuts on both ends, where nails still stuck out.

She could work one of those nails loose, but they looked too thick to fit into the lock.

But maybe she could use the board.

If she could figure out how to take her captors by surprise.

She glanced around the empty room again. What could she do? What could...?

The carpet.

She had a chance, a tiny chance, but she'd make the best of it.

She wasn't going down without a fight.

# CHAPTER THIRTY-THREE

Surrounded by detectives paying no attention to him, Braden shoved his cell into his pocket. He'd told Klein what he'd learned, and the detective had promised to send a couple of officers to the Deerfield to see if anything looked *fishy*. "If we're right about where he's going," Klein said, "we'll be there in fifteen minutes."

If he wasn't right, then those fifteen minutes could mean the difference between life and death.

Klein was a pro, though. Maybe Oscar was leading them straight to Carly. Maybe she wasn't at the Deerfield.

But Braden wasn't risking the woman he loved on a *maybe*.

He hurried to the small room where the families waited and burst inside. "Dad, I need your keys."

His father stood. "What's going on?"

"I think I know where she is. The police are going to the wrong place." He held out his hands, itching to take off. "They impounded my truck."

Mom stood beside Dad. "Sweetie, you can't go by yourself. Let the police—"

"Dad." He ignored his mother's pleading voice. "If it was Mom, if it was Shannon..."

His father swallowed. "I'm with your mother on this one, son."

*Son.* Dad was the only person who got to call him that. But in that moment, even coming from his father's lips, it grated on his nerves.

Dad stepped closer, his expression filled with compassion. "You need to let the police—"

"I got my car."

Braden turned at the voice and saw Pete standing at the door.

"But I'm coming with you," he added.

Braden managed to swallow the first words that came to mind. Because Pete was a lot of things—lazy, demanding, selfish. He'd never been protective.

But the person across the room seemed determined to be exactly that.

"Dad?" Danielle's voice was high and filled with terror.

Pete focused on his younger daughters. "I'm gonna get your sisters. You two stay here and"—his gaze flicked to Braden's parents—"pray." He turned to Braden. "Let's go."

Braden's mind had snagged on one word. *Sisters.*

Pete was concerned for both Sophia and Carly.

Ignoring his parents' worried expressions, Braden followed Pete out the door.

The winter sun was sinking behind the buildings as they drove toward downtown. The Friday afternoon traffic was heavy, and the two-mile drive took more than twenty minutes. When they reached the Deerfield, Pete passed it and found a spot by a fire hydrant and parked.

No police cruisers on the street. Apparently, the cops hadn't seen anything fishy, if they'd bothered to drive by at all.

"What do we do, just walk in the front door?" Pete turned in his seat and surveyed the eight-story red brick building through the rear window.

"Maybe a back door, or..." Braden climbed from Pete's car and studied the area. An alley ran along one side of the building.

Pete's car door closed. Another slam had Braden turning his

direction as Pete joined him on the sidewalk, something dangling from his right hand.

A tire iron.

Pete shrugged. "Wish it were a gun."

"Any chance you have a second one of those?"

"Nope."

Weaponless, Braden started down the alley. At the back of the building, the entrance to an underground parking garage gaped in darkness. They walked down the ramp, keeping to the shadows along one side.

First glance told Braden it was empty. He tried to believe that was good news. That if Carly and Sophia weren't there, then maybe Klein was on the right track.

He and Pete continued around a corner.

A black Honda CR-V was parked right beside the elevator.

He gripped Pete's arm and, keeping his voice low, said, "That's their car. I'm calling Klein."

They stepped nearer the SUV, and Braden snapped a photo of the plate and texted it to the detective, then dialed.

Klein didn't answer.

A word he tried not to use anymore slipped out. As soon as the detective's voice mail beeped, he said, "I'm at the Deerfield. Wiley's SUV is here. I'm calling 911."

He hung up and did just that, relating what he knew while Pete skulked around the rest of the garage. The dispatcher promised to send help and told him to get out of the building and wait a safe distance away.

Braden hung up, though the dispatcher was still talking, and found Pete on the far side of the space. Just beyond him, a sedan was covered with a tarp that had a fine film of dust on it. It clearly hadn't been moved in a couple of days.

Pete stood beside a metal door.

Braden told the older man what the 911 operator had ordered them to do.

"You gonna leave?" Pete asked. "Just wait and hope the cops get here in time?"

"The thing is, Carly's the only witness to Murphy's murder. Maybe they'll surrender. Maybe they'll kill her and try to get away." He closed his eyes, prayed for wisdom, and felt nothing but the itching desire to go after her. He opened his eyes again. "I'm not taking that chance."

"Me neither." Pete rapped his knuckles against the door behind him. "Stairwell. There's another by the elevator. Lynch said the building's being renovated, so it's probably empty. No cars confirms that. Yeah?"

"Agreed."

"They'll use the elevator, especially with their tools and whatnot. And set up near it, I think. Easy access. People are inherently lazy."

Pete would know. Braden shook off the ungracious thought. "We go up these stairs, farther away." Braden saw what Pete was getting at. "Good idea."

The sound of an engine had them turning toward the bottom of the ramp. Headlights bounced against the concrete wall, and Braden and Pete backed behind a cement pillar. Braden peeked around it and watched as a silver sedan parked beside the SUV.

Two men stepped out. They both wore jeans. One had on a jacket while the other wore a T-shirt, which showed off well-built arms. And a bulge where a gun was holstered. Bodyguards or thugs. The kinds of guys who did the dirty work.

A third man exited the back seat and started toward the elevator, buttoning his suit jacket over a paunchy middle. He was five five, maybe five six, balding.

Oscar Shaw.

After making sure his phone was on mute, Braden lifted the cell and snapped a photo, hoping it would come out in the darkened garage.

The men pressed the button for the elevator. A moment later, it arrived, and they stepped on. When the doors closed, Pete hurried across the space and watched as the numbers above the lift lit up.

Braden dialed Klein again. Voice mail, again. He left another message. "I don't know who you're following, but Oscar Shaw is at the Deerfield. Sending you a photo. Already called 911. Somebody better get here fast."

He ended the call as Pete jogged his direction. "Fourth floor."

"Let's go."

# CHAPTER THIRTY-FOUR

CARLY WAS as ready as she could be when the door opened.

The man who regarded her from the doorway was far from intimidating. He wasn't just shorter than her five eight, he was small-boned and narrow-shouldered. But his eyes... There was something cold and calculating in Oscar Shaw's eyes.

She had no doubt that Preston was right about his uncle. He didn't look intimidating at all, but fear dripped down her spine at the sight of him.

If Preston or Wiley or anybody else entered with Oscar, her plan would surely fail, which was why she'd been praying since the nephew walked out that Oscar would come alone.

*Let him underestimate me,* she'd asked more than once. *Let him think I'll be easy to handle.*

It seemed God had answered that prayer, because she hadn't heard voices before the door opened, and nobody stood behind Oscar now.

His expression was one of amusement and satisfaction. "Well, well, well. You've been hard to pin down, Miss Garcia." His voice. High, almost feminine. Yet menacing. Distinctive. This was the man who'd killed Ian. If she'd harbored any doubts, they were gone now.

"Sorry to be such a bother."

He waved her off as he stepped inside, closing the door. "I wish it hadn't come to this."

"You and me both."

His smile was conciliatory, as if he sympathized. "You've had a very difficult week."

He still didn't move forward. The longer he stood there, the worse her chances got.

She didn't shift her gaze from his. "I've had better."

"Though, I suppose the fact that you got to live all those days—Monday through Thursday, almost to the end of today. One must be thankful for the simple things."

Oscar wasn't wrong. If not for what happened Monday, Carly wouldn't have reconnected with Braden. She wouldn't have understood how he cared for her. She wouldn't have come to terms with her own inadequacy. The knowledge that she couldn't do what her mother asked, that she wasn't capable of taking care of her sisters and taking care of herself, would have escaped her.

In a blink, she remembered that moment at Mama's bedside, her mother's weak grip on her hand. She remembered exactly what Mama had said.

"You're stronger than you think you are. Take care of them."

"I will, Mama. I promise."

But Mama had shaken her head, as if that wasn't what she meant at all. "And let them take care of you."

How had Carly forgotten that?

Pete and his daughters had never tried to take care of Carly. If they had, would she have allowed it?

No. She'd worn their wellbeing like an albatross.

Her mother hadn't stopped there.

For the first time since Mama had taken her last breath, Carly remembered the rest of what she'd said that day.

"I love Pete, and I love those girls. But you"—she'd squeezed Carly's hand—"you are my treasure, the best part of me. Grieve me. Learn to trust God, and be happy."

Carly had gotten caught up in the grief and the promise she'd made—the promise Mama hadn't asked for. And she'd discarded the most important part of Mama's final words.

Maybe, maybe deep down, she hadn't believed she could be happy.

And then she'd taken up with Ian, and she hadn't believed she *deserved* to be happy.

Now, though... Now that it was too late, she wanted nothing more than to do exactly what her mother had said.

All those memories came and went in a flash while Oscar studied her.

"Where was it?" he asked. "The evidence Murphy collected. We'd been searching that place for days, and then my guy saw your friend take off with something. Your boyfriend's notebook full of proof, we believe."

"Ex. Longtime ex."

He nodded, conceding that. "Your ex got drunk and shot his mouth off about how he was figuring out who was behind the crime in the neighborhood."

Ian and his big, boasting mouth. He got himself killed.

And maybe Carly. And maybe their child.

*Please, God.*

Oscar smirked as if he were disgusted. "I wish I could blame my guys, but I spent an entire night there myself searching. And then cleaning the place to make it look as if we hadn't been there. Didn't want to let on anything was wrong, in case the police actually believed you."

"No risk of that, though."

"O'Malley was smart enough to plant doubts about you before he took off Monday. Told his replacement you were known for calling with crazy stories about your ex. Suggested you had mental problems. That kept them off our tail for days."

That explained why Klein hadn't taken her seriously at first.

"So, where was it?"

"In his box spring."

Oscar's expression shifted as if he were impressed. "And you found it how?"

"I saw Ian hiding something there once, before we broke up."

Oscar took one small step toward her.

She needed him to take another, and faster.

"You were dead the moment we walked into that shop on Monday morning," he said. "You just didn't know it yet."

She saw the gleam in his eyes. He was the one with mental problems, so eager to inflict pain. Maybe it was that anticipation that had him taking the next couple of steps faster.

If he'd been looking, if the room had had adequate lighting, he might have seen the obstacle, though perhaps not. The overhead light created few shadows on the floor, and the carpet was dark.

And his gaze was on her, not on where he was going. He opened his mouth to say something else, perhaps continue his banal banter. But the words were cut off when he tripped over the carpet she'd painstakingly yanked up from the floor and bunched in the middle of the room.

Before he could catch his balance, she snatched the short two-by-four she'd propped just inside the unfinished closet and swung.

It connected with his skull, and he went down.

Everything in her vibrated with fear and horror, but she ignored the sensations and, as he spun, reaching for his pocket, she hit him again.

His gaze collided with hers as he stumbled, reached for her.

She reared back and hit him one more time.

He collapsed.

His eyes closed.

Was he out, really out?

She was tempted to whack him a fourth time, just to be safe, but he wasn't moving.

Crouching beside him, she dug through his jacket pockets and swiped a key and a pocketknife. She searched for a cell phone and handgun but found neither. Carefully, she patted his pockets, around his waistband, even his ankles, thinking for sure there was another weapon, but she found nothing else.

The small pocketknife she opened and slid into the pocket on her sweatshirt.

She swiveled toward the door and prepared to stand.

His hand snaked around her wrist.

A scream crawled up from her chest and got caught in her throat.

He yanked, nearly pulling her off balance. His mouth opened, and a small sound came out. He sucked in a breath. She knew, she knew, that he would scream as soon as he got enough air.

She snatched the board from the floor beside her and rammed it into his stomach.

His breath rushed out, and he struggled to inhale.

She brought the board down hard against his head.

He gasped. His grip on her arm loosened.

His eyes closed.

He didn't move. Was he dead? She didn't know, couldn't let herself care.

Every muscle trembled, but she managed to stand and fit the key into the lock. She turned the handle and peeked out the door. The large room was empty. Low voices carried from down the hall to her right.

She closed the door behind her as quietly as she could, made sure it was locked, and turned to the left, pulling the knife from her pocket and depositing the key there. She crouched low, not that there was anything to hide behind in that large room.

Finally, she reached the hall on the opposite side from the voices. On the far end, an exit sign glowed red.

A staircase.

She just needed to get there.

Here, the cheap industrial carpet had been replaced with dark hardwood. This part of the renovation seemed to have been completed. Offices lined the wide hall, five open doors on each side, darkly stained wood and trim. She crept forward and passed the first two doorways, then the second two.

Light spilled from one of the three pairs of doors. She approached slowly, cautiously.

"Darling." Preston's voice came from inside. "It won't be much longer, and then you and I will have the whole weekend together."

"What about my sister?" Sophia asked. "I need to get her home."

"I'll drive her myself. And then, what do you say we get out of town for a few days? Have you ever been to the Bahamas? I have a place down there you're going to love. White sand beaches, warm water."

Sophia giggled. "That sounds perfect." But the lighthearted tone was off. She was playing her part, but not convincingly.

Carly didn't doubt Preston could see through Sophia's facade.

It was all one big game to him.

If there were any way to separate Sophia from that disgusting man, Carly'd do it. But even with the knife, she doubted her ability to take Preston out, certainly not before he raised the alarm.

If Carly distracted Preston long enough, Sophia could probably escape. But not both of them.

A week before, even just a few days before, Carly wouldn't have thought twice about sacrificing herself for her younger sister. But Braden was right. She had another life to protect, an innocent life. Unlike Sophia, the child in Carly's womb hadn't gotten herself into this mess.

No. Carly would have to escape and call for help. But to do that, she had to get past the door. Did she dare with the two of them inside?

A shout carried from behind her.

*No!* They'd discovered she was missing.

She ducked through a door and pressed her back against the wall.

Seconds later, Preston swore, the sound coming from the

hallway where she'd just stood. "Something's wrong. Go back to the other room."

"But baby—"

"Now, Sophie. Go."

A muffled sound. Was Sophia walking away? Was she safe?

Voices rose from the large room down the hall.

"She's gone!" one yelled.

Another, "He's waking up!" Then, "Guard all the exits. We can't let her escape!"

Men shouted in response, telling their whereabouts.

Preston said nothing.

Was he still there?

Waiting in front of the stairwell door?

Despite the faraway noises, she heard footsteps in the hallway. He was close.

A door closed softly, then another. Another.

He was looking for her.

Gripping the knife tightly, she told herself she could do it if she had to.

She could.

She would.

She had no desire to kill a man, but to save her child...

*Grieve, learn to trust God, and be happy.*

To save herself, she would do it.

But she was running out of time. Better to face one man than four. Or more, if Oscar hadn't come alone.

*Rescue me, Lord. I need You!*

If she didn't get out of there, she would be recaptured. She had to move.

She had no choice. No choice at all.

She stepped away from the wall in the dark room and looked into the hallway. She couldn't see much beyond the space right in front of the door. No sign of Preston.

No sound from him, either.

She inched closer.

Leaned out to look. Nobody was coming from deeper in the building.

But the other direction...

Preston stood halfway down the hall between her and the exit, Sophia in front of him. His hand covered her mouth.

Her eyes her wide with terror.

His gun pressed to her temple.

"I knew you'd show yourself eventually."

Carly's gaze flicked from Preston to her sister.

He opened his mouth to say something else, probably shout to alert the others that she'd been found.

But a figure pushed through the stairwell door behind him.

Another captor, there to guard the exit?

Preston turned to see, the gun slipping away from Sophia's head.

Something metal glinted in the dim red light from the exit sign, a flash.

A muffled thud.

Preston collapsed.

Sophia's mouth opened, and Carly waited for the scream she knew was coming.

"Silence." The man's voice was familiar, but Carly couldn't reconcile the sound with the situation.

She was still trying to make sense of that when another figure jumped over Preston's body. It looked like... but it couldn't be.

He barreled into her. By the time her body registered the terror, his hand had covered her mouth. Her shriek was muffled behind the palm. She shifted the knife, prepared to stab him.

"It's Braden."

She lowered the knife. But it couldn't be Braden.

Was she hallucinating?

But the arms were Braden's. The scent was Braden's. The heartbeat beneath the ear she pressed against his chest—even that was Braden's.

He set her far enough away for her to see him, and she looked up into those beautiful blue eyes.

"I got you," he whispered. "We have to hurry."

He backed up and reached for her hand, stopping when he saw the knife. She held it out to him, but he said, "Keep it. We're not out of here yet."

A hiss came from down the hall. "If you two are finished..."

They turned to see Pete dragging Preston's unconscious form into an office.

Pete. How was he there? How were either of them?

Sophia was standing against the wall. Stunned.

Pete snatched Preston's gun as Braden urged Carly and Sophia into the stairwell.

Now, to get out of the building.

# CHAPTER THIRTY-FIVE

It took all of Braden's self-control to hold the stairwell door until it quietly closed.

As soon as it did, Pete whispered, "You first, then the girls."

The man was older, but he'd dealt with Preston Shaw deftly and wasn't even breathing hard. He could handle himself taking up the rear.

Braden was happy to lead the way.

He didn't let go of Carly's hand—might never again as long as he lived—and started down the stairs. Sophia followed, and Pete stalked behind, Preston's gun in hand. If anybody came, Pete would take him out.

During the ride on the way there, Braden had learned that the guy had military experience. He'd seen action in the Gulf. Carly had never mentioned it, but maybe she hadn't known.

In any event, Pete seemed to know what he was doing. Better than Braden did.

Taking out bad guys. Another class he'd missed at MIT.

But Pete had planned it from the start. They'd been hiding in the stairwell with the door cracked, listening, when they heard someone raise the alarm that Carly had escaped. It had been torture, utter torture, not pushing through that door to find her, but

Pete had kept his hand on Braden's arm, the grip tight. "Wait," he'd whispered. "Just wait."

*For what!* He'd wanted to scream, but he did what the older man asked.

The silence had been torture.

And then, a man had spoken. "I knew you'd show yourself eventually."

They'd pushed the door open just enough to see outside. After they took in the three figures in the dark hallway, Pete whispered so low, Braden hardly heard him. "I'll take out the gunman and keep Sophia quiet. You keep Carly from screaming."

Braden had agreed.

Somehow, it had worked.

A miracle from God, no doubt about it.

They passed the third-floor landing and kept going. They were nearly to the next landing when the door below opened.

A man stepped in. Raised a gun. Aimed at Braden.

Braden dove into him, gravity propelling him fast.

The weapon fired, but not before the gunman had shifted to defend himself.

While Braden collided with the man, sending them both crashing into the heavy door and concrete floor, he registered the sounds behind him.

A quiet gasp.

Pete's voice. "No! Oh God, no!"

Someone had been hit. Sophia or Carly.

Braden landed on top. With his left hand, he held the man's gun against the cement. With his right, he punched his ribs, his kidneys. Blow after blow, ignoring those the gunman landed.

Ignoring the sounds of the people behind him.

He fought for Carly's life and that of the baby she carried. Not to mention Sophia and Pete.

He felt no pain.

He felt no fatigue.

He felt no fear.

And he knew there was no margin for error.

He punched and punched and punched. The man's gun arm no longer struggled to get free. The gun had slipped from his hand. No more blows reached Braden's midsection.

Was he down? Really, had Braden bested him?

He pushed himself away. Stringy blond hair, glazed-over eyes. It was Wiley, the one who'd tried to kill Carly. Just for that, Braden wanted to punch him again.

But Wiley wasn't fighting back.

"Braden, we have to go."

Carly's voice penetrated, and she gripped his arm. She'd said the words more than once, though he was only now realizing it. He forced himself to stand.

Carly's eyes were wide. "Hurry. We have to go. Sophia..." Her voice cracked. She had blood on her hands, her shirt. Smeared blood, though. Not hers. Thank God.

Pete held his oldest daughter in his arms as if she were eight, not eighteen. Her top was stained red, as were her jeans where Pete's hands held her. "Grab the gun."

He got Wiley's. Carly held Preston's.

Braden led the way down the stairs. If anybody else popped out from doors, he'd shoot.

But they reached the first-floor landing without incident.

After checking the weapon in his hand for bullets—it was loaded—he inched open the door. The lobby was empty, but flashes of blue and red lights beamed through the front windows and against the walls.

They hurried to the front door. It wouldn't budge, but he found the mechanism above and unlocked it, then slowly pushed it open.

"Show me your hands!"

He poked both hands out, Wiley's gun dangling from his right, and peeked, just to be sure. Uniformed police officers stood on the sidewalk, their weapons trained on Braden.

He dropped the gun, then took the one Carly'd been holding

and dropped it too. He kicked them both across the concrete toward the steps leading down to the sidewalk. Hands held high, he stepped into the opening. "Braden Reilly. I'm the one who called. We have Carly Garcia and Sophia Lancaster with us. Sophia's been wounded."

"Come out slowly," one officer yelled.

Braden held the door open, and Pete carried his daughter into the cold night. Streetlights added to those on the emergency vehicles. It barely looked like nighttime at all. Countless cruisers idled on the road, not to mention a fire truck and, mercifully, an ambulance.

Ignoring the police and their weapons, Pete hurried that direction and laid Sophia on a gurney.

Uniformed officers approached, separated Braden from Carly, and patted both of them down. Braden tried to answer the officer questioning him while keeping one eye on Carly.

She was safe. Thank God.

Now that she was out of the building, all Braden could think about was Sophia and that bullet. Though the police were asking him questions, he couldn't concentrate. He stepped nearer Sophia as paramedics worked on her. They seemed calm as could be. Maybe that meant the wound wasn't as bad as it looked.

Maybe they were calm because they didn't know her. Didn't love her.

And they hadn't been the reason she was shot.

He felt Carly's presence beside him and slipped his arm around her. "I'm so sorry."

She angled to face him. "What?"

"He was aiming at me. I thought, when I dove, he'd shoot me, and you guys would get away. But he must've jerked when he saw me coming. His bullet went high."

Carly was safe, but Sophia...

Carly stepped between Braden and the ambulance and put her hands on Braden's cheeks. "Look at me."

He did, swallowing the fear he should have felt in that stairwell. All he'd felt was cold fury and determination not to lose Carly.

"You saved our lives," she said. "Oscar would have killed us both."

"Probably not." His gaze flicked back to the paramedics surrounding Sophia. "The police would have gotten you out."

"No, they wouldn't have." She sounded so confident, he focused on her. "Preston told me they had a way of escape." She pointed to the roof. "He bragged that he'd figured a way to get from this one to one of the others. Not sure which, but the police are covering them all."

Braden only then realized the cops were moving to cover the block. One was shouting into a radio something about more manpower.

He prayed there'd be enough.

"They wouldn't have let me live," Carly said. "I knew too much. And Sophia had seen too much. I think that, the minute they saw the police outside, they'd have killed us and tried to get away. Or tried to take us with them and kill us later. You saved us, Braden."

The paramedics rolled the gurney into the back of the ambulance, and Braden and Carly walked that direction.

Pete swiveled and wrapped Carly in a tight hug. "I'm sorry." Before she could respond, he backed away and surveyed her from head to toe. "Are you all right? Did they hurt you?"

"I'm fine. How's Sophie?"

"Bullet didn't hit any organs. I think she's gonna be all right."

"Thank God."

Pete turned to Braden and embraced him too. "Thank you. Thank you for saving my girls."

Braden's eyes stung, and he blinked the emotion back. "We did it together."

Pete climbed in the back of the ambulance. "I'm going with Sophie."

The paramedics closed the doors, and the vehicle pulled from the curb with a blast of its siren.

Carly leaned against him. "She's going to be okay."

He couldn't speak past the relief that filled his throat. He pulled Carly close and held on. If it were up to him, he'd never let her go.

# CHAPTER THIRTY-SIX

IN THE HOSPITAL, in a private waiting room roughly the size of a walk-in closet, Carly gripped Braden's hand. He hadn't left her side, and she hadn't wanted him to. She gave Detective Klein her statement. They were seated in three of the six chairs pressed against the walls, so close Braden's knees were only inches from the detective's.

They learned that, thanks to Preston's having tipped her off about Oscar's escape plan, six men had been apprehended. Both Preston and Oscar had been admitted to the hospital for observation. Preston had a severe concussion and might have to stay overnight. Oscar's wasn't as bad. He'd have the privilege of being transferred to jail that night, where Wiley and the other men were already behind bars.

The notebooks, which Oscar had been so eager to get his hands on, had been collected from the B and B and transported to BPD.

"We got enough to charge him with multiple crimes, including assault and arson. And of course"—Klein tipped his head her direction—"kidnapping. With your testimony, we'll add murder to those charges. Oscar won't be getting out of prison anytime soon."

"What about the others?"

"Wiley Cuthrow's going down for attempted murder. Preston

Shaw too. Everybody we caught is guilty of kidnapping, at the very least. We'll figure out the rest of the charges after we've completed our investigation."

In the chair beside hers, Braden said, "What about Lynch?"

"He claims he had no idea what Abecedarian was up to. We'll see what we dig up."

"He's the one who told me about the Deerfield."

She turned to Braden. "He was? You didn't tell me that."

He kissed her forehead. "We haven't had much time to talk."

They hadn't. They'd been transported to the hospital, where Braden's parents and Carly's other stepsisters waited. After hugs and quick explanations, Klein had ushered them away to give their statements. He'd wanted to talk to them each separately, but neither Carly nor Braden had been keen to let the other go.

Klein had grudgingly allowed them to both accompany him.

Now, Carly reveled in Braden's closeness. "We will have plenty of time to go over it," she said. The rest of their lives, if it were up to her.

Klein said, "Even if Lynch is guilty, the fact that he helped us find you will go a long way with a judge. Maybe not the voters."

"I don't think he's guilty, though," Braden said. "I don't think he knew anything."

"I tend to agree," Klein said. "We'll get the whole story, one way or another."

"None of them will be getting out of jail, right?" Carly asked.

"Can't ever tell what a judge will do, but I wouldn't count on it. Even if they did, they have no reason to hurt you now."

"She's the only witness to Ian's murder." Braden's voice went from conversational to angry in the space of a second. "That seems like reason enough."

"I guess I haven't told you that part." Klein leaned forward, clasping his hands between his knees. "During our search of the Deerfield, we found an old green Chevy Camaro in the garage."

Carly's heart raced. "Ian's car?"

"Yup. His body was in the trunk, wrapped in a tarp. Forensics is working on it already. Fingerprints, DNA... We figure it's just a matter of time before we link the men we arrested today with Ian's murder. The DA'll probably offer the underlings a deal to bring down Oscar and Preston, but they should still serve time."

She slumped back, and Braden slipped his arm around her shoulders and pulled her close. "So it's over." She needed to hear the detective say it. She needed to be sure.

Klein's smile showed all his teeth. "It's over, and you're safe. You two..." He pursed his lips. "I'm sorry I didn't believe you. As soon as we find O'Malley, he'll face charges."

"Oscar told me he claimed I had mental problems."

Klein smirked. "Never crossed my mind he was lying to me, not until you two were shot at. It was one thing for *you* to be crazy, but"—he inclined his head toward Braden—"either you found an equally crazy partner, or you were both telling the truth." He pushed up from his seat, and Braden and Carly did the same. Klein held his hand out to Braden, which Braden shook. "Doesn't usually work out so well when civilians take matters into their own hands. Glad you weren't hurt." He held Braden's hand a moment too long and leaned in. "Next time you're told to stand down, though, I recommend you do it."

Braden backed away, rubbing his side. She'd caught him doing that a lot, but he'd brushed off her concern. "I don't intend for there to be a next time."

"Even better." The detective focused on her. "Sorry I doubted you."

"But God was with me."

The older man's eyes narrowed. "I think you're right."

And then Carly remembered...

"Wait. That bag of cash Ian gave me...?"

"Right. I'd forgotten. How much was in it?"

She shrugged, but Braden said, "Ten thousand two hundred seventy-four dollars."

She focused on the detective. "He's a freak."

Klein chuckled. "We'll need to get that from you."

"It's at Braden's house. He can put it in the mail, or...?"

"I'll bring it down," Braden said. "I'll be coming back soon."

She looked up to face him. "You will?"

"I certainly hope so."

Klein's gaze flicked between them. Finally, he said, "I'd appreciate that, sooner rather than later."

After Braden's nod, Klein held his hand out to her. "Friends?"

She laughed and shook it. "It never hurts to have a detective for a friend, I guess."

He chuckled as he left the room.

She started to follow, but Braden snagged her hand and pulled her against him. She didn't fight it, just melted against his chest, taking in his perfectly unique scent.

"How are you, really?" he asked.

She backed away to face him. "Tired. Hungry." A short burst of laughter had his eyes widening. "Relieved."

"You're sure you're not hurt? The baby...?"

She pressed her hand against her abdomen. "They didn't hurt me. Not like they did you."

He brushed that off with a shake of his head. "Carly, I know I didn't handle it well, your news. I hope you can forgive me. I can't... I don't want to lose—"

She cut off his words with a kiss. What she'd meant to be a short peck turned into something else, something that had the fatigue and rumbling stomach and fear for her sister and nerves all taking a backseat.

None of those thoughts could compete with the feeling of Braden's lips against hers.

His hand on her back. The other in her hair and sending a million sensations through her body.

When he stopped, she wanted to pull him close again. But he backed away, held her face in his hands, and gazed into her eyes. "I love you, Carly Garcia."

His words spread warmth all the way to her toes. "And I love you. Every moment since that first awkward kiss when we were fifteen, I've loved you. I'm sorry I didn't—"

But his lips cut off her apology. They were well on their way to another mind-blowing experience when, once again, he ended it. "Let's forget the past. Let's just go forward from here."

The perfect solution, except... "I'm carrying Ian's child. Do you think you can learn to love her? Or him?"

Braden leaned back far enough to rest his palm against her belly. "I already do."

Oh. Tears stung her eyes. She didn't know what to say.

But Braden wasn't waiting for a response. "I don't know what this will look like or how it'll work. If I need to quit my job—"

"You don't." She thought of his little house in the woods, the peace she'd felt there. Someday, she hoped that could be her home. For now... "I'm sure there are apartments in Coventry. Or Plymouth. Maybe I could start school again."

His grin spread and lit up his whole face. "You'd move to New Hampshire?"

"I'd move to Timbuktu, if that was where you were."

"What about Pete and your sisters?"

"They're not my responsibility. Never were." She thought of the real promise Mama asked Carly to make. She'd grieved. She'd learned to trust God. There was one more thing to do. "I'm going to be happy."

# CHAPTER THIRTY-SEVEN

It was too good to be true.

Braden could hardly believe it. Carly was going to move to New Hampshire.

He stretched in the tiny twin bed that had been his growing up, staring up at the bunk that had been his brother's. Trophies lined the walls, John's from sports, Braden's from math and science competitions. He smiled at the memories, at the hope the morning brought.

Because Carly had agreed to move to New Hampshire. He'd wait an acceptable amount of time. A couple of weeks? No, a month, at least. Give her time to get settled.

And then he'd propose. He wanted to marry her before she started showing, but if she wanted to wait until after the baby was born, he could do that. Whatever Carly wanted, as long as they could be together.

They'd live in Coventry. He'd work at BNB. Maybe she'd work on her degree, maybe not. He could afford to support her and the baby. Hopefully, there'd be more babies to come.

Whatever she wanted.

And, if something happened with BNB, if he lost that job...?

Then he'd get another one. And if they had to move, then

they'd move. If he'd learned nothing else in the previous few days, he'd learned that he couldn't control the future. He couldn't even control the present. And security wouldn't come from Braden's planning or scheming or clawing his way into positions he didn't need.

God had rescued them from evil men.

God could certainly figure out how to provide for all their needs.

They hadn't gotten back to Braden's parents' house until nearly four in the morning, which explained why he'd slept until eleven. He checked his phone. Not the burner. Thank heavens he had his own powered on. Nothing from Carly, but then, her cell was at his house, her burner smashed. He texted Pete's number, which the man had given him the night before. *Please have Carly call me when she gets a chance.*

A response came in immediately. *Will do. She's still sleeping.*

Good. She needed it.

Then, he texted Jacqui. *I need to talk to Andrew. Can you share his number?*

She, too, responded immediately. *Everything OK? Been praying for you and Carly.*

*Long story, but all is well. I'll tell you about it Monday.*

A moment later, Andrew's contact information popped up on his screen.

He dialed, and the man answered.

Braden launched himself out of the bed, nearly banging his head on the top bunk. Had it always been so low? "It's Braden Reilly."

"Did you get your stuff worked out?" the man asked. "Your girlfriend doing okay?"

"Yup, she's good. Listen, we need to talk. I did a little digging on you."

That remark was greeted with silence.

"I assume Jacqui doesn't know you spent time in prison for embezzlement."

Again, silence. But only a moment of it before Andrew said, "My sentence was overturned."

"Still..."

"I assume"—his voice was measured, the words delivered carefully—"that you heard the whole story."

"About the gambling debt? About how you changed the books?"

"I had no idea what I was doing." Still, his words were flat, almost emotionless. As if he didn't care. No. Not that. As if he'd defended himself many times in the past, and he was tired of it. "I had no idea—"

"The prosecutor believed that. The DA came to believe it."

Andrew added, "The owner of the company did, too, eventually. When my supervisor fessed up."

Braden waited for more explaining, more excuse-making. But Andrew surprised him.

"Jacqui doesn't know any of that," Braden clarified. "Right?"

"Who contacted you? Was it—?"

"Nobody contacted me."

"Somebody obviously tipped you off. Otherwise, why—?"

"I overheard your conversation in the parking lot Tuesday night. I overheard you tell somebody you wouldn't be blackmailed."

Andrew blew out a long breath. "And I won't. Not by him, not by you."

"I'm not—"

"What do you want?"

What did Braden want? At one point, he had been so sure of the answer to that. He was still sure. But the answer had changed dramatically. "Do you still gamble?"

"No. Never. That was one stupid football season. I got lucky the first weekend, then dug a hole for myself the next few. Once I got those debts paid off, I was done forever."

"Nothing else—?"

"Look, I love it here. And I love the company. Jacqui's brilliant but also... kind. You don't see that every day. BNB's got good people, a great work environment. I think I can be an asset. But if you want me to leave, I'll leave. I don't want the information going public."

"What about the guy blackmailing you?"

"What about him? I called his bluff. Well, I thought it was a bluff until you called. Now, I'm not so sure."

"Nobody told me—"

"Just tell me what you want," Andrew said. "You want me to quit, I'll quit. You don't like me, don't want me at BNB. Fine. I love this job, but I'm not gonna risk my whole future for it."

Braden had him. If he told Andrew to resign, the man would be on his way out of town before Braden returned. He could step into the vacuum Andrew would leave, and he could do a decent job of it.

But he couldn't manage BNB anywhere near as well as Andrew could.

"I want you to do your very best to make BNB a success," Braden said.

The silence on the other end of the line stretched a long time. "That's it?"

"I love my job too. I expect you to manage the company so well that nothing threatens it."

"I don't understand," Andrew said. "You're not going to tell Jacqui?"

"I'm not. You should, though. If I know Jacqui—and I think I do—she'll understand. If she hears the story from you, if she hears what I heard, she'll accept it. It won't jeopardize your job or your future. But if she hears it from a stranger..."

"Or you," Andrew said.

Braden hated how close he'd come to being the one to spill Andrew's secrets. But he hadn't. In the end, he'd decided to do the right thing. "She's not going to hear it from me."

"If you and I get into a conflict—"

"She's not going to hear it from me. But she should hear it from you."

Braden waited through another long pause. Andrew wasn't a quick-to-speak sort of guy. "Okay, then. I'll think about that."

"Good. I'll be back Monday. I'll see you—"

"Hey, wait. Jacqui's gonna tell you something Monday. Just know... That was in the works before this."

"What? What's in the works?"

"I just want you to know it has nothing to do with this conversation. Just something we decided last week when you were gone."

Braden had no idea what he was talking about, but it seemed Andrew wasn't going to satisfy his curiosity. "Okay. I guess I'll figure it out Monday."

"Yeah. And, uh... Thanks, man."

Braden ended the call, content. He'd leave the managing of BNB to Andrew and Jacqui. He'd do what God had created him to do, and he'd trust God with the rest of it.

After all, he had what he really wanted. He had Carly, and he intended to do everything in his power to keep her forever.

# CHAPTER THIRTY-EIGHT

Carly stood on the sidewalk in front of the house she'd lived in for years. She hugged Danielle and Laurie. "You two promise to help keep this place clean?"

"Promise," Danielle said.

"Promise." Tears welled in Laurie's eyes. Tears, as if she'd miss her. "I wish you weren't going so far away."

Not long before, New Hampshire had seemed a million miles from Dorchester, but Carly had been back and forth enough in Braden's old Monte Carlo in the last few weeks—securing an apartment and finding a job—that it no longer seemed that far at all. "Two hours in traffic, tops," she said. "You can come visit me."

Laurie's eyes widened.

Danielle said, "We can? Maybe next weekend?"

Carly glanced at Pete, who said, "Why don't you give Carly a little while to get settled. Then we'll talk about it."

Carly squeezed the younger girls' hands and turned to Sophia.

Her oldest stepsister was slightly hunched over, her hand pressed to the still-healing wound on her side and leaning on the stair rail that led to the front door. Carly had tried to say good-bye in the house, but Sophia had insisted on walking her out.

Carly hugged her, careful of her injury. "I'll miss you, sis."

Sophia leaned back, her eyes filled with tears. Her face was scrubbed clean of makeup. She wore a long-sleeved T-shirt and jeans and looked as innocent and sweet as she had when Carly'd first met her. "I'm so glad things worked out. And I'm so—"

"We're done with that, remember?"

Sophia clamped her lips closed against the apology. Carly had forgiven her. Sophia had even let her tell her about Jesus, and she'd listened. She hadn't been convinced yet, but Carly believed her faith would come, in time.

"You'll come see me too?"

Sophia nodded, then leaned against her father, tears spilling over.

Carly turned to Pete, who pulled her into an awkward one-armed side-hug. "You call if you need anything."

She backed away, and his gaze lifted over her head. "You take care of her."

Behind her, Braden said. "I intend to."

"And that little one." Pete's voice cracked. He swallowed whatever else he'd planned to say.

They looked so forlorn. "It's not forever, you guys. I'll be back to see you. And you can come see me."

But tears streamed down her sisters' faces and had Pete tilting his head back as if he could stem them with gravity.

They weren't perfect, these stepsisters and stepfather. But they were hers, and she would miss them.

"No matter where I live," Carly said, "we'll always be family."

Beside her, Braden slipped his hand into hers and squeezed.

His parents had come to help her load her things into the trailer, and she felt their presence at her side.

Her old family. Her new family. She thought of the little life growing in her belly—her future family.

Soon, Braden would slip a ring on her finger, and they'd make it official. He'd been given a promotion at work. It seemed that his absence had highlighted for Jacqui and Andrew just how important he was in guiding the other researchers in their tasks. When he'd returned that Monday morning, he'd been made lead researcher, a position equal to Andrew's. Turned out, he wasn't nearly as replaceable as he'd feared.

Not at BNB, and certainly not in her life. Soon enough, she'd be his bride. For now, she was content to know that she was loved, and not because she took care of others. Not because they couldn't do without her. Even though her mother was gone, Carly was loved. She was loved because... because she was loved. It was as simple and as extraordinary as that.

Pete, the girls, Braden's parents.

Braden.

They loved her, and she loved them, and that was all she needed to know.

Her future looked very good indeed.

THE END.

I HOPE you enjoyed Carly and Braden's story. I used to live next door to the Museum of Fine Arts and went to Northeastern University, where Carly rested after her harrowing bicycle escape. It was fun to revisit my old stomping grounds.

If you liked TRACES OF VIRTUE, I think you're going to love TOUCH OF INNOCENCE. Turn the page for more about book five in the Coventry Saga.

From a USA Today bestselling author comes a gripping story of mystery, romance, and pulse-pounding suspense.

**How can she save the little girl next door from being exploited if nobody believes her?**

Grace used to try to save people, but that was before she realized how powerless she is. Now, she avoids emotional ties, working from her

secluded cabin, content with her aloneness. When eight-year-old Lily starts hanging around, Grace enjoys her company but carefully keeps her distance—until she discovers the girl is being exploited. Little though she wants to, she must get involved, even if it means risking her own safety to secure Lily's.

Andrew can't help but be drawn to his new neighbor and her beautiful foster child. When he learns about Lily's disturbing history, he offers to help Grace prove her suspicions about the girl's father. But the more they learn, the more puzzling Lily's history seems. They work together to unravel the mystery, determined to ensure Lily ends up with a family who loves her.

But Lily's father isn't giving up his muse—or his obsession—that easily. He believes Lily is rightfully his, and he'll do anything to get her back.

# ALSO BY ROBIN PATCHEN

The Coventry Saga

Glimmer in the Darkness

Tides of Duplicity

Betrayal of Genius

Traces of Virtue

Touch of Innocence


The Nutfield Saga

Convenient Lies

Twisted Lies

Generous Lies

Innocent Lies

Beauty in Flight

Beauty in Hiding

Beauty in Battle

Legacy Rejected

Legacy Restored

Legacy Reclaimed

Legacy Redeemed


Amanda Series

Chasing Amanda

Finding Amanda

Standalone Novellas

A Package Deal

One Christmas Eve

Faith House

# ABOUT THE AUTHOR

Robin Patchen is a *USA Today* bestselling and award-winning author of Christian romantic suspense. She grew up in a small town in New Hampshire, the setting of her Nutfield Saga books, and then headed to Boston to earn a journalism degree. After college, working in marketing and public relations, she discovered how much she loathed the nine-to-five ball and chain. After relocating to the Southwest, she started writing her first novel while she homeschooled her three children. The novel was dreadful, but her passion for storytelling didn't wane. Thankfully, as her children grew, so did her writing ability. Now that her kids are adults, she has more time to play with the lives of fictional heroes and heroines, wreaking havoc and working magic to give her characters happy endings. When she's not writing, she's editing or reading, proving that most of her life revolves around the twenty-six letters of the alphabet. Visit robinpatchen.com/subscribe to receive a free book and stay informed about Robin's latest projects.

www.ingramcontent.com/pod-product-compliance
Lightning Source LLC
Chambersburg PA
CBHW071724190726
48292CB00003B/600